ALSO BY JENNY WHITE

The Sultan's Seal
The Abyssinian Proof

the winter thief

Jenny White

W. W. Norton & Company

NEW YORK   LONDON

For information about permission to reproduce selections from this book,
write to Permissions, W. W. Norton & Company, Inc.,
500 Fifth Avenue, New York, NY 10110

For information about special discounts for bulk purchases, please contact W. W. Norton Special Sales at specialsales@wwnorton.com
or 800-233-4830

Manufacturing by Courier Westford
Book design by Brooke Koven
Production manager: Anna Oler

Library of Congress Cataloging-in-Publication Data

White, Jenny B. (Jenny Barbara), 1953-
The winter thief / Jenny White. — 1st ed.
p. cm.
ISBN 978-0-393-07017-0 (hardcover)
1. Special prosecutors—Turkey—Fiction. 2. Armenians—Turkey—
Fiction. 3. Socialism—Turkey—History—19th century—Fiction.
4. Turkey—History—Autonomy and independence movements—Fiction.
5. Turkey—Politics and government—19th century—Fiction.
6. Massacres—Turkey, Eastern—Fiction. I. Title.
PS3623.H5763W56 2010
813'.6—dc22

2009040403

W. W. Norton & Company, Inc.
500 Fifth Avenue, New York, N.Y. 10110
www.wwnorton.com

W. W. Norton & Company Ltd.
Castle House, 75/76 Wells Street, London W1T 3QT

1 2 3 4 5 6 7 8 9 0

In memory of Carl Leiden

Beneath these lilies sleep lions,
and beneath the lions is all the world.

—APOLLO GRIGORIAN
Tiflis, 1890

the winter thief

Istanbul

CHRISTMAS DAY, JANUARY 6, 1888

THE ELDERLY PUBLISHER put on his spectacles to examine the enameled pin in his hand. It displayed a symbol of broken chains draped across a sword, an ax, and a red flag. He handed the pin back to the young woman as if it were poison.

Vera had gotten lost in the twisted lanes leading to Bab-i Ali, the publishing district, and ended up down by the harbor, then had to work her way back up the hill on the boulevard, where she might be seen. But she had been late for her meeting with the publisher and didn't want to risk getting lost again. It was only five o'clock, but already dark from the approaching storm. The street was nearly deserted. The few men she passed were wrapped up against the cold, and she could see only their eyes. As she approached the center of the district, the buildings became more substantial, with ornate porticos, but their windows were blank, reflecting back the gray sky. All the Armenian businesses were closed for Christmas. Her own family's house in Moscow would be blazing with warmth and light, Vera thought with a pang of regret. She hurried along Jalaloglu Street, peering at the names across the entrances, and finally, gratefully, turned into a doorway marked Agopian Brothers Publishing House.

Now Vera was sitting in a chair before the publisher's desk. Curls of auburn hair, darkened by moisture, stuck to her cheeks. He reminded her of her grandfather, whom she remembered sitting at a desk much like this one, waiting impatiently for his granddaughter to speak her mind. The logs in the fireplace throbbed deep red. Shelves were crammed with books, and a long table was heaped with manuscripts. The publisher's desk, however, was as organized and tidy as the man himself. Vera noticed a vase of pine boughs in a window niche. Beside it lay a pomegranate, symbol of luck in the New Year.

"I'm sorry to interrupt you on Christmas Day," she said, pocketing the pin, the symbol of the Armenian socialist Henchak organization. "But I wanted the chance to speak to you alone. Thank you for coming to your office."

"I wish you a blessed Christmas, my daughter. What can I do for you?" They spoke in Armenian, his voice cultured and precise, hers heavily accented. Her parents had spoken only Russian at home. What she knew of the language, she had learned from her grandmother and, later, from fellow Armenian students studying in Geneva.

Vera reached inside her coat and pulled out a manuscript. She placed it on the desk between them.

"*The Communist Manifesto.*" The publisher read the title out loud. "By Karl Marx and Friedrich Engels." He flipped through the pages. "It's in Armenian."

"Exactly."

"You want me to publish this?"

"Yes."

"Look here, Madame . . . What did you say your name was?"

"Lena," she lied. "Lena Balian," using the name of a childhood friend in Moscow. "Will you do it?"

A look of irritation passed over his face, disguised immediately by official blandness.

"Explain to me why I should publish this."

"It's the duty of educated Armenians like us to protect those of our people who are vulnerable, the peasants and the workers." Her words sounded hollow and rehearsed. She wished she had Gabriel's eloquence. He had grown up in the shipyards of Sevastopol and had acquired his many languages in the cauldron of the street. She had studied at a privileged academy in Moscow, but what had she learned that was useful? "The Armenian people will find the strength to resist oppression only by joining the International Movement, by standing shoulder to shoulder with other oppressed peoples around the world."

Her face was flushed from the overheated room. "The *Manifesto* has already been translated into English, French, Russian, Spanish, Polish, and Danish. It's a scandal that there's no Armenian translation."

The publisher placed his spectacles on the desk and said gently, "Madame Balian, I appreciate your sentiment, and to some extent I agree that we need to stand together, but from what I've heard, this is the stuff of sheer anarchy. If you remove the state altogether, do you really think men will support one another from the goodness of their hearts?" He shook his head. "No, I don't agree. If you remove the state, they'll rush to tear out each other's throats."

"They'll do that anyway. This way we can resist. There's strength in numbers."

"Something has to hold people together, madame. We're Armenians. That's enough. We don't need someone else's utopia."

"An Armenian landlord has more in common with a Turkish agha than with the peasants plowing his fields. The fact that landlord and peasant share the same nationality is irrelevant. It doesn't mean the landlord will treat his workers any better. Peasants have to stand together, no matter if they're Turk or Armenian. Nationality divides people; socialism unites them."

"Where is your family on this Christmas Day?" the publisher asked gently.

Vera was startled by the sudden change in subject. "My family? In Moscow." The revelation made her feel vulnerable.

"Are you not a member of the landed class yourself?"

"Why would you think that?"

"Your clothing, the way you speak. You've had a good education. Perhaps in Moscow it means something different to be an Armenian than here in the empire."

"What do you mean?"

"Maybe in Moscow you have the luxury of being Armenian however you choose—by going to church, or speaking the language, or just baking cheoreg. But here we Armenians have a common fate, peasant and landlord alike."

"Fate," she repeated. "That sounds very Oriental. What use is a life without struggle?"

"Ah, madame, we have enough struggle to satisfy several generations. We are not short of struggle."

"I mean, struggle for a better society where everyone is equal, where no one starves just because they don't own any land."

"Everyone wants to offer us a utopia," he said sadly. "No one offers us peace."

Vera hesitated. The conversation was becoming too philosophical, and philosophy, like poetry, had no end. "What harm would it do to publish this?" she asked. "If, as you say, Armenians don't exploit each other . . ."

"I never said that," he interrupted.

"If Armenians are united despite their differences, then this would link them to something greater. Do you want to deprive the Armenian people of their right to participate in the greatest global movement of the century?"

He thought about that, drumming his fingers on the manuscript. "I'm not averse to publishing this text, but I can't publish it under the names Karl Marx and Friedrich Engels. It would be immediately recognized by the Ottoman government for what it is—socialist propaganda. My publishing house would be closed down, perhaps worse. Then what have we gained?"

"What are you saying? That you'll publish it anonymously?"

He shrugged. "We could publish it under your name instead."

"Then it would be seen as Russian propaganda."

"A woman's name is less dangerous."

"That would be like sending a man into battle with a blunt sword." She rose abruptly, stifling her disappointment. "Please reconsider," she pleaded.

"Madame Balian, you must know that Russia is threatening the empire's eastern provinces," he said with thinly disguised exasperation. "The sultan suspects us Armenians of collaborating with them. This is not the time to publish Marx's work here." He held out the manuscript, refusing to meet her eyes.

She stuffed the papers into her coat, her face stern so he wouldn't notice the tears. Her gloves fell unnoticed to the floor.

The publisher walked to the window and glanced out at the street. He hesitated, then picked up the pomegranate and handed it to Vera. "I didn't have time to break this on my office doorstep in the New Year, so I suppose I've missed my luck. Take it. May it bring you luck and success."

"Blessed Christmas," she answered softly, tucking it into her pocket.

IT WAS dusk and the buildings at the end of the block were invisible amid a swirl of snowflakes. Vera turned down a side street that she thought led in the direction of their rented room in Fatih. The grand buildings of the boulevard gave way to meaner houses, three-story tenements with crumbling balconies arrayed like broken teeth along narrow, rutted lanes. Vera scanned the sky above the buildings for a minaret. Mosques were set in public squares where she might be able to orient herself. Gabriel would laugh at her for being such a novice, she thought.

She fumbled to close the top button of her coat and realized she had lost her gloves. Expensive kid leather gloves that her mother had bought for her to take to Geneva. The thought of her parents brought on more tears. They would be devastated to learn that their daughter was a revolutionary working to overthrow the very system that allowed them to send her abroad to study. They didn't seem like the class enemies she had read about. They were kind to everyone. She missed them. Vera reached down and washed her face with snow. If Gabriel was in their room when she returned, he mustn't know of her weakness.

She vowed to herself that she wouldn't go back to Geneva with her very first mission unaccomplished. They had been in Istanbul for two weeks and Gabriel had been gone most of that time, engaged in activities of his own, about which he told her nothing. He had tried to send her home after just one week, and she knew that he regretted allowing her to come along. She twisted the silver ring on her finger that he had given her as a Christmas gift last night, one of the few nights he had slept in their room. There had been no feast, no family, no anushabour, the sweet barley Christmas pudding that she loved. There had been grilled fish, onions, wine, and Gabriel. Her face heated at the memory of their lovemaking. They had been married shortly before leaving for Istanbul, and there hadn't been time for a ring or even a ceremony. There had been no privacy on the train and ship. Last night had been their wedding night.

Two feral dogs with scarred flanks and matted fur began to follow her. She picked up a stone and hurled it at them, but they only shied to the side, then resumed their pursuit. Hearing the call to prayer, she followed the sound and, to her great relief, emerged into a large square. The dogs paused at the mouth of the street, sniffed the air, then trotted away. Near the mosque, a group of ragged men and veiled women crowded around its soup kitchen. Smoke rose from its chimneys and Vera caught the scent of freshly baked bread. Her stomach clenched with hunger.

Recognizing the square, Vera hurried down the lane behind the mosque complex toward home, hoping Gabriel would be there. The snow deadened the footfalls of the man following her.

2

KAMIL PASHA, magistrate of Beyoglu, strode into Yorg Pasha's reception hall carrying a rifle. He was trailed by the liveried doorkeeper and two secretaries, who seemed unsure about their right to halt the unannounced intrusion of the tall young pasha, equal in status to their lord, and appeared unnerved by his weapon. As a compromise, they expressed their disapproval by sticking close to Kamil's coattails and uttering obsequious inquiries, none of which Kamil deigned to answer. His face was lean and determined, his moss green eyes aimed straight ahead. He was dressed in a fashionable dinner jacket, now rumpled and grimy.

Yorg Pasha sat on a raised dais at the front of the hall in an armchair decorated with gold lion heads. He himself looked like an aging lion, his broad chest accentuated by a robe embroidered in gold thread that made him appear even more massive. His face beneath his turban sagged with age and fatigue, but his eyes missed nothing. Three secretaries sat at writing desks by his side, and a phalanx of other staff stood at attention along the wall beneath a painted frieze of wild animals gamboling in a forest.

Kamil knew that Thursday was Yorg Pasha's receiving day, when his employees, clients, and anyone else wishing to make a complaint, beg a favor, or pledge their fealty could approach him. A portly man dressed as a prosperous merchant fell to one knee on the dais, his face bowed over Yorg Pasha's hand, and kissed his heavy gold ring.

Kamil pushed his way through the crowd of waiting men and stepped onto the platform. The merchant rose and, at the sight of Kamil's gun, stumbled backward. Yorg Pasha gestured at a grim, narrow-shouldered man in a fez whom Kamil recognized as the pasha's secretary, Simon. A few moments later, the pasha's guards pushed the crowd out the door, some objecting loudly that they needed to speak with the pasha. "Come back next week," the guards answered.

Yorg Pasha patted his stomach and said amiably, "Kamil. It's been months. Last time I saw you was at the Swedish ambassador's house. Lovely wife, but the food." He shook his head and grimaced. "What brings you here?"

Kamil indicated the servants in the hall. "In private."

Simon helped Yorg Pasha to his feet, then stepped back and bowed. Yorg Pasha lumbered down from the dais and led Kamil to a silk-paneled room at the back of the receiving hall.

They sat facing each other over a small table, surrounded by a forest of silk-screened palms and clambering monkeys, stalked by other beasts. "You're looking well," Yorg Pasha offered. Kamil had been up all night at the docks and had just come from a frustrating interview with the British ambassador. He was in no mood for small talk but reached gratefully for the tiny porcelain cup of coffee the pasha's servant offered him. He sipped the thick brew scented with cardamom and waited for the room to clear.

"What's happened, Kamil?" Yorg Pasha asked, leaving his coffee untouched. "I lied. You don't look well at all."

Kamil was caught off guard by Yorg Pasha's tone of concern. The old man had been a close friend of his father, Alp Pasha, when he was governor of Istanbul. Yorg Pasha had taken an interest in the lonely boy in the governor's mansion, and Kamil had spent many hours in his company learning the inner workings of clocks, one of the pasha's hobbies. When Alp Pasha committed suicide two years ago, Yorg

Pasha had sent for Kamil and sat with him, recounting stories of Alp Pasha in his youth. It was a gift of family history Kamil had been grateful to receive, for his father had spent little time with him.

A chime struck four times and reminded Kamil of the waning afternoon. A British-owned ship full of armaments had been discovered in the harbor last night, and he was no closer to finding out who had sent them or for whom they were meant. Yorg Pasha was an arms dealer.

"Pasha," he said formally, placing the rifle on the table between them, "I'm sure you know about the shipment of rifles last night. Forgive me for asking, but do you know who they belong to?" Kamil meant, Were they his?

Yorg Pasha ignored the gun. "I hear they're all Peabody-Martinis, the best. You've confiscated them?"

"The gendarmes have. Yes." The local police didn't have the manpower to guard a thousand rifles and pistols, so Kamil had called in the military police. A contingent of soldiers now surrounded the ship. The British ambassador had insisted the ship was British property and that it be released immediately. Kamil had refused, arguing that if the British claimed the ship, then they would also be accepting responsibility for the illegal arms, creating a diplomatic incident between the British and Ottoman empires. The ambassador had backed off, but Kamil suspected it was merely a tactical retreat. He had a premonition of unseen forces assembling to impede his investigation.

"If you need to dispose of them when the case is over . . ."

"Do you have any idea where they're from and who they're meant for?" Kamil asked again, knowing that despite their relationship, the pasha wouldn't answer such a question, even if he knew, without receiving something in return.

Yorg Pasha picked up the rifle and examined it carefully, then took a magnifying glass from a drawer and peered at the serial numbers. "Standard forty-five-caliber Peabody-Martini rifle from the Providence Tool Company in the United States." He sniffed the barrel. "This has been fired, but not recently."

"All the guns appear to be used. It's a British-owned ship, but the captain is Alexandrian and claims he had no idea he was carrying guns. They were in barrels, supposedly salted fish." The captain and crew were now guests of Police Chief Omar Loutfi in the Fatih district jail. If they knew anything, Kamil was sure Omar would find it out.

Yorg Pasha placed the rifle gently on the table. "Where was the ship coming from?"

"Malta via Cyprus. Before that, the manifest says New York."

"These probably were loaded at New York. They don't salt fish on Malta, not in these quantities." Yorg Pasha rumbled a laugh.

Kamil thought back to the British ambassador's denial that morning. He had seemed sincere enough, even shocked when Kamil told him how many guns were involved, more than a thousand. But it was typical of the British to vow support for the Ottoman Empire while undermining it. British ships had delivered Martini rifles to the Iraqi Bedouin by way of Kuwait, ostensibly to protect them against tribal disputes. They had given gifts of guns to tribal sheikhs and the heads of dervish convents around the Arabian Gulf. Now those rifles were trained against the Ottoman Sixth Army. No, Kamil didn't rule out British meddling, even if the guns had originated in the United States. But who were the British supporting and why Istanbul? Perhaps the guns were meant to be moved elsewhere.

"I suppose the British could have bought them in New York. Who in the United States would have a reason to ship illegal weapons to Istanbul?"

Yorg Pasha didn't answer. Kamil thought he looked worried. Despite his affection for the aging pasha, Kamil didn't trust him. He was the unseen middleman in procuring many of the Ottoman Army's weapons, but Kamil had heard of problems, jammed mechanisms, rotted stocks. Nothing was ever traceable back to the pasha himself.

After a few moments, Yorg Pasha said, "You have a difficult job ahead of you, my son. I wish I could help you, but I can't. The empire's enemies are countless. You know that. Armenians, Greeks, Russians, the British, the French, Young Turks sitting in the Porte, plotting to reinstate the parliament. They all have support abroad, and all could use a shipment of guns." He regarded Kamil for a moment with an affectionate smile, then reached across the table and rested his hand on his arm. "Come and visit me again soon and tell me how your investigation is going." He pushed himself to his feet. Simon hovered nearby, not quite touching the pasha's elbow as he followed him from the room.

Yorg Pasha's labored breathing reminded Kamil of his father, and he felt his heart contract. His parents were dead, and soon all the people who had known them best would be gone, erasing their presence in the world even further. He sat for a few moments, pulling his mind back to his work, and tried to parse what the pasha had said. He knew from experience that Yorg Pasha never spoke idly. A group with foreign support needed a shipment of guns to plot against the empire. That much was obvious. But which group? The pasha had said he wanted to help Kamil but couldn't. Did that mean Yorg Pasha was involved in the shipment? The thought saddened Kamil. The guns could have cost many lives. But Yorg Pasha had invited Kamil to return, and that Kamil resolved to do.

After a servant brought his horse, Kamil rode uphill toward the suburb of Nishantashou, where his brother-in-law lived. Huseyin worked at Yildiz Palace and had the ear of Sultan Abdulhamid. He would have heard if there was a revolution afoot in Istanbul. Kamil didn't know Huseyin's exact function at the palace, but his brother-in-law always seemed to have his finger on the pulse of information.

3

"CAN'T YOU PAINT us one at a time?" Huseyin asked irritably, catching his eight-year-old daughter Alev's arm as she tried to rise from the sofa. "Stay here, my girl."

"I'm bored," Alev sighed, pulling at her lace collar.

"Me too," her twin sister, Yasemin, chimed in, squirming against her mother, Feride. The girls wore matching dresses, their red hair gathered in satin bows. Feride was elegant in a white gown, a square of silk draped across her hair and pinned in place by a jeweled comb. Her face was long and pale with the cool repose of marble, her features finely chiseled, and her eyes the color of dark jade. When she looked at her husband and daughters, her eyes betrayed a fragility, as if she didn't quite believe they were real. She embraced Yasemin and leaned across to lay a steadying hand on Alev's knee, causing her to sigh crossly. Feride gave the artist a pleading look. "Can't we take a break, Elif?"

"One more moment." Elif bent closer to the easel, her blond hair falling forward and brushing her cheek. Her features were suspended in concentration, like a sculpture in bronze, revealing an unexpected immobility, possibly a hardness beneath her delicate beauty. Elif had sought refuge with her cousin Huseyin the previous year. An artist whose career had been cut short by marriage and the war in Macedonia, she had begun to paint again, but only landscapes, evocations of light and color, sea and sky. This was the first time she was attempting to capture people since her flight, since she had sketched her five-year-old son's death mask by the side of the road with charcoal and the boy's blood.

She stepped back from her easel and her expression eased. "There. You can all go now. I've done a sketch, so I won't need you together as a group anymore. From now on, I'll do individual portraits."

"Better paint the girls while they're sleeping," Huseyin suggested, drawing both of his daughters onto his lap, where they leaned contentedly against his chest. Yasemin idly fingered the gold and diamond medallion that hung from a ribbon around his neck.

Alev broke free of her father's embrace and sped across the room. "Uncle Kamil."

"Wouldn't it be simpler to have a photograph taken, brother-in-law?" Kamil asked with a laugh, bending down to embrace his niece.

"That advice would put all of us artists out of work," Elif retorted. She didn't look at him, but Kamil could have sworn the color rose in her face. She wore a cherry-colored tunic over wide pants, the eclectic, half masculine—half feminine style she had developed since arriving in Istanbul dressed as a man to aid her flight. Her golden hair was cut short as a boy's and unadorned.

"A photographer would give me a portrait of the family I actually have instead of the glorious creation Elif is painting. Every one of us will be gorgeous. Especially my wife." Huseyin reached over and tried to draw Feride onto his now-empty lap. Embarrassed, she struggled to get away. Huseyin planted a kiss on her cheek and let her go with a pat on her behind.

"Huseyin," she scolded, her face red. Kamil thought she looked secretly pleased and wondered at the unfathomable mysteries of married lives.

Feride took a closer look at her brother and frowned. "You look as though you were in a brawl at the opera."

He laughed. "Close enough. I was called from a formal reception last night to look into a case."

"And I'll bet you haven't slept or eaten, my dear. Dinner will be ready in just a few moments." Feride signaled the girls' governess to take them to change their clothes.

Elif smiled at Kamil, then busied herself with her paintbrushes and easel.

"Can I help you carry these things?" Kamil and Elif had become close after her arrival. She had trusted him enough to confide the story of the deaths of her husband and son. He had tried to let her know how much he cared for her, but she had disappeared from his life into one of her own. This was the first time he had seen her in months.

"It's good to see you," Elif said, her voice low in her throat.

"And you. You're looking well." What he really wanted to say was that he missed her company. Instead he asked, "How are your classes?"

"The students are wonderful. I'm honored to be teaching them." She snapped shut her paint box. "I have to go." She gave no explanation but raised her hand for him to shake. He took her hand and kissed it, holding it against his lips a moment too long.

She averted her eyes and, when he released her, fled the room.

Feride swept up Kamil's arm and led him into the dining room. Like the sitting room, it was dominated by enormous mirrors in gilded frames and still life oil paintings. Kamil wondered what Elif thought of the orchestrated scenes of fruits and flowers. They were masterly in execution, but very different from her own lively, impressionistic use of color. He found the pictures in his sister's home fascinating in an awful way, so true to life, yet simultaneously barren. He was sure they expressed Huseyin's taste, not Feride's.

Huseyin was already seated at the head of the table. He wasted no time. "So, brother-in-law, I'm surprised you kept your trousers on in there. I thought you were going to explode with desire."

"Huseyin, you're impossible," Feride scolded. "It's hard to believe sometimes that I married you."

"I know, my delicate flower. I'm a disappointment to you."

Kamil tensed at what he feared might be an evening of bickering. He had always wondered why Feride had chosen Huseyin from among her suitors. He was a distant relation of the royal family's, and very wealthy, but seemed to revel in his overbearing boorishness. Still, the previous year Huseyin had helped Kamil with one of his cases and shown himself to be a shrewd judge of character. When Kamil overlooked his brother-in-law's ostentation and bad taste and his tendency to needle Feride, he managed to like him.

A servant placed a slice of spinach pie on his plate and a bowl of yoghurt beside it. The scent of the fresh-baked pastry reminded Kamil how hungry he was. Huseyin drank wine, as he did with almost every meal, but Kamil asked for water, which calmed him and cleared his mind.

He noticed a pin in Feride's hair, a shower of teardrop-shaped rubies that winked in the light when she moved her head. The hairpin was more exuberant than his sister's usual modest attire, and Kamil complimented her on it. Feride was a beautiful but reserved woman. He knew that she deeply desired the kind of close friendships she imagined other people had but held herself back. She had few real friends, though she kept up a hectic schedule of visits and activities with the women in her social circle. She had once complained to Kamil that they bored her to tears. Since their father's death, she had become even sadder and more reserved. Only with Elif and on occasion with her husband had Kamil seen his sister open up. He remarked on and treasured any sign of joy in his sister's life.

"It's a gift from Huseyin," she responded shyly.

"Only the very best for the very best," Huseyin explained between bites. "What are you working on these days?" he asked Kamil.

"Is there something brewing in the city?" Kamil asked. "We've intercepted a cargo of weapons." He refused a servant's offer of wine but pushed his fork with relish into the next dish, charred eggplant cream topped with morsels of stewed lamb.

"On a British ship," Huseyin added pointedly. "I know the British are arming terrorists in the provinces, but what are they thinking sending weapons like that to Istanbul? This is a city, not a desert sheikhdom. If you start shooting here, before you know it, you'll have a pile of bodies so big it would fill the harbor. Don't tell me Nizam Pasha has assigned this case to you."

"He has. He wants me to find out who the shipment was for and its purpose." The imperious and inscrutable minister of justice, Nizam Pasha, had made Kamil special prosecutor in charge of the investigation. Kamil was never sure whether these difficult assignments were a recognition of Kamil's skill or an invitation to fail.

"More of these British games. They distribute fuel drop by drop, year after year, thinking no one notices, and then they hand out matches." Huseyin drank from his glass, gave a satisfied grunt, and then turned his attention to his plate.

"Who would the British be arming here in Istanbul?"

"Sultan Abdulhamid suspects the Armenians of colluding with Russia. There are rumors of something going on in the Kachkar Mountains. Foreigners have been seen there, agitating the locals. They'll be arming the villagers next. The Kurdish irregulars will put an end to it, one way or another."

"What do you mean?" Feride asked, staring at her husband. "Are you saying they'll just kill everyone and that will be the end of the problem?"

"Of course not, my delicate rose." He reached out and laid his hand over hers. "We shouldn't be discussing business over dinner."

Feride pulled her hand away. "I find politics interesting, and I don't like being treated as a child."

Huseyin looked to Kamil for support. "Do I deserve this?"

"A rose with thorns, as you often put it," Feride retorted, placing her napkin beside the plate and pushing her chair back as if preparing to leave the table. "Would you like me better if I were all soft petals?" Kamil could hear the hurt in her voice.

Huseyin reached out a restraining hand and said in a cajoling voice, "I like you the way you are, my wife, with both thorns and petals."

"I agree with Feride," Kamil interjected, hoping to ease the tension. "We have a well-trained army. Why send irregulars known for their brutality? They're no better than bandits in the service of the state. If our Armenian subjects do revolt," he warned, "it'll be against the sultan's heavy-handedness."

"We don't want the Kurdish tribes civilized," Huseyin said, glancing at Feride, who sat stiffly but was following his words. "At least one of our knives has to remain sharp. Don't be naïve, Kamil. The Russians have been trying for centuries to grab a piece of the empire. They took Artvin ten years ago, and now we have the border right up to our ass. These disturbances are taking place on our side of the border, in the Choruh Valley, where Armenians live. Of course the Russians are trying to extend their reach. They think we're weak now. They think they can get another arm of the empire, and the Armenians will get a finger in return." Huseyin speared a piece of meat and held it up. "And the British lie in wait under the table for the scraps."

"That may be so," Feride broke in, "but killing Armenian villagers isn't going to make them loyal."

"So what would make them loyal?" Huseyin growled. "Do you think there's enough gold left in our treasury to buy them?"

"Most of them are loyal now," Kamil pointed out.

"And if they feel respected and safe and that their children have a future," Feride added, "then they'll stay loyal."

Huseyin stared at them incredulously, wineglass paused in midair. "I'm married into a family of fools."

"Look more closely and you'll find not foolishness, but wisdom," Kamil, offended, told him.

Huseyin laid his hand across his heart. "I apologize." He nodded at his glass. "Blame it on the grape or on a bad upbringing, but I have no control over my tongue. I would rather cut it out than say a bad word about my honored wife, whom I respect more than myself." He looked into Feride's eyes. "Am I forgiven?"

Feride lowered her eyes, then nodded briefly.

Huseyin turned again to Kamil. "Do you think the British are behind the weapons shipment?"

"It makes no sense," Kamil observed. "If the British wanted to arm the Armenians on the Russian border, it would be much easier to send the weapons through Syria. Anyway, the British would never help the Armenians if that meant helping the Russians."

"True enough. The British are devious, but not suicidal. The socialists, on the other hand, they're an unpredictable lot." Huseyin took another sip of wine.

"Socialists?" Kamil exclaimed. "Isn't that rather far-fetched?"

"They have alliances all over Europe, so you're not dealing with just Armenians or Greeks or Russians. You're dealing with all of them, plus the Irish, the Americans, and Allah knows who else has swallowed their ridiculous ideas." He held out his glass. "You should try this. It's good. From my favorite vineyard in Ayvalik. If you like it, I'll send you a case."

It was a gesture of peace. Kamil allowed the servant to fill his glass and took a sip, then nodded his approval. He noticed Feride drinking deeply from her own glass and thought he saw the glint of tears in her eyes, but he didn't know what to say. She would have to find her way in this marriage. He gave her a sympathetic smile, then turned back to Huseyin. "What's the reaction in the palace to the weapons?"

"What do you think? Our great padishah has been convinced by his advisers that other nations have riddled us with spies like mold in a loaf of bread and that he needs a secret service to counter their influence. For now, the sultan has set up a new security force called Akrep as a branch of the secret police, but mark my words, Akrep is the first step in establishing a Teshkilati Mahsusa, a vast secret service like the one the British have." Huseyin took another sip from his glass, letting the wine roll on his tongue before swallowing. So out of character, Kamil noted, for a man who devoured his food with wolfish abandon. "Akrep is going to ferret out these revolutionary cells, unlike the secret police who just spy on everybody and write reports. Akrep is going to go after these people, the Armenians, the Greeks, the socialists, and all their foreign collaborators."

Any expansion of the secret police alarmed Kamil, much less the formation of a new security network reporting directly to the sultan.

"Akrep means scorpion. The scorpion that hides in your shoe," Feride mused. "Or is it an acronym? Does it stand for something?"

"I have no idea." Huseyin threw down his napkin and got up. He gave Feride a kiss on the cheek. "I've got to go. A meeting."

"At this time of night?" Feride asked. Kamil saw the light go out in her eyes.

"Business is best conducted over a meal with raki, my dear wife. That way, your opponent's brain is in his stomach and you can take advantage of him." He patted his ample stomach. "I've already eaten, but that's never been an impediment. I eat in the line of duty."

"Take Vali, Huseyin," Feride urged, referring to their driver. "I don't like it when you go out drinking and use a hired carriage."

"Wine is king and raki is queen, and a good marriage they make. Like ours." He leaned over and kissed her cheek. "Don't worry, my rose."

"When will you be home?"

"I'm not sure." He kissed her again. "See you, brother-in-law." Huseyin winked at Kamil and strode out of the room.

Kamil and Feride said nothing for a while, busying themselves with their coffee cups. Then Feride gave a self-conscious laugh and said, "You've resisted all my attempts to marry you off, dear brother. But maybe it's better that way, to marry only when you're tired of chasing about."

"I don't 'chase about,' Ferosh," Kamil responded with mock indignation.

Feride wagged her head and intoned, "Everything reaches my ears."

Kamil was glad to see a spark in her eyes. She laughed, revealing a row of pearllike teeth.

Then she surprised him by saying, "Elif needs time, brother. She looks happy enough with her art and she loves teaching. But she's still mourning." Feride twisted her napkin. "Her example makes me impatient with my own foolish fears."

Kamil went to her side. He pulled his thumb across her forehead as he had done as a child to soothe her and was rewarded by a sad smile. "I'm always here, Ferosh."

4

WHEN THE BLAST hit, the first thing Vahid looked at was the porcelain ball hanging from a chain in the middle of the ceiling. His mother continued tatting in her chair by the stove, undisturbed by the noise. He wondered if she was going deaf, although she seemed to hear what she wanted to hear. Her eyes were clouding over with cataracts, slowly blinding her. She didn't need to see in order to wrest tiny shapes from the thread that slipped through her still-nimble fingers. Almost every surface in the small house was decorated with doilies, laces, and the embroidered cloths she had brought as part of her dowry when she married Vahid's father. His death, like his life, had left no imprint on the house at all.

The decorative ball was useful as a quick earthquake indicator. Tonight it hung unmoving from the painted ceiling, a still fulcrum in a field of peeling stars and flowers. Not an earthquake then, but a powerful explosion somewhere in the city. He checked the time. Eight o'clock. He opened the window, letting in the smell of damp charcoal and wood fire. A foul-smelling yellow mist insinuated itself into the room. Flakes of snow settled on his sleeve.

To the northeast, above the dark hulks of houses, the sky was abnormally bright. He heard shouts in the distance. Beneath his window, a group of men stood talking excitedly. "The bank is on fire," he heard one of them say. Vahid marveled at the speed of gossip. The Ottoman Imperial Bank was on the other side of the Golden Horn, the inlet that divided the old city from the new. Certain that this was no ordinary fire, Vahid drew on his coat and boots.

"Are you going?" his mother asked in a reedy voice.

"Yes," he responded curtly, thinking, as always, that it was obvious that he was going, but feeling guilty about his annoyance. He descended into the dark street.

He followed the commotion down the hill toward the Eminönü pier. A pall of white smoke rose from the opposite shore. He pushed his way through the crowd across the Galata Bridge. In Karaköy Square, men with flares ran about, shouting. As he approached the bank, torches were no longer necessary. The fire was at a wooden taverna across from the bank. The blaze was enormous. Both floors must have been crowded with diners, he thought. Vahid never frequented this taverna, popular with bankers and bureaucrats from the Sublime Porte, the center of government just across the Golden Horn.

The fire brigade pumped water from a tank into the flames. When the fire died down sufficiently, men dashed inside and began to pull out bodies. Those still alive were laid on a covered cart. The air stank of charred flesh. Vahid pulled a handkerchief from his pocket and held it over his mouth. He surmised the victims were rich men making deals or entertaining their mistresses. Many of the corpses were naked—their clothes had burned off—mouths cooked open, blackened hands curled in supplication. Snowflakes settled on them, melting immediately. The cart carrying the wounded began to groan up the steep hill.

The street echoed with shouts and coughs, the moans of the wounded, the murmur of the crowd. A woman screamed, "My daughter, my daughter," bucking against the bystanders who held her back from the burning building.

A burly, broad-shouldered man whom Vahid assumed to be the

police chief was shouting at his men, "Keep the hell out of there, you idiots. It's going to collapse and crush your stupid skulls. Where the hell is Rejep?"

Sure enough, there was a loud creaking and the taverna lurched as the second floor crashed down upon the first. The chief ran into the rubble, hauling and kicking planks out of his way, and pulled out one of his men. There was a cheer from the bystanders.

As he approached, Vahid noted with surprise that part of the stone facade of the bank also had collapsed. The explosion must have been there, with the fire spreading across the lane to the wooden taverna.

An explosion at the bank was sure to unsettle Sultan Abdulhamid. It was an attack on the financial center of the empire. As he surveyed the scene, Vahid began to see the destruction before him as a rare opportunity. As head of Akrep he commanded hundreds of agents and spies who would track down these criminals. Before long, they'd be hanging on a meat hook in Bekiraga Prison. Perhaps they were revolutionaries with bigger designs on the empire than a simple robbery. He could make sure they confessed to such a plot before they died. When Sultan Abdulhamid saw that Vahid had saved the empire, he was certain the padishah would appoint him chief of the Teshkilati Mahsusa, the enormous secret service that was now only in the planning stages.

As head of the Teshkilati Mahsusa, Vahid would command thousands, not hundreds, of men. They would infiltrate towns and cities all over Europe, not only the Ottoman Empire. He would have direct access to the sultan, instead of having to work through the vizier. The vast networks and resources would make him feared by even the highest-ranking men in the empire. There were those who didn't believe him worthy of such an exalted position, men who would rejoice if he failed. But Vahid knew in his heart there was no one more capable than he, and he would prove it, possibly now with the help of this remarkable twist of fate.

The snow had let up, and he could see the corpses at the side of the road. At a distance they all looked alike, oozing black and red, mouths open in interrupted screams, claws instead of hands. The police were wrapping each body in a sheet. One man stopped to retch into the gutter.

Vahid walked over to examine the bodies more closely. The patrons of this taverna had been powerful men, but in death they were indistinguishable from those they had commanded.

He recognized her hair. Waist-length golden curls that turned in on themselves like a nautilus. He had never seen another woman with such hair. It had miraculously escaped the flames and unfurled across the pavement. He knelt and reached out to stroke it, avoiding looking at her body. When his hand touched the curls, his fingers stiffened, and for a moment he was unable to breathe, as if his own hands and lungs had been immolated in the fire. With great effort, he turned and inspected her face. It was Rhea. What an hour before had been a delicate face with an engaging smile and alabaster skin had become the bloated black and red mask before him. He remained motionless for a long while, then retrieved a silver hairpin set with rubies from her hair. When two policemen came to move the body, he stood and stepped away.

What was the woman he loved, the woman he was going to marry, doing at a taverna? Overcome by rage at the thought that she had been with another man, he squeezed his hand around the hairpin in his pocket, lacerating his palm. He would find this person and do to him what the man had done to Rhea.

As Vahid walked away from the scene, lost in thought, a man approached him. "Sir," the Akrep agent said discreetly, "there's been a new development."

5

VERA TOOK OFF her sodden coat and hung it over a chair, then dried her hair with a dirty underskirt. She opened the iron stove. Chunks of coal lay on top of kindling, ready for her to light. Silently thanking Gabriel, she wondered if he would come home tonight. She heard a commotion in the street. She peered out the grimy window, noting a strange brightness to the air, but could see nothing through the storm. After a few minutes, the sounds receded. Who knew what strange things happened at night in a city like this? Better to stay close to the fire and wait for Gabriel. She sat down next to the stove and examined her wool gown for signs of wear, fingering the embroidered sleeve that betrayed her family's wealth.

She smoked a cigarette and threw the stub on the floor. Bored and hungry, she went to the cupboard and took out the remains of last night's meal. If only Apollo had come to Istanbul with them as planned, she would have had company now. Her dear friend Apollo Grigorian, whose words poured like brilliant water over his listeners, soothing and inspiring them. He gave the revolution a charmed life, as if it had already happened in their minds and there was no longer any need to fret. Most of all, Vera remembered that he had held her hand when she felt homesick, and had healed her without saying a word. She knew that Apollo's absence weighed on Gabriel, who had counted on his help for the project he was carrying out in Istanbul. With a stab of anxiety, she wondered whether something had befallen her friend, but then scolded herself. Messages were lost and carts overturned. She knew that Apollo would pick up the spilled apples and move on.

Vera wrapped herself in a quilt and sat back down beside the stove. She would go home to Moscow, she decided. Gabriel didn't want her here, and she was a failure at being a socialist, a revolutionary, a wife, and, she added for good measure, a daughter. She smoked another cigarette and threw the butt into the stove, then lay down on the quilt. She kept the lamp turned low in case Gabriel should return. She thought about the beaded velvet gown her parents had given her last Christmas. She could almost feel the softness of it on her fingertips. Her baby sister, Tatiana, would be wearing it now. She remembered the weight of Tatiana's heavy black hair in her hands as she plaited it and the smell of geraniums wintering on the windowsill.

She was asleep when Gabriel slipped through the door and shut it quickly behind him. Gabriel Arti was a tall man with slightly rounded shoulders and a pleasant, undistinguished face with a mustache and clipped beard. He pulled off his wool cap, releasing a shock of sandy hair, and tickled her cheek with it until she woke.

"Where were you this afternoon?" he asked, dropping his coat in the corner.

"I went to see that publisher."

"God damn it." Gabriel squatted down beside her, extending his hands to the fire. They were scraped and bleeding. "I told you not to go."

She got up and went to a ceramic jar in the corner of the room. "Let me heat some water to wash your hands." She dipped a copper bowl in the water and set it to heat on top of the stove.

"Well, did he agree? Was the fact that you put us in danger balanced by the publication of some tract that only five people will ever read?"

"I wasn't followed," she insisted. "It was snowing. Why are you being like this?"

"What difference would snow make, except to make it impossible for you to see whoever was following you?"

"That's unfair. I have a mission too, and you have no right to keep me locked up here." She lit another cigarette. "Where were you? You never tell me where you go. Why do I have to report to you?" She threw the cigarette to the floor.

Someone spoke in the street, a snatch of sound, then stopped suddenly. Gabriel rose to his feet so quickly he knocked the water from the stove. He put out the lamp and peered cautiously out the window. "Get your coat on."

"Why? I told you no one followed me."

Gabriel grabbed her by the shoulders and shook her. "We have to leave right now," he said through gritted teeth. "Now. Now."

She threw on her coat and grabbed the small leather satchel that contained their money, travel papers, and the manuscript.

"Are we coming back? What about the suitcase?"

"No." He took the satchel from her hand and pushed her toward the door.

She pulled away from him and in the dim light of the stove began to throw her few things into the suitcase. He pulled it out of her hands and flung it across the room.

"I'm taking my things," she shouted, sobbing, retrieving it. "You don't care about me at all. Why did you marry me? Just as a convenient cover?"

"Shut up, Vera. You're being stupid." He glanced nervously at the door.

Vera placed the suitcase next to the chair and sat, arms folded tightly across her chest. "I won't be spoken to like that. Go ahead. I'm staying."

"You'll get us both killed." After a moment, Gabriel pulled himself together. "All right," he said. "I'll go to the hostler on the corner and rent a carriage to carry my lady away. Is that acceptable?" He made a formal bow, but his smile was forced.

Vera wiped her eyes with the edge of her scarf. "Thank you. I'm sorry I made such a fuss."

"It won't take more than five minutes. Take your suitcase and whatever else you want to pack and wait for me at the back door to the alley. Five minutes," he warned. "Be very quiet. If you see anyone, run into the alley and hide." He reached into the satchel and handed her a small booklet, her Russian passport. "Put this in your pocket, in case we get separated."

"I'll be ready." She jumped up and retrieved her suitcase from across the room. Hearing his shoes clatter down the back stairs, she worried that he was not wearing boots.

$$\infty$$

IT TOOK more than half an hour to find a hostler so late at night, agree to terms, and harness the horse. Gabriel would have to find a way to return the carriage tomorrow so as not to arouse further suspicion. Tonight of all nights, with the gold safely hidden, he had wanted to celebrate by making love to Vera. He wished he still had his driver, Abel, and the carriage, but after the robbery they had driven to the pasha's stables in Bebek to stash the gold, and then Abel had dropped Gabriel off and gone home.

Gabriel wiped the snow from his eyes and slapped the horse's rump with the reins. It was senseless to rail at Vera for her naïve enthusiasm, which had made her forget the basic rule of any mission—make sure you're not detected. But he could no longer risk staying here. It was crucial that he not be arrested. The entire project, years of preparation, would be destroyed. New Concord commune needed the weapons and the gold to survive. Vera didn't know about the robbery and the guns or their link to New Concord, so how could he expect her to understand what was at stake?

Over the past eight months, fifty pioneers of the socialist International from Europe, Russia, and the United States had made their way to the Choruh Valley in the Kachkar Mountains to begin a grand experiment Gabriel had conceived and spent the last ten years bringing to life—the first truly socialist community in the world. This was his dream and the dream of dozens of comrades who were risking their lives to realize it.

Last year, he and three associates had traveled by ship down the Danube past Budapest and Belgrade to Trabzon on the Black Sea. From there they rode through the mountains and followed the rapids of the Choruh River to the village of Karakaya, where in the name of the New Concord Foundation, the commune had bought a parcel of land, an orchard, and a ruined monastery that it planned to restore. The valley was a paradise of alternating rain and brilliant sunshine, with stands of poplar and neat orchards of olive, pomegranate, and fig trees. The streams were alive with trout. Villages clung to the slopes below dizzying ascents through forests and alpine meadows. It reminded him of Geneva and made him think of the Garden of Eden. It was the perfect place to begin the human experiment anew, without the sin of greed.

Gabriel left the rented carriage at the end of the dark alley and waded through the snow to the back door of the tenement. Vera wasn't there. Perhaps she had gotten cold and gone back upstairs to wait by the stove.

He pushed open the door and climbed the stairs. His feet were wet and cold, and he thought he'd change into his boots, which were drying by the fire.

Inside, the suitcase was open, its contents strewn across the floor, but Vera was gone. He looked down and saw a bloody mass beneath his shoes. He stumbled backward, then realized, to his relief, that it was a crushed pomegranate. He wondered where it had come from. Maybe Vera had kept the fruit until they could make their luck together. The pomegranate told him that she had struggled. He walked around the room, his fists balled, but there was nothing else to tell him what had happened.

He ran down the stairs to the front of the house, noticing muddy smears on the treads. He peered out into the empty street. The snow gave off a nacreous glow. A glint of candlelight appeared in a window across the way. He could see carriage tracks, but snow had already filled them in, leaving only shallow depressions.

He went back upstairs and examined the room again. An object on the floor, embedded in the crushed flesh of the pomegranate, caught his eye. He picked it up and wiped it clean. It was Vera's passport. A corner of the first page had torn away.

Gabriel pulled from his pocket the wool cap, a kind local workers wore, tucked his scarf around his face, and stepped into the street. He walked slowly and deliberately in the opposite direction from where he had left the carriage.

He felt rather than saw the men behind him. Gabriel was skilled at evasion, learned as a boy in the brutal dockyards of Sevastopol and honed in two decades of political organizing. He leaped sideways into an alley, leaving no tracks, then moved from one doorway to another, trying to land on dry surfaces. Before long he had lost his pursuers.

He walked much of the night, not daring to hail a carriage. Keeping the Bosphorus in sight to his right, he headed north. The road wound through a forest at the crest of the hill, then dipped steeply and rose again. He stumbled in the darkness under the trees and more than once became mired in drifts. In desperation, he left the road and struggled down the slope, pushing his way through undergrowth and brambles, toward the waters of the strait pulsing far below.

He came to a village, dark and shuttered against the storm. A thin stream of smoke drifted from a stovepipe chimney protruding from the side of a house, and Gabriel was momentarily entranced by the scent of burning wood. He imagined his sister sitting beside him on a quilt. It was satin. He could almost taste the bright pink color. He had stolen it from a porch where it was being aired and brought it to their shack in the forest. Whenever his sister stroked the slippery surface, her face took on a soft, faraway look. Gabriel was gripped by a powerful impulse to sit down beneath the chimney and lose himself in his memories.

The thought of his naïve childlike wife in the hands of the police pushed him forward. He stumbled past the houses and found a path that he thought might connect this fishing village to the next. It was barely discernible in the storm, but at least it was level.

After several more hours, his hair and beard were frozen and he could no longer feel his limbs. Like a leper, he moved forward insensibly, not caring whether he was freezing to death. It didn't matter. Why had he left Vera alone?

He thought he felt the warm winter breeze of Sevastopol on his face, the wetness on his cheeks was salty sea spray. His sister kissed his cheek softly. He caught her scent of hyacinths and thought he should stop and embrace her. He had believed his sister was dead, but he was mistaken. The realization filled him with happiness. He resisted the desire to sit down and let the snow cover him. He had to stay alive to get Vera back.

6

THE WINDOWS of Kamil's villa glowed invitingly as he rode up the drive, wrapped against the icy wind in a heavy wool coat and a kalpak of Persian lamb. His cook and housekeeper, Karanfil, made it a point to place lamps near the windows when he was out, a habit she had developed when he was a child and sentimentally kept up now that he was a grown man. He could see the elegant silhouettes of his orchids on the sills, the long sprays of flowers preening in the limelight. He would have to remind Karanfil again not to put the lamps so close to the delicate blooms. He looked forward to one of her meals and to an hour in his winter garden before returning to the problem of finding the guns.

The firearms meant that something unusual was brewing, something that could tear at the belly of the empire, already made vulnerable through massive debt to European banks and loss of territory in decades of wars and revolts. The Ottoman state had created a stable system, fairer than most, that allowed every subject to participate, regardless of faith. Ottoman laws respected people's differences and accommodated them. None of those who broke away and founded their own nations could say the same, Kamil thought. These new states on the empire's receding fringes were cradles of blood in which nothing grew but hatred. The streets of Istanbul were crowded with refugees from massacres committed by people newly freed from the Ottoman system of law, acting with impunity or, worse, with a nod from their national leaders. Kamil was determined to keep the center strong, serving the empire like his father and grandfather, who had both been governors.

Karanfil's son, Yakup, who acted as Kamil's manservant, ran from the house and took hold of the bridle before Kamil could dismount. Yakup's ascetic, high-boned face was grim.

"I was just about to fetch you, pasha. Chief Omar sent for you. Someone blew up the Ottoman Imperial Bank. A taverna next door burned down. There are many dead."

Kamil turned his horse and galloped back through the gate. He was surprised to receive the summons from Omar. The bank was located in the Karaköy district. Omar was the police chief of Fatih, on the other side of the Golden Horn.

Half an hour later, he slowed to maneuver through the traffic that thronged the steep, winding streets even at this late hour. Below him, he could see a black funnel of smoke twisting upward and expanding into a ghostly white cloud lit from below. He descended to Karaköy Square, where horse-drawn carts, porters, pedestrians, handcarts, and peddlers jostled one another, churning the snow into a brown paste. He spurred his horse through the crowd of onlookers until he heard Chief Omar's familiar, booming voice, then dismounted, giving his horse to one of the constables.

Black smoke boiled into the night. There was a cacophony of screaming, shouting, and the crack of smoldering wood. The confusion was fitfully illuminated by men running back and forth with torches. A crowd of onlookers was gathered at the end of the street, barely held back by a handful of policemen. Others were at work carrying people from the wreckage. Italian nuns, their lips moving in prayer, watched from the rectory windows of Saint Peter's Church, directly behind the bank.

Two fire brigades pumped water from their portable tanks onto the taverna. One group of firemen had relayed a long hose into the Golden Horn and was pumping water from the harbor. Despite the cold, the firemen were shirtless and their bodies gleamed with sweat in the torchlight. Kamil wet his handkerchief and held it over his mouth and nose.

He identified himself to one of the policemen, who led him to the area between the bank and the burning taverna. The bank, a three-story granite building, was still standing, the coat of arms on its façade blackened but undamaged, although the entrance had been smashed into rubble. Across the lane, the timber shell of the restaurant glowed red like a backlit stage set. Occasionally a man emerged from the wreckage or disappeared inside. Istanbul's firemen were as famous for their physical prowess as for their almost foolhardy bravery.

Kamil saw the charred bodies lying on the pavement and stopped in horror. Some were still alive. Cracked, bloody hands grasped feebly at the air. As he watched, two firemen brought out the naked body of a woman, her face burned beyond recognition. They laid her on the ground and ran back to the fire. A woman in a black charshaf checked her pulse and then draped a sheet gently over the body. The woman's veil had fallen away from her face and Kamil saw that she was old, her chin covered in tribal tattoos, her teeth bared with tension. Men carried the wounded to carts lined up at the narrow crossroads. Kamil took hold of one of the victims and helped carry him to a cart already crowded with other victims. Viscous fluid seeping from the wounds stuck to Kamil's hands. He fought down nausea.

"Where are they taking them?" Kamil asked a bystander as the cart began its way uphill.

"Probably the nuns," the man responded, his eyes held by the flames. "That's the closest place."

"They're taking the wounded to a church?" Kamil wiped the palms of his hands on his trousers, but they remained sheathed with soot and blood.

"Austrians." The man's eyes were red, and tears streaked his face, from smoke or weeping. Kamil couldn't tell. "They set up an infirmary

during the last cholera outbreak. Right up there"—he pointed—
"below the tower. They might be taking them elsewhere too. It isn't
very big."

An empty cart pulled up. Kamil and the men worked quickly, since
every touch seemed to cause the wounded great pain. Kamil forced
himself to be calm. He thought of the orchids in his summer garden,
his mind walking along the pebble-filled trays, listing one Latin name
after another—*Acineta hrubyana, Cephalanthera rubra, Orchis lac-
tea, Orchis pinetorum*—while his hands grasped slippery limbs, the
victim's lungs too burned to moan, but his eyes wild with pain.

When all the wounded had been taken away and the remaining bodies checked, wrapped in sheets, and stacked in carts, Kamil
washed his hands thoroughly in a bowl of warm water the old woman
brought him. Then he slumped down against the side of a building.

After a few minutes he became aware of a familiar voice and
caught sight of Chief Omar arguing with a man in uniform, presumably the chief of the Karaköy police district. When he saw Kamil,
Omar, black from head to foot with soot, but looking smug, came
over.

"The Karaköy police will survey the neighborhood," he announced.
"They're good at that; they know everybody. We'll do the hard thinking, of course. Good thing I happened to be in the area." He grinned.
"I'll share the credit with them, naturally." His teeth were glaringly
white against his dirty skin. He was a big, barrel-chested man with a
thick neck, an overly loud voice, and doleful brown eyes that expressed
undisguised pleasure at being in the thick of things.

Kamil stood and faced Chief Omar. "What the hell is going on?"
he asked in a hoarse, cracked voice, angry at the police chief's levity.
He wondered if Omar's experience as a soldier had hardened him to
such carnage. Kamil hoped he would never think of any death as less
than the highest tragedy.

"The most damnable thing," Omar exclaimed. "There was an
explosion at the bank. The fire spread across the street. Eighteen
dead so far. Four of them bank guards, the rest were in the restaurant.
A fast fire." He gestured at the smoldering ruin. "Most in the taverna

died. One bank guard survived. Don't know if anyone else was inside the bank. It was closed."

"Well, we had better find out." Kamil surveyed the pile of rubble that had been the bank entrance, then bent over and heaved a length of marble facing to the side. The physical effort helped him regain some semblance of control over his emotions. He and Omar's men worked by the light of torches in a pall of acrid smoke. The clap of bricks landing and the coughs and curses of the policemen mingled with the shouts of the fire brigade next door and the sound of wood settling. Half an hour later, a contingent of heavily armed gendarmes arrived from the direction of Karaköy Square. Kamil had called in the military police to guard the bank, just as they were guarding the ship carrying the guns.

Kamil paused to give instructions to the gendarme captain, who then ordered the soldiers to surround the building and to help clear the rubble. They wouldn't be able to go inside until the debris was cleared and the building stabilized.

"This will take all night," Omar said, disgusted. "We might as well go home. What's that up there?" he asked, pointing to the raised carving on the wall.

"This used to be the residence of the French ambassador a hundred or so years ago. I think it's his coat of arms."

"They told me the building belongs to Saint Peter's Church. Isn't that Italian?"

Kamil raised his hands in helpless surrender, unable to decode the twisted strands of property relations in this, one of the city's oldest districts.

Kamil asked the gendarme captain to send for them when the bank was considered safe to enter. As he and Omar walked to the stable where their horses were kept, they passed the imam from a nearby mosque and a Greek Orthodox priest huddled deep in conversation, presumably deciding where to take the bodies that couldn't be identified. The taverna was owned by Christians.

"Did you find out anything from the ship's crew?" Kamil asked Omar.

"The barrels were loaded in New York, but I think the crew didn't know there were guns in them. There were a lot of barrels on board, most of them full of salted fish just like the manifest says. The recipient in Istanbul gave a fictitious name, so we couldn't trace him." He coughed and spit out black phlegm, then gestured over his shoulder at the demolished bank. "Do you think the same people did this?"

Kamil stopped and stared at the crowd in the square, livid that they were carrying on as if Armageddon hadn't just happened a block away. He could feel Omar watching him and knew the gruff ex-soldier understood. "A shipful of illegal weapons and an attack on the Imperial Bank in the same week? I doubt it's a coincidence," Kamil said in a quiet voice.

7

$\mathcal{V}$ERA WAS EXPECTING someplace cold and dark, not this comfortable armchair in a warm room hung with kilims. After Gabriel left, two men had burst into the room and, after a brief struggle, thrown a greasy blanket over her head, carried her out, and pushed her into a carriage, where the blanket was replaced by a blindfold. It had taken no more than a moment; she couldn't even remember their faces. After a long ride, they emerged and walked along a gravel path—the snow had been cleared, and she could hear the delicate crunch of stones beneath her feet—and down a flight of steps into this room. The men politely asked her to remove her boots. They had taken them away and in their stead given her slippers that were too small.

As soon as they left, Vera pulled the blindfold off and tried the door, but it was locked. On a small table beside the glowing stove was a glass of hot tea. She settled herself in the armchair and, warming her hands with the tea glass, tried to figure out who these men might be.

Had Gabriel been detained and sent his allies to snatch her to safety moments before the police arrived to arrest her? She knew

Gabriel had been right to worry about her carelessness and regretted acting like a child when what her husband had needed was a smart comrade-in-arms. She had struggled against the men, out of surprise and alarm, and dropped the pomegranate from her pocket onto the floor, although what message Gabriel could take from that she didn't know. She checked her coat pocket for the tenth time. Except for a torn fragment, her passport was gone. It must have fallen out of her pocket with the pomegranate.

The key turned in the lock. In spite of her coat and the proximity of the stove, she was shivering. The man who entered was tall, with an imposing head and a jutting nose. His cheeks were pitted with acne scars, partially hidden beneath a black, pointed beard and a precisely trimmed mustache. His hair was thick as an animal's pelt, sleek and shiny. There was something military in his bearing, although his clothing was that of an ordinary civil servant. His movements were careful, tidy, as if minutely thought out. He stood just inside the door, staring at her with a slight tilt of the head as if he had recognized her and were trying to place her. He was not attractive, she thought, but there was a gross sensuality in his reddish lips, the too-luxuriant hair. She looked away, uncomfortable, and put the tea glass on the table, slowly and deliberately, as if not to disturb him.

The man sat down in the chair facing hers and said something in Turkish. When she didn't understand, he said, "Welcome, Lena," in poorly pronounced Armenian. "My name is Vahid." Behind a curtain of thick lashes, his eyes were dark amber. She could read neither concern nor threat in them, only a barely suppressed interest.

It took her a moment to realize he thought her name was Lena Balian, the false name she had given the publisher. The kind old man would never have reported her name to the police, she thought. He must have noticed that she was being followed and asked his acquaintances to snatch her away to a safe place. Did these men work with Gabriel too? She didn't think they were Armenian, despite Vahid's few words of the language, so they must be socialists. Gabriel sometimes talked about the men supporting his mission in Istanbul.

He had described one of the men as having a big face like a horse. Was this that man?

She gave him a wavering smile. "Thank you." She wasn't sure for what.

"You don't like the tea?" He indicated her full glass.

She shook her head yes. She liked the tea. She didn't want to seem ungrateful. The intensity of his gaze made her anxious. Should she tell him her real name? She realized she had been playacting at politics. This now was real. She must make the right decision and not disappoint Gabriel again.

"You were in danger, Lena. But you are safe here. And your friend, where is he?" the man asked, head cocked to the side, his eyes never leaving her face.

What was she supposed to answer? She looked down at her hands.

"We had hoped to bring him here as well. He's also in danger."

Vera said nothing, thinking furiously. It nagged at her that he hadn't said Gabriel's name. Surely he knew him, one of the most famous socialist leaders in Europe. Vera began to shiver.

"You are young, Lena," Vahid said with a tight smile that was not reflected in his eyes. "Your friend appreciates you?" It didn't surprise her that he didn't know she and Gabriel were married. They had told only their close friends. She made a decision.

"Which friend?" she asked. She saw the flash of anger but wasn't prepared for the blow that knocked her from the chair. For a moment her vision went black. She crawled along the floor until her back was against the wall. Her mouth was filling up with blood.

"You're an intelligent girl, Lena. I know we'll get along. You'll see."

8

AT FIVE O'CLOCK IN the morning, Yakup roused Kamil from his bed with a glass of strong tea. A gendarme waited in the entry hall to tell him that the rubble had been cleared from the front of the bank. It had stopped snowing. A thick fog wrapped the city in muslin and deadened all sound, so that the tick of their horses' hooves on cobble was very loud.

Through the mist, the bank looked undamaged. Across the street, the taverna was now just a blackened pile. Kamil walked up the cracked marble stairs into the bank. The gendarmes had set up scaffolding to keep the entryway from collapsing. It opened onto a high-ceilinged room decorated with blue tiles and lit by torches and lamps. Along a marble counter were the tellers' cages and a woman's section where the bank teller was obscured behind a wooden lattice. Benches ranged along two sides of the room. Except for the entrance, the bank seemed unscathed.

The gendarme captain saluted Kamil, and Omar sauntered over. "About time. I'm almost ready for another breakfast." He waved his hand around the room. "Not as bad as we thought."

"The explosives were set at the entrance," the captain explained. "It looks like a hasty job, meant more for show than damage."

"Was anything taken?"

"We waited for you," Omar announced, running his finger over his mustache. "The vault is downstairs. It's open," he added meaningfully.

He led Kamil to an iron gate at the back of the lobby, beyond which narrow steps descended. Kamil pointed to a polished wooden slide that ran from the head of the stairs into the basement. "This must be where they send the bags of coin down to the vault."

"About ten years ago, they had a robbery here, an inside job," Omar told him. "One of the clerks was sneaking into the reserves and replacing gold coins with silver. It was years before they noticed the adulterated bags. By that time he had stolen about eighty thousand British pounds. I heard that after that, they developed a new, foolproof security system. Wait until you see it."

At the bottom of the stairs a corridor led to a thick wooden door. It stood open, a key protruding from the lock.

"This explains why the empire is bankrupt," Omar said, his voice dripping with sarcasm. "We don't need a treaty to hand our wealth over to our European friends. They can just come in here, jiggle the lock, and take what they want."

They crossed the threshold and found themselves in a brick chamber with a vaulted roof, lined with shelves of ledgers. There was no gold.

Omar pointed to two doors at the far end of the room, each behind a gate of iron bars. "Strong rooms. Well, at least that."

The outer barred gates could be opened with a key, but the strong room doors appeared to be of solid iron and had double locks. One of them was ajar. Kamil pushed it open and stepped inside. The air was musty and smelled of leather, ink, and old paper.

The walls, floor, and ceiling were welded iron sheets. Wooden shelves held leather bags, chests, metal strongboxes, bundles of banknotes, and stacks of securities. One set of shelves near the door was bare, the floor littered with gold coins from a leather bag that had fallen and split open. Kamil picked up one of the coins and tossed it in his hand, then placed it on the shelf. "I wonder how much is missing." Several European countries stored their assets in this bank.

"I bet it won't be pigeon shit. Do you think they were just run-of-the-mill thieves or that they're going to use this money to raise hell? I'd put my money, if I had any, on raising hell. Why else the fireworks? Either way, our padishah is going to be very unhappy."

" 'Unhappy' isn't the word I would use." Sultan Abdulhamid would assume a connection between the weapons smuggling and the robbery and put pressure on the minister of justice, who in turn would blame Kamil for not apprehending the smugglers in time to prevent the robbery. Kamil was certain Nizam Pasha would assign him this case as well. He often gave Kamil important cases with one hand and with the other undermined his ability to prosecute them, as if he couldn't decide whether he wished Kamil to succeed or fail and so routinely prepared the way for both.

"Can you imagine if they had gotten hold of the guns too?" Omar whistled. "It must be something big they've got planned."

"With this gold, they can buy ten shiploads of guns."

9

IT WAS NEAR DAWN when Gabriel approached Bebek, a village north of the city on the Bosphorus shore. It had stopped snowing, and everything was muted by mist, the quiet punctuated by the raucous laughter of gulls. The muezzin called the faithful to prayer from a nearby minaret. A faint pink wash outlined the Asian hills on the far side of the strait, a band of tarnished silver against the black landscape. Gabriel came to a high wall and lifted a thick fall of ilex with numb hands, unmindful of the avalanche of snow this released onto his head and shoulders. He forced the gate and slipped into the barren garden of Yorg Pasha's mansion.

The guards were suspicious, but at Gabriel's insistence they fetched Simon, the pasha's secretary, who Gabriel had previously noted seemed never to sleep. Simon arrived in minutes, fully dressed in a crisp stambouline frock coat and tie. If he was surprised to see Gabriel, he gave no sign.

Gabriel told him he had to see Yorg Pasha.

"It's six in the morning, Gabriel. The pasha isn't available. Perhaps I can help you."

Gabriel considered making his request to Simon, but the matter was too important. "I need to speak with the pasha directly." He didn't trust either of them, but he had no one else to turn to.

"That's not possible. If this is in regard to business, I'm the one to speak to. The pasha doesn't get involved in that sort of thing."

"It's a personal matter," Gabriel blurted out, unsure what other argument he could make to convince Simon.

Simon looked at him oddly, perhaps with a glint of amusement. "You'll have to tell me more if I'm to convince the pasha."

"Look, if this weren't urgent, I wouldn't have walked here in the middle of the night. All I want is ten minutes of his time. Please just tell him that."

Simon looked Gabriel over, considering. "Very well, I'll tell him, but I promise nothing." He pointed to Gabriel's hands. "It looks like you have frostbite. I'll send someone to look after that."

A servant arrived and brought Gabriel to a small marble bath, where he was instructed to place his hands into a basin of warm water. Gabriel's entire body ached, but when he removed his hands from the water, the pain shocked him. Two of the fingers on his right hand had turned purple. The man returned with a lamp and looked over Gabriel's hands. He pointed to the cuts on the fingers, which Gabriel had gotten from the brambles on his slide down the wooded hill, and explained in French, the shared language of foreigners in Istanbul, that if the cuts didn't heal, he might lose those fingers.

Brought to a room, Gabriel sat waiting, staring at his bandaged hands. The servant had given him laudanum to quell the pain, but the memory of it remained with him like the border of a large continent he was always just about to cross.

He no longer trusted himself to know what to do. The room looked out over the Bosphorus, and as he stood there, the color of the sky gathered and thickened between the hills directly across the strait into a deep apricot stain so intense it seemed alive. A cat scrabbled to get in, but Gabriel was mesmerized by the glowing disk, still partially obscured by trees, that was rising from the Asian hills, increasing in brilliance until he was forced to look away.

He pulled the curtains shut and went to lie on the bed. He tried to sleep but could not keep his eyes closed against the vertigo of visiting scenarios of his young wife in the hands of the secret police. He ceased to hear the scratching of the cat.

Finally, a messenger came to tell Gabriel that Yorg Pasha would see him as soon as the pasha finished breakfast. While Gabriel waited, another scene played in his head. The chests filled with gold liras had been pushed up against his knees in the carriage, its leather window flaps drawn as it turned into Karaköy Square to mingle with the evening traffic. An enormous blast sounded behind them. He was tempted to open the flap but could not risk exposing himself. After they had passed through the wooded hills north of the city and were unloading the chests, he had asked his driver, Abel, about the explosion.

"It was dark," Abel responded. "I don't know."

Abel was a member of the Istanbul cell. Gabriel planned to give him and his sister, Sosi, who had helped get the keys to the vault, enough money to disappear or travel to the commune in Karakaya. Once the chests were unloaded, Abel had taken him back to the city, dropped him off, and then disappeared. The carriage would be needed one more time—or so he had thought—to take him, Vera, and the gold to the ship that would transport them and their cargo to Trabzon. From there they would travel through the mountains to Karakaya.

A decade of political organizing, his dream within reach, and he was lying in a gilded room wondering whether his moment of weakness in marrying Vera would destroy everything he had worked for.

They had robbed the bank for gold to buy tools and building materials, livestock, more land, and rifles and pistols to replace those lost when their shipment of weapons from New York had been impounded in Istanbul's harbor.

The commune's proximity to the Russian-Ottoman border was a risk. The Russians might try to extend their territory again, as they had only a decade earlier. At the end of that war the Ottomans had ceded Artvin, which was less than a day's travel from Karakaya and the commune. Gabriel and the settlers thought that the unstable dirt tracks winding through the mountains in place of roads and the vertiginous drops and long screes on either side would keep away the Russians with their heavy artillery. Still, the hundreds of pioneers that Gabriel envisioned for New Concord needed enough firepower to hold off a battalion of invading infantry.

The Russians weren't the only danger. Without gold, without weapons, the community would starve or, defenseless, be slaughtered by the Ottoman authorities, who would feel threatened by a system with no privileged leaders and no distinction between rich and poor. None of the members of the commune were peasants, although several had grown up in the countryside and others had studied modern agriculture and animal husbandry. All would receive weapons training. If they got through the first year, word would spread, and as more people joined them, the commune would become self-sustaining. He had an image in his mind of white homespun cloth drying on a line before the restored walls of the monastery. He saw his sister lift one of the sun-soaked sheets and walk through into shadow.

Gabriel rose from the bed and moved the curtain aside. The light reflecting from the snow blinded him momentarily, but then he saw that the morning was well advanced. There was no sign of the cat. The gold was out there, he thought with satisfaction, just a few meters away beyond the frozen garden. When he first arrived in Istanbul, Gabriel had asked Simon's permission to store some supplies in the pasha's vast stables. After the robbery, he had simply added the chests from the bank, well camouflaged, to the jumble of other chests and supplies he was accumulating for his trip to the east. As long as the gold was safe and within reach, there was a future.

Gabriel tried the door to the room, but it was locked. He balled his fists and pounded on it, ignoring the pain that blazed through his hands, but there was no response. There was still Vera. He had to find his wife.

10

OMAR TRIED THE DOOR to the second strong room, but it was locked. "Well, at least they didn't rob this one."

"I wouldn't make that assumption," Kamil corrected him. "They could have gone in and then locked the door again. They appear to have had the keys. None of the doors were forced."

Omar nodded.

"We'll need an account of what's stored in these rooms," Kamil told him. "I'm surprised there aren't already bank officials here. Weren't they notified?"

"I was busy with the fire, getting people out. Maybe the Karaköy police sent word." He called over one of his men. The policeman was young, with the face of a much older man. His eyes were serious and attentive. "Rejep, go ask Chief Muzaffer where the bank officials are."

"The keys to this room might still be here," Kamil suggested, looking around. He set two of the gendarmes to search the bank systematically. They came back with handfuls of keys taken from various offices. None of them fit.

Rejep returned, red-faced. "Chief, Chief Muzaffer said to tell you . . ." He hesitated, and Omar bellowed at him, "Just tell me what that rat-faced excuse for a policeman said. I'm not going to kill the messenger."

"Yes, Chief," Rejep rattled off. "He said that if you want to be the cook, you have to also peel the onions."

Omar turned back to Kamil and translated. "No one has told the officials, although you'd think they could smell their bank burning even in the suburbs. Rejep, find out who the top officials are and where they live."

"Just a minute," Kamil interjected. "The central cashier is a Frenchman named Montaigne," he said. "The comptroller is British. Swyndon is his name, I think. There's a third official, a German, but I don't know him." He had met the bank officials several times at social events. Kamil remembered Montaigne as a narrow-eyed man who tippled champagne. Swyndon had a leonine head and a loud voice. He generally could be found in a gathering holding forth on some obscure subject, like the best way to hunt tigers, and tended to be the center of attention of a group of admiring ladies.

Omar gave Kamil a surprised look, as if he had suddenly remembered that Kamil was a pasha and not a simple ex-soldier like himself. "The addresses," he reminded Rejep.

The policeman began to move off, but Omar called him back. "And keep track of what the Karaköy police find out. Talk to the neighbors and people in the restaurants around here yourself. Find out what they saw." He explained to Kamil, "I only trust my own sources."

"As you command, Chief." The policeman turned to go.

"Rejep," Omar called out again. "Make sure you write it all down. The magistrates like fat reports." He winked at Kamil.

They climbed out of the basement into the smoke that still filled the lobby. A crystal chandelier hung from the ceiling. Pieces of it lay splintered across the floor like a spill of diamonds. The tellers' stations were behind cages of gilded wrought-iron bars. Bars that had kept no one out, Kamil noted grimly.

Beside him, Omar huffed, "Why bother blowing anything up when you have the keys? If they hadn't made all that racket, the theft might not have been discovered until morning."

"Probably they meant to kill the guards. They might have recognized them."

"Don't you think blowing up the building is an exceptionally elaborate way to kill a few guards?"

"Have you spoken to the surviving guard?"

"He wasn't in any condition to talk last night. They took him up to the Austrian infirmary. I hope he's still alive. From what I saw, the burns looked bad."

The sun was rising, flushing the sky orange, as they strode up the hill to the Austrians. Nuns with broad white wimples tacked across the unpaved yard like sailboats, carrying baskets of laundry, buckets, and trays of food between the two-story wooden house that served as their residence and a former barracks they had turned into an impromptu infirmary. As one of the wimples moved inexorably in their direction, Omar fell a step behind Kamil and muttered, "Allah protect us."

"From what?" Kamil scoffed. "Nuns?"

"Women," Omar responded with a growl. Kamil smiled, knowing how much Omar, despite his gruffness, doted on his wife.

"I am Sister Hildegard," the nun announced loudly in passable Turkish, then paused to give her visitors the opportunity to state their business. She tilted her head to the side, which made the entire starched wing of her headpiece tilt as well. Another solid-looking expanse of starched linen extended over her bosom. Her robe was blotted with blood and other fluids.

"Bulletproof," Kamil heard Omar comment sotto voce behind him.

Kamil explained that they were looking for the wounded bank guard. Sister Hildegard nodded once, then swung around and led them to the infirmary.

A line of beds stretched down both sides of the cavernous stone room. Between the beds a row of coal-filled mangal braziers exuded warmth, but the room was still chilly. An iron chandelier holding dozens of oil lamps hung from the ceiling and cast delicate shadows across the walls, the beds, and their occupants. Kamil heard groans and the keening sound of someone crying. He felt a deep pity for the featureless forms wrapped in white bandages that inhabited the beds. A novice who was tending the braziers jumped to her feet when she saw Sister Hildegard.

"Suzanna, bring our guests some tea," Sister Hildegard told her.

Kamil nodded toward the patients. "Have you identified the burn victims yet?"

"Most of them. Their families heard about the fire and came to look for them. Those that didn't find their loved ones here went on to the mortuary."

Omar clucked his tongue in disapproval. "Such needless pain. If you're going to kill someone, just shoot them." Sister Hildegard flashed him an unfathomable look.

The bank guard's body was invisible under a casing of bandages, but his face was burned red, the skin blistered along one cheek. His lips were black and his eyes squeezed shut. He seemed unaware that they were beside his bed.

Omar leaned close to the guard's face and said softly, "Fuat, tell us what you saw, so we can go get the bastards. I'll bring you back their left ears."

The guard's lips twitched. He opened his eyes and, after a few hoarse attempts, managed to speak in a whisper. Kamil leaned in to hear.

"The bank closed at five. Just after dark, a carriage pulled up. Monsieur Swyndon came out of the bank with a man I hadn't seen before. They took two big chests from the carriage and carried them inside, one after the other."

Omar threw Kamil a puzzled look. "Swyndon was there?"

"Monsieur Swyndon is the comptroller. He often works late, so I didn't think anything about it. About a half hour later, they carried the chests back out."

The guard closed his eyes again and breathed heavily. "I was lucky," he said, his voice straining. "I didn't inhale the fire. I threw myself to the side. What about my mates?" His eyes focused on Omar's. No one responded and Fuat closed his eyes again. "Kismet," he whispered. "Allah knows everything." A tear trickled from beneath his eyelid. Omar and Kamil looked away.

After a few moments, the guard continued. "The chests looked heavier going out, so our captain offered to help, but Monsieur Swyndon said no."

Kamil picked up a glass and, holding the guard's head up, dribbled water between his lips." What did the stranger look like?"

"Tall. He had a cap on and a scarf around his face, so I couldn't see much. He wore regular shoes, not for the snow. I thought he was a customer. Only the very poor or the very rich walk around in shoes in the snow, poor men because they have nothing else, rich men because their feet never touch the ground."

Omar chuckled. "I'll have to remember that. I bow before your philosophical mastery."

The guard looked up at Omar to see if he was making fun of him, then, satisfied that the chief was genuinely impressed, stretched his scabbed mouth into a rictuslike grin.

"Then what happened?" Kamil prompted him.

"They went back inside. Then the stranger came out and left in the carriage. The driver was in and out too, helping carry the chests and other stuff."

"What other stuff?" Omar asked.

"He went in with two heavy bags."

"Did he bring them out again?"

The guard thought for a moment. "I don't remember."

"So Swyndon stayed in the bank?"

"I didn't see him come out, but there's another door down the street. Haraf was guarding it, but he got caught in the explosion." Kamil saw the guard struggle to contain his emotion. "He had come over to ask me if I would be his son's sponsor at his circumcision. That's the last thing I remember."

Omar took down the guard's address and the names of the other guards and promised to notify their families.

They walked down the row of beds toward a table where the novice had placed a tray of tea and pastries. "Well, now we have our top official robbing his own bank," Omar announced.

They passed a shelf lined with blackened objects, scorched and scarred by fire. Each was neatly labeled with a number tied on with string. Kamil stopped, intrigued, and called Sister Hildegard over. "What's all this?" he asked.

"Those are things we found on the patients. It helps family members identify them. Do you have any idea what this is?" She reached into a cabinet, pulled out a partially melted object, and handed it to Kamil. "You can see why I keep it out of sight." Kamil cradled the medal in his hand. It was a gold starburst decorated with diamonds. A bit of scorched blue ribbon still clung to the back.

"Allah protect us," he said in a soft voice. It was an order just like the one Huseyin had been wearing for Elif's portrait.

"Do you recognize it?" Sister Hildegard asked, picking up the alarm in Kamil's voice.

"It's a royal order, but I'm not sure which kind. My brother-in-law, Huseyin Pasha, has one. But I'm sure he's not the only one who does." Sultan Abdulhamid used royal orders to reward the loyalty of his top men. "There's no number attached to this."

"We found it in one of the carts that had carried both dead and wounded. It's heavy. It must have slipped off the body. We have no idea who it belongs to." She added, with a sympathetic look, "I'm sorry. Was your brother-in-law injured?"

"I don't know." Kamil was already walking back toward the row of bedsteads, followed closely by Omar. In the first bed, the patient's breathing was labored, each breath accompanied by a faint bubbling sound. Of the face, Kamil could see only the eyes, closed in sleep or exhaustion.

"We know who this man is. But three are unidentified," the nun explained, "the ones with a green or red cloth tied to the bed. The red one is a woman. But several more seriously injured patients were moved to another hospital with special facilities. The foreign embassies already took their people away." She shrugged. "They think their medicine is better."

"Where?" Omar asked.

"The German hospital, probably." Sister Hildegard rubbed her eyes with the heels of her hands and Kamil saw that they were red with exhaustion. "Oh, you mean the badly injured ones," she said. "Eyüp Mosque hospital. They have a burn specialist there."

Kamil stood over one of the beds marked with a green cloth and regarded the swaddled figure that lay there. Thick black hair curled from the head. The figure was slim, even under the carapace of bandages. The man in the adjacent bed was too short to be Huseyin. The coals in the braziers hissed. The smell of carbolic barely masked the stench of pus, blood, and urine.

"May I keep this?" Kamil asked Sister Hildegard. "If it's not my brother-in-law's, I'll return it." The nun nodded her assent, and Kamil slipped the medal into his pocket.

Omar followed him out into the cold. "Do you want me to go to Eyüp with you?"

Kamil shook his head no. They waited for the stableboy to bring their horses.

Omar tucked his hands under his arms and stamped his feet against the cold. His breath formed a white cloud before his face. "Swyndon either went along with the robbery and took off, or he was coerced and then eliminated. But then where's his body?"

Kamil tried to focus on what Omar was saying, but his mind was full of Feride's anguish if she learned that Huseyin was either dead or so terribly injured that he had been unable to tell anyone who he was. "We couldn't get into the second strong room," Kamil suggested.

"You mean you think the manager might be in there?" Omar was skeptical. "That makes no sense."

"Why not? What better way to get rid of a witness?"

"For all the thieves knew, the bank would just unlock the door the next day and let him out. And if he's dead, why bother locking him up?"

"You have a point," Kamil admitted.

"Better to check, though. Thieves aren't always the smartest of Allah's creations."

THE AUSTRIAN infirmary was just a few blocks above the bank, so they instructed the stableboy to follow with their horses and waded down the hill through ankle-deep snow. Kamil saw movement behind the windowpanes as residents peered into the street. The air felt scrubbed clean by the storm. The stove fires had died out during the night, so the noxious smog had dissipated. Istanbul's chilled inhabitants, fresh from sleep, were stacking kindling and smudging their hands with coal and ash, shivering until the new fires caught, and gazing in wonderment out their windows at the accumulated snow. Snowstorms weren't unknown in Istanbul, but they were rare.

When they reached the bank, Kamil shouted at the gendarme captain to bring some men to the vault. Kamil picked up a brass weight from a scale, pushed it through the bars of the gate, and banged on the door of the locked strong room. "Hello," he called out in English. "If you're in there, make a sound." He waited but heard nothing. He knocked again and repeated his message. Again they waited, and again there was only silence.

Omar shrugged ostentatiously. "He's long gone. We give the Franks salaries the size of Mount Ararat and still they rob us blind. Europeans are about as trustworthy as weasels in a larder." Seeing Rejep come down the stairs, he asked, "Have you got the addresses?"

"Yes, Chief." He handed Omar a piece of paper. "I found out about the keys too. The central cashier has the key to the main vault and the barred gates. The assistant director and the comptroller each have one key to the double locks on the strong room doors. You need all three keys at the same time to get into the strong rooms."

"Fine," Omar grumped. "but have you got anything useful?"

"There's only one set of keys," Rejep added triumphantly.

"Well, fuck a donkey," Omar exclaimed. "Can you imagine? One of the managers wanders out the door with his key and falls into the Bosphorus and suddenly the entire gold reserves of the empire and half a dozen countries are unavailable." His voice was thick with incredulity. "If that's not crazy, then call me a donkey's whore."

They contemplated the locked strong room. "What do you think?" Kamil asked the gendarme captain.

"It would take a long time to break through that door by force," the captain concluded. "It would practically take a military operation. It would be better to get a locksmith, although I don't know anyone with experience in opening doors like this."

"Or a safecracker," Omar said, smiling broadly. "I know just the man." He sent Rejep to fetch him.

Within half an hour, Rejep returned, leading a man who reached only up to Kamil's chest. Despite his short legs and odd gait, he moved swiftly. A large growth on his back bent his head at an angle, but his face was handsome and confident. He wore a padded jacket and a leather satchel hung from his belt.

"Hagop, my good friend"—Omar beamed—"we need your peerless skills."

"Well, Chief, we meet again. What do you have this time?"

"We'd like you to crack this strong room." Omar pointed at the locked door.

Hagop coughed. "You want me to rob the Ottoman Bank?"

Omar looked offended. "Of course not. We're all representatives of the law here."

Hagop glanced at the policemen and gendarmes standing around the room. "Whatever you say, Chief." He opened his satchel and spread out a variety of mysterious tools. He inserted a thin piece of metal into the lock of the barred gate, and within moments a latch clicked and the gate swung open. Hagop then turned his attention to the strong room door. He ran his fingers over every crease and rivet, then spent some time examining the lock. He finally turned to Omar. "This won't be easy, but I can do it. The same deal?"

"Same deal."

Kamil wondered what kind of regular deal a police chief would have with a safecracker, but he had learned that some things about Omar he was better off not knowing.

Hagop asked for more lights. "Bring me some water, then get out," he commanded. "I'll tell you if I need anything else."

OMAR AND Kamil went outside to reclaim their horses. The morning sun had burned through the mist and the destruction was more evident. Crowds of curious onlookers milled about the street. A few men were picking through the charred remains of the taverna.

Omar called over one of the gendarmes. "Get those men out of there before they break their legs.

"There's one thing I don't understand," Omar said, placing a restraining hand on the neck of Kamil's horse. "If you need three keys to get in, where did Swyndon get the other two?"

"That's what I'm hoping he'll tell us."

11

*V*AHID SANK INTO THE leather chair in his new office. Akrep occupied a large stone villa near the outer perimeter of Yildiz Palace, not far from the forest. He treasured the thick walls, the solitude, the secluded corners of his new realm. Mounted on the wall behind him was a matching backdrop to the chair, the framed leather padded and tufted into large diamonds like a quilt. He understood the need for certain trappings to induce respect and obedience. He had had most of the other furniture removed so that the high-ceilinged room seemed even more imposing. Two straight-backed chairs were placed before his desk for visitors.

In a locked room in the basement he kept a bloody sword. Vizier Köraslan's only son had stabbed his best friend with it in an act of rage over a woman. Vahid had spirited the friend's body away, and it was later discovered in the Belgrade Forest, where presumably the young man had been robbed and set upon by bandits. Vahid had arranged for some bandits to be killed by the police, just to put the minds of the city's inhabitants at rest, as the forest was a favorite spot for outings. Vahid had also let the grateful vizier know that the bloody murder weapon with his son's insignia was in a safe place and that he had paid a witness to the murder to be quiet. That the witness didn't exist was immaterial. It was the perfect solution. Vizier Köraslan could continue to lie to himself about the nature of his vicious son, and Vahid had been promoted and given this building to run Akrep.

Vahid instructed his assistant not to disturb him. He brought out Rhea's hairpin and placed it on his desk. The tines were silver, shaped to conform to the head. It was crowned with a spray of rubies, each framed in gold and attached by a tiny chain to the crest. He held it up against the light so that the rubies spilled from the comb like a sparkling waterfall. An expensive pin. How had Rhea acquired it? Her father owned vineyards on the Aegean coast and sold his wine by the barrel. He knew Rhea was—had been—her father's favorite, but he was unlikely to give the youngest of his six children a valuable ruby ornament. It was the sort of thing you gave a wife. He thought about his own father, who had never given his mother a kind word, much less a gift.

Vahid ran his fingers over the tines. He should have been the one to give Rhea this gift. Instead, just like his father, he had demanded everything but given her nothing. She would have married him if he had given her jewels like this. Women always responded when you gave them what they wanted. But he had never been able to understand what it was that Rhea wanted.

"I respect you, sir," she had said in a voice so warm that he was convinced she liked him. They met every Saturday afternoon in the private room of a café overlooking the Golden Horn. There she let him touch her golden hair, the shafts of it flexible between his fingers. He held her dimpled hand with its translucent pink nails. Once she let him guide her trembling head onto his shoulder. Her hair smelled of lemons.

But she refused his offer of marriage, saying her father wouldn't allow it. He then talked to her father, a man who could have used a powerful son-in-law. Her father put him off, once saying she was too young, another time that he did not yet have the money for a dowry. Vahid understood that Rhea's father was afraid to refuse him, and he took comfort in that small hope. Lately he had put pressure on her father to hasten his decision. One of the father's warehouses had burned, ruining a season's production. Vahid wondered if Rhea had guessed the origin of the fire. Could that have been the reason she had refused to see him the past two weeks? He pressed his thumb against the tine of the hairpin with such force that it buckled. He could master men, he thought, but whenever he reached for love, it was wrested from his grasp.

He opened a drawer and took out a small, sharp, and pointed knife, a bottle, and a latched box. He rolled up his sleeve, revealing a swarthy arm seeded with scars like grains of rice. He pressed the tip of the knife to the skin just below the crook of his elbow and for a few moments let the sting penetrate like a balm. His heart beat faster. Lowering the blade, he increased the pressure ever so gently, until he broke into a sweat, his eyesight blurred, and a cascade of pleasurable feeling washed over him. He removed the knife. He was breathing rapidly and his heart pounded. Carefully averting his eyes from the line of blood, he took a piece of cotton from the box, poured on alcohol solution, and tied it to his arm with a cotton strip. He rolled up his sleeve, flexing his arm to feel the sting. He put on his jacket, slipped Rhea's hairpin in his pocket, and left without a word to his assistant.

12

ESPITE THE EARLY HOUR, Kamil rode first to Feride's house. He had to know whether Huseyin had come home. Deep shadows beneath Feride's eyes revealed that she hadn't slept. She was dressed in the same gown she had worn at dinner the night before. Elif sat beside her on the sofa and held her hand. Kamil thought Elif must have stayed the night. He imagined the steep streets of Galata, where she lived, had been made impassable by the storm.

Two anxious servant girls waited just inside the door. Glasses of tea and a plate of breakfast chörek rested untouched on the table beside the sofa. A fire roared in the grate.

"Kamil!" Feride jumped to her feet. "What are you doing here so early?" She turned to one of the servants. "Tea, and bring some breakfast."

"I can't stay long, Ferosh." Kamil could see the tension around her eyes. The furrow that had appeared between her eyebrows after their father's death had deepened. "Is Huseyin here?"

"Has something happened?" Her voice was steady, but he could hear her anguish moving like water beneath a thin sheet of ice.

He wasn't sure what to tell her. In truth he knew nothing. "Do you know where he went last night?"

Elif stood also, her slight figure in a crumpled shirt and trousers. Her feet were bare. She looked at him questioningly, not wishing to upset Feride further by asking outright.

Kamil indicated with a shake of his head that he didn't know, but there was a moment of understanding between them. She took a deep breath and put her arm around Feride.

"I think he has a mistress," Feride said, her tone brutally frank, as she pushed Elif's arm away.

"Nonsense, Ferosh," Elif countered. "You're jumping to conclusions."

Feride looked unconvinced, the pain evident on her face, but she grasped Elif's outstretched hand.

With a look, Kamil tried to communicate to Elif his gratitude that she was there to support his sister.

"Does he often stay out late, Ferosh?" Kamil asked. "Has he stayed away all night before?"

"He's rarely away in the evenings without telling me where he's going. A few times, especially in the last month, but he's never stayed away all night without letting me know."

"What's different about the past month? Did something happen? Have you had unusual visitors?" Or a fight? Kamil wondered silently.

Feride thought, then shook her head. "Nothing out of the ordinary. Huseyin's friends come and go, but I know most of them."

The servants appeared and set down two trays of hot tea, freshly baked bread and pastries, cheese, olives, and honey.

"Business people? Tradesmen? Servants?" Kamil didn't know what he was searching for. An alternative to death, he supposed, as an explanation for Huseyin's absence. A business deal, a mistress.

"I wouldn't know. My housekeeper handles all of that."

They stared abstractedly at the food, but no one made a move to take anything.

Elif spoke up. "The vintner came a few weeks ago."

"He comes once a month to take Huseyin's wine order," Feride said dismissively.

Elif looked as if she might say something more but closed her mouth.

"Tell me more, Elif," Kamil coaxed.

"They were in Huseyin's study and . . ."

"Really?" Feride exclaimed. "But he always sees tradesmen in the receiving room at the side of the house. What were they doing in his study?"

"Huseyin was trying to convince him of something, but I didn't hear what. I thought the man said the name Rhea. You were out, Feride, and I had come back for some painting supplies I left behind. I noticed the vintner's carriage when I left, so I assumed it was him." She shrugged. "But maybe it was someone else."

"Rhea." Feride rose and walked to the window. She held aside the drapes and stared out into the gray shimmer of the day. "Rhea," she repeated. "I'll get hold of the vintner and find out what this is all about. They're all the same, those Greeks," she said, her voice breaking. "The women have no shame."

"You're upset," Elif responded, taking her arm. "I may have been mistaken. They might have been talking about a new type of grape."

Feride went to the desk in the corner of the room and picked up a piece of paper. "I sent a messenger to Doctor Moreno's house. You remember him, don't you, Kamil? He was a friend of Baba's. They used to play chess together. He's a surgeon at Yildiz Palace now. I thought he could find out whether Huseyin had been held up at the palace." She handed Kamil a note. "Here's his response. I know it doesn't look good for me to be chasing my husband across the city, but I have to know." She closed her eyes and shook with the effort of keeping her emotions under control, then opened them again. "Doctor Moreno is discreet."

Kamil remembered Doctor Moreno, a tall Jewish surgeon with graying locks that hung like women's curls down either side of his face. He had long, graceful fingers that picked up a chess piece with as much delicacy as a scalpel. Moreno's note said that he hadn't seen Huseyin for several days and knew nothing about a business meeting the night before. He placed himself at Feride's service and said he would make some inquiries and come by in the morning, but that she shouldn't worry.

Kamil wondered at the cavalier way men treated one another's disappearances. It was as if every man was assumed to have a secret life and was expected to disappear into it from time to time without having to account for his absence. He hoped Feride was right. The tragedy of Huseyin's keeping a mistress was nothing compared with his own worry.

"Where does Huseyin go during the day?" Elif asked.

"I don't know. I suppose he must have an office at the palace. Do you know, Kamil?" Feride turned to him, a puzzled frown on her face. "I never realized until today how little I know about what Huseyin does when he isn't at home."

Kamil wasn't surprised. Muslim men of Huseyin's class never sullied their hands directly with commerce but guided the acquisition of wealth and power by Christian and Jewish merchants from the lofty heights of a bureaucratic admiral's bridge. They did business with the help of many informal agreements rarely recorded or shared with their fellows, and certainly not with their wives. "He has an office in the Great Mabeyn," he said. "That's the building at the palace where the sultan meets with his staff and visitors." Kamil had seen Huseyin's enormous office and staff, appreciably larger than his own, but had little idea what exactly his brother-in-law did there. Perhaps the gold medal had belonged to another loyal subject of the sultan's, Kamil thought, and it was premature to tell Feride about the fire. His momentary relief left him ill at ease. He knew he didn't believe it.

Kamil took a sip of tea and encouraged Feride and Elif to eat something and then sleep until Doctor Moreno arrived. They both looked haggard. He saw in Elif's face the shadows that had been there when she had first appeared on Huseyin's doorstep after her harrowing escape from Macedonia.

Neither woman had any appetite, and Kamil left them sitting on the sofa, waiting. What he wanted to do was ride directly to Eyüp and check the hospital for Huseyin. Composing himself with difficulty, he spurred his horse toward the bank official Swyndon's house instead.

AFTER KAMIL had left, Feride excused herself and went to her dressing room. There she opened an almost invisible door, painted white to match the wall. It led to a small, oddly shaped room that appeared to have been added by the architect of the mansion without a thought to function. Feride closed the door behind her. This was her space, where she could take off the social mask she was required to wear. The servants entered only to clean and keep the mangal coals alive so the room was always warm. Its single window looked out onto the top of a chestnut tree. She settled into a high-backed armchair. A footstool and a small table were the only furniture in the room. She watched the pink-breasted doves huddle on the ledge by the warmth of the slightly open window.

She thought about the early days of her marriage. She had seen Huseyin twice at formal meetings set up by their families after he had made his intentions known. She had agreed, even though she had two other suitors. What was it about Huseyin that had attracted her? He had rudely looked directly into her eyes and then smiled. What had he seen there? She was shy, and people had mistaken that for submissiveness, an attractive quality in a bride. Only Huseyin had seen what she needed, when she herself hadn't known. She blushed when she remembered their first weeks after the wedding, the mad dashes about the rooms. He had laughed and licked her up and down like a cat, and finally she had turned on him and bitten him with her small teeth. They had laughed until tears came. After that Feride had ceased to be quite so afraid, as long as Huseyin was beside her.

She tried to imagine her husband licking another woman's skin, but the image remained indistinct, a flickering shadow that presaged a darkness she knew she couldn't bear. Worse was the thought that he would leave her, push her aside for a second wife. Or that he would die. For a brief moment, she considered that it would be better for him to die than to reject her, but at that the darkness descended. There was a frantic burst of flapping at the window as the doves fled, leaving behind a soiled windowsill.

13

KAMIL LEFT FERIDE'S HOUSE in Nishantashou and rode the short distance to the Swyndons'. He passed a small army of servants wielding shovels and brooms, clearing the streets of snow. Omar got out of a waiting carriage, and they walked together up the drive to Swyndon's house. It was set on a hill in a terraced garden rimed with snow and afforded a spectacular vista of the Bosphorus glittering in the morning sunlight.

Inside, the view was quite different—heavy draperies, a clutter of waxed furniture, and dark oil paintings. Mrs. Swyndon was a heavy-boned Englishwoman with beautiful gray eyes that regarded Kamil steadily while she absorbed the news of the robbery. Kamil's English had the burnished pronunciation he had learned at Cambridge University, with an Oriental lilt.

"My husband didn't return home last night," she confirmed. "That's all I can tell you."

Except for tightening her grip on the wool shawl around her shoulders, Kamil thought she showed little reaction to the news that her husband had been seen at the bank during the robbery but was now missing.

An English neighbor, fetched by Mrs. Swyndon's servants, arrived. When she entered the room, as if on cue, Mrs. Swyndon began to cry, effectively dismissing the men. They got up to leave. As they retreated down the stairs, Omar commented, "My wife would never mourn me like that."

"She'd be grateful to be rid of you."

Omar smiled.

At the base of the stairs, a plump, red-cheeked girl of about seven stared at them from behind the skirts of a frightened-looking nanny.

While Omar waited at the end of the hall, Kamil stopped and asked the nanny her name.

"Bridget, sir." Her face was that of a woman in her early twenties, but she was very short, barely taller than the child, and her frame so shrunken within her woolen gown that Kamil wondered if she was ill.

"And who is this?" Kamil smiled at the child, who disappeared behind Bridget.

"Alberta, sir."

Kamil sat on a damask-covered slipper chair, bringing the level of his head closer to the nanny's. "Are you English, Bridget?"

"Yes, sir. From Canterbury."

"How long have you been in service here?"

"Two years, sir."

"Have you noticed anything unusual in the house over the past month? Visitors? Any tensions?"

The young woman colored and looked down. "I'm sure I can't say, sir."

"Now, Bridget, you know that Mr. Swyndon has gone missing, so anything you tell us might help us find him. I'm sure no one would see anything disloyal in that."

"No visitors other than the usual, sir. The missus's friends and then the families that come for dinner."

"Anyone coming to see Mr. Swyndon?"

She looked puzzled. "Mr. Swyndon doesn't do any business here, sir."

Alberta darted out from behind the nanny's skirts and blurted out, "But you had a visitor!"

Bridget looked alarmed. "You weren't to tell anyone, Alberta. You promised."

Alberta looked at her defiantly, then turned her back.

Near tears, the nanny told Kamil, "I'm not allowed visitors here, you see. I could lose my post if Mrs. Swyndon found out. But sometimes"—she wiped her eyes—"it just gets lonely."

"Who was this visitor? A friend?"

"A local girl. She came by selling sweets—I do so have a weakness for them. She spoke some English and when she said she'd like to learn more, I agreed to help her. I offered to come to her house on Monday afternoons, which is when I have time off, but she told me her brother wouldn't permit a stranger in the house. So she came here."

"How often?"

"Once a week. On my half day off. We went up the hill there." She pointed. "There's a small orchard. But when the weather got cold, we stayed in my room."

"I'm going to tell," the little girl announced. "She took my bracelet."

Bridget crouched down to the child, stroked her hair, and said in a soothing voice, "Albie, darling, you don't want to do that. If I go, who will take care of you? Can anyone else take care of you like I do?"

The girl shook her head no, offering up part of her victory.

"Thank you, Albie." Bridget kissed her cheek and stood up, holding the girl's hand in her own. "We'll find your bracelet. I'm sure you just left it somewhere. You're always playing with it."

"I'm sorry to have caused you any trouble," Kamil said sincerely, touched by the young woman's tenderness toward this difficult child. It was not the first time he wondered whether he was cut out for fatherhood if this is what it entailed. He adored his nieces, but it was Feride who dealt with the spirited girls day after day.

"It'll be all right, sir. Albie's a good girl, aren't you, Albie?" She beamed at her charge, the smile lighting up her face so that she seemed almost pretty.

"May I ask your friend's name and where she lives?"

"Sosi. She said she lived in . . . it sounded like Bangali."

"Pangalti?" It was a nearby district populated mainly by Christians. The French Catholic Cemetery, a Protestant cemetery, a Greek Orthodox school, a synagogue, and an Armenian church were all within sight of one another. Sosi was an Armenian name. It was probably an innocent friendship. Nevertheless, he'd set a watch for the girl.

THEY FOUND Montaigne and Hofmeister, the other two officials, inspecting the damage at the bank and watching Hagop suspiciously as he worked on the lock to the second strong room. The captain of gendarmes stood between them and the scowling safecracker. When the officials saw Kamil, they demanded that he stop the break-in. Kamil ignored them and asked instead where Swyndon was. They didn't know, nor did they know how he could have opened the other strong room without all three keys. After some argument, during which Kamil pointed out that the keys no longer locked anything in, each man gave Kamil his key. Neither of them turned in the locks.

14

WHEN THE MESSENGER CAME again to say that the pasha was with his family and wouldn't be long, Gabriel could no longer contain his anguish. He stormed past the servant into the hall leading toward Simon's office, beyond which he believed lay the pasha's private quarters. Guards with drawn swords rapidly converged on him, and, too exhausted to fight, he slumped against the wall. The guards accompanied him back to his room.

He took another draught of laudanum to ease the pain in his hands and lay on the bed. He was awakened by a peremptory knock on the door and the sound of the key turning. Simon walked in and announced that the pasha would see him. Gabriel glanced at the window. Judging by the light, he guessed it was nearing noon.

When Gabriel entered Yorg Pasha's receiving room, he was momentarily disconcerted by the painted creatures and forest scenes on the silk-paneled walls. In the flickering light of the fireplace, the animals seemed to roam through the foliage. Gabriel turned his attention to Yorg Pasha, seated in a velvet armchair. Although the man's face sagged and the backs of his hands were knotted with veins, Gabriel had the impression of immense strength. It was the first time they had met. Until now all of Gabriel's dealings had been with Simon, who stood at the pasha's shoulder.

Yorg Pasha motioned for Gabriel to sit by the fire. "You appear to be in difficulty," he said conversationally, brushing his fingertips along the armrest.

Gabriel nodded, not sure whether Yorg Pasha was referring to the state of his frostbitten hands or the confiscation of the shipload of weapons. The pasha couldn't know about Gabriel's involvement in the bank robbery.

Yorg Pasha had a reputation abroad as a reliable arms dealer with good connections in the government and police. Thinking he needed a powerful local protector in this unfamiliar territory, Gabriel had made a deal with him, or rather with his secretary, Simon, to bribe the necessary officials to make sure the ship passed customs. In return, Simon had demanded the steep price of three hundred rifles and a hundred pistols, more than a third of the shipment. Gabriel had told him that the guns were destined to arm the villagers directly on the Ottoman-Russian border, which cut through the mountains just east of Trabzon, against a possible Russian incursion. It was a ludicrous story on the face of it, given that Gabriel was himself Russian, but Simon had seemed to accept it. Gabriel assumed that the pasha and his secretary didn't care what the cover story was, as long as they were paid.

But Yorg Pasha and Simon had failed. Almost as soon as the ship had docked, the guns were confiscated by the police. Someone must have tipped them off. Gabriel leaned in toward the heat of the fire, hiding his furious face, wondering whether the pasha or his secretary had betrayed him, and why. A servant handed around porcelain cups of Turkish coffee set in wrought silver sleeves, then withdrew. Gabriel fumbled the cup with his nerveless fingers. Annoyed, he put it down on a side table, where it tipped over and leaked a brown ooze onto the inlay.

"I'm concerned about your health," Yorg Pasha said. "No one will benefit if you freeze to death."

"You needn't worry," Gabriel retorted, knowing as he spoke that it was a mistake, that he should be conciliatory if he wanted the pasha's help, but unable to rein himself in. "I imagine you'll find a way to be paid, even though you didn't hold up your end of the bargain."

Simon moved fractionally, but at a slight lift of Yorg Pasha's eyebrows, he became still again.

"Debts are always paid, one way or another," Yorg Pasha said mildly, ignoring the insultingly direct mention of money.

"Isn't there anything you can do about the shipment? That was your part of the bargain, to make sure it passed customs." Damn the guns, Gabriel thought. It was the ship he needed now, so he could take the gold to New Concord. With the gold he could buy new guns. And he needed to find Vera.

"Do you know who informed the police about the shipment?" Yorg Pasha asked.

"The only person who knew about it was your secretary." Gabriel shot a glance at Simon, who opened his mouth as if to speak, then shut it again.

Yorg Pasha regarded Gabriel with a direct gaze that made him uncomfortable. No one spoke.

"I'm not saying you did it," Gabriel backtracked. "Why would you? You drove a hard bargain. But I don't see another explanation, do you?" He took up a fire iron and began to stab aimlessly among the coals.

"Surely more people knew about the ship than just the three of us in this room," Yorg Pasha suggested reasonably. "Who was going to help you off-load it? How were you going to get the cargo to the east?" Gabriel noted with contempt that the pasha delicately avoided using the word "guns." But he was struck by the truth of what the old man had said.

Their socialist network here was thin and full of leaks, he thought. The eight men in the cell that the International had contacted to help him in Istanbul all were Armenian, rather than of mixed heritage like socialist cells in Europe. This herd mentality of like with like was infecting the movement in Europe too. Vera had joined a new socialist group in Geneva called Henchak, of which all the members were Armenian. Gabriel had wanted her to quit, but their friend Apollo had been a founding member, so out of misplaced loyalty she had refused. It was a contradiction, he had insisted, to claim allegiance to socialism while clinging to an outmoded and divisive identity. Gabriel was convinced that in their hearts the Armenians were nationalists who would rather have their own Armenian pashas, priests, and landlords than join with peasants and workers around the world against these oppressors.

He had discovered that rather than accept his lead in the project, the Istanbul cell obeyed a priest, Father Zadian, whose permission Gabriel was forced to obtain for his every move. Gabriel didn't trust Zadian, just as he didn't trust this pasha, a merchant without principles, who helped them only in order to turn a profit. But the pasha was right. Father Zadian had known about the shipment of guns.

Where the hell was Apollo? Apollo had failed to arrive at the train station in Geneva, and they had received no word from him since. The doleful Armenian Russian philosopher with the silver tongue would have known how to handle Yorg Pasha and Father Zadian and his unreliable cell of Armenians. And Apollo would have kept Vera company so that she wouldn't have embarked on her ruinous campaign to get Karl Marx published in Armenian. Gabriel stabbed furiously at the coals, aware of the uncomfortable silence in the room.

The pasha waited, his hands resting calmly on the arms of the chair. Gabriel could see blue veins under the papery skin. Simon stood behind him, watching Gabriel closely.

"It's possible," Gabriel admitted. "It might have been one of the socialists here in Istanbul. Maybe one of them got drunk or told his mistress, who knows? But what are we going to do about it?" He tossed the iron onto the hearthstone. "Look, I need help."

"I thought as much." The pasha nodded, his eyes hooded.

"I need a ship. Small, fast."

"You can arrange that with Simon," Yorg Pasha sounded impatient. "Surely that isn't what you wanted to drag me out of bed for."

"My wife," Gabriel surprised himself by saying. "She was followed and then taken from our room last night."

"You brought your wife on this mad adventure?" Yorg Pasha seemed nonplussed. "Didn't you have enough other things to worry about?"

"Yes, of course. But I still have to find her before . . ."

"What do you want me to do?"

"Can you find out if the secret police have her and help me get her out?"

"Do you think members of the secret police lie about like apples in the orchard? Do we know anyone in the secret police?" he asked Simon.

"No, pasha."

"And we don't want to know them. May I point out that in your present circumstances, the last people you want anything to do with are the secret police."

"I was hoping you would make the inquiries for me, pasha." Gabriel knew what he was asking. Yorg Pasha did not want to attract attention. He was an arms dealer, and not just through official channels. But Gabriel had no other options. None of the socialists he knew had sufficient connections to remedy all that had gone wrong, and he no longer knew whom among them he could trust.

"Explain to me why I should put myself in any further danger in order to help you?"

"For ten thousand gold liras."

"Don't mark me for a fool," Yorg Pasha said in a low voice. "I expect those with whom I do business to be straight with me." Anyone listening from outside the door would have been fooled by the friendly tone, but Gabriel froze.

"What do you mean?" he asked. "I told you I don't know why the weapons were discovered, but there's no way the police can link them to you, so you have nothing to worry about."

"Don't I? What about those two chests filled with gold in my stable? I believe they belong to the Imperial Ottoman Bank, which was recently robbed."

Gabriel was flabbergasted. Were there no secrets in this country at all? "What makes you think I had anything to do with that?"

"The pasha knows everything that goes on in his house," Simon answered. "I've examined the contents. You've done well. I'd estimate the value at about eighty thousand British pounds. Clever to take the jewels. They're easier to carry."

"So you see," Yorg Pasha pointed out, "I was right. Debts are always paid."

Gabriel panicked. "You can't take the gold. It's not mine."

At that Yorg Pasha laughed, a startling, deep well of sound. "Well, that's true enough."

Gabriel faced the fire, then turned back to Yorg Pasha. He had thought things couldn't get any worse, yet in the space of an hour they truly had. He had no idea what to do now. His confusion must have been apparent because Yorg Pasha said in a conciliatory tone, "Gabriel, the chests are guarded, so don't think you can spirit them away from under my nose. But I'm a fair man. Tell me what you planned to do with the gold and then I'll consider our options."

With the feeling that by doing so he was condemning all his comrades in Karakaya to death, Gabriel told Yorg Pasha about the commune. He tried to convince the pasha of the beauty and justice of their cause, of the fragile hopes of their community at New Concord, hoping to appeal to the pasha's sense of honor so that he would release the gold and not be tempted to turn them in.

When he had finished, the pasha sighed deeply and said, "Very noble, although I feel obliged to tell you, also incredibly naïve. The news that foreigners are gathering in the Choruh Valley on the Russian border," he emphasized, "has already reached the ears of Sultan Abdulhamid, and he's about to order troops into the area. By spring your friends most likely will have no use for weapons or gold or anything else. They'll all be dead."

Gabriel turned white.

Yorg Pasha considered him for a moment, pity showing on his face. "There's more. You need to hear this so that you have a complete picture. Your friends won't be the only people to suffer. If the sultan sends in troops, they'll likely be Kurdish irregulars. Judging by their previous interventions, I expect they'll lay waste to the entire region. And do you know why Sultan Abdulhamid would send his least discriminating and most feared troops on this particular mission?"

Gabriel's mind whirled with images of the sun-laced villages and orchards of the Choruh River valley put to the torch, its inhabitants arrested or killed. "Why?" he rasped, knowing what the answer would be. It was his fault.

"Because a shipload of illegal weapons was found in the Istanbul harbor and the next day the Ottoman Bank was robbed and blown up. Your incompetence has convinced the sultan that there's a major revolt afoot."

Gabriel's head jerked up. "But I didn't—"

Yorg Pasha cut him off, his voice rising. "And, dare I mention it, you have dragged me into the center of this enormously dangerous plot by using my house and my name to carry it out." At this, the pasha's anger broke through, and he slapped his hand against the arm of his chair. He stood and added, "And you come here asking me to help you find your wife." He nodded once at Simon and headed for the door.

Gabriel jumped to his feet. "I didn't blow up the bank," he called after the retreating pasha, desperate to save at least a shred of his honor.

Yorg Pasha turned around. "What do you mean?"

"I only took the gold. I heard an explosion, but I was already on the road. I had no idea it was the bank."

"How do you explain that?"

"I have no explanation," he stuttered.

Then suddenly Gabriel remembered. His driver, Abel, and his odd unconcern about the explosion. Abel had been sitting atop the carriage and would have seen it. He must have known it was the bank. Abel would have had time to set an explosive charge while Gabriel was inside gathering the gold and jewels. Was it Abel who had told the police about the weapons shipment? To what end? Why undercut their mission?

Gabriel sank back into his chair. Somehow he was certain that Father Zadian was behind this. He buried his head in his hands, unaware that he had been spinning these thoughts silently.

Yorg Pasha stood quietly for a moment, then walked over and let his hand rest on Gabriel's shoulder. "You remind me of a friend's son. Like you, he's always chasing shadows. But I'm glad to say he's a lot more competent." He sat down in his armchair.

"Now, tell me who did blow up the bank."

LATER, AFTER Gabriel had returned to his room, Yorg Pasha thought about what the hotheaded young man had told him about the commune, an experiment the pasha suspected would be short-lived. He couldn't help being unpleasantly reminded of his own twisted path through Ottoman society, a world that he had always believed was ready to crush his every initiative in the vise of tradition. He had had innovative ideas and had hoped he could leave a progressive mark on his world, but now the remnants of his idealism wouldn't fill a thimble. There was no escaping a system that even controlled the roads leading away from it. He had listened to Gabriel's ideas and, whatever he thought of the man—and he thought him a fool—the idea of the commune inspired him. He was too old to join such an endeavor now, but he thought there should still be a place in the empire for dreaming.

15

ERA SAT IN THE CHAIR by the stove and considered what she could do to protect herself when Vahid returned to the room, as she was certain he would. After hitting her in the face, he had become gentlemanly, helping her to the chair, patting the blood on her chin with a handkerchief. He spent another half hour in the room with her, sitting so close that their shoulders were touching, saying little, and running his hands through her hair. Stunned and frightened, she didn't move. Only when she saw him reach into his jacket pocket and pull out a knife did she start away.

He smiled at her, a smile that could have been mistaken as sweet if she hadn't seen his eyes, hard black onyx that gave her reflection back. He took a handful of her hair and sliced it off at ear level. The knife was sharp, so she felt no more than a slight tug, but when he pulled his hand away, her head felt disembodied. She reached up involuntarily now, as then, and felt for the phantom weight of her missing locks.

She was no match for him physically, she thought, so when he came back she would have to outsmart him. He had seemed interested in her in some odd way. Perhaps she could use his attraction to convince him to bring her to another place, somewhere she could escape. A bedroom. She beat back thoughts of Gabriel. She had caused him enough grief. She would be the revolutionary wife he wanted and she was ready to make any sacrifice for the socialist cause. The words sounded hollow. The thought of being with a man besides Gabriel was monstrous.

She heard the key turn, but it wasn't Vahid. Two men entered, both wearing polished black boots, black breeches, and tight-fitting jackets without insignia. They grabbed her arms and marched her out the door and down the corridor, thrusting her into a small room lit by a single lamp. It contained little more than a platform, a bucket, and a table on which were jumbled objects that she could not identify but that frightened her.

The men took off her coat, then pulled at her dress. Despite the pain still shooting through her head, she tried to remain calm. Afraid they would rip it and leave her nothing to wear, she unbuttoned the dress herself. When they pulled down her stockings, she fought blindly for a moment, then relented when she realized how insignificant and feeble her resistance was.

VERA WOKE up on the floor. Her back and legs were stiff, and her neck hurt. It was completely dark, a blackness so thick she felt for a moment that she couldn't breathe. Her disorientation lasted a full minute until she fought down her panic and began to remember.

Gabriel, she thought, anguish like bile in her mouth. Gabriel must never know. The men had used only their hands, but she felt as violated and humiliated as if they had done the rest. Worse than the physical damage, her memory of her wedding night had been perverted. She would never be able to undress before her husband again, to lie with him and bear his touch without these men's hands sliding alongside his. When she looked up at him, it would be their lust-glazed eyes and obscene lips she would see.

Then she leaned over and vomited. She reached up to wipe her mouth, but jerked back in pain when she touched her bruised face. Her tongue felt swollen in her parched mouth. Where was she? Her palms rested on a carpet. Was she back in the original room? She struggled to her feet and shuffled cautiously forward into the dark. They must have taken the lamp, or perhaps it had gone out. She had no sense of the passage of time.

She remembered the room in flashes of color. There had been a chair beside the stove. The stove. She focused her eyes in the dark and finally saw the faint glowing eye of the stove like a distant pulsing star. Using that to orient herself, she inched her way across the room, edging each foot forward gingerly, until her knee encountered the chair. Her slippers were lost, her feet cold. There had been a small table with water. She almost tipped over the carafe, but caught it in time and slaked her thirst, ignoring the pain of flexing her mouth. Worse things could happen. Worse things had happened to her comrades, worse things happened to peasants all the time. She was a soldier in the fight against injustice. For once the words struck a chord in her and didn't just seem like a callow wish.

She shivered and blew at the embers through the slots of the stove. The fire swelled and shed enough light so she could see herself. Her dress and coat were unbuttoned, and her stockings sagged between her legs where they had been inexpertly drawn up. Once she had adjusted her stockings beneath her skirt and buttoned her coat, she felt calmer, as if she had gathered and smoothed her heart beneath her fingers and the circumstances of this room were now encompassed and controlled. Sitting in the circumference of the fire's eye, Vera considered what she needed to do.

16

AMIL AND OMAR LEFT the carriage at the police station in Fatih and continued on horseback to the district of Eyüp to look for Huseyin. The Eyüp Mosque was located at the inland tip of the Golden Horn where two rivers spread through meadows to replenish the estuary. They found themselves in a broad expanse of kitchen gardens now heaped with hay against the frost. In the distance, the stately cypress groves of the Eyüp cemetery fenced off the sky.

"Let's hope he's here," Omar said.

"It's worth a try. But he could be in any of the hospitals or infirmaries." Or he could be dead, Kamil thought.

"If he's not here, I'll get my men to look in all of them," Omar assured him.

The mosque and its complex of buildings were enormous compared with the poor structure that served the Austrian nuns in Galata. Kamil and Omar left their mounts at a hostlery and took a shortcut through the cemetery, where for some reason the snow had not accumulated, as if the ground were hot with decay. The sour smell of the soil permeated the air. After several wrong turns, they found the hospital, a broad-backed stone building of great age set within a garden. Kamil breathed in the scent of herbs, growing in a sheltered spot. He recognized sprigs of salvia and melissa, round mallow leaves, spikes of purple foxgloves, and the hard brown capsules of opium poppies. He brushed against a low shrub, causing it to release a scatter of black berries. He identified it as *Atropa belladonna*, or deadly nightshade. Rose hips gleamed red on the spiky remains of stems.

Inside the building, the wards were neatly lined with beds, but except for the patients, the hospital seemed strangely deserted. They found the director's office, a small whitewashed room with a desk almost obscured by stacks of books and ledgers. A window looked out onto the herb garden. The coals in the brazier were gray and gave off only a meager warmth. Behind the ledgers sat a thin man wearing a tunic with greasy sleeves, his hair a limp fringe beneath his fez. His face was furrowed as if the padding of flesh beneath his skin had melted away.

"We're looking for a victim of the bank fire," Kamil said.

The director glared at them. "Do you think this is a hotel where we register guests? If they want to tell us who they are, that's their business. If their relatives come to pay, that's even better. But in the meantime I have fifty-eight patients, one man who claims to be a physician but is nothing more than the imam's nephew, and five lazy orderlies. If you want to figure out which one is your friend, they're in Ward Three." He shouted for an orderly.

"We've been rude not to introduce ourselves," Kamil said. "This is Omar Loutfi, chief of the Fatih police, and I am Magistrate Kamil Pasha."

"You think that impresses me," the director answered belligerently. "You have no idea what I have to do to keep this place running. Don't come in here holding your titles over me. I'll quit. It would be the best thing I ever did for myself."

"I've been appointed by Sultan Abdulhamid as special prosecutor in charge of investigating the fire at the bank."

At the mention of the sultan, the director grew wary.

"I heard you have a special treatment for burns here," Kamil continued. "What exactly do you do?"

"We alternate exposure therapy with topical application of silver nitrate, zinc oxide when we can get it, and collodium. Mostly we try to determine the toxin that is poisoning the body and draw it out. We administer laudanum for pain, and once the patient can eat, we provide a nourishing diet to build up his life force. Depending on the severity of the case, we also use baths and surgical treatments. We've had some good outcomes with skin regeneration. Pressure bandages seem to inhibit scarring."

"That's very impressive. Can you do that with so few staff members?"

"You see my point," the director shouted, half rising from his chair. "I can't. I just can't do it all. Tell our padishah please that we need more staff, not more patients!" He collapsed back into his chair.

"I'll see what I can do," Kamil promised. "In the meantime, we're looking for Huseyin Pasha. We think he might be among the victims from the bank fire."

"I have fifty-eight patients and you're looking for a pasha," the director muttered. He barked at the orderly who had appeared at the door and went back to his paperwork without another glance at Kamil and Omar.

"You'd think being attached to a mosque would sweeten his spirit," Omar grumbled as they followed the orderly through frigid corridors and courtyards in the centuries-old building.

When they found Ward Three, it turned out they had reached an impasse. Three patients were Huseyin's general height and weight, but unrecognizable behind their bandaged faces. Their eyes were closed, the flesh around them scraped and charred. Kamil tried speaking to each of them, but only one opened his eyes. They were hazel; Huseyin's were brown. The other two appeared insensible.

"One of these may be Huseyin, but no way to know, short of ripping their bandages off," Kamil observed. "Make sure you keep a special watch on these two," he told the orderly. He didn't say that he wanted special treatment for them. He could see that the hospital was already doing everything it could, despite being short-handed. Although the floors were grimy and a slop pail stood unemptied in the corner, the bandages were clean and dry. He reached into his jacket pocket, pulled out two handkerchiefs, and tied one to each bed.

17

ENDIT'S GOLD SHOP was opposite the corner fountain in the Covered Bazaar. The great iron-studded gates to the bazaar hadn't opened yet, but Vahid went through one of the many side doors used by the merchants. He found Bendit pulling his wares from a strongbox that had been locked up overnight in the Inner Bedestan, the guarded central area of the bazaar, and laying them out on velvet-spanned trays in his narrow shop. Vahid refused the dealer's offer of a cushioned seat and tea. He laid the hairpin on the blue velvet tray. The merchant turned it over in his hand, then examined the stones under a loupe. "Do you want to sell it?" he asked. "It would fetch a good price."

"No," Vahid said. "I want to know who bought it."

The gold merchant started to say something, then thought better of it. Vahid had been to see him before on such matters. The man had never bought anything, but like all the other storekeepers in the bazaar, Bendit believed that service brought friendship and loyalty. Eventually, if the man wanted to buy gold, he would do so from Bendit's shop. So he smiled and said, "If you're willing to leave it with me for a few days, sir, I'll ask around."

"I'll wait." Vahid sat.

Ten minutes later, Bendit returned, looking pleased. "This was easy to trace. It was made by—"

Vahid interrupted him. "Who bought it?"

"Huseyin Pasha. He bought two."

18

OMAR SETTLED HIMSELF on a stool in a corner of the Fatih police station and gestured that Kamil should join him. "Have some tea and then let your frustration out on that mangy dog of a ship's captain." Around them the station bustled with petitioners and curiosity seekers. Policemen sat at their desks, taking statements. An old man wandered in, carrying a box of stuffed mussels, followed by a vendor with a tray of simit breads. Both found takers, and before long work ground to a halt as the policemen sipped their tea and snacked. The young policeman Rejep brought a glass of tea to an old woman in a much-mended charshaf who was sitting on a bench, waiting to make a complaint.

Kamil refused the tea and Omar's offer of a simit, but lit a cigarette. "What have you found out so far?"

"He's Alexandrian, so I sent in one of my men who's an Arab from Antakya to talk to him. Tariq over there." He pointed to a burly policeman with a luxuriant mustache and thick, curly black hair, who was sitting at a desk, cleaning his weapon. "I figured before long they'd be buddies. Sure enough, the Alexandrian broke down, but all we got was an earful of his marital woes. Seems his wife got tired of his being gone all the time and had him declared dead so she could remarry. The new husband paid him to disappear, but the man misses his kids."

Kamil finished his cigarette, then followed Omar down a corridor to the holding cells at the back of the station. Omar turned the key, and the thick oak door creaked open. "Rejep will be right outside if you need anything," he told Kamil. Then to the captain, "Old man, tell Magistrate Kamil Pasha about the ship." He stepped aside to let Kamil enter, then locked the door behind him, leaving the barred window set into the door open.

The captain was propped on his elbow on the narrow cot in his cell, as comfortable as if he were in a hammock belowdecks. This was perhaps more comfort than the man was used to in the tight quarters of a ship, Kamil thought, and offered him a cigarette. The captain was a lean twist of weathered leather, his forearms knotted, and his face burned black by sun and wind. Kamil was surprised to learn he was only thirty years old.

The captain pulled deeply at the cigarette and his eyes flared with pleasure. "What do you want to know?" he asked in heavily accented Turkish. The language seemed to rasp from deep within his throat. "I already told them I picked up the load of salted cod in New York. There are six hundred barrels on board. You think I looked in every one of them?"

"Who was the expediter?"

"The same company we always deal with, Orient Company of New York. It's on the manifest. Who they got the load from, I can't say."

"Who was on the receiving end?" When the man didn't answer, Kamil pulled out his cigarette case and held it open. The captain raked together half of the cigarettes with a long, dirty forefinger and made them disappear inside his shirt.

"Hope Enterprises. But the names don't mean a thing. They're always just middlemen, fronts with no backs. I can't tell you the number of times I've been stuck with merchandise rotting on my ship because no one shows up to off-load it and no one has ever heard of the company I'm supposed to deliver it to. I end up dumping it cheap just to earn a few kurush on the load."

"You realize that you're in serious trouble. Illegal weapons were found on your vessel. If you have anything useful to tell us, it would help your situation."

The captain scratched his chest and looked unconcerned. "I was thinking of retiring anyway."

"Do you understand that you'll be put in jail for years, and that could be the most agreeable outcome?" Kamil's expression was cold.

"I've been in worse jails. What do you think a ship is like for months at sea? I've done my time." He sat up. "On the other hand, cigarettes and women. You don't get those at sea and you don't get them in jail, I suppose."

Kamil assured him he wouldn't.

"Well, then, if I tell you something useful, will you let me go?"

Kamil reluctantly agreed. He had learned that this sort of deal was common in Omar's world—letting a small fish off the hook in exchange for information leading to a bigger catch—but Kamil hadn't reconciled himself to the slippery nature of the law when it was applied in the streets. He thought justice shouldn't be bought and sold like grain at auction.

"It was in New York. The barrels were stored in a warehouse, and as soon as we laid anchor I went down to take a look at the cargo. I like to know right away what's coming aboard, so I can talk to my men before they disappear into the city and come back too drunk to take orders. It was pretty late at night when I went to the warehouse. I didn't use a light. I don't need a light to see in the dark." He pointed to his eyes, sharp bits of flint under leathery sheaths. "There were five young men there, marking the barrels. I watched them for a while and listened. Nothing better to do. I don't go in for drink and didn't have the money for a woman. Now my ears, they aren't as good as my eyes. Too much wind and rigging. But I could hear some of what they said, all right."

Kamil held out his cigarette case. The captain took two, lit one, and stuck the other in his shirt. "Two of them were speaking Armenian. I get to know a lot of lingos out there." He swept his hand toward what Kamil assumed was the sea. "It was Armenian, but I don't speak it, so I can't rightly say more than that."

Kamil felt a tug of excitement. It was frail evidence, but it finally pointed him in a specific direction. But an Armenian revolt against the empire? Not only was there no reason that he could think of for such a revolt, but it was doomed to fail. What could they hope to accomplish with even a thousand guns against a corps of Ottoman soldiers? It would be suicidal. There must be another explanation. And why take the risk of smuggling in a thousand guns when you're planning to rob a bank of enough gold to supply a small army. He was about to rise when the captain stuck out his hand and grabbed Kamil's sleeve.

"Wait. There's more. One of them called the other 'comrade.'" He leered at Kamil. "You know what that means."

"You're saying they were socialists?"

"That's right. And you know what the marks were on the barrels?" He sprang up, all agile muscle, picked up his cigarette butt, and drew on the floor with the crushed remnant of tobacco.

"What is it?"

"An ax."

"So what does that mean?"

"Well, that's your business, not mine." He threw the butt down, folded himself back onto the cot, and sucked at his cigarette. "I'm a seaman. Retired."

When he refused to say anything more, Kamil got up to leave.

"No jail, right?" the captain called out.

"If your information is of use." The captain must have known the marked barrels were contraband. Kamil already regretted the deal.

Omar was waiting in the front room of the police station, still sitting on a low stool, smoking and drinking tea. Kamil had never seen him sit at his desk, a vast mahogany ship marooned in the middle of the room.

"What's an Armenian socialist ax?" Kamil asked as he sat down beside him.

"Is this a riddle?"

Kamil managed a smile, but he was sick with worry about Huseyin and not in the mood for levity.

Omar looked penitent. "Just trying to lift your spirits. As for your riddle, the Henchak symbol is a chain, a sword, an ax, and a red flag." He called one of his men to bring him a pen and drew a sketch on a corner of newsprint.

"Henchak, the new Armenian socialist group. I remember hearing it was founded by some Russian university students studying in Geneva. What does it have to do with us?"

Omar shrugged. "I don't know much about it. In Fatih we mostly have people breaking each other's heads over money or impugned honor. One of my Armenian neighbors showed me their symbol."

"I thought socialists didn't go in for nationalism. How can there be Armenian socialists? Isn't their slogan something like 'Workers of the world, unite,' not 'Armenians, unite'?"

"They're fools if they think that. It's always 'Armenians unite.' That's human nature. We run in packs like wolves."

"It's an interesting idea, though, you have to admit," Kamil mused. "To rise above the pack mentality and come together around a cause— like helping peasants and workers better their lot."

"More like pull down the rich and powerful, a very wolfish thing to do. And then what have you got? Do they really think unlettered peasants will be able to govern themselves? They're in for a rude awakening. Believe me, I had a bellyful of peasants in the war. They're as greedy as the wealthiest nabob and as ready to slit your throat over a loaf of bread."

Kamil rose to his feet, unable to bear any longer the anxiety that had been building in him. "I can't sit here and talk politics, Omar. I have to tell Feride."

19

THE PITCHER WAS EMPTY and the fire had gone out. Vera pounded on the door and called out, "I need water. I'm freezing." The door was of heavy wood. She could feel loops and shapes beneath her fingers. There were ornamented doors like this in her family's home in Moscow. Was this someone's home? She tried to remember the room as it had been when it was light, but could recall only disjointed flashes. She didn't remember seeing any windows, but she searched for one anyway, gliding her hands over the walls around the entire periphery of the room. Surely someone would come. She squatted in a corner and waited. She stroked the cloth of her dress and coat over and over, memorizing the different textures, the feel of stitching beneath her fingertips, trying to keep panic at bay.

After what seemed an eternity, she heard a faint sound like slippers scuffing and then the key turn in the lock. The door swung open. Vera closed her eyes against the sudden light.

When she opened them, she saw a plump, frightened-looking teenage girl in a marigold-colored robe, holding a lamp in one hand, a basket by her feet. She lugged the heavy basket into the room. Seeing

Vera, she came over and knelt beside her, then reached out a small white hand and stroked Vera's hair. Vera noticed that the backs of her hands were marked with cuts, one above the other like a ladder. A strong smell of perspiration hung about her, and an unpleasant musk rose from her clothing. The girl poured a glass of water and handed it to Vera, then watched as she put it to her lips and let the cool water course down her throat.

"Who are you?" Vera asked in broken Turkish. "Where am I?"

The girl looked around, as if afraid to be seen talking with Vera, with the prisoner, Vera thought. She wondered if this girl was also a prisoner. "What's your name? My name is Vera Arti." She couldn't bring herself to lie to this brutalized girl.

The girl looked surprised. "Gabriel Arti?" she asked.

"My husband," Vera said triumphantly. "Do you know him?"

The girl nodded. "I'm Sosi," she said in Armenian. She looked at the door and frowned.

"Do you know where my husband is?"

"Not now," Sosi whispered, glancing at Vera to see if she understood.

Vera nodded, disappointed. The girl drew a cotton shawl around her lower face and slipped out of the room. Vera heard the key turn. Sosi had taken the lamp with her, leaving Vera in darkness again.

Vera reached out and pulled the basket closer. She felt the contents and was delighted to recognize the textures of kindling, coal, and matches. She dragged it toward where she thought the stove would be. In the process, she stumbled and twisted her wrist. Ignoring the pain, she made up a fire and by the light of the flames examined the rest of the contents. There was a loaf of bread, slices of dried meat encased in red paste, soft goat's cheese, a ceramic pot of olives, and another of yoghurt. She drank more water, then, afraid she would drink it all, put it carefully aside and tasted the food. It was all very salty but tasted better than anything she could remember eating in a long time, except Christmas dinner with Gabriel.

The thought of Gabriel made her want to weep. She didn't know how, but she was certain she had endangered his mission. He would worry about her when he should be concentrating on his work. She was just a fool, she berated herself, the soft daughter of bourgeois parents, brought up in a cocoon with no skills to survive by herself. She should have married the man her parents had chosen for her, a kind young doctor, instead of insisting on going abroad. Why had she gone to Geneva? She admitted it to herself. Because she had been bored. The socialist cause had given her life an exhilarating edge, a meaning greater than the books she read for class and the fashionable shoes she bought with her parents' money. The socialist community in Geneva was her family, but she didn't deserve them now. Kneeling by the open stove door to warm herself, she crammed cheese and bitter olives into her mouth.

20

ON HIS WAY TO FERIDE's house, Kamil made a detour to his office in the courthouse on the Grande Rue de Pera. The avenue crested a hill in the Beyoglu district, or Pera, as it was commonly known, and was bustling with shoppers and tradesmen making deliveries. The air rang with a hundred different tongues. The merchants were mostly Armenian and Greek-speaking Ottoman subjects, but many French and other foreigners lived in Pera as well. It had been the foreigners' section even in Byzantine times, a thousand years ago, when the Genoese and Venetians set up trading posts here. The peaked tower of the Genoese fortifications still dominated the skyline of Galata, now a Jewish district that unfurled down the hill toward the confluence of the Bosphorus and the Sea of Marmara and the inlet of the Golden Horn that served as Istanbul's harbor.

Elif lived in Pera, in a building owned by the wealthy Jewish Camondo family that had taken her under its protection. Kamil had visited her there only once, in the apartment overlooking the water that the Camondos had given her and that she had turned into a studio, the room flooded by light, the sea beyond, the paintings and the room merging. Even though the building was only steps from the courthouse, at her request he had never again visited her. Thoughts of her and an uneasy feeling of regret were never far from Kamil whenever he walked down the Grande Rue de Pera.

Kamil handed his horse to a stableboy and strode up the courthouse stairs. He hadn't been to his office in two days and dreaded the pile of files and paperwork that would have accumulated on his desk. He had asked Nizam Pasha several times for more staff, but the minister had refused, arguing that Kamil had access to the police and the gendarmes for his investigations. They didn't do paperwork, Kamil thought, his head throbbing.

The doorkeeper greeted him. "You have visitors, pasha."

Kamil nodded absently. Most likely plaintiffs who should have been sent to the scribes to draw up an official petition, then to his assistant Abdullah for processing. Why did he have assistants if they didn't assist him? It was as if the sourness of the Eyüp cemetery had stayed with him, settling in his head and bones.

He entered the gilded door to his outer office and stopped dead. Feride, Elif, and Doctor Moreno sat on the divan meant for clients of the court. Their heads turned to him in unison. Abdullah had brought them tea, which they held in their hands like tiny bouquets. Feride, putting her glass down so suddenly that it jumped on its saucer, rushed toward him.

"Why didn't you tell me about the fire?" she cried.

Kamil ushered them into his private office, then closed the door. He bowed to Doctor Moreno and asked them to sit. Feride refused. "What are you not telling me?" she demanded, loosening the veil that covered her lower face.

"I told you I didn't know anything, Ferosh." Kamil tried to keep the frustration and worry from his voice, but Feride knew him too well. She looked him in the eyes, arms crossed, waiting.

"I've been to that taverna with Huseyin," Doctor Moreno explained to Kamil, "so when I heard about the fire, it occurred to me that he might have been caught up in it, especially since he didn't come home that night."

"He should have told me he was going there, even if it was to meet his mistress," Feride insisted.

"You don't know that," Elif scolded. "I'm sorry I said anything." She had been wandering about the office, examining the books on Kamil's shelves, all leather-bound law books, and the paintings on the wall, naturalistic oils and watercolors of flowers. She was dressed in a man's suit, with a broad hat that she removed, letting her chin-length hair swing free. Kamil had never completely adjusted to Elif's impersonation of a man in public, at once high-strung and aggressive. He wished that Elif as a man would be kinder to his sister.

Kamil reached into his pocket and handed the medal to Feride. She ran her fingers over the diamonds and enamel decoration. "It looks like his," she announced dispassionately, although Kamil could see her hands shaking. "Where did you find it?"

Kamil explained where the medal had been found and the fact that many of the wounded were unrecognizable. "There are two patients at Eyüp Mosque hospital who could be Huseyin. I went to check after we spoke this morning, and I was on my way to tell you."

She slipped the medal into her purse and took him aside. "I know you mean well, my brother," she insisted in a low voice, "but I don't need to be protected from news about my husband. I'll be fine." She attempted a shaky smile. "Huseyin always calls me his thorn."

"And his rose," Kamil reminded her, passing his finger across her cheek to wipe away a tear. "We still don't know anything for certain," he said, as much to remind himself as to comfort Feride.

"I'll go to Eyüp," Feride announced. "I know you're busy, but maybe Doctor Moreno would accompany us?"

"I'd be honored." Moreno met Kamil's eye, and he nodded lightly.

"Thank you, Doctor, but I'd better take you there so I can tell you which patients I mean. They're very short-staffed and I doubt anyone would be able to show you."

Kamil crammed the stack of files on his desk into a leather satchel, put on his kalpak, and led the way out of the courthouse.

"Where are your servants?" he asked Feride, seeing only a single coach and their driver, Vali. Usually his sister traveled with an entourage of ladies-in-waiting and guards. Seeing her so unprotected made him suddenly anxious.

"I didn't tell the staff. I wanted to get here as fast as possible to find you, to find out whether he's alive. Oh, why didn't you tell me?"

"I will always tell you everything," Kamil assured her. He helped her into the coach. "Take some guards with you from now on, Ferosh. Promise me."

"Yes, my dear brother." Feride reached out and touched his cheek.

Kamil mounted his horse and led the way over the crest of the Pera hill, followed closely by Feride's carriage. The streets had been cleared of the worst of the snow, but it took almost an hour to reach Eyüp through the afternoon traffic, snarled by an overturned coal wagon.

"The hospital is over there." Kamil pointed.

In the entry hall, they stepped aside to let an orderly carrying a bundle of bedding pass. Kamil led them down the corridor to the director's office.

The director jumped to his feet when the four visitors crowded into the room. Seeing Kamil, he snapped, "Back again? This isn't a social event." When he remarked the quality of his visitors' clothing, his tone suddenly became ingratiating. "If you're here to contribute to the hospital, of course, that's different."

"We're here to see. . . " Kamil started to say, when Feride interrupted him.

"Are you the head doctor?"

"Yes, madame." The director stood and made a formal bow. "Amadio Levy, surgeon and director of Eyüp hospital."

"I am Feride Hanoum, and this is Doctor Moreno and my cousin Elias." With the latter she indicated Elif, wrapped in her greatcoat, hat still on her head. She stood with arms crossed just outside the office door. "You've met my brother, Kamil Pasha."

"Yes, madame." A note of impatience crept into the director's voice.

"What is it that you need?" Feride asked.

"Madame?"

"For the hospital."

The director became animated. "Salaries, mainly salaries so we can hire more orderlies and nurses. We have no nurses. You have no idea, madame, how hard it is to handle so many patients with no staff. I myself am on bedpan patrol first thing in the morning. If we don't get to them in time, they soil the linens and the bandages, which are also in short supply, especially after all the recent burn victims. Their bandages have to be changed constantly."

"Please make me a list. I'll take it with me on my way out," Feride told him. "Now I'd like to see my husband, Huseyin Pasha."

"Your husband, madame?" the director stuttered, looking at Kamil.

"The two men in Ward Three," Kamil reminded him. "We saw them this morning."

"Yes, of course." The director brushed by Kamil and strode rapidly down the hall. They had to run to keep up with him.

Sunlight streamed through the deep, arched windows of Ward Three. Kamil's handkerchiefs were still in place, but one of the two beds was empty.

Feride examined closely what was visible of the remaining patient's hair and face and shook her head no. Kamil went from bed to bed looking at the other patients, but the one he had thought might be Huseyin was gone.

He turned on the director, fairly shouting, "Where is he?"

Feride looked stricken. "Is he dead?" she asked in a whisper.

Elif stood beside another bed, looking down at a woman whose face was so puffed and bruised that her eyes were no longer visible. Her nose had been broken and was in a splint, so she breathed loudly through her mouth. Kamil could see Elif's shoulders trembling and went to stand by her side. The patient had been badly beaten, most likely by someone in her family. Kamil wondered what memories this raised in Elif. He wanted to put his arms around her, but it would have been scandalous, whether she was a man or a woman. He drew Elif away.

"She's going to be all right," he assured her.

"She'll never be all right," Elif responded. "Someone she loves did that to her."

Kamil found himself reluctant to agree that something so heinous was a daily occurrence, even though he knew better.

"It's ugly," she said, half to herself. "Violence is always ugly. I don't know why some people love it so much."

The director, nonplussed, stared at the empty bed festooned with Kamil's handkerchief. "There were no deaths recorded in Ward Three today," he said in a dry, matter-of-fact voice. "And no transfers authorized. I'm responsible for this hospital, and I'll find out what happened here. There's only a limited set of possibilities."

"Which are?" Kamil asked.

"One, the patient died and the orderlies called the imam to fetch the body for burial without notifying me. Two, the orderlies transferred the patient without permission. Neither of these things has ever occurred under my watch."

"To your knowledge," Kamil added.

The director looked at him. "To my knowledge." Then he turned and walked out of the ward.

Kamil and Feride followed. When they reached his office, he was sitting behind his desk, squinting at a ledger. "I was correct," he announced triumphantly. "No deaths, no transfers."

"So where is he?" Kamil couldn't keep the anger from his voice. He was losing patience.

For a moment, the hospital director fell silent. Then he said, "I'll find out. Come back tomorrow." He returned to his ledger.

Kamil walked up to the desk and slammed the ledger shut. "Start now."

The director made a sour face."My dear sir, I was looking to see which orderlies were on duty. If you permit." He opened the ledger again, found the right page, and pulled his finger down a column of neat writing. Then he closed the ledger. "That orderly has already gone home."

Feride sat in a chair by the door. "I'll wait here until you bring him." She looked up at Kamil, who stood in the middle of the room with his arms crossed. "Brother dear, you have other important matters to deal with. I'm in good hands."

Doctor Moreno nodded at Kamil, his sidelocks bouncing beneath his hat. "I'll make sure they get home safely."

Kamil took Feride's hand and held it briefly to his lips. "May Allah guide you."

Feride smiled at the unaccustomed religious sentiment. "Go, you," she told him, and turned back to the hospital director, who was now deep in conversation with Doctor Moreno.

Kamil placed his hand on Elif's arm as he left and indicated that she should follow him. Kamil was worried about her. She looked as if she were in a trance, her eyes glazed with unshed tears, and despite her heavy coat, she was shivering. She seemed tensile as glass, as if she might shatter at any moment.

They walked wordlessly down the corridor until they came to an alcove where they wouldn't be seen.

"What is it?" he asked her. "What can I do?"

Elif's blue eyes sought his but then slipped away again, focusing on the wool of his cape. Without another word, Kamil put his arms around her shoulders, so frail beneath the bulky coat. He took off her hat and cupped his hand around the base of her head and held it tight against his chest until she stopped shaking.

21

THE DOOR OPENED AGAIN, and someone entered carrying a lamp. Vera shut her eyes against the bright light. Her body curled into a ball, preparing for whatever was to come.

"What happened to your light?" Vahid asked pleasantly, pushing aside the remains of food and placing the lamp on the table. In his other hand, he held a glass of steaming tea. "I see you received the food I sent. I've brought you some tea." He set the glass down beside her. "Is there anything more you need? You have water?" He looked at the empty carafe. "I see not. I apologize. I'll have more sent right away."

Vera found herself gaping. Did he have no idea what had just happened to her? Had those men acted without his knowledge?

Vahid sat in the chair beside her and crossed his legs, revealing a slim ankle in a white silk sock. Vera found the sight of the white silk so moving it made her want to cry for the lost innocence of her Moscow childhood. Pull yourself together, she told herself crossly. She forced herself to focus on Vahid's face. He was smiling patiently, like a family doctor making his patient comfortable enough to reveal the wretched failures of her body. He indicated the tea with a nod of his head. "Drink something. You look chilled. I took the liberty of adding sugar."

Vera reached for the glass. It rattled against her teeth, but the warm, sweet liquid calmed her. She should tell him, she thought with rising fury and indignation. They would be punished for what they did.

"I brought you something." Vahid reached into his pocket and pulled out a silver hairpin. Red stones depending from delicate chains clicked softly against each other. He stood behind her and ran his fingers through her thick auburn hair, avoiding the area he had cut off. Vera was frozen with terror, wondering what he would do next. Suddenly he twisted her hair into a knot and clumsily inserted the pin so that it scratched her scalp. Her hair fell free again at once, but the pin remained entangled.

Afraid to move, Vera concentrated on controlling her breathing.

Vahid sat back admiringly. "You look lovely like that."

"Thank you." Vera breathed out slowly through her nose so he wouldn't see her chest rise and fall in panic. She sensed it would be worse if he saw how frightened she was. She sat up and attempted a smile. "You're very kind, sir."

"You're welcome. It's of no importance. I want to make sure you're comfortable here."

"I'd like to leave."

"My dear Lena, there are men outside waiting to arrest you. I hope they haven't already captured your friend. Here you are safe."

Vera felt confused. Was she not already under arrest? If these men weren't the secret police, who were they? "You've been very kind. But . . ." She felt tears coming on and struggled against them.

"Please, my dear girl," Vahid said, leaning toward her solicitously, "just tell me what's bothering you, and I'll see to it that it's taken care of. You're under my protection here."

Did he really not know? Vera wondered, confused. "Your men came in," she began, but found herself unable to continue.

He looked puzzled. "My men? I sent a girl with the food."

Vera took heart that he hadn't known about the men. Perhaps they did it believing she would be too ashamed to tell. The comb looked expensive. Maybe he would help her. "They came in here and took me out. To a room down the hall."

Vahid waited, frowning with concern. He reached out and took her hand. "Go on, my dear girl." His hand was warm and Vera found comfort in the gesture.

"They did things to me." To her horror, she began to weep, her plan to remain in control in shreds. Vahid squatted beside her chair. His hand tangled in her hair and pulled her head to his shoulder, where she wept uncontrollably.

When she had calmed somewhat, he sat back, keeping his arm around her shoulders, his lapel wet with her tears. "Tell me what they did, my dear, and I'll look into it."

Taking a ragged breath, Vera said, "They took off my clothes and touched me everywhere."

"What do you mean by everywhere?" Vahid asked with a frown. "Please explain."

Vera forced herself to say, "Where only my husband should touch." It was all she could utter. She couldn't look at him. She began to feel uncomfortable in his embrace and wanted to push him away, but remembering her plan for escape, she forced herself to remain still.

"You are married?" Vahid asked, glancing at the silver ring on her finger.

"Yes."

"What is your husband's name?"

This might be a trick to get Gabriel's name from her. "Ivan Balian."

She felt his arm tighten around her shoulder. "Is he here in Istanbul?"

"No, in Moscow."

"You are here alone, Lena? How can that be? It's very dangerous for a woman alone in a strange city. Anything can happen."

He stood, towering over her. "I'll see that those men are punished. They won't bother you again." He clicked open a silver cigarette case and offered it to her.

She wiped her eyes on her sleeve and took a cigarette. "Thank you, Monsieur Vahid."

"Vahid." He lit the cigarette for her. His smile showed a line of perfect white teeth beneath his mustache. "You may call me that."

"Thank you, Vahid." Vera forced herself to look at his face and smile back. The aromatic smoke in her lungs intoxicated her.

"I will send more water." He removed the pin from her hair and put it back in his pocket.

When Vahid had gone, the key once more turned in the lock, Vera realized she still had no idea who he was or what he wanted from her. She was sure he was interested in Gabriel, but she wouldn't lead Vahid to him. She had no idea where Gabriel was now, but perhaps Vahid didn't know that. If she convinced him that she had no useful information, would he let her go? She knew the answer. She would be the lure to bring Gabriel out in the open. Her only option was to get out first.

22

KAMIL THOUGHT ABOUT THOSE moments in the hospital hallway all the way back to Eminönü. Elif had once told him the story of her husband's death, how Ottoman soldiers had come to the house and shot him because he had a Slavic name, how he had taken days to die, while their neighbor, a surgeon, had refused to treat him. The families had been best friends. They had bought her husband's paintings, their children had played together.

When her husband finally died, Elif told Kamil, she had made a funeral pyre of his paintings, stolen the neighbors' carriage and horses, and, taking her young son, set out for Istanbul. Armed and dressed as a man, she had made her way through lawless territory until her carriage was stolen. Then, watching her son be killed by bandits, she had lost whatever remained of the woman she had been.

Kamil had met her soon after she arrived in Istanbul at her cousin Huseyin's door. Under Feride's calm attention and Huseyin's firm hand, Elif had slowly come back to life. She was painting again and had found a teaching position at the Academy of Fine Arts. But when she moved into her own apartment, it seemed as though she no longer needed or wanted Kamil's companionship.

Now he felt he had been given a second chance. Despite the tragedy of Huseyin's disappearance, Kamil felt full of joy as his horse
cantered through the streets of Fatih, down the hill to the Eminönü
waterfront, and across the bridge to the Ottoman Imperial Bank.

IT HAD taken Hagop most of the day to defeat the vault. The door
stood wide open, the lock seemingly undamaged. Omar was inside
and grimaced when he saw Kamil. "I hate it when I'm wrong, especially when that means you're right."

"Swyndon was in there?"

"Banged up, but able to talk. They took him to the German hospital. He said a man came to his office yesterday afternoon and showed
him his daughter's gold bracelet."

"How did he know it was hers?"

"He had it made for her, set with turquoises."

"Do you remember?" Kamil prompted him. "The child said Sosi
had taken her bracelet."

"The man told Swyndon that he had an accomplice at his house
and if he didn't open the strong room, the kid would be dead by the
time he got home."

"Probably a bluff."

"But as effective as if it weren't. What parent would take the
chance? Swyndon told him that he couldn't open the door without the
keys kept by the other managers, and the guy held out the keys."

"Someone stole the keys and replaced them with fakes. Sosi again?
I bet we'll find the other two managers' nannies also had a mysterious
friend with access to the house. How was Swyndon wounded?"

Omar sniggered. "You could say he beat himself up. He tripped
and hit his head on the metal shelf, knocked himself out. There, you
can see the blood on the edge."

23

GABRIEL MOVED QUICKLY AND soundlessly through the lanes of the Kurtulush district until he came to a small cottage ringed by a garden wall. The papery trunks of poplar trees in the garden glowed in the slanting afternoon light. His driver, Abel, and Abel's sister, Sosi, lived in this cottage with their aging father, an irascible man who was blind in both eyes. Gabriel had visited them before.

He planned to confront Abel about the explosion at the bank. What on earth did he hope to gain, Gabriel wondered, by attracting the attention of the secret police? There must be a reason, he told himself. Perhaps it could be explained as the excesses of immature, would-be revolutionaries, but he was furious at their lack of discipline. They had ruined the entire mission. As had he, he reminded himself ruefully. Still, he wanted an explanation.

The blue-painted door was ajar. Gabriel pushed it open and went inside. It took a moment for his eyes to adjust to the gloom, but he could already smell the blood and feces. Abel, dead, was naked and tied to a chair, his body livid with bruises, cuts on his arms and round burn marks, probably from cigarettes, on his genitals. Gabriel stepped on something and jumped back. On the floor were two of the man's fingers, neatly severed at the joint.

Gabriel's mind flashed back to Sevastopol, his sister's broken body, the pink quilt stained with her blood, the fingerless woolen gloves the men had heedlessly left behind, their hands hot with stolen life. Gabriel moaned and dug his fists into his eyes until the vision receded and he was once again inside his skin, in this Istanbul room with Abel's body.

That's when he saw Abel's father hiding inside the quilt cabinet, his milk-white eyes staring and his mouth slack with shock. "Sosi?" the old man whispered, trembling.

"Not Sosi, but a friend," Gabriel reassured him. "Where is Sosi?"

"He took her."

"Who did?" But Gabriel could find out nothing more from the terrified old man. Was it the secret police? Gabriel wondered. They would be after him and the gold. Abel knew where the gold had been stored. He must have told them. He had no reason to protect Gabriel. If the secret police knew that the gold was at Yorg Pasha's mansion, then the old man was in danger as well.

Given Abel's inexplicable perfidy at the bank, though, Gabriel realized there could be interests at play about which he knew nothing at all. Still, the young man's brutal murder shocked him, and he worried about Sosi. He had met her when she delivered the keys to the vault she had stolen from the bank managers. He knew what happened to women taken by the secret police. Vera. Sosi. He fled the house, moving surreptitiously through the lanes of Kurtulush to Father Zadian's church.

24

THE MEAGER AFTERNOON LIGHT barely lit the parlor where Mrs. Swyndon sat on the sofa, clutching a glass of whiskey. She was dressed in a floral gown that seemed oddly out of season. Her hair was swept up into two gray wings held back with combs.

"We have good news about your husband, Mrs. Swyndon," Kamil said.

"Yes, one of your men told me."

Kamil and Omar exchanged a puzzled look. "Who?" Kamil asked.

"The man from the police," Mrs. Swyndon said, outraged. "Don't you know your own people? Is this some kind of joke you play on foreigners?"

"I'm sure there's an explanation," Kamil said in a tone of voice he used for calming skittish horses. "We're glad that you received the good news."

"Would you please describe the man who was here?" Omar added.

Mollified, she reached for a decanter and refilled her glass. She held the whiskey out to them, but Kamil and Omar declined. "You're Muslims, of course. I forgot." She got up and went to the window, looking down at the silver waters of the Bosphorus. "What a lovely view. I'll be sorry to leave it."

Omar repeated the question.

"Oh, yes, I'm so sorry. He was tall, with dark hair. His face was pockmarked. And he had one of those sharp little beards and a mustache." She laughed. "Well, except for the pockmarks, that about describes the entire male population of Istanbul, doesn't it?"

"May I speak with your nanny, Bridget?" Kamil asked.

"The nanny, whatever for? Anyway"—she waved her glass—"the girl's gone off her head for some reason. The native maid gave her a potion to calm her down. As soon as she's well enough, she'll be on the next boat to England. My sister warned me about engaging a cripple, and now not only is there no one to watch Alberta, but the staff have to take care of the nanny as well."

"What do you mean by 'off her head'?"

"The cook found her curled inside the cupboard, her arms full of blood. Seems she'd been cutting at herself with a kitchen knife. Nothing deep, just enough to get our attention. As if we didn't pay her enough attention. Can you imagine? I mean, she's a servant. It's pathetic." She refilled her glass. "Frightened Alberta half to death. She was screaming like a banshee."

"I'd like to see Bridget nonetheless." Kamil struggled to keep his rising annoyance from his voice. He saw Omar glance at him with what he guessed was amusement.

"She's not speaking. Probably ashamed at all the trouble she's caused." She led Kamil and Omar down a corridor to a room at the back of the house. Kamil was glad to leave the claustrophobic atmosphere of the parlor, but the sight of the nanny's room infuriated him further. A water stain spread across the ceiling and part of one wall, and the yellow paint was peeling. The wardrobe was missing a door, and the girl's paltry bits of clothing were on display. Still, someone had covered Bridget with a brightly stitched quilt. The girl's bandaged arm lay on top of it. Her face was white and clammy, and her eyes twitched beneath the closed lids.

"She's feverish," Kamil said. "Have you sent for a physician?"

"The Turkish maid sent for one of the local healers." Kamil saw

Mrs. Swyndon's hand stroke the cover admiringly, an acquisitive look in her eye.

"Madame"—Kamil turned on her—"a local healer will write a Quranic verse on a piece of paper, throw it in a glass, and have the patient drink the inky water. I really think you should send for some-one competent."

"What I do is none of your business," Mrs. Swyndon retorted, and left the room, slamming the door behind her. Relief swept through Kamil. He had rarely taken such a dislike to anyone.

"Someone cared enough to do a good job of wrapping the wounds," Omar noted, his tone excluding Bridget's mistress.

"Let's take a look." They unwound the bandage just enough to see the even shallow cuts on the inside of her forearm, one above the other like a ladder.

"She didn't do that herself," Omar decided. "By the third cut she wouldn't have had the control."

Just then a Turkish maid entered the room and, seeing the loose bandage, sternly asked what they were doing.

They identified themselves. "Do you know how this happened?" Kamil asked.

"Someone did that to the poor girl. No one believes me, but I'm glad they called the police finally." She wrapped her arms around herself. "There's a crazy person with a knife on the loose, cutting women."

"How do you know she didn't do it herself?"

"Well, she couldn't have, could she? The cuts are as neat as if a tailor made them. And the child saw someone, although no one believes her either. It's as if we're all cabbages with no eyes or brains in our heads."

"Alberta? What did she see?"

"She says 'a black man.' There was a visitor earlier today who had black hair, but I don't know who it was she saw."

"Can I talk to her?"

The woman hesitated, plucking at her embroidered cotton head-scarf. "I'm not sure Madam would approve, but. . . come with me. Don't tell her, though?"

"Don't worry." Omar smiled at the kind peasant woman. "Was it you who called the healer?"

She spit, "Those people call themselves healers. A lot of mumbo jumbo. I called the midwife, who knows what to do about fevers."

Omar's smile broadened.

KAMIL KNELT beside the bed and stroked the little girl's forehead with the tip of his finger. "Wake up, Alberta," he said. Asleep, the girl looked like a cherub. When the long-lashed eyes fluttered open, he smiled and said, "Remember me? We met yesterday. I'm Bridget's friend." He waited until Alberta nodded. "Can you tell me what happened to her?"

The child's eyes grew wide and frightened.

"Don't worry. Nothing will happen to you." Kamil hoped that was true.

"He hurt her," Alberta whimpered.

"Who did?"

"The black man."

"What did he look like?"

"He had a black beard. He asked me about Sosi, but I didn't say anything." The last turned into a wail. "Bridget told me not to say, and I didn't. It's not my fault."

"Of course it isn't. None of this is your fault." Kamil stroked her hair until she calmed down. "What was he wearing?"

"Black clothes. He hurt Bridget," she whispered.

"What did he do to Bridget?"

Alberta turned her head away and mumbled, "Cut her. With a knife."

The maid sat on the bed and took the girl in her arms.

"I was afraid," Alberta insisted, "but I didn't tell."

"You're a brave girl, Albie," Kamil said softly, and kissed her sweet-smelling hair. Anger built inside him, blackening the horizon like a storm.

25

WHILE THEY WAITED FOR the orderly to be found, Director Levy gave Feride, Elif, and Doctor Moreno a tour of Eyüp Mosque hospital. He was proud of the facilities. "You see we have a lot of room, many beds. The Mosque Foundation is very generous. We have bandages and food and water. But it's not enough for a hospital of this size. The foundation doesn't understand that the sick don't just lie in a bed until they get well. They have to be treated." He emphasized the word. "The burn victims especially need continuous care. Poisons build up in their bodies. We should do tests to identify the toxins, so we can counteract them. We need a laboratory, and most of all, we need a bigger staff.

"I pay the orderlies very little," the director explained as they walked back, "and I suspect they supplement that with some pilfering of supplies, but I have no choice."

Feride was fascinated by the way the hospital worked. It was like a healing machine, despite the blood-soaked cloths in buckets, the unemptied bedpans, and the dirty floors. She pictured it clean and properly supervised. "How much assistance would you ideally need?" she asked.

"A pharmacist, trained nurses, orderlies, cooks, laundry workers.

You can't imagine how many sheets we go through every day. Another surgeon would be nice," he added wistfully, looking at Doctor Moreno, who smiled in return.

Imagining the hospital's needs, Feride was surprised to learn that she enjoyed hearing about how things worked after a lifetime of having the mechanics of living hidden behind the servants' walls. It salved her mind, which was raw with fear about Huseyin's fate and, she was ashamed to admit, pent-up anger. If she was honest with herself, a mistress wasn't strange at all. She had heard complaints from many women in her circle. It seemed that almost every man of consequence eventually found one, especially now that taking a second wife was increasingly frowned upon as unworthy of a modern man. She supposed mistresses were also cheaper than second wives, who demanded their own separate households. She should have been suspicious at Huseyin's uncharacteristic gift of a jeweled hairpin. Had he bought Rhea her own apartment, then, and was the pin for his wife meant to assuage his guilt? Had he bought Rhea a pin too? She would speak with the vintner with whom Huseyin had discussed his precious girl. The thought that he would confide such personal matters to a tradesman sent a spasm of anger through Feride.

Feeling suddenly weak, she caught herself on a bedframe. Why was she so angry at him now when she should care the most? He put up with her bleak humors with a wink and a fond pinch. She knew many, even Kamil, found him boorish. Feride would never have believed such a man could draw her out of herself, make her laugh. Now, even if he were returned to her alive, that joyful rapport would be gone. She wanted to hate him for that. If she didn't find him, she thought, these feelings would eat at her soul.

Elif came over and laid a hand on her arm, her face questioning. "Are you all right?"

Feride nodded. Elif had taken off her hat but kept on her greatcoat in the chilly hospital. She looked like a child, a young boy in a too-large coat.

Only the patient wards were kept warm with braziers, Feride realized. "How much does it cost to heat the hospital?" she asked the director. "It must be quite expensive to heat such a large stone building." Secure that he couldn't see her expression behind her veil, she tried to concentrate on the director's response.

IT WAS two hours before Director Levy's assistant found the orderly and brought him back to the hospital. He was obviously drunk. "What's so important that you take me away from my family?"

"Come with me," Director Levy said, and led the way to Ward Three. He pointed to the empty bed marked with Kamil's handkerchief. "Where is this patient?"

"How do I know?"

"He was your responsibility. You were on duty."

"Well, I can't watch everyone all the time. Maybe he got better and walked out."

To everyone's surprise, Elif stepped up to him and backhanded him hard in the face. She stepped nimbly aside when the orderly grabbed for her. Feride was astounded. Her friend seemed at times to be two quite different people, one calm and tenderhearted, the other impatient and fierce.

The director and Doctor Moreno moved between Elif and the orderly, who looked confused and fell back, overturning a stool. Several patients craned their necks and looked on curiously.

Feride said something to Elif, who pulled a silver coin from her pocket and grudgingly handed it to the orderly. An avaricious gleam passed through the man's eyes.

"Now, please tell us where the patient is."

The orderly raised himself up and crossed his arms. "Only if I keep my job."

Feride turned pleading eyes toward the director, who told him, "All right. But one more infraction—big or small—and you're out."

"His relatives took him away," the orderly announced.

"Why didn't you note that in the log?" the director asked.

The orderly shrugged. "I was going to. The family said they wanted their son treated by believers, not by infidels." He glanced with sly satisfaction at Director Levy.

"Where did they take him?"

The orderly didn't answer until Elif dropped another coin in his hand. "Üsküdar." He claimed to know nothing more than the name of the neighborhood, nor did he know their names. It was clear to Feride that he was lying. How could he have entered the patient's move in the log if he didn't know the name. Perhaps, ashamed of their prejudice against Jews, the family had paid him to hide their identity.

Üsküdar, she thought with dismay, was on the other side of the Bosphorus. It was getting dark.

26

VAHID THREW THE REINS to the liveried servant and looked around in disgust at the wide, graveled drive, somehow clean of snow when the city was suffocating in it. Did Yorg Pasha have his servants melt it with their hot breaths or throw cauldrons of boiling water on it? These were the excesses that softened the empire's belly, on which foreigners chewed like rats. The empire was being eaten alive because its leaders, like this pasha, traded their loyalty for gold, for fat, for unnaturally clean roads.

He strode forward, overtaking the servant who had come to greet him. The guard stood at attention and let him pass, just as if he had been expected. The massive gilded double doors were held open by yet more servants. This gave Vahid pause, as he had expected to surprise the pasha with his visit.

The pasha's arms dealing was well known, and Vahid suspected that he had had a hand in the illegal weapons shipment. He couldn't prove it, but Abel had told him the name of the bank robber and that he had stored the gold from the robbery in Yorg Pasha's stable. Vahid thought about Abel's sister, her resilient young body, the sharp note of desire in her voice. He caught his breath. The desire to live. It was intoxicating. Bridget had led him to Sosi, and Sosi to her brother, Abel, and now he was here in the home of one of the most powerful men in the empire. At this very moment, two Akrep agents, disguised as newly hired day laborers, were combing the stables.

Vahid swept into a mirrored entry hall. There he stopped and gaped in amazement. The walls and ceiling were painted with fantastical creatures, horned men with the legs and hooves of beasts, birds with women's breasts. The images were repeated endlessly in the mirrors. The shamefulness of it—in an entry hall where everyone would see—chilled him. It transgressed any number of laws and norms of society. The worst kind of idolatry, it depicted the human form in a display of lewdness to which no decent woman should be exposed. Clearly only the debauched ever crossed this threshold.

He turned and saw a tall, dour-looking man standing by the entrance to a marble-paved corridor.

"Selam aleykum," the man said. "I am the pasha's secretary, Simon."

"Aleykum selam." Vahid shed his cape and laid it across a table inlaid with semiprecious stones. He was dressed in immaculate black trousers and a high-collared stambouline frock coat. He dropped his gloves on the table. "My business is with the pasha."

"And you are?" Simon asked.

"Vahid. I'm a business associate. Please tell the pasha I wish to see him."

Simon appeared unflappable. "I'll see if he's available," he said mildly, turning and walking down the hall. After a moment, Vahid followed him.

He trailed the secretary down connecting corrridors, each hung with lavish tapestries with scenes he could not make out. Vahid wondered about the secretary's name. Was he Jewish?

He almost stumbled into Simon's back when the secretary abruptly stopped.

"Please wait here." Simon opened a door, entered, and shut it behind him.

Vahid hesitated in the hallway, then he pushed through the door.

The room was empty. The secretary had vanished.

The small room was hung with tapestries, one of a hunt, the other of a horse with a single horn on its forehead trapped in an enclosure. Vahid wandered around the room, examining the embroideries, pulling one up occasionally to see if an exit lay behind it.

A door clicked open, so cleverly designed that it was indistinguishable from the wall. A dignified older man in a brocade robe entered, his sharp eyes taking the measure of his guest. Despite his advanced age, the pasha filled the room with his size and presence.

He smiled and gestured at a comfortable chair. "Please, Vahid. Join me in a cup of coffee. I've just received a shipment from Yemen. The beans have been fermented in the bellies of goats that live in trees. You'll find the flavor most delicate."

More fantastical creatures, Vahid thought. Coffee shat by goats. The old man watched him as if he could read his mind.

The pasha took a seat opposite Vahid in a large armchair. He smiled politely, waited for Vahid to respond, and, when he didn't, nodded at Simon. Vahid saw the secretary hesitate before he left the room. Well, at least the Jew had enough sense to fear him, Vahid thought with satisfaction.

"I'm interested in doing business with Gabriel Arti. It would be to your advantage also. I understand he's staying with you."

Yorg Pasha rested his chin on his fist and regarded Vahid thoughtfully. "Are you in the caviar business as well, or do you simply wish to supply your house?"

The caviar business? That was almost funny. At least Yorg Pasha didn't deny knowing him. "Neither," Vahid answered. "I'd like him to handle a shipment of goods from Istanbul to Trabzon. If you agree, your secretary could act as expediter and draw up the documents. It's a sizable cargo, worth around eighty thousand British pounds."

"What kind of cargo is it?"

Vahid almost said "salted cod," but that would have been too obvious, or unbelievable if the pasha didn't know about the arms shipment, which Vahid didn't for a moment believe. "That's between me and Monsieur Arti. Suffice it to say that it involves something of historic significance originating in the Choruh Valley."

If Yorg Pasha knew anything about Arti's real purpose in coming to Istanbul, Vahid thought, he would have understood his coded communication by now. That it would be to his benefit to give the man up, and that Arti's cause was lost, the settlement in Karakaya discovered, that they had tracked eighty thousand British pounds' worth of loot to Arti and Arti to Yorg Pasha. Even if the pasha was just Arti's unknowing pawn, he might still tell him where the socialist leader was or, as important, the gold. Vahid itched to have his men search the mansion, but Yorg Pasha was powerful, and without any proof of wrongdoing, Vahid's hands were tied. Still, if he could prove that Yorg Pasha had harbored a terrorist, then the pasha's property would be forfeited and he would be reduced to living like the rest of the world.

Yorg Pasha shook his head and said in an aggrieved voice, "I would warn you off doing business with Gabriel Arti, Monsieur Vahid. He left yesterday morning with several of my best horses and a carriage. Without paying for them. He seemed such a respectable gentleman."

With a rush of anger, Vahid understood that the pasha was not going to cooperate. "Do you know that your guest is also a wanted terrorist?" He sat back to see the effect of his words on the pasha but was disappointed.

"A terrorist? How remarkable. What is he accused of?"

"Murder, theft, inciting a revolt against the empire." He leaned forward and continued in a concerned voice. "Do you realize the danger this puts you in?" The pasha was silent, but Vahid could see the fingers of his right hand stroking the velvet of the chair arm. "You could be accused of harboring a terrorist." Vahid crossed his legs. "The penalty for treason, may I remind you, is death."

"My dear sir, the coffee will be here in a moment. In the meantime, let me tell you a story," the pasha said. "It's a sad story about a boy whose father didn't want him but preferred another boy, an illegitimate son whose mother had taken him away when he was very small. The father enshrined that missing boy in his mind as a golden child that outshone all else in his life—his job, his wife, even his legitimate son. The golden boy's name was Iskender, and he was the product of the union between the man and his Greek mistress."

All of Vahid's muscles contracted. He wanted to smash the pasha's head so he would shut up, but instead Vahid found himself paralyzed. How could Yorg Pasha know about his father, about his half brother, Iskender?

"His family desired a better match and refused the marriage," Yorg Pasha continued, "so the woman took her son and moved to another city, where she married and her son shone or didn't shine with another father in another family. But to the man left behind, the universe had gone black. He married the young virgin of a good house his family had chosen for him and did his duty by her. They had one son. The father lived with them but cared nothing for them. Perhaps he didn't even see them. When he died, he left no inheritance but bitterness and loss. What do you think happened to that boy, the second son? What could ever make him whole?"

"What nonsense are you spouting, old man?" Vahid found himself on his feet. He paced up to one of the tapestries. A familiar pain had arisen just under his skin, beneath his jaw, along his back, over his heart. His hands itched with it so that he wanted to tear his skin from his flesh.

In the lines of the tapestry, he saw his father standing by the rail of the Galata Bridge, where he stood every night, looking down into the black water. Vahid, a young boy of seven, beside him, heart pounding, not knowing what his father would do. Scold him for disturbing him, ignore him? Anything would be better than silence. If only his father let him stand there, Vahid had pleaded desperately with fate. Passersby would know he was his father. They would be thinking, Look at the man and his son watching the ships together. Just then his father reached down without moving his eyes from the water and put his hand on the boy's thin shoulder. Vahid remembered closing his eyes, terrified that his father would remove his hand. When the moment came, it was almost a relief. Vahid had blinked back tears of love, of gratitude, of released fear and looked up at his father with a small, tentative smile. His father flung his cigarette over the railing and, without looking at him, began to walk away. Vahid could still hear his father's voice calling to him over his shoulder, "Let's go, Iskender."

Vahid came to, staring at an image of a hound in the tapestry. He swung around. "I tell you you're facing the hangman," he snapped, "and you tell me a fairy tale." He found the pasha's sympathetic look unbearable. Vahid took a step forward.

Simon moved between them. At that moment a servant entered the room carrying a tray. At the sight of Vahid, he stopped. The room filled with the chink of fine porcelain shivering on the tray. Then there was a crash as the china hit the floor.

The servant squatted to pick up the shards. "Leave that and bring fresh coffee," Simon instructed him, keeping a wary eye on Vahid.

"Where is Arti?" Vahid demanded, using his anger to push away the image of his father. "If you tell me—and after all, what is he to you?—I'll keep your involvement in his crimes quiet, and you can continue amassing your goat shit coffee and your obscene decorations without hindrance"—he gestured nonchalantly—"at least by me."

He felt certain that the terrorist was still nearby. He decided to take a further risk. "By the way, Arti has an acquaintance, perhaps more than an acquaintance, a woman named Lena Balian. I feel certain he would like to know that she is well and under my protection. If Gabriel Arti wishes to see her, he just has to let me know. Tell him that if you happen"—he emphasized the word—"to see him."

Vahid watched Yorg Pasha carefully, but he seemed not to recognize the name. Perhaps he had the wrong woman after all, not Arti's wife or lover but simply a stupid girl.

"Have you met a young Russian woman by the name of Vera, by any chance?" Yorg Pasha asked suddenly. "She's the daughter of a business acquaintance. She disappeared several days ago and her father is very worried."

Vahid looked up sharply. Was the pasha agreeing to trade Gabriel for this Vera? The pasha's eyes were on the tapestry behind Vahid's shoulder, on the delicate penned horse with the horn on its forehead.

"What's her family name?" Vahid would send his men out to

look for her. He noted the fractional hesitation before Yorg Pasha
responded.

"Ivanovna. Vera Ivanovna."

Vahid was certain her name was Vera Arti. He rose. "If I learn
anything, I'll let you know."

Yorg Pasha nodded politely, "Go in peace." He looked exhausted.
Like a man out of options, Vahid thought triumphantly. As soon as
his men located the stolen gold in Yorg Pasha's stable, not even the
pasha's high position would save him from a charge of treason.

As soon as he was inside the carriage, Vahid fished in his pocket for
a piece of wire and wound it tightly around his hand. Then he made
a fist so that the wire cut into his flesh. His shoulders buckled at the
pain, at the sweet release.

When his breathing and heartbeat returned to normal, he put the
wire away and wrapped a handkerchief around his hand. His mind
cleared of shadows, Vahid banged on the roof of the carriage. They
moved off down the drive, but when they were just outside the walls,
the carriage slowed. A man approached the carriage door.

The Akrep agent leaned in. "Nothing," he told Vahid. "There's no
gold in the stables."

Vahid's fist punched the seat beside him. "Then tell our agent
inside the house to look around," he ordered. "Discreetly," he added,
recalling the broken china. He slammed the door shut.

The carriage rumbled off. Vahid vowed that he would burn the
pasha and his obscene house to the ground. No one but Vahid had
the right to his memories.

27

"**I** CAN'T GO." Gabriel sat shivering by the fire. He thought he would never feel warm again. The beginning of a thick russet beard covered the lower half of his face. He looked a decade older than three days ago, when he had berated Vera for visiting the publisher with the manifesto.

"You'll do more harm by staying," Simon told him. "Akrep knows you're here, and it won't help your wife if you're sitting in jail too. There's nowhere you can hide in this city that Akrep can't find you. Trust me. We'll try to get your wife out. What can you do? Nothing. He's using her to lure you into a trap. Don't give him the satisfaction."

Gabriel fixed his eyes on the floor, trying to beat down feelings of shame and impotence. He wanted to hit Simon, to beat him with his fists. Gabriel no longer resembled the peaceful man who had spent the last ten years forging his idyllic vision on the anvil of labor and self-denial. Instead he was back in the woods of Sevastopol again, driven by rage and bloodlust. He hated himself.

"A grain boat is on its way from Thrace to the Black Sea. It leaves Karaköy pier tomorrow morning. I've booked you a berth. In your cabin you'll find a trunk with warm clothing. You'll need it in the mountains, so you don't lose your fingers altogether." He nodded at Gabriel's bandaged right hand. "There's also a rifle and some ammunition, although it doesn't look to me like you'll be doing any shooting for a while. The trunk has a false bottom with gold liras and jewels from the bank worth thirty thousand British pounds." Simon held out a key.

Gabriel looked up, the question clear on his face. He took the key clumsily. The cuts on his hands had begun to heal, but the tips of two fingers on his right hand remained lifeless.

"It's enough to last your group through the winter and to buy food, guns, loyalty—whatever it is you need. We deducted what you owe for our assistance in facilitating the shipment."

"But I never received that shipment."

"That wasn't our fault. You said yourself one of your own men probably tipped off the police. The amount we retained also includes our commission and the cost of your trip to Trabzon. The shipping company will help you purchase supplies. You'll need a fleet of animals and carts. The mountain roads can be impassable in winter. Wait a couple of months before you try to bring in supplies. If you want to buy new guns, I'd be happy to help you do that."

Gabriel put the key in his vest pocket. Simon's businesslike tone made it seem almost sensible that Yorg Pasha was keeping more than half the gold, were Gabriel not aware of what was at stake in the eastern mountains. Dozens of comrades should have arrived at the commune by now from all over Europe and America, each bringing weapons and supplies. Surely, they would survive the winter without him. The valley had seemed so fertile and protected. They had even seen lemon trees on their previous visit. But he was unconvinced. He pictured them freezing in the unheated monastery, starving, unable to defend themselves against marauders. He had little faith that the local landowners would come to their assistance.

Simon waited by the door, arms folded, his forehead creased in a frown. "The pasha has been accused of treason for harboring you. He could have gotten out of it by handing you over, but he didn't, for reasons that escape me." He lifted a heavy fur cape from a chair by the door and threw it at Gabriel. "Get ready. Every moment that you're here is another length of the pasha's shroud."

Gabriel dropped the cape on a chair and went to stand beside the fire, massaging his forehead. "I can't leave without Vera," he announced. He felt disgust at his inability to protect anyone who had ever been in his trust.

He heard Simon take a deep breath, the only sign betraying the secretary's impatience. "Do you know anyone named Lena Balian?"

Gabriel's head jerked up. "That sounds familiar." His fingers burrowed into the fur of the cape, his eyes far away. He saw Vera giggling by the waterfall, a crown of daisies slipping from her hair. They had strayed from the group on a spring hike in the mountains around Geneva and found a secluded meadow where they could be alone. He had splashed her with water and, shivering with cold, she had slipped so naturally into the circle of his arms. He recalled the silken curls of her hair, strewn with white petals, and her voice as fresh and voluble as the waterfall as she talked wistfully about her family in Moscow, her sister, their dogs. That was it. Lena Balian was the daughter of the forester who trained Vera's father's dogs.

"She's a friend of Vera's in Moscow. Why do you ask?"

"I think we may have found your wife."

Gabriel's mood soared. "Where is she?" he cried out.

"Where you thought. She's being held by the secret police."

"Can you get her out?" Gabriel realized as he spoke these words that he had now abdicated responsibility for helping Vera to Yorg Pasha. Simon was right. There was nothing he could do on his own. Redemption, he thought with a pang, was short-lived.

28

ERA HEARD THE KEY TURN in the lock. As the door opened, she forced herself to stand, back straight, eyes alert. Even if she wasn't a proper comrade, she was the daughter and granddaughter of generals. She didn't know what she would do if the men came for her again, but stoked her anger because that helped.

A plump face wrapped in a shawl peered cautiously into the room. Seeing Vera, the girl nodded and touched her hand to her mouth. She put the basket and her lamp on the floor and, after another glance into the corridor, closed the door softly. She wore the same marigold robe. Vera noticed it was grimy and torn. The girl's eyes were bruised and vacant, and she looked more frail than she had the day before.

Vera held out her hand, but the girl pulled hers back. They were latticed with fresh cuts, some still bleeding. The girl reached into the basket and brought out two long, black charshaf veils. She shoved one toward Vera. "Hurry."

Vera dropped the garment over her head and was enveloped in scratchy wool smelling of unwashed bodies. A tickle ran across her neck—lice. She forced down her revulsion.

Sosi was tying up her charshaf, which was too long for her. Then she pinned the veil over Vera's mouth. The girl picked up the lamp, opened the door and looked out, then slipped through, Vera following. Sosi closed the door, grasped Vera's hand, and pulled her down the corridor.

They had gone only a short distance when Sosi opened another door and pushed Vera through. Inside, Vera froze. She recognized the room as the place where the men had taken her. The table with leather restraints and metal clasps loomed in the light of Sosi's lamp. Sosi tugged at her arm, but Vera doubled over, gasping with pain, and ripped the veil from her face. Her stomach heaved but brought forth only a thin drizzle of bile.

"Be quiet," Sosi whispered, taking a length of her skirt and wiping Vera's mouth. Vera took a deep breath and nodded. Sosi turned to the back wall, pulled a wooden panel aside, and shoved Vera through.

On the other side, Vera saw several chairs facing the paneling, each chair situated in front of a peephole that gave a view of what was going on inside the room. She realized that Vahid had been behind this panel during her humiliation.

Sosi pulled at Vera's sleeve. The girl's face was white and greasy with sweat. She put out the lamp, fumbled a key from her sash, and unlocked a door. The smell of loam carried on the chill night air.

Vera pulled the charshaf tight around her face and stepped into a small courtyard cleared of snow. Keeping their backs against the wall, she and Sosi moved through the yard like shadows, then set out across open ground, ducking behind bushes, until they came to the edge of a grove of trees. There Vera began to run, the rocks and brush lacerating her bare feet. She heard Sosi's footsteps behind her until her own breath and heartbeat drowned out all other sound.

29

"Hanoum Efendi," Feride's driver Vali pleaded with his mistress, "it's too dangerous. It's dark on the water and there's a fog. There are too many ships out there. Even if we were to reach the other side without mishap, we'd never find the right hospital. And we have no guards. We should send a message home for the house guards to go with us. They can meet us at the pier. But really we should go tomorrow when it's light. It's just not safe."

Feride was convinced that the stolen patient was her husband, and she was determined to find him. Every moment she wasn't by his side was a moment in which poor care might bring him closer to death. If he wasn't already dead. It appeared he had already been moved twice, from the Austrian infirmary to Eyüp and now clear across the strait. She gritted her teeth. There was no time to assemble a larger party from her home.

"We'll lose at least two hours waiting for them. Let's drive to Beshiktash. That's the closest point to Üsküdar. Surely someone there will rent us a boat. For enough money, they'll carry us over on their backs." She stopped before Elif, who sat on a broken column, seemingly lost in thought. "Come on, let's go," Feride said, her black cloak and veil blurring in the dusk.

Elif didn't budge. "What's the matter with you?" Feride asked, her voice tense.

She was becoming increasingly impatient with Elif's unfathomable moods. Her friend had become a stranger. She wondered if she had been wise to bring her along. Given what she had been through, perhaps the sight of damaged people was more than Elif could bear.

Doctor Moreno looked for a moment as if he would intervene but then thought better of it.

"Well, I'll go by myself then." Feride climbed into the carriage. "We can't wait until morning. Doctor Moreno said there's a danger of sepsis if the poisons in a burn victim's body aren't drained. Isn't that right, Doctor?"

Doctor Moreno agreed, setting his gray curls in motion. He laced and unlaced his slender hands. "It's unsafe to go," he told Elif in a gentle voice, "but probably worse if we don't."

Elif stood and said, "Let's go. I know a way." She gave Vali directions and climbed into the carriage after Feride. The doctor followed.

The driver frowned and took up the reins.

They drove slowly through the city, delayed by drays hauling wood and coal, carriages, street vendors, pedestrians, and dogs, then more quickly up through the wooded hills above Beshiktash. There they turned onto a lane that wound steeply downward. The road was slick with snow, and the carriage shifted and slid, tumbling its passengers into one another. They could hear Vali cursing as he maneuvered the horses.

Finally the carriage stopped. They climbed out into a mist that completely obscured the Bosphorus and everything on the shore beyond a meter away.

"Where are we?" Feride asked uncertainly. Elif had refused to tell them anything more in the carriage.

"Come with me," she commanded brusquely, and set off into the fog. Feride and Doctor Moreno hurried so they wouldn't lose sight of her.

They came up against the side of a wooden boathouse. Feride could hear the water reverberate inside it. She couldn't see any of her companions and felt completely alone, but not frightened. In fact, for the first time in her life, she felt that she inhabited herself fully. She pressed her face against the heartbeat of the building until Doctor Moreno found her.

Elif reappeared, accompanied by a barrel-chested man with enormous arms, carrying a lamp so bright that it turned the mist around them into a white, almost solid mass.

"This is Nissim," Elif said, "chief of the Camondo boatyard. He can get us across." The Camondos were Elif's wealthy patrons. Nissim clearly recognized Elif in her man's clothing.

The boatman gestured with his lantern and they followed him into the building. Only tendrils of the fog penetrated inside, and Feride had the sudden sensation of seeing again. The boatman led them to a sturdy rowboat tethered just inside the water gate. He attached his lamp to the front and gestured that they should get in.

The danger of crossing the strait in this weather became clear to Feride for the first time. "Maybe I should go alone," she suggested. "Why should you risk your lives because of me?" We should all go tomorrow in the daylight, she thought, but Huseyin might be dead by then.

"Nonsense, my dear," Doctor Moreno said in his calm voice. "Do not meet troubles halfway."

Vali took a position by one set of oars. Nissim returned with an enormous contraption like a leather bird with wooden wings that he made fast to the back of the boat. Doctor Moreno sat nearest to it, and Nissim showed him how to work the bellows. As he did so, an extraordinary moaning issued from the device.

"Clever," the doctor commented. "A bagpipe operated by a bellows."

"Keep it going all the time," Nissim admonished the doctor. "Other boats will hear us, even if they can't see us."

"Who else would be out on the water in a fog like this?"

"There are always fools abroad." The boat swayed as Nissim got in and took up the second set of oars. A boy slid open the water gate. The craft edged out into the current. Feride clutched her charshaf around her, glad of the heavy veil protecting her against the wind. Around them all was brilliant white as if they were trapped inside a cloud. The bagpipe moaned into the blind night.

THE STABLEBOY AT THE HOME of bank comptroller Swyndon remembered seeing a carriage parked in the road the day the mysterious "policeman" had visited the household. One of the horses, he noted with professional interest, had a thick pink scar on its flank. The same carriage with a scarred horse, Kamil learned, earlier that same day had brought the "policeman" to the Montaignes', where he asked to speak to their governess. The girl was away and so presumably was spared Bridget's treatment.

Someone was following the same trail of clues and frightening their witnesses. Kamil wondered whether the "black man" seen by little Albie might belong to the Akrep organization Huseyin had told him about. How else would the man be aware of what Kamil and Omar had only just learned themselves. Omar had put it more colorfully. Presumably the "black man" thought, as they did, that Sosi was the means to finding the other thieves and the gold. He hoped, for Sosi's sake, that they found her before the "black man" did.

While Omar returned to the Fatih police station to see what his network of spies had managed to discover about Sosi, Kamil turned his horse toward Nishantashou, where he hoped for a late dinner with

Feride to learn whether she had discovered anything about Huseyin's whereabouts. Surely Elif would still be with her, he thought, aware that it was the delicate golden woman who sent the blood spinning in his head. He realized that his primary motivation was to see her, not his sister, and he was disgusted at himself for his disloyalty.

When he arrived, he was disturbed to find Feride and Elif still out. Doctor Moreno had promised he would bring them home safely. Their driver, Vali, was with them, but given what he had learned that day about his mysterious adversary, he worried that they hadn't taken any guards with them.

Having left instructions to send a message when Feride returned, he rode slowly home through the banks of fog that made the night seem impenetrable. He was relieved when Karanfil's lamps, magnified by the mist, bloomed in the darkness before him, and he crossed over the threshold of light.

Yakup came out with a lamp and took the reins. When Kamil had discarded his wet coat and hat in the entry hall and wiped his face with the towel Karanfil held out to him, he saw on the salver the letter with Yorg Pasha's seal.

❧

"I APOLOGIZE FOR bringing you out so late, my boy, and on a vicious night like this. Would you like a whiskey?"

Kamil sat on a divan in a part of Yorg Pasha's mansion he had not seen before. It was in the old Ottoman style with cushioned benches around three sides of a raised, carpeted platform. Below the platform extended a marble-paved floor, where a small fountain burbled. The ceiling was painted with fantastic birds. Yorg Pasha half reclined on the facing divan, propped on cushions, in his hand a narghile pipe, his eyes half lidded. A brass mangal brazier warmed the air.

Kamil accepted the glass of whiskey Simon brought him. Yorg Pasha famously kept a cellar of the finest wines and other heady liquids for his guests, though he himself never drank alcohol. The amber potion opened a welcome path in Kamil's chest. Yorg Pasha sipped from a glass of boza, sweet, fermented millet. He passed Kamil a dish of roasted chickpeas.

"To tell you the truth, amja," Kamil said, presuming on their closeness, "I'm glad to be here. This hasn't been a good day and I'm bone tired."

Kamil saw Yorg Pasha's eyes glow with pleasure when he called him uncle. The old pasha had three sons, but respect required them to be distant and formal with their father, as Kamil had been with his own. Why was that a virtue, Kamil wondered, when sons hungered for their fathers? Surely it was natural for fathers to desire their sons' affection. Because they were not related, Kamil realized sadly, he and the old pasha were free to like each other. Suddenly the whole world tasted sour, and he felt so tired he had to fight not to lie down on the divan.

"I've had two interesting visitors lately," Yorg Pasha began. "One of them has robbed a bank but claims he did not blow it up."

Kamil sat up, fully awake, and put down his glass.

"The other," the pasha continued, "would like to trade a Russian lady for the bank robber."

Kamil had a hundred questions but chose to wait.

"It's already a dilemma worthy of a saint," Yorg Pasha said. "But there's more. The gold my first visitor stole is meant to support a commune in the Choruh Valley populated by a group of naïve socialists who are courting death either through starvation, irritating the local landowners, sheer idiocy, or official eradication by order of our padishah. My question to my guest was, Who then blew up the bank that caused the latter to become the most likely outcome? Can you guess?" Yorg Pasha smiled, clearly pleased with the effect of his riddle.

"Socialists in the Choruh Valley?" Kamil repeated stupidly.

"They're setting up these utopias everywhere these days. From Ukraine to Palestine. Foolish young people come to a place with no knowledge of farming, local conditions, or even the local languages— just a head full of dreams."

"I've heard of the Palestine settlement," Kamil replied. "I suppose I thought it was an admirable thing to attempt, naïve perhaps, but, well, someone needs to dream. An egalitarian society may not work, but where's the harm in trying?"

"My thoughts exactly." Yorg Pasha surveyed Kamil over the mouthpiece of his water pipe. "Perhaps I've delegated some of my own dreams to you, more so than my own lazy children. I cannot afford to have dreams myself. I'm too old and fond of power."

"Pardon the question, amja, but are you sure this settlement is harmless?"

Yorg Pasha nodded. "Simon has looked into it. The locals doubt it'll last the winter, and it seems many hope it won't. They're right to be suspicious of outsiders. It can only bring them trouble."

"And this socialist claims he didn't blow up the bank? I find that hard to believe."

"His name is Gabriel Arti. He thinks his driver, Abel, did it."

"Why? It would have been smarter to leave quietly and not draw attention to the robbery."

"They're Armenians."

"The socialists?"

"The socialists hark from many nations. Their only commonality appears to be their naïveté. Gabriel is Armenian, from Russia. His driver also is Armenian, a local man from Kurtulush."

"I didn't know there were Armenian socialists in Istanbul."

"As far as I know, there aren't. An Armenian socialist is a mythological beast that doesn't exist in nature. The Armenians want their own state, but an Armenian one, not a socialist one. I suspect Gabriel Arti doesn't understand the difference. An Ottoman Armenian can no more be a socialist than a fish can fly."

"One hand working against the other. I suppose that's possible. But why the explosion?"

"Think about it." Yorg Pasha waved the mouthpiece of his narghile in Kamil's direction. "What did the explosion accomplish that a robbery might not have?"

"Well, it certainly captured the interest of the palace. A robbery would cause concern, but a violent act sends a shiver up the spine of the government."

"Exactly." Yorg Pasha agreed, drawing deeply on the mouthpiece of his pipe. "Explosions draw the secret police like honey draws a bear."

Kamil watched the smoke curl from the pasha's mouth toward the ornate ceiling. He would have liked a cigarette himself, but it would be rude to light up before an elder. His father had never seen Kamil smoke. Society's rules were there to create order and civility out of the rabble of our emotions, he reflected. You may hate your father, but by not smoking in front of him, you show your respect. He hadn't hated his father, but he hadn't known him either, and this seemed to him as great a tragedy, the inadmissibility of love.

"I don't understand the motivation of the local Armenians, though. All they've accomplished with their explosion is to endanger their own people. What's the point of their playing along with the socialists only to undermine them? If they object to the socialists setting up a commune in an Armenian valley, the local residents can just drive them out. You said they were barely surviving anyway."

"This is a radical group within the Armenian community. They wouldn't be the first to orchestrate an attack on their own people in order to get attention for their cause. It's brutal, but it works. They grafted their own interests onto Gabriel's socialist experiment. They set him up. Now it will all look like his doing. And if there's a massacre of socialists and Armenians, the blame will fall on the socialists and their commune for inciting it. The British press, no friends of ours, would pick up the news of a massacre and push for their government to get involved. The Armenians would expect the British to help them carve out a homeland where they'd be safe. That's what they're hoping anyway. A remarkable plan."

"Let me understand this. A group of Armenians in Istanbul are hoping that blowing up the bank will prod the sultan into cracking down on the Armenians in Choruh?" Kamil shook his head in disbelief. He leaned back and let his eyes play over the colorful plumage of the birds pictured on the ceiling. He smacked his hand hard on the divan. "I bet it was the local Armenians who reported the weapons shipment to the police. And told them about the commune. How else would the secret police know about the settlement in the Choruh

Valley? Someone inside Gabriel Arti's circle must have told them." He emptied his glass, feeling energized as ideas clicked into place.

Yorg Pasha exhaled a plume of sweet-scented smoke. "The male of a certain species of spider allows himself to be devoured by the female after they've mated," he said. "It's his final, magisterial investment in the success of his offspring."

Kamil grimaced. "That's grotesque."

"It's heroic. The Cause is always greater than individual lives."

"The second guest you mentioned," Kamil asked, "was he tall, with a pointed beard?"

"Ah, well done. Always a step ahead. His name is Vahid, commander of Akrep, the sultan's very own poisonous creature." The pasha set down his pipe and reached for the glass of boza. Simon stepped up from the lower room, picked it up, and handed it to him. "Unlike our selfless spider, the scorpion paralyzes its prey with venom." He drank some of the boza and wiped his mouth on an embroidered cloth. "Perhaps it toys with its prey for a time before eating it," he speculated. "The prey is only immobilized after all." His eyes sought Kamil's. "Imagine the terror of seeing those small claws attached to the scorpion's jaw come closer, take small, delicate bites. Watching yourself being slowly dismembered."

Kamil listened carefully. He had a feeling that the pasha, who never wasted words, was telling him something important.

"Yet surprisingly," Yorg Pasha went on, "for such cruel beings, scorpions are actually quite timid. They'll run from danger or they remain very still. It's when they're still that you must be particularly careful. And you must never, never," he repeated, "allow a scorpion to mistake you for prey."

"What does he want?"

"He wants people to be in his power. His is the voice whispering in the sultan's ear."

"Where's this Gabriel Arti now? And the gold?"

"On their way to Trabzon."

Was it a slip of the pasha's tongue, or had he meant to reveal to Kamil that he knew where the gold was? The realization disturbed

Kamil, but he found he wasn't surprised. He tried to remember that he needed to be wary of the pasha. "How?" he asked.

"Steamer. You won't catch up with him now." Yorg Pasha waved his hand dismissively. "Forget these socialists. They aren't a problem, except to themselves. Vahid is where you should focus your attention."

"I can't leave the city right now anyway." Kamil told him about the fire and Huseyin's disappearance. "Feride and Doctor Moreno are looking for him in the hospitals."

"Ah, vay, ah, the poor man. And my dear girl, Feride, what a tragedy. I hope it will not come to that and you will find him well. Perhaps a different accident has befallen him, a broken leg in the snow?"

"We would have heard. Huseyin isn't the quiet type."

Yorg Pasha chuckled, breaking the tension that had been growing between the two men. "Yes, that's so."

Kamil passed his hand across his face. "Sometimes I feel the task is beyond me."

Yorg Pasha came to sit beside Kamil and laid his hand on his shoulder. They sat in silence for some moments before Yorg Pasha said softly, "Your father loved you as he loved life itself. I know this."

Kamil nodded his head in acknowledgment. He smiled to cover his confusion and, after a few moments, got to his feet, swaying with tiredness.

"Stay here tonight," Yorg Pasha suggested. "It's a cold night." He stood up with difficulty. Kamil offered his hand, but Yorg Pasha waved him away, muttering, "Even in winter, the lion can roar."

"Thank you. That's most generous, but I have work to do tonight." He stepped down from the divan platform into the marbled hall. "You mentioned a woman," he added, almost as an afterthought.

Yorg Pasha shook his head in bewilderment. "The fool Gabriel brought his wife along. I've looked into this Gabriel Arti. He has a reputation as an experienced activist, but he was groveling on his knees because he's allowed his woman to fall into the grasp of Akrep." The pasha leaned on Simon's arm to step down from the platform. The secretary then retreated, following the pasha like a shadow.

Yorg Pasha and Kamil walked side by side through the glittering lamplit rooms. Beyond the window sashes, the black mass of the strait heaved in the night.

"There was something about a sister," Yorg Pasha continued. "She lived with Gabriel in Sevastopol. One night while he was out, she was murdered, and I gather that he went on a rampage. Some men were killed, but it was never established that it was Gabriel who killed them, or that these were truly the men who had murdered his sister. But none of those distinctions mattered to the Russian police, who needed to arrest someone for the crime. Gabriel fled to Geneva to avoid arrest and joined the socialists."

"A man with nothing left to lose is dangerous."

"And a man with a wife is vulnerable."

"What's her name?"

"Vera Arti, but Vahid thinks the name of the woman he holds is Lena Balian. I hope I convinced him that Lena Balian is the wrong person and useless to him as a lure for Gabriel. But I dread to think of what she's already endured. If there's any way to bring her out . . ."

Kamil felt tired and overwhelmed. He wanted to focus on finding Huseyin. Now Feride and Elif were missing, and here was another person lost, pieces of a puzzle that seemed to shift in three dimensions. But he could say he had found the bank robber and the gold, he thought with a glint of hangman's humor. He could put a pin on the map and say they were on a ship between Istanbul and Trabzon. And Vera Arti was probably being held in the Akrep headquarters. That would be easy enough to locate. Another pin. Yet the entire roster of lost persons was insignificant compared to the match he now saw being held up to a corner of the map, the conflagration that would devour an innocent population.

"I'll do my best, amja."

"Yes," the pasha said with a worried look. "You always have." He gripped Kamil's arm with surprising strength.

31

THE FOG WAS NOT AS thick in Üsküdar. An icy rain seemed to have swept the air clean as the little group made its way across the square opposite the boat landing and into the alleys leading uphill to the Valide Mosque hospital, the largest in the district. The cold had frozen the mud into troughs, so they walked slowly, Nissim in front and Vali bringing up the rear, each carrying a lamp. A strange calm possessed Feride as she followed Elif and Doctor Moreno. She stumbled once and caught at Elif's coat. After that, Elif came to walk beside her whenever the lane was wide enough. No one spoke.

Before long, the way opened up into a lane that passed between orchards and vineyards. A pack of bony dogs followed them, remaining just outside the light. Whenever one of them approached, Vali hurled a rock at it. The rain had stopped. There was an odor of pine and soil, and the stars had reappeared. In the dimness, Feride made out the dome and two minarets of a mosque flanked on either side by buildings, which must be the complex of monasteries, schools, soup kitchens, hospitals, baths, and shops that accompanied all great mosques.

Nissim led them to an adjacent building. They entered a grand vestibule that led to a caravanserai where travelers spent the night. Several men sat by a fireplace, and Nissim asked them the way to the hospital.

Their stares caused Feride to look at her companions with new eyes—a blond foreigner, an old Hasidic man with sidelocks, a veiled woman, and two burly workingmen, assembled here at a suspicious hour.

Nissim led them around the back of the building. He pounded on a locked door until it was opened by a bearded man in a turban.

"What do you want, you ruffian? This is a hospital and you're frightening the patients."

Doctor Moreno stepped forward and introduced himself as a physician at Yildiz Palace. The man's expression changed immediately, and he stepped aside and welcomed them in.

Doctor Moreno explained whom they were looking for.

"A patient with burn wounds transferred from Eyüp Hospital yesterday or today?" The man rubbed his beard. "I don't recall anyone like that. In fact, as far as I know we have no burn patients here. I'll have to wake the director."

He led them through a door at the opposite end of the vestibule, then across a colonnaded courtyard, where he knocked tentatively, then more loudly at a door. A tall, lanky man in a hastily donned robe emerged, settling a fez on his balding head. "What is it?" he asked.

Doctor Moreno stated his case again.

"Come, let's look through the wards," the director said, glancing curiously at the doctor's associates, "but I can assure you that we have no burn patients. Are you sure he was sent here?"

Feride took a lamp and stepped into the first ward. It was cleaner than the Eyüp hospital and had fewer patients. She walked among the patients, then halted beside a man whose head was wrapped in bandages. She knew without a doubt it was Huseyin. This was the husband who had always supported her, even when her father committed suicide and, blaming herself, she lapsed into melancholia for months. This was the husband who adored his twin girls. The thought of them growing up without their father made her begin to weep.

The director rushed over. "Now, now, this is just a bad rash," he explained gently. "Nothing life-threatening. A local man. Not your husband. Certainly not."

Elif drew her arm through Feride's and they continued to the next ward. After they had looked through all the rooms, she asked the director, "Where else could he have been brought in Üsküdar?"

"Patients with wounds that severe generally would be brought here. But there are several smaller infirmaries attached to the mosques." In her exhaustion, Feride had let her veil fall open, and he politely avoided looking at her face.

"If such a patient appears, would you immediately send word?"

The director bowed. "Of course, hanoum." He turned to Doctor Moreno. "I can make chambers available for you and your guests if you'd like to spend the night. It's a dangerous crossing."

"That it is," muttered Nissim.

A COCK CROWED nearby and Feride opened her eyes, then sat up, startled by the unfamiliar room. A stone cupola arched above her, and a narrow window gave out onto a courtyard. It wasn't the cock's crow, she realized, that had awakened her. It was still night. Light flared across the window as men with lamps ran past through the courtyard. Feride put on her charshaf and stepped outside. The director was buttoning his jacket. He had forgotten his fez and his head looked pale and vulnerable. He saw her and said in a breathless half shout, "Please, hanoum, go back into your room and lock the door."

As soon as he was out of sight, a figure detached itself from the shadows and pulled Feride aside.

"Elif!" Feride exclaimed, relieved. "What's happening?"

Elif looked as though she hadn't slept at all. "The doorman was murdered. They think we had something to do with it."

"Why would they think that?"

"Because one of the patients also died." She grasped Feride's hand. "The man with the bandaged head."

32

THAT MORNING, Kamil woke before dawn and rode directly to Omar's house in Fatih. Omar's wife, Mimoza, was already stoking the fire in the potbellied stove. She bade him sit, and returned after a moment with a glass of tea. At the door, her adopted son, Avi, slipped off his shoes and handed Mimoza two loaves of bread, still warm from the community oven.

"I saw you, but I couldn't catch up with you." He beamed at Kamil, then followed Mimoza to the kitchen.

A few moments later, Omar appeared, tucking in his shirt.

"Welcome, pasha, to our humble home." He settled heavily beside Kamil on a cushion. Avi came in with the teapot. Omar waited until the boy had gone before he told Kamil in a low voice, "We found Abel. They had buried him already, but we dug him up."

They sipped their tea in silence while Mimoza brought in a pan of poached eggs and spinach, settled it in the middle of the tray, and tilted a big spoon against it. She gave them a curious glance and disappeared again.

"Two fingers cut off," Omar whispered, one eye on the corridor. "Burn marks on his yarak. Who would do something like that?"

"Akrep commander Vahid, no doubt," Kamil responded, remembering Yorg Pasha's warning. "He found Sosi through the nanny Bridget, and Sosi led him to her brother, Abel. Any sign of the girl?"

"The priest said she was abducted. On her engagement day, no less. She'll be conspicuously dressed, which might make her easier to find. We talked to her fiancé, but he doesn't know anything. He was under the impression that she lived a sheltered life at home. Their father was in the house when it happened, by the way. He's blind, and now they say he has brain fever. We couldn't get a coherent sentence out of him."

"Yorg Pasha knows the man, Gabriel Arti, who carried out the robbery." Kamil told him Arti's suspicions about his driver, Abel, and about Vera Arti's arrest.

"Yorg Pasha runs in dangerous circles," Omar commented, "but that doesn't surprise me. Now Abel setting off the explosion to draw attention to the Armenian cause, that surprises me. That's like blowing off your behind to loosen up your bowels." Omar let out a deep breath. "Well, they certainly got the palace's attention."

Mimoza coughed before she entered with the rest of their breakfast. They ate to Avi's chatter and good-natured sparring between Omar and his wife. Kamil felt unaccountably lonely and wondered for the hundredth time where Feride and Elif were. No message had arrived.

When the dishes were cleared and the tray removed, Omar asked, "Do you think Gabriel took revenge on Abel for messing up his nice, neat robbery?"

Kamil remembered Yorg Pasha's description of Gabriel. "I don't think so. He has bigger problems. But I have a favor to ask of you."

33

T HE NORMALLY PLACID Doctor Moreno was flushed with anger. "Of course, we're leaving. You can't possibly think we had anything to do with these murders."

"As a man of science," the director said, "you must admit it's unlikely to be a coincidence that right after you arrive, the man who let you in and the man you mistook for Huseyin Pasha are both dead. We wait for the police."

"Has it occurred to you, Director, that we might also be targets?" Feride pointed out. "Keeping us here puts us in danger as well. Whoever did this apparently wanted to kill"—her voice broke—"a man he believed, or thought I believed, was my husband."

"I'm sorry, hanoum," the director said in a conciliatory voice. "Of course, I understand that." He peered at her. "Do you know why someone would want to kill your husband, especially as he is already incapacitated?"

Feride heard the slight pause before the word and knew the director thought that Huseyin was either dead or as good as dead.

"Ask the orderly who was on duty in the room," Elif suggested in a boyish voice.

It was the first time she had spoken to the director, and he looked at her curiously. "Excellent idea, monsieur," he told Elif, then called his assistant and told him to find the orderly.

"He's the only one who could have seen me at the man's bed," Feride added, suddenly afraid.

After a few moments, word came that the orderly was missing.

Feride went to warn Vali and Nissim, who were keeping watch across the courtyard.

"Someone followed us here? Through that fog?" Nissim was incredulous.

"They could have gotten the location the same way we did," Vali noted, "from the orderly at Eyüp hospital. He'd sell his mother for a kurush."

"Who are these people?" Feride asked, near tears. "What should we do?"

"Not wait for the police." Nissim turned to Vali. "Is there a carriage?"

Vali disappeared for a few moments, then returned and shook his head no. "We'll have to walk."

"We should go now," Nissim urged.

Feride went to fetch Elif and Doctor Moreno, who was still arguing with the director.

"If you don't remain," he was saying, "you will place yourself under suspicion."

"I doubt that." Struggling to keep her voice steady, Feride said in as haughty a voice as she could muster, "I am the wife of Huseyin Bey, and Doctor Moreno is employed at the palace. We are easily found, and should the police wish to speak with us, I'm sure we would be happy to accommodate them. Isn't that so, Doctor? My brother is the magistrate of Beyoglu, and naturally I would like to consult with him before I answer any questions."

"It wouldn't do, sir, for a lady to be interrogated like a criminal," Doctor Moreno added. "Surely you see that."

When the director nodded uncertainly, Feride indicated to the others to follow her. Nissim was waiting by the gate. They heard a carriage clattering toward them at great speed.

Nissim stepped off the road into a vineyard. "Hurry."

Doctor Moreno and Elif took Feride's arms and pulled her into the shadows just as the carriage rounded the corner into the square.

34

VERA RAN DOWNHILL THROUGH the forest until she came to a high wall. She followed it and found a gate. There was no guard, at least on her side, but it was locked. She looked behind her and listened, but couldn't hear Sosi, only the baying of dogs. Breathless, she burrowed into a pile of leaves and pine needles behind a large boulder where she couldn't be seen. It hadn't occurred to her that they would send dogs. Dogs noticed movement, she remembered from home, though they also had an excellent sense of smell. She looked around wildly. Where was Sosi? She didn't dare call out to her.

The gate in the palace wall opened and two guards rushed in. They stopped at the edge of the forest and listened intently, then had a hurried conversation.

Vera didn't understand what they said, but while they were distracted, she scrambled up and, keeping her body low, ran through the gate as fast as she could, expecting at any moment to be cut down.

35

"*I* WANT TO CHECK the other infirmaries," Feride insisted. "We came all this way. I'm not going back to the city without finding him. He must be here somewhere." She didn't care anymore that he had a mistress. She just wanted him alive and home. Someone was trying to kill him, and it made her furious.

They were crowded into a farmer's single-room house. Silver coins had persuaded him to host them. Feride, Elif, and Doctor Moreno sat on stools before a brazier, drinking the hot water with lemon juice the farmer's wife had served them before withdrawing with her family into the attached stable. She had left them yoghurt and honey and some flat bread. A brindled cat wound itself around Feride's feet. Vali and Nissim took turns standing guard outside the door.

Doctor Moreno agreed. "If Huseyin is suffering from burns, we must find him as soon as possible. Every minute is crucial."

"Who knows what those small infirmaries are like? They probably don't even have a doctor," Elif added, coughing. The air was thick with fumes from the burning charcoal.

Feride thought Elif looked thin and unwell. Deep shadows circled her eyes. When Elif arrived at their home from Macedonia, she had been gaunt, a ghost evading every human contact. But her work at the Art Institute seemed to have revived a spark in her. Feride could see that spark dying. It had been a mistake to bring Elif on this quest. She should have seen that her friend wasn't strong enough yet.

Üsküdar was a center of shipping and trade. The farmer had given them directions to three infirmaries, all attached to mosques. They were often full, he told them. The previous year, he had brought his son to one after he had broken a leg, but the crew of a ship had fallen ill and taken up every bed. The local bonesetter had gone home to his village to help with the harvest, so the boy wasn't treated and now walked with a limp. Feride flinched at the pain he must have endured. She could understand that there was no free bed, but surely someone could have set the boy's leg or stilled his pain with laudanum.

They filed out of the cottage. Vali carried a lamp. The sky was dark, but with that deep fragility that preceded dawn.

"I still say we should wait until it's light," Nissim growled.

Doctor Moreno put his head close to the burly boatman's ear, but Feride heard him say, "The hanoum is worried, and so am I," before they disappeared over the crest of the hill.

Feride put her hand on Elif's arm and held her back. "Are you well, my sister? You look very tired."

Elif smiled. "Of course, my dear. We're all tired. But we'll find Huseyin. Don't worry."

"If you'd rather . . . ?"

"No," Elif said hurriedly. Her voice was strained. "I'm fine. Really. Let's go on."

Vali returned, holding the light.

"We're coming," Elif said, and followed him down the hill into the vineyards. The light went with them.

Feride stopped for a moment and looked up at the fading stars, tiny specks of ice in an infinite sky that cared nothing about a small boy's pain. She turned around, startled by the sound of a twig breaking. She opened her mouth to shout and began to run down the hill after the others, but could no longer see Vali's light.

36

ERA WOKE SHIVERING so hard she thought her bones
would break. She was curled up in a coil of netting under
a tarpaulin that had kept out the wind but not the cold.
The movement of the boat and the sound of water slapping against
the sides had awakened her. Pangs of hunger and thirst made her sit
up and cautiously peek out from under the canvas. It was still dark,
but a silver sheen meant dawn wasn't far away. The walls of Yildiz
Palace gleamed on the hill above her, enclosing the woods through
which she had run. Below the wall, small cottages tumbled to the
shore along wooded lanes. Was Sosi hiding in one of those cottages?
She hadn't had a chance to ask her about Gabriel.

Her throat ached for water. She pushed the tarp aside and stumbled out. She had to get off the boat before anyone saw her. To her
dismay, she saw that the boat was no longer docked. They were in
the middle of the Bosphorus. She looked up into the startled eyes of
a young fisherman.

37

AMIL WANTED THE ELEMENT of surprise, so he used Huseyin's name to gain admission to Yildiz Palace instead of announcing his business to the gatekeeper. He drove through the gates in a closed carriage.

He had learned that the Akrep headquarters were in an isolated section of the palace grounds that backed onto the forest. When they were nearby, but not yet in sight of the building, Kamil ordered the driver to head onto a path behind a stand of rhododendrons. He surveyed the building through the spear-shaped leaves. Unlike the ornate wooden confections of the other imperial villas, this was a squat stone cube, two stories high and unadorned except for a marble stairway leading up to the front door. Its windows were flanked by heavy black shutters. The small guardhouse with a peaked roof at the end of the drive seemed almost frivolous in comparison. He heard men shouting but could make out only that someone had escaped. Dogs barked wildly in the forest.

Kamil then drove up to the front of the building and got out. A guard in black uniform carrying a rifle challenged him. Kamil noted the insignia on his collar—a stylized scorpion stitched in gold.

While a second guard went into the headquarters for instructions regarding the visitor, Kamil continued his examination of the house. Hedges obscured the sides of the building, but he saw an opening where a rounded trellis held the remains of last year's roses. He wandered over, ignoring the guard who followed behind him, and bent over one of the dried yellow blooms, letting his eyes roam into the courtyard beyond. A gravel path led to an open door, and as he watched, three men in civilian clothes emerged, the one in front hurling abuse at the others. When he saw Kamil, he stopped, the curse dying on his lips. He turned on his heel, and after a low, muttered conversation with the other men, they went back inside, slamming the door shut behind them.

The second guard returned and ushered Kamil in. Despite its drab exterior, the building's interior was lavishly appointed. The walls were faced with colored marble, and the grand hall was furnished with Western-style sofas and tasseled curtains. A massive pink and green Murano chandelier hung from a coffered ceiling. The guard led Kamil through double doors painted white and gilded, as if he were being ushered into the presence of the sultan himself.

Kamil knew Vahid immediately. The impeccable black hair, sensual lips, and cold eyes could have belonged to no one else. He wore ostentatiously high black boots and a tightly fitted, wide-shouldered black uniform with no emblem.

Vahid stood behind his desk and smiled when Kamil entered the room.

"Selam aleykum."

"Aleykum selam. Thank you for receiving me."

Vahid gestured for him to take a seat on an uncomfortable-looking chair, set at an angle, so Kamil would have to look up and sideways at Vahid.

"I'll stand."

"As you like." Vahid sat down on his padded leather chair." I've heard of you, Magistrate."

"Have you?"

"You're the sultan's hunting dog. Whenever there's a problem, he sends you to sniff it out and break its neck. You're quite good, I hear."

Being compared to a dog was an insult, but Kamil heard the guarded respect. Good, he thought, let him fear me. He scanned the room, noting entrances and exits, the position of the room vis-à-vis the rest of the house. If Akrep was keeping prisoners here, they would most likely be held in the basement. He walked to the window and leaned against the sill. It wouldn't do to bring up the subject of Lena Balian directly, thereby giving her importance in Vahid's eyes.

"Well, what can I do for you, Kamil Pasha?" Vahid asked, unable to keep the impatience from his voice. "I'm sure you came here for a reason." He squinted at Kamil, who was backlit against the window.

"I'm investigating the Ottoman Imperial Bank robbery. I believe you also have an interest in that case. If so, I suggest we're better off pooling our information, rather than working at cross-purposes."

"You mean you need our help." Vahid leaned back in his chair and laced his fingers. "Lost your bite, Magistrate?"

Kamil ignored Vahid's smirk. "If it's a matter of assigning credit, then by all means take the credit. I don't care about that."

"You have nothing to offer me, my friend. It's a much bigger case now, and your investigations, to be honest, are irrelevant."

"I don't know what you mean. We get the gold back. We arrest those responsible. That's the case."

"Hardly. The robbery was the first shot fired in a revolution against the empire. Terrorists have set up an armed camp, ready to take the entire east and place it in Russian hands. They're aiming to assassinate the sultan himself."

"What are you talking about?" Kamil asked, completely at a loss.

Vahid tilted his head and chided him. "You really have not been keeping up, Magistrate. There's a terrorist camp in the Choruh Valley, and the entire population has gone over to them. They're armed. They even have howitzers. The stolen gold is financing them, and that shipload of weapons we diverted would have made matters worse. It's proof of the danger. Sultan Abdulhamid realizes it now too. My main concern is to protect our padishah and to eradicate that Armenian scum in the mountains."

It dawned on Kamil that Vahid was talking about a massacre. He thought of all the refugees crowding Istanbul's streets, having fled just such carnage in the empire's provinces. He remembered Elif's gaunt, horror-filled face when she first arrived from Macedonia. The killings wouldn't stop at the Choruh Valley. It would galvanize Armenians who had been loyal citizens to take up arms against the sultan, and it would certainly draw the attention of the Europeans and the Russians. So far the foreign empires had been content to chew away at the edges of the Ottoman lands, but the massacre of a Christian minority would provide the excuse to invade the empire's core outright. It would be a disaster of the greatest dimension.

Kamil stared at Vahid and the thought came to him that by using the knife in his boot now, he would save countless lives. It took all his moral strength not to do it. No man's death is unaccountable, he told himself firmly.

Vahid watched Kamil with a contemptuous smile on his face, as if he knew what Kamil had been tempted to do but was too weak to carry out.

"You're misinformed," Kamil told him. "That group in Choruh is an international socialist commune. They have no plans to join Russia—the czar's troops would throw them all in prison." In the back of Kamil's mind a suspicion nagged—was it he who was misinformed? How far could he trust Yorg Pasha's information?

"Ah, so you know about them," Vahid said, drawing the words out. "Yet you were silent. Do you think a group of armed socialists is nothing to worry about?"

Kamil felt that he had been put on the defensive. "So you do know that they're socialists and not Armenian revolutionaries."

"What's the difference? What matters is what our great padishah thinks. And he's already ordered his troops to put all those traitors to the fire."

"And you'll have saved the empire," Kamil said, his voice sharp with sarcasm.

"And Sultan Abdulhamid's life. We've learned that there's going to be an attempt on it soon." He stood and moved to the front of his desk, where he could better see Kamil against the glare from the window.

The man had said this too blithely, Kamil thought, almost as if he had planned it himself. He didn't think Vahid would be capable of assassinating the sultan, but a failed attempt would bring him greater power. Kamil was horrified and amazed at Vahid's ambition and insensitivity to human life and honor. He thought of Yorg Pasha's description of the blind cruelty of the scorpion, but he also remembered something he had seen on one of his botanical trips to the east. The village boys had built a ring of burning vegetation and set a scorpion in the middle of it. As the ring of fire drew close to the animal, the scorpion buried its stinger in its own back, preferring to kill itself. If only he could trap Vahid in his own lies.

He should warn the sultan, but without evidence, no one would believe him. They'd probably put it down to professional jealousy, part of the eternal turf war between the judiciary and the secret police.

He walked up to Vahid, so close that Kamil could smell the cloves he chewed on his breath. "Do you play chess?"

Vahid didn't answer. Kamil could sense his discomfort. The odor of stale sweat became stronger.

"I'm sure you know what 'checkmate' means, don't you?" Kamil felt certain that the only way to deal with someone as unscrupulous as Vahid was to get him off balance, to inspire fear and doubt. After all, Vahid had no idea how little Kamil knew, and Kamil was sure that this was a man with a great deal to hide.

"This is not a game." Vahid took a step backward and put his hands in his pockets, giving Kamil a cynical smile. "Or perhaps it is, my pasha." His smile didn't reach his eyes.

Kamil turned on his heel to leave.

"Kamil Pasha," Vahid called to him. "There's no need to end on such a sour note."

Kamil waited as Vahid came up to him, holding out his hand. Reluctantly Kamil held out his own, but to his surprise, Vahid used

Kamil's hand to pull him close, patting the back of his jacket with the other hand.

Kamil jerked away from this overly intimate embrace, certain that Vahid was up to something. Irritated and on edge, Kamil turned to pass through the door but found it partially blocked by Vahid. As Kamil brushed past him, Vahid jammed his shoulder into Kamil's so hard that it hurt. In the blink of an eye, Kamil slipped the dagger out of the sheath in his boot and pressed it against Vahid's throat. Two of Vahid's men came running from the outer office. They hovered close by, hands on their weapons, uncertain what to do.

Vahid, careful not to move his head, held up his hands, palms out. "Please forgive me. It was an accident," he said with an ugly smile.

Kamil snapped back his wrist and, sliding the dagger into his belt, where it would be in easy reach, strode out the door. He knew what he had to do. First he had to find out the truth. Then he must warn Sultan Abdulhamid, even though he would be taking a grave risk if the sultan didn't believe him. He thought about how he might gain access to the padishah, perhaps through Yorg Pasha or through his own boss, the minister of justice. Kamil had never met Sultan Abdulhamid but knew his reputation. The sultan was as distrustful of his own countrymen as he was enamored of European culture. He was fanatically religious and tirelessly modern. In other words, he was unpredictable. But Kamil wouldn't stand by while the population of the Choruh Valley was massacred to feed the ego of a madman like Vahid.

WHEN KAMIL'S carriage was outside the walls of the palace, it pulled over, and Omar and Rejep unfolded themselves from their hiding places inside the hollow seats.

"Well," he asked them impatiently, "any sign of the Russian woman?"

"We found the back door you told us about, but the place is buzzing like flies on shit, so I had Rejep go in by himself. He told them he was there to clean the rooms." He nodded at the young policeman, who was dressed in the wide breeches and tunic of a palace worker. "Tell him what you saw."

"The door led into the basement, which is six rooms along a corridor, three on either side. All the doors were locked except two. One was a sitting room. The other room had a table fitted with restraints and a partition with peepholes so someone could stay hidden and watch."

"Allah protect us," Omar muttered.

"I went around sweeping"—Rejep handed Kamil a scrap of paper—"and found this on the floor."

Kamil recognized Cyrillic letters. It had been torn from a document.

38

ERA BACKED AGAINST THE BOW of the boat, but her foot tangled in the fishing net and she stumbled and sprawled onto her back. The young fisherman approached and squatted before her. His hands, red and swollen from hard labor, hung between his knees like skinned animals, and he stank of sweat, and brine, and unwashed clothes. He's not married, Vera thought out of the blue, or someone would have washed his shirt, which she could see was torn and crudely mended.

He must have noticed her glance. He pulled self-consciously at his thinly padded jacket. His eyes were round with awe, but she thought she saw a dawning glint of avarice. A woman on his boat. If something were to happen, no one would be the wiser.

She glanced around for a weapon but saw only rope and net and winches. Everything heavy was attached to the deck. When she looked back, the fisherman was gone. She heard sounds from the cabin. If Sosi were here, she'd be able to speak with him. Had she escaped? Vera hoped so. The girl could return to her family, she thought. At least Sosi had somewhere to go.

Quickly she disentangled herself and moved to the side of the boat nearest the shore. It didn't seem impossibly far, but she had never learned to swim. The water was choppy and looked cold, the color of iron. She would have a better chance against the fisherman, she thought. She wondered if he could swim.

Just then he returned. In one hand he held a cup, in the other, a tinned copper bowl and a spoon. He extended them to her, not approaching.

Vera moved cautiously forward and took the cup. She gulped the water and returned the empty cup. The man put the beans down, took the cup, and disappeared inside the cabin. The moment he was gone, Vera grabbed the bowl and began to eat. The oily beans tasted better than anything she could have imagined.

The man returned with a full cup and watched while she ate and drank, the expression on his face that of a hunter sighting a fox and not wishing to scare it off. Vera kept her eye on him. He was around seventeen, with matted brown hair and hazel eyes, the outlines of a boy still visible beneath his weather-chapped face.

When she finished, she put the bowl and cup on the deck between them and said in her poor Turkish, "Thank you."

The man looked startled, then a sweet smile dawned on his face. "You're welcome." His voice was surprisingly gentle. "You are lost?"

VERA STUMBLED into the doorway of Agopian Brothers Publishing House. Her feet were wrapped in makeshift boots that the fisherman had fashioned from sailcloth and bound to her feet with as much care as if she had been his sister. He had left her at Eminönü pier and she had made her way through the back alleys up the hill to Bab-i Ali. It was midmorning as she pushed open the entry door.

"No beggars," the doorkeeper announced, flapping his hands at her.

She drew herself up and said in French. "I'm here to see Monsieur Agopian."

Staring at her tattered clothes and filthy rag-bound feet, the door-keeper asked her name.

"Lena Balian."

39

Running through the dark toward the vineyard where Vali's light had disappeared, Feride stumbled and nearly fell. She twisted her head in the direction of the sound that had spooked her and tried to calm herself. It was probably a dog, she thought, embarrassed by her overreaction. Just then a powerful arm encircled her waist and lifted her off the ground. She tried to scream, but a hand covered her mouth. Fear took over her body, which in its rage to be free, arched and bucked. She tried to bite, but her teeth only grazed the beefy palm pressed against her mouth. Suddenly she couldn't breathe and struggled frantically until the man, realizing the source of her distress, moved his hand from her nose.

This brush with death had the effect of banishing Feride's panic. In order not to die, she realized, she needed her wits. Ignoring her racing heart, she tried to look about her. They were moving through the vineyard, the man dragging Feride under his arm, another man keeping pace beside him. The moon's dim light revealed the tortured shapes of bare grape stocks. Where were Nissim and Vali and her companions? She had been only a moment behind them. Surely they would notice her missing and return to look for her.

"Are you sure this is the pasha's wife?" the man holding her asked.

"Has to be," Feride heard the other man say. "She's the only woman in the group."

"Tell me again why we're bothering with his wife? I don't think she knows where her husband is."

"Well, we can't find him either. Do you want to go back and face the commander with empty hands?"

"I guess not."

The men spoke in city dialects, Feride noticed. They weren't peasants or common highwaymen. Who was their commander? Who would even know her, or that she was here? What did they want with Huseyin? She was shocked by the realization that the men holding her had likely murdered the patient in the Valide Mosque hospital, thinking he was Huseyin.

She sagged to her knees, forcing them to stop. The hand over her mouth slipped momentarily, and she managed to emit a loud bleat. She had to alert the others. Nissim and Vali would put these men to flight in an instant. Then she heard it—shouts and the muffled thud of bodies. A man cried out. Was that Vali? Had they been attacked too?

Cursing, the man picked her up and, holding her tightly against his chest, set off at a fast pace toward the edge of a forest. One arm was grasped tightly by the man who carried her, but with some experimentation, she found she could move her head and the arm pressed against his chest. She lowered her head and raised her arm so that she could pluck from the side of her veil the sharp needle that pinned it closed around her face. It took several tries. When the pin was in her hand, she leaned back so she could see the face of the man carrying her. This close up, she thought he too looked afraid. Then she thrust the needle backhanded at whatever it might reach.

He screamed and dropped her. Feride scrambled to her feet and ran. After a moment's confusion, the man's partner raced after her. Feride threw off her charshaf and thrust it beneath his feet. He stumbled, kicking his foot to clear it of the tangled cloth. Feride hurtled between the rows of vines down the hill, the grape stocks tearing at her skirts.

In the gray dawn she saw a tangle of bodies between the vines, and the glint of metal. Elif's thin figure rose above the rest, legs spread wide. She swung a long curved knife before her like a scythe, over and over, and Feride could hear the dull thunk of the knife as it hacked into flesh.

"Elif?" Feride called out uncertainly. She couldn't be sure what she was seeing. Surely an apparition, a distortion of the mist and dawn.

At the sound of Feride's voice, Elif looked up, her face invisible inside a helmet of pale hair. The hand holding the knife hung by her side. Nothing else moved.

Feride ran toward her, afraid to speak. Elif's vacant face stared in her direction without seeing her.

Suddenly, as if she had just awakened, Elif looked down at her feet and her face took on an expression of utter horror. She began to scream, a bloodcurdling cry of anguish that spilled like black ink across the lightening fields.

40

K AMIL KNELT BEFORE Sultan Abdulhamid, his eyes on the intricate blue and red designs of the silk carpet beneath his knees. He remained that way until Vizier Köraslan indicated that he should rise and present his petition. They were in a reception hall adjoining the sultan's study. Dozens of splendidly dressed guards and servants were grouped about the room, all in a state of hushed attentiveness. The sultan had received Kamil in his private quarters, rather than in the Great Mabeyn, where everyday business was conducted. Kamil had pulled every string possible to arrange an audience that morning.

The wood and stone structure of the sultan's residence was designed to look like a Swiss chalet and seemed to Kamil, as he walked up the marble steps, too whimsical to house a man with such enormous power. Inside, the rooms were decorated in European fashion with gilded mirrors and heavy drapery. The ceilings were painted with landscapes. He had heard that Sultan Abdulhamid had crafted some of the furniture himself. Each sultan was required by tradition to learn a craft, and Sultan Abdulhamid was renowned for his furniture-making skills. He was also expanding the empire's railroads and rebuilding its cities with European-style boulevards. All the latest English mystery books were translated as soon as they were published. An aide read them aloud from behind a screen at the insomniac sultan's bedside. An enlightened monarch, he neverthe-less jealously guarded his fears and delusions and would visit them whenever the mood took him. This, all his subjects knew, made him unpredictable and even dangerous.

The sultan sat on a wide cushioned chair inlaid with mother-of-pearl. Like Kamil and the vizier, he wore trousers, a frock coat, and a fez, but his coat was heavily brocaded in gold thread, with gold epaulets at the shoulders. A red and green grosgrain sash spanned his chest, and his white-gloved left hand loosely held the pommel of a sword. The haughty stillness of his face spoke more of power than any action or insignia. His hooded eyes gave nothing away.

Vizier Köraslan stood to the right of the throne. He was a tall, imposing man with a neat sandy beard, and his deep-set eyes roved continually around the room. He had a reputation for incorruptibility, but he was also known to be ambitious. There was no higher position in the empire to which he could aspire, but there was always more power and more wealth to be accumulated. Kamil imagined that every vizier wanted to be seen as indispensable to his ruler. Viziers were famously expendable. Some sultans had deposed them on a whim, others had put their advisers to death. Kamil didn't envy the man his position, one foot on a very high pinnacle.

Eyes lowered, Kamil stated his name and rank, but inside he fret-ted. How to convince the sultan that the head of his secret police was planning to fake an assassination attempt when Kamil had no evidence, and that an attack on the Choruh Valley would be a mistake without implying that the Great Lord was mistaken? Could he do that without mentioning the socialist commune, which the sultan might take to be a different kind of threat? In other words, he thought with a feeling close to despair, he had to make convincing arguments about two life-and-death situations without actually saying anything. He decided to enter the conversation on neutral ground and feel his way along.

"As your special prosecutor," Kamil began, "I wish to report on my progress in the Ottoman Imperial Bank robbery."

"Isn't that a matter you should be discussing with your superior, the minister of justice?" Vizier Köraslan interrupted impatiently. "You said this was urgent."

"I would like to assure His Majesty that neither he nor the empire is in any danger on that front." Kamil wished he knew that was true. He was taking an enormous risk.

"That's not what I heard." Sultan Abdulhamid's voice was testy, but curious. "My sources tell me there's a revolution afoot. What do you say to that, Kamil Pasha? It seems you are uninformed. That disappoints me."

The last thing Kamil wanted was to disappoint the sultan. The incremental approach to delivering his message clearly wasn't working. To convince the sultan, Kamil decided, he would have to tell him what he knew.

"I'm aware of the situation in the Choruh Valley, Your Highness. A group of young people has begun an experimental farm there, in Karakaya Village near the town of Ispir. They're not revolutionaries."

"How do you know that? Have you been there?"

"No, Your Majesty. I was informed through trusted sources."

"And you believed them," the vizier said, barely disguising his sarcasm. "We too have our sources, and they tell us otherwise."

There was a tense silence. Kamil knew the vizier was referring to Akrep.

"How is this farm experimental?" the sultan asked. "And who are these young people?"

Kamil remembered that Sultan Abdulhamid had a particular interest in agricultural reform. "They're socialists, Your Highness, who have traveled there from a number of different countries. As I understand it, it's a social experiment, a community where the members share the labor and profit equally."

"Our religion encourages us to share profit and share loss with others in our community. You needn't be a socialist to do that." He tapped his sword on the carpet. "Their intent is admirable, but their implementation is godless, is that not so?"

"That is so, Your Highness," the vizier agreed. "They are godless infidels."

Kamil kept his eyes averted from the sultan, as protocol required, but saw him reach up a bejeweled hand to grasp his chin in thought. Finally the sultan turned to his vizier and said tersely, "I want a report on these socialists. I've heard of them, but I want details. If they're active in the empire, I should know about it. You told me they were Armenians."

"I was told that they are Armenians as well as socialists."

"Those are not the same thing. Find out what species of animal this commune is."

"At your command, Lord of the Two Lands and the Two Seas." Vizier Köraslan made a deep bow. "Perhaps Kamil Pasha might wish to discover the truth of the matter himself and report back to Your Highness."

Kamil was taken aback by the suggestion that he travel all the way to the Russian border. The sultan had his own trusted men. Why send him?

"An excellent idea. I would appreciate your unbiased impression," the sultan told Kamil earnestly. "I had been under the impression that this was a revolutionary movement that required a military response, but if indeed this is a peaceful valley and the socialists are not pawns of the Russians, as my advisers have told me, then I would be committing an unforgivable crime." The sultan's voice rose by a fraction, but given his previously measured speech, it gave the effect of shouting. "It is haram to spill innocent blood, and may Allah preserve me from it."

The vizier looked very uncomfortable. Kamil realized he had made another powerful enemy. Kamil had caused the sultan to question the vizier's judgment, and he would never forgive that. But Kamil realized he had a more immediate problem. It seemed the sultan had taken the vizier at his word.

"Go and find out the truth of the matter yourself," the sultan continued, "then report back. I'll put a company of my household cavalry under your command, and you can take one of the royal steamers. I'll give the order to crush the revolt in thirty days unless you convince me otherwise."

Kamil held his breath. "The mountains are inaccessible now in high winter, Your Highness."

"Very well, bring me news by the end of March. You'll be able to get through by then, and so will my troops," he added meaningfully.

When the sultan raised a finger from the arm of his chair, the vizier stepped forward and told Kamil brusquely, "You may withdraw."

"One more thing, Your Highness," Kamil said hurriedly. "With regard to the threat . . ."

"The impertinence," the vizier shouted. "You have been dismissed." He beckoned the guards.

The sultan raised his finger again, at which all movement in the room ceased. "Go on, Kamil Pasha."

Kamil felt the sweat run down his sides. "Your Highness, I wish you health and long life. It is my duty to warn you against trusting your source in this. I believe it is possible that the Akrep commander is planning an attack in order to gain your trust by appearing to save you from harm."

Sultan Abdulhamid's face showed no trace of emotion. He stared at Kamil, deep in thought.

"On what evidence do you base this serious accusation?" Vizier Köraslan asked, outraged.

"No concrete evidence, my lord. Some words said, that in themselves might mean nothing but that together with other things I've learned indicate at least a need for caution."

"You're both working on this bank robbery, you and Vahid," the vizier said, as if the explanation were dawning in his mind. "So you think that by undermining his reputation, you'll get him out of the way and take the credit for yourself. How despicable," he growled. "The bigger crime is that you have wasted the padishah's precious time."

"You forget yourself." The sultan addressed the vizier in a neutral voice without even a glance in his direction, but the man immediately fell to his knees, his forehead to the carpet, and apologized abjectly.

"Get up," he told the vizier. "Your warning is noted, Kamil Pasha. I'll expect to hear from you by the end of March."

Kamil murmured the formulas of departure from such an august personage, ending with a call to Allah to rain blessings on the sultan. Head lowered, he backed slowly out of the room to avoid the unforgivable offense of showing one's back to the padishah, the Shadow of God on Earth.

The meeting with the sultan had left him with an equal mixture of elation and unease. The sultan had listened to his warning, but Kamil had made an enemy of Vizier Köraslan, the second most powerful man in the empire. He would never forgive Kamil for having witnessed his humiliation. And Vahid would probably take Kamil's accusation about him to the sultan as a declaration of war. Still, Kamil felt satisfied that he had at least postponed an attack on the valley and the commune, even at the price of his having to make the journey east himself. He considered the reprieve he had gained of almost three months. Although the mountains of eastern Anatolia would be snowbound even in March, he would have plenty of time to prepare.

He now thought of Feride and Elif, who had been gone since the day before with no word. He reached into his pocket for his watch but didn't find it. In the confusion of the past few days, he must have left it at home. Feride and Elif had probably visited a friend and spent the night, he told himself—not surprising given the snow and fog. He should stop worrying.

A flash of orange in a corner of the palace garden caught his eye. He approached and found a tree festooned with kumquats. Kamil picked one and scratched the skin with his fingernail, then held it to his nose and inhaled the citrus scent. Why exactly was he going to the east? His duty was to capture Gabriel and return the gold to the bank. But his ultimate purpose now, it seemed, was to produce proof of the commune's innocence and preserve the valley from harm. Wouldn't that be akin to proving the innocence of thieves? He wondered at his own logic.

41

*V*AHID THRUST THE WINDOW open to let out the smoke that hovered like a noxious cloud in the room. Then he opened the stove door, blew on the embers, and added a ragged chunk of coal. He emerged coughing and wiped his fingers on a rag.

Socialists. Vizier Köraslan had summoned him to ask about socialists, implying that he was wrong about an Armenian revolt brewing in the Choruh Valley. Despite the cold, Vahid was sweating beneath the collar of his wool jacket. He didn't think Vizier Köraslan would dare demote him, but he needed the vizier's goodwill and trust if he wanted to become head of the secret service. Sultan Abdulhamid was sending Kamil Pasha to the valley. Vahid would have to make sure that what the pasha discovered when he arrived were armed Armenian revolutionaries. That meant Vahid would have to go east himself to make sure that no one remained alive who could contradict the vision of the valley he had spun for the vizier and, through him, the sultan.

He took off his jacket, folded it neatly, and laid it over the back of a chair. A lace doily, yellow and stiff with age, fluttered to the floor. He picked it up and threw it into the stove.

His mother was asleep in her chair, gnarled fingers tangled in her tatting, snoring softly through lips that hung slightly open. His mother's lips reminded Vahid of worms after a rainstorm, and he turned away. No wonder his father had preferred the Greek woman. He chided himself for the thought.

Rhea's lips came to his mind, plump cushions that she had a habit of pursing as if she were sucking on hard candy. He wondered what Lena Balian's lips tasted like. When his men picked her up again, he would find out. There was no place in Istanbul where she could hide. She had the same pink translucent fingernails as Rhea, and her hair curled around his finger like a baby's fist. He had smelled her fear and it aroused him. The smoke from the stove brought to his mind the smell of charred flesh. He strode into the kitchen, picked up a knife, and pressed the point against the palm of his hand just hard enough to hurt without breaking the skin.

That bitch Sosi had waited until his men were on a tea break and had let Lena Balian out. Where had Sosi gotten the keys? It had been a mistake to keep her alive. She was too clever. He didn't like clever girls. He should never have sent her into Lena's room with food. Women couldn't be trusted.

"Are you back?" he heard his mother call.

"Yes, Mama, I'm back," he answered, trying to keep his voice even. He poured water from a clay jar into the belly of the samovar and lit the flame beneath it. "Would you like some tea?"

42

𝒱ERA SAT ON A VELVET-covered sofa in the publisher's parlor, dressed in his daughter's clothes. His wife fussed over her, refilling her tea and extending a plate of savory pastries. She was a comfortable-looking matron with snow-white hair swept up in a cloud above her face. Her daughter, with the same heart-shaped face, sat across the room, smiling at Vera, unable to hide the curiosity in her eyes.

Vera fought the urge to cry. She was reminded so strongly of her home in Moscow and of the kindness and decency of people, from the humble fisherman to this bourgeois family. She and her comrades believed that people were arrayed into opposing camps, the capitalist and the working classes, and that it was acceptable and even necessary to destroy one for the other. Yet here on the Agopian family's sofa, their daughter's satin slippers on her salved and bandaged feet, she sensed the contradiction of it and wondered idly what Gabriel would think of her finding refuge in the familiar surroundings of middle-class family life. She noted without emotion that it didn't seem to matter to her whether he approved or not.

She concentrated on what she had to do next. She knew that her jailers had most likely been the secret police. But why were they holding Sosi? Did that mean they had arrested Gabriel too? Had Sosi managed to escape? Vera was unsure how much she could ask Monsieur Agopian to help her.

The publisher had made no inquiry when she had stumbled into his office, simply expressed his dismay at her condition and brought her home. Reluctant to tell him where she had been and what had happened, she was grateful that he didn't press her. She hadn't even told him her real name, which made her feel a bit ashamed. But she was reluctant to admit to lying to him at their first meeting. And somehow she had become used to being Lena Balian.

The publisher cradled a meerschaum pipe in his hands and nodded, his eyes on Vera's face. She had the impression that he knew who she was and where she had been, although that was impossible. He leaned toward Vera and said in a warm voice, "Lena, if there is anything you wish to tell me in confidence, I can assure you it will go no further. Please let me help you."

Vera wanted to tell him everything, but she seemed to have acquired a habit of suspicion that wouldn't allow her lips to shape the words she wished to speak. "My name is Vera Arti," she wanted to say. But then she would have to relate what had happened to her, and that she couldn't do. Instead she nodded and said, "Thank you," in a strangled voice.

Vera closed her eyes. Why didn't she just ask Monsieur Agopian to help her find Sosi and Gabriel? He would send out word to the Armenian community, and the answer would flow back like driftwood on the tide of relations. Could things really be that simple? If she just sat here long enough, warm and comfortable and pampered, Sosi would come and sit by her side, and Gabriel would take her in his arms. She felt herself fall down a deep well toward oblivion.

43

KAMIL SENT YAKUP to Doctor Moreno's home to see if he had returned, while he rode to the hospital where he had left them two days before. He galloped over the Pera hill, across the New Bridge and along the Golden Horn to Eyüp, and burst into the hospital director's office.

The director looked up from his ledger, and his furrowed face broke into a smile. "Ah, you're back. I hope you've found your brother-in-law." He squinted at Kamil's face and sighed. "Bad news then. I was afraid of that. Burn wounds are so—"

Kamil interrupted. "Where are they? Where did you send them?"

The director frowned. "To Üsküdar. A family took him away, thinking he was their relative. The orderly didn't record the move, so we didn't have more specific information. Why? Has something happened?"

But Kamil was already out the door, cursing.

44

DAWN LAID A LIGHT shroud of mist over the fields. Feride gasped at the scene before her. Elif's cry had faded, and now she stood between the gnarled wine stocks, her hands slick with blood and her shirt spattered with it. At her feet lay the bodies of three men, their heads and limbs carved open, weapons scattered about them on the rocky ground. Feride looked behind her, but the men chasing her were gone, perhaps as terrified as she was by Elif's scream.

Trembling, Feride approached the bodies. They were strangers.

"Where's the doctor?" she asked Elif, shaking her arm.

When Elif didn't respond, Feride stumbled through the vines and searched along the rows. She tripped over what she thought was a root, but realized it was an arm. She fell to her knees beside the massive body of Nissim. His throat had been cut.

"Doctor Moreno?" she whispered, her voice hoarse with fear. "Vali?"

She heard a faint sound, thin as a breath of wind, and called out again. The sound was repeated. She made out, "Here." She crawled through the dirt until she came to Doctor Moreno's prone form.

Beside him sat Vali, propped against a rock, holding in his fist a tourniquet tightly bound around the doctor's leg. But Feride could see that Vali was weak and could barely speak. She couldn't tell where he was wounded, although his eye was swelling. If Vali let go of the tourniquet, she thought, Doctor Moreno might die. She didn't know what to do. She had to get help, but she didn't want to leave them alone.

"Elif," she screamed, and when she didn't respond, ran to where she had left her. She was gone. Then Feride heard a gasping sound. She found Elif on her knees vomiting. When Elif raised her face, it was barely recognizable, all planes and angles and dark hollows.

"You have to help me, Elif," Feride sobbed. "I don't know what to do. Please help me."

Elif stared at her red hands and began to scrape them across the ground. "My hands are dirty," she said in a hollow voice.

Dirty hands, Feride thought, remembering with a sharp pain her two daughters. Dirty hands were something she could deal with. She picked up a knife and, hitching up her skirts, cut away the lower half of her chemise. She handed a piece of the white linen to Elif, then cut the rest into strips.

Elif stared at the cloth, then began to wipe the blood off her hands.

"Over here." Feride led her to the two men. Vali had fallen unconscious, and blood streamed from Doctor Moreno's leg where the tourniquet had loosened.

Feride quickly tightened the tourniquet, which she recognized as part of Vali's turban, and, after cutting away the cloth of Dr. Moreno's trouser leg, bound several linen strips tightly across the wound.

"Is this right?" she asked Elif. When her friend didn't respond, she shook her, then slapped her across the face.

Elif pushed Feride so hard that she fell. Feride grabbed Elif's leg and pulled her down, and soon the two women were tussling in the dirt between the vines. Finally Elif yelled, "Stop. Stop. Stop. Stop." Sobbing, the women held each other.

Feride scrambled up and returned to the men. "Is he alive?" she asked Elif, who was squatting over Vali, examining him. Doctor Moreno lay slumped beside him, his wound seeping slowly into the makeshift bandage.

Elif cradled Vali's head. "He's breathing," she said. Her hand came away bloody. "Let me have one of those strips." They bound Vali's head as best they could, then Elif examined Doctor Moreno. "He's lost a lot of blood."

"What should we do?" Feride cried.

"The bandages should keep him from bleeding anymore," Elif said. "But we have to get help. And we must get away from here."

"There were two more men." Feride looked nervously up the hill. A couple of wild dogs had appeared over the crest, sniffing the air. "Maybe the farmer can help us." She remembered with longing last night's companionable room and shared tea.

"One of us should stay here." Elif's voice sounded far away.

Feride gave her friend a worried look, wondering whether it was better for her to stay amid the carnage or to step into the unknown up the hill.

"They're more likely to help if you ask them," Elif pointed out.

Feride squeezed Elif's hand and got to her feet. She collected a pile of stones for Elif to throw at the dogs, then started to walk, carrying more stones in a fold of her skirt.

At the top of the hill, she retrieved her charshaf and put it on so she would look somewhat respectable, wiping her blood-smeared hands on its ample folds. The dogs had disappeared, so she emptied her skirt of the stones, keeping one in her fist, more a talisman against harm than a weapon. She hurried through the vineyard, then along the path to the farmer's cottage, now clearly visible in the morning light. She knocked. There were voices behind the door, but no one answered.

She knocked again and called out, "Selam. It's your guests from last night."

"Go away," the man yelled. "You're evil djinns. We know you now and won't open our doors again."

Feride pounded on the door using the stone. "We need help. Two of our friends are wounded. They've had an accident. Please help us. I will pay you." But there was no response. The stone slipped from her hand.

As she stepped back, the hem of her charshaf swept over the cat. It was lying in front of the farmer's door, a blood-encrusted gap at its throat. The sight of the lifeless body threatened to tip Feride into hysteria. No wonder the farmer refused to open the door.

She peered into the dark interior of the stable adjoining the house and rejoiced when she saw a donkey. There was no cart, but she found a stack of large wool grain bags and some rope. She loaded a dozen bags onto the animal and led it through the vineyard to where Elif waited beside Doctor Moreno and Vali.

THE TWO women layered the long, heavy grain sacks to make a padded stretcher, then tied Vali and Doctor Moreno on and hitched it to the donkey. In this way, they made their way laboriously downhill, the sacks catching on the grape stocks and threatening to overturn, until they reached the road leading to the port area. Despite the thick wool pads on which the men lay, the road was full of bumps and loose stones that Feride was sure caused the wounded men pain.

They attracted curious and sometimes disapproving stares from the few passersby out this early. They must make a strange sight, Feride thought, a blond foreign man and a Muslim woman in a soiled cloak and veil, pulling two wounded men behind a donkey. If anyone was hunting for them, they wouldn't have to look far. By breakfast, the whole town would be talking about them.

One of the locals must have alerted the imam of a nearby mosque, who huffed his way up the hill toward them. Two small boys ran behind him, their thin legs churning up dust.

"Selam aleykum."

"Aleykum selam," Feride responded.

"You are in need of assistance," the imam said, exposing brown teeth. "May I help?"

"We were fallen upon by bandits, and these two men were injured defending us. One is a doctor, the other, my driver. Another of our party lies dead in the vineyard above, having valiantly resisted these criminals. Two of the bandits escaped. Several others lie vanquished in the dirt. We need immediate medical care for these men, the best that can be had, and I would like to send a message to our people in the city."

Feride's upper-class intonation and vocabulary hadn't escaped the imam, who sent the boys scurrying off with messages.

"Honored hanoum, I've sent a boy to fetch the doctor from the Valide hospital and a cart. If you will come to the mosque, my wife will be pleased to make you comfortable and your travel companion can rest and change into a clean robe." He looked curiously at the blond foreigner.

Feride declined his invitation, saying they preferred to remain with their wounded companions. Elif had again become unresponsive.

While the imam sent off for stools and refreshments to be brought to them, Feride hovered over the two wounded men, neither of whom had regained consciousness. She swallowed a sob that had begun to rise in her throat. She wished Kamil were here. Her brother would know what to do. She tried not to think of Huseyin. The sight of so much death today had made her husband's likely death seem real for the first time. Perhaps she was chasing a ghost and risking the lives and sanity of her dearest friends for nothing. Had she really wished Huseyin to be dead rather than to leave her for another woman? The thought filled her with shame and an inchoate fear that by thinking it, she had brought it about.

45

B Y THE TIME KAMIL reached Üsküdar, it was early afternoon. It had taken him two hours to ride back to his
house in Beshiktash, which was the closest point across
the Bosphorus from Üsküdar, and for his boatman, Bedri, to row
him and his servant, Yakup, across the strait. They came armed with
knives and pistols. He also had sent word to Omar. Feride might well
be staying with friends in Üsküdar. But his conversation with Yorg
Pasha and his meeting with Vahid had raised his level of caution, and
he felt inexplicably tense. If he were indeed a dog, Kamil thought,
his hackles would be raised.

Upon arriving in Üsküdar, they hired a carriage and drove up
the hill to the Valide Mosque. Kamil instructed Bedri to wait by the
carriage while he and Yakup went inside. Instead of a doorkeeper, a
policeman opened the gate and challenged them to identify themselves. When Kamil told him he was the magistrate of Beyoglu, the
chastened policeman ushered them into the courtyard and hurried
to fetch the director.

Kamil noticed two other policemen standing guard in front of a
padlocked door.

"Find out what's going on here," he told Yakup in a low voice. The tall, impeccably dressed servant sagged into the posture of a defeated workingman and twisted his sash around to expose its plain cotton lining. He then lifted his fez and ran a hand through his hair, making it stick out wildly. His weapons concealed inside the folds of his wide trousers, he loped off in the direction of the kitchen, following the smell of freshly baked bread.

The director of the Valide Mosque hospital, a thin man with a meager frizz of hair jutting from beneath his fez, hurried over, trailed by the worried-looking policeman.

"Kamil Pasha, selam aleykum. Welcome to our hospital," the director said, holding out his hand.

"Aleykum selam." Kamil shook his hand and looked around curiously. "Why are there so many policemen here?"

The director looked flustered. "We had some suspicious visitors last night and then, Allah protect us, two murders," he added in a low voice.

"Who?" Kamil's voice caught. Were Feride and Elif dead?

"The doorkeeper and a patient."

Kamil breathed again. "And the visitors?"

"That's the odd thing." He led Kamil to a table in a small winter garden, heated by a stove, and bade him sit, then summoned a servant to bring cups of coffee. "The wife of Huseyin Pasha turned up last night, accompanied by a doctor from the palace and a Frankish man. She told me her husband had been badly burned and was missing. For some reason, she thought he was here. I told them we had no burn patients, but they looked around the wards anyway. There was a man with his face bandaged, and she thought for a moment it was her husband, until I explained that the patient was a local merchant with facial eczema, which we were treating with a sulfur poultice."

"Where are they now?" Kamil broke in impatiently.

"They spent the night here, and the next morning we found the doorkeeper and the man with eczema dead. The police were summoned, of course. They suspected the visitors of having something to do with the murders. I told them it was absurd to think that a distinguished hanoum or the doctor could have had anything to do with it. The foreign man, I can't say. There was something odd about him." He stood and took up a watering can." On the other hand," he continued, eyeing the soil in each pot before adding a calibrated stream of water, "the patient who was killed was the man the hanoum had mistaken for her husband. Surely there's something important in that." He turned toward Kamil, the half-empty can dangling from his hand. "It's as if they meant to kill Huseyin Pasha." He put down the can and sat again, waiting silently while an orderly placed a cup of coffee before each man.

Kamil's nerves were so taut that the click of cup on saucer sounded as loud as an explosion.

"The police wanted to detain them," the director went on, "but they left, which I thought was wise at the time. But this morning the hanoum returned. She and her associates said they had been attacked on the road. The doctor and one of their servants are quite badly wounded."

Kamil rose, knocking against the table and spilling the coffee. "And the women?"

Looking confused, the director unfolded his lanky body from the chair. "There was only one woman, Huseyin Pasha's wife. She and the foreign man accompanied the wounded here."

"Where are they?" Kamil grasped the back of his chair, his knuckles white.

"The police have them locked up," the director explained in an anxious voice, making propitiatory motions toward Kamil with his hands. "I told them they couldn't treat exalted personages like that, but it was like talking to stone. I did what I could to make them comfortable. I put the hanoum in the guest room. The Frank was covered in blood and by rights should be in the infirmary, but the police took him away." The director righted Kamil's cup. "Would you like to see them?"

Kamil stood by the door, barely able to control his impatience as the director opened it and preceded him out into the hospital courtyard.

"I can't tell you what a relief it is that you're here, Magistrate," the director babbled as he led Kamil through the arcade and across the path to the padlocked door Kamil had noticed when he arrived. A policeman in a gray wool uniform and peaked helmet, armed with a rifle and sidearm, slouched against the wall beside the door. When he saw Kamil and the director, he jumped to attention.

"Kamil Pasha would like to speak with Huseyin Pasha's wife," the director told him.

The policeman threw back his shoulders and proclaimed loudly, "Impossible without permission from my commander."

"Where is your commander?" the director asked.

Before the man could answer, Kamil stepped close to his face and snapped, "Open it. I am a special prosecutor for the sultan."

The policeman fell back, "Of course, Your Eminence." He bowed, clutching his fist to his heart. "I didn't know. I wasn't told."

"Kamil!" he heard Feride cry out through the window.

The guard pulled the key from his pocket. Kamil grabbed it from him, unlocked the door, and flung it open. Feride ran into his arms.

"My sister," he barked at the director and the astonished policeman.

Kamil was appalled at Feride's appearance. Her charshaf was ripped and spattered with mud and what looked like blood. Her face was bruised and strands of hair escaped from beneath her veil. She hadn't bothered to cover her face, and he could see that her lip was swollen.

"Allah protect us," he called out. "What's happened to you?"

Instead of answering, she pulled her veil across her face and pleaded, "Where's Elif? You must find her." Her voice had an edge of hysteria.

Admonishing the director to take care of Feride, Kamil grabbed the policeman by the back of his uniform. "Where's the foreign man?" He felt deep in his bones that she was in great danger. She was so frail in body and lately in spirit that it would take little to snuff out the flame.

The policeman led Kamil along an unlit hallway and unlocked a door.

Kamil stepped inside, but at first saw nothing in the darkness. His eyes adjusted quickly, and he saw Elif slumped against the wall, covered in blood. He enveloped her in his arms and carried her out.

$\mathcal{V}$ERA WOKE IN A ROOM with an icon of the Blessed Virgin on the wall before the bed and lace curtains at the sunny window. It took her several moments before she understood where she was.

The Agopian girl was sitting beside the bed, embroidering. She ran from the room, calling, "Mama, Papa, she's awake."

Madame Agopian bustled in carrying a dress and an armful of other garments. "Lena, welcome back to us. I'm sure a sleep did you good. When you're ready, we can serve a late lunch." She piled the clothing at the end of the bed. "I've had a few things altered to fit you. My seamstress can come and make any last-minute adjustments." She looked down at the pile, frowning. "I didn't want to wake you, you see, so I chose some things I thought would be practical. I hope you like them, but if not, please tell me and we'll find something else. You will do that for me?"

Her face was so creased with worry that Vera almost laughed. She was certain she would never again worry about the cut of her clothing. "Thank you, madame. I'm sure it's lovely. You've been so generous and kind." She sat up and flinched. Her whole body ached. Her feet were blistered and scraped and throbbed beneath the bandages.

She fingered the brushlike swatch where Vahid had cut off her hair.

When she had dressed, she joined the family in the dining room. Ravenous, she devoured the lamb and vegetable stew set before her and drank several glasses of water.

"Eat more, child," Madame Agopian urged Vera, telling the maid to refill her plate. Her daughter watched their guest from beneath lowered lids.

Monsieur Agopian sent his plate away untouched. "Are you planning to return to Geneva?" he asked Vera. "I can arrange a berth for you on the next ship. I'll cover the cost, so you needn't worry. You must be anxious to get home." At Madame Agopian's startled glance, he added, "There's no rush, none at all, but if I can be of help . . ."

It seemed to Vera that he was in a hurry for her to leave. Perhaps she should take him up on his offer. She could be in Geneva within the week. But she couldn't leave without learning what had befallen Gabriel, and she wondered what to do about Sosi. If Sosi had been recaptured and Vera remained silent, the girl would be lost. Should she try to find her family? Gabriel had mentioned that his cell was based in Kurtulush, but she had no idea where that was. She wondered what Gabriel would do and found that she couldn't imagine.

They moved to the sitting room. Sleep had cleared her mind, and she began to think about her predicament and what to do. Vahid knew her by the name Lena Balian. She realized that the only person who knew her by that name, and who could have told Vahid, was the grandfatherly gentleman sitting here before her, smoking his pipe. Yet without the Agopians' help, she didn't know what to do about Gabriel and Sosi. She was saddened by the thought that she couldn't trust any of them. Still, if Vahid learned she was here, not only she but the Agopian family would be in danger.

When Madame Agopian and her daughter left the room, Vera asked, "Do you find it easy to be a publisher here in Istanbul, monsieur? I had the impression from our first conversation that you were under some pressure by the state."

"Do you know the fable of the fig tree?" Monsieur Agopian asked her.

Vera shook her head no.

"One day the gardener asked the fig tree, 'Why do you spread your branches so low to the ground?' The fig tree replied, 'I have many enemies. I bend low so that they won't break my branches, and I serve them sweetness so that they forget evil.' "

Vera thought about this for a few moments, then asked, "Doesn't that mean you condone evil?'"

"Not at all, my dear girl. It means that the weak must try to sweeten the bitterness of the strong by being humble and by serving them. We don't really have another alternative."

"You could grow the fruit higher and starve them."

He chuckled at her naïveté. "They'd just pull the branches down or come with an ax. What have we gained by that? No, we must think of survival. There are good times and bad. We make our peace with the bad and save our strength to take advantage of the good."

"But people aren't trees," Vera protested. "People can do things differently. They could themselves take up the ax."

Monsieur Agopian stared at her for a moment, then said gently, "Young people always believe that survival is their God-given right, if they even think about it at all. But as we get older, we realize how weak and vulnerable we are—and the people we love." He glanced at the door through which his wife and daughter had disappeared.

Vera nodded, her suspicion of the publisher suddenly softened by understanding. He had so much more to lose than she did. But she couldn't ask him to help her find Gabriel and Sosi, and she knew that she had to leave. She wished she could report Sosi's imprisonment to someone in authority she could trust. There seemed no one left in the world who matched that description.

47

KAMIL, ACCOMPANIED BY Feride, carried Elif's limp body into the infirmary and laid her on a bed. Her hair, face, and hands were crusted with dried blood and her clothes stiff with it. There were no other patients in the room, and Kamil told the hospital director to lock the door. Feride held Elif's hand.

"Elif is a woman," Kamil explained to the director. "I want no one but you to see to her."

The director didn't seem surprised. "I thought he seemed rather odd, not a boy, not a man. I wondered for a moment if he had been castrated. No matter. Let's tend to her."

He called for hot water, bandages, salve, and a tisane to be made from some herbs from his garden. While Kamil waited by the door for the supplies, the director pulled over a mangal to heat the area by the bed. When the hot water arrived, Feride washed Elif's face and hands, which were covered with cuts. The deep ones began to bleed again. The director smoothed on a salve, then wrapped Elif's hands in bandages. He examined her face, but when the blood and filth had been washed off, it appeared as pale and unmarred and distant as the moon.

Gently, Feride peeled off Elif's shirt and trousers, exposing her fragile, birdlike chest, her small, pointed breasts, and hips slender as a boy's. On the inside of her thighs, Feride saw two ragged scars in the shape of carnations, as if the skin had been scraped or burned away and had regrown pale and puckered. She wondered what could have caused them. There were no recent wounds that she could see, so she tucked a quilt around her.

Kamil sat beside Elif's unmoving body and found that his mind had gone entirely blank. He had been too busy with work to protect the two people he loved most in the world. Now that it was too late, he understood that none of his work counted for even a kurush against their lives.

"Why isn't she awake?" Feride asked the director.

"I don't know," the surgeon admitted. "Did she fall or bump her head?"

"She walked here with me, but she hasn't spoken in some time—since we were in the vineyards. It's as if her body was there but she wasn't in it."

"What happened in the vineyards?" Kamil asked. "Why was she so covered in blood?"

Feride told them of the attack and what she thought she had seen in the vineyard.

"She couldn't have killed three men by herself," Kamil said, his speech slow and thick.

"Maybe I just saw her standing over the bodies," Feride admitted. "I'm not sure now. It was dark and I was frightened."

"I've seen the bodies," the director said. "The police brought them here. A woman of her size would have been no match for them. Likely they were killed by your men and Elif Hanoum witnessed it."

"Nissim was the Camondo family's boatman. Someone should let them know," Feride suggested, her voice flat.

"I'll take care of that, chère hanoum." The director gently raised one of Elif's eyelids to examine her pupil. He slapped her lightly on the cheek, but there was no response. "It's shock. I've seen it happen to men after battle."

"How long does it last?"

"Sometimes they wake up and it's over. Sometimes it's a lifetime."

Kamil bowed his head until it rested on the quilt beside Elif's matted hair.

48

VERA TOLD THE AGOPIANS that she wanted to visit a friend in Kurtulush, and they allowed her the use of their coach. By finding Sosi's family, she hoped to find Sosi, her only link to Gabriel. She had no idea how big the district was, but she had a plan.

She asked the coach to stop outside a house that she had picked at random. Late-afternoon shadows pooled in the cobbled lanes that wound up the hill from the small square. The house was quiet, its lace curtains shutting out the street, a cat snoozing on the windowsill. A young girl peered out and, seeing the strange coach, turned back inside. The door opened, and a man emerged and called out to the coachman.

Vera placed a neatly folded note addressed to Monsieur Agopian on the seat, then slipped out of the carriage on the side away from the house and disappeared into the lane. After walking for some time up and down the slopes of Kurtulush, she spied the belltower of an Armenian church.

Out of breath and sweating in her borrowed coat, she knocked on the door of the adjoining residence. It was opened by a man wearing a priestly robe. A curtain of gray hair and a long beard framed his face. Below his alert eyes were pouches of fatigue. Vera introduced herself in Armenian and told him she was looking for the family of a woman named Sosi.

The priest's eyes shifted behind her as if to make sure that no one had overheard, and then he pulled her inside. In the dim light of the parlor, he bade her sit on the sofa, while he stood by the door. "I am Father Zadian. Why are you looking for Sosi?"

Vera considered what she could tell him. "We employed her at one time and owe her back wages."

"I see." Vera could tell from the tone of his voice that he was suspicious. "May I ask what service Sosi performed for you?" he asked. "And what is your name?"

Vera hesitated but decided to trust the priest. "My name," she said finally, "is Vera Arti."

"Are you related to Gabriel Arti?" The priest sat down in a chair opposite her.

"He's my husband," she said, her voice betraying her excitement. Someone else who knew Gabriel. "Do you know where he is? I'm looking for him."

"He's in the east."

Vera was stunned. She had thought he was in hiding or perhaps under arrest. It had never occurred to her that he would simply continue his project, leaving her behind in the hands of the secret police. He would have had to make a choice, a difficult choice, of that she had no doubt, but in the end he had chosen the movement. As she absorbed this news, she monitored her heart but found only a cramped emptiness where there had been joy.

"Where in the east?"

"The New Concord commune." The priest seemed surprised. "You didn't know?"

"I was . . ." She forced herself to go on. "I was being held by the secret police, and I just escaped." As she uttered it, she realized it seemed a fantastic claim.

The priest drew in his breath and muttered a quick prayer. She saw him glance at her expensive coat.

"I went to the only person I knew in the city." She told him about the kindness of the Agopians.

"Do they know you came here?" the priest asked.

"No." She thought of the note she had left in the carriage for Monsieur Agopian in which she had thanked him for his help and explained that, not wishing to put his family in any difficulty, she had decided to leave Istanbul. She hadn't said where she was going. He might worry about her, but he would be relieved.

"I don't want to speak against them," Father Zadian said. "They're good people, and God knows we all have to make our peace with the powers above us, but, well, it would be best if you didn't let them know too much."

"I understand. They don't know my true identity." It reinforced what she already suspected. She remembered Monsieur Agopian's fable of the accommodating fig tree.

"Father," she said urgently, "I need to find Sosi's family." She told him about their escape. "I think they caught her. She needs help." Her mind shied away from how they might punish the girl for attempting to escape.

The priest's face was grim. "This is monstrous. Let me think about what can be done." He regarded Vera huddled in her coat on the sofa. "Can you give us a detailed description of the building? I know some people who can try to free her."

"Who?" she asked, thinking of the socialist cell Sosi belonged to.

"You needn't concern yourself. The less you know, the better."

She saw the pity in his eyes, not knowing whether it was for her or Sosi, and recoiled.

A housekeeper appeared at the door and brought a tray of tea and choereg, still fragrant from the oven. At the sight of the glossy braided rolls sprinkled with sesame seeds that her family's cook in Moscow baked every Sunday, Vera put her face in her hands and wept.

49

"**H**USEYIN PASHA IS Kamil Pasha's brother-in-law," Vahid mused. "I love the efficiency of it. Did Feride Hanoum lead you to her husband?"

"No, Commander." The Akrep agent shifted his stance uncomfortably before Vahid's desk. There was a bandage beneath his right eye. "The hanoum was traveling with four men, a Jew, a Frank, and two servants. We followed them to the Valide hospital in Üsküdar. An orderly told us she had identified one of the patients as her husband, so we dealt with him."

"Excellent," Vahid said, a surge of pleasure rising in his chest at having bested both his rivals, Huseyin and Kamil, and avenged Rhea. He repressed a smile.

"Unfortunately it wasn't the pasha, sir," the agent admitted in a subdued voice. "The doorkeeper was killed too; that was an accident. When they discovered the bodies, the director called the authorities and we went in disguised as policemen, but the hanoum and her group had left before we got there. It took us a while to locate them. They spent part of the night in a peasant's hut. We found them just before dawn."

"And then you tracked them through the woods. What is this?

A fairy tale?" Vahid's disappointment was doubly bitter at having imagined Huseyin dead.

"It was me and four agents, Hilmi, . . ." He began to name them, but Vahid cut him off.

"Just tell me what happened."

The agent crossed his arms, then dropped his hands to his side. Vahid could smell his anxiety. "I thought we could bring the pasha's wife in to be questioned about where her husband was. It wasn't working to follow her around. We weren't finding out anything, and we were making people suspicious."

Vahid's voice rose with exasperation. "You wanted to bring the wife of a pasha in for interrogation." He slammed the palm of his hand on the desk. "Are you insane?"

"She's just a woman. And the pasha would be dead anyway, as soon as we found him."

"Did it occur to you that she doesn't know where her husband is?"

The agent's shoulders were hunched, and he looked down at his hands, clasped before him.

"Go on," Vahid commanded.

The agent fastened his eyes on the wall behind Vahid. "I took the hanoum, but she stuck a knife in my face and ran off." His hand reached up involuntarily to touch the bandage on his cheek. "Then we heard a sound, I tell you honestly, it made my hair stand on end. It was surely a djinn."

Vahid leaned forward and stared at the agent. "What do you mean?" This account was getting worse and worse. A mistaken murder, the involvement of the local police, an attack on Huseyin Pasha's wife, and now his agents believed they had been attacked by djinns. A feeling like ants crawling invaded his extremities. He clenched and unclenched his fingers. He could feel his heart beat against his collar. "Go on."

The agent's eyes widened. "One minute our men were fighting, the next they were lying there in pieces like dog meat. Hilmi and I backed up a bit to . . . to reconsider our strategy."

If he wanted to build Akrep into an organization to be feared,

Vahid thought, he'd have to weed out superstitious cowards like this.

"How many agents dead?"

"Three," the man admitted softly.

Vahid's finger tapped on the desk, a steady drone like water dripping. "And Huseyin Pasha's wife?" Kamil Pasha's sister, he added to himself with the satisfaction of knowing that destroying Huseyin would also wound Kamil. The symmetry of it gave it the stamp of fate.

"She was gone. The next thing we knew, they were all back at the hospital, except for one of their party, who was dead."

Vahid rose to his feet. His chest was so tight that he could barely breathe. "This whole operation was a disaster," he pointed out in a deceptively gentle tone. Vahid was considering what might happen if Vizier Köraslan or Sultan Abdulhamid discovered that he had been using Akrep resources in a personal vendetta against one of the empire's most highly placed and respected citizens. Vahid was aware that to the old elite families, he was little more than a roach underfoot, one they tolerated because he was useful but wouldn't hesitate to crush should that become necessary.

There were limits even to his hold over the vizier. An attack by a lowly bureaucrat on a member of the royal circle would not be tolerated. Now both Huseyin Pasha and his wife would have to die to make sure the attack could never be linked to Vahid. This was all a consequence of the colossal incompetence of his agents, he thought, turning his glare on the man standing before him.

The agent had gone pale. He bowed his head, hands pressed to his sides. "I have no excuse, sir."

Vahid let the silence stretch out until, finally, he said, "Are you satisfied with your work here?"

The agent looked surprised. "Yes, Commander."

"But you could always use more income, isn't that right?"

"Yes, Commander." The man's eyes sought the window, as if he wished to escape.

"You have two daughters, don't you?" His finger tapped once.

The agent stiffened. "Yes, Commander." His voice had fallen to an uneasy whisper.

"Despite your abject failure, you'll find that I'm a fair man. Bring the youngest in next week, and we'll find some work for her here."

The agent took an involuntary step backward. "But . . . I can't. She's been very sheltered."

Vahid gazed at him with interest, wondering at the predictability of human interaction. "Of course you can. She'll be very happy here, I assure you, and her salary will be half of yours." He smiled, exposing his perfect white teeth above his pointed beard. "I'm looking forward to meeting her."

50

A NUN CARRYING SLOPS in the early morning had found the body by the courtyard wall of Saint Peter's Church. The girl's body was draped across the rosebushes, her marigold robe pinned by thorns as if she were a rare specimen of butterfly. Her face was creased as if in pain, a discolored, swollen tongue protruding from her mouth. There were bruises on her neck.

When Sister Balbina touched her, an object fell from the dead girl's hand. The nun screamed and ran to wake the others.

CHIEF OMAR gave Rejep instructions, then faced the nuns. "Did any of you move anything?"

Sister Balbina stepped forward and handed him a silver pocket watch. "This was in her hand."

Omar glanced briefly at the elegant timepiece, trying to keep his face expressionless, then slipped it into his pocket. He had seen the magistrate pull this watch countless times from his vest to check the hour. Someone wanted to set Kamil up as a murderer. He thought he knew who that might be.

"Anything else?" he asked brusquely.

"Take a look at her arms," Sister Balbina insisted. The girl's sleeve was pushed up around her elbow. The flesh inside her forearm was ravaged with punctures, burn marks, and cuts, some healed, others fresh. "We should take her down." She headed for the rosebushes. "She's been through enough."

"Hold on," Omar bellowed. The girl had been strangled. What else she had endured would have to await the arrival of Sister Hildegard, the nun from the Austrian infirmary, whom he had sent Rejep to fetch. It would take hours to track down the police surgeon in Fatih, across the Golden Horn. He had muscled his way in on another police chief's turf, and he would have to improvise. The Austrian nun had seemed efficient and cold-blooded enough to deal with a girl's corpse, unlike this flock of Italian nuns who fluttered about in morbid excitement.

He told one of his men to string a rope across the end of the garden and keep an eye on the nuns so they didn't enter. He didn't trust them. When nuns were convinced that something was right, not even Allah could stop them.

A few minutes later, Sister Hildegard hurried through the gate, accompanied by Rejep, who carried a bulky leather case. She made her way directly to the girl caught on the bush. "Get her down," she ordered Rejep, who looked helplessly at Chief Omar.

Omar nodded. He had looked the body over carefully and noted where and how it had fallen. She hadn't simply been tipped over the top of the wall. If that had been the case, the weight of the body would have crushed the bushes and it would have come to rest on the ground. No, someone had carried the girl into the garden and arrayed her neatly across the top of the rosebushes, spreading her robe around her. The girl was small, so she rested easily on her bier of thorns.

Sister Balbina ducked under the rope and joined Sister Hildegard and the policemen. In a babble of languages, they took the girl down and laid her gently on a cloth-covered table under a tree. It had lost its leaves, but wizened yellow apples decorated it like a tree of wishes. The other nuns had retreated into the church, and the murmur of their prayers leavened the air.

"We'll need to know . . ." Omar began.

Sister Hildegard raised her hand. "I know, Chief Omar. I regret to say that I've done this sort of examination before. Much too often."

Omar wondered at this. He had thought nuns to be aloof from the sort of sordid crimes he had to deal with. Sister Hildegard was clearly a nun who got her hands dirty.

The women rolled up their sleeves and bound them at the elbow, and Sister Hildegard opened her leather case.

Omar left them to the examination of the body and, together with Rejep, went over the crime scene again to see if he had missed anything. He had already examined the soil for footsteps, but the pack of nuns had trampled most of it. In other places, the ground had been swept. He could make out the telltale parallel grooves of a broom.

He walked over to the gate, his head bent to the ground. There it was: the imprint of a boot. A new boot, with a clear circumference instead of the amorphous shape of the well-worn shoes most people wore. A sharply outlined heel. He could even see the faint impression of a line of stitches along the front and, more important, a small nick where the leather had been cut by a sharp stone. Hand-sewn soles were expensive, but as prey to the city's razor-sharp rubble as the meanest slipper. Judging from the size, he estimated that the man would be about two heads taller than himself. Omar told Rejep to place a stool above the footprint, so no one would blunder over it. He wanted to show it to Kamil, who, he now remembered, had mentioned that Vahid was tall.

He hadn't been able to get hold of Kamil. The messenger sent to his house had returned saying the pasha had gone to Üsküdar. What on earth was Kamil doing in Üsküdar? No matter. He would deal with this himself. Certain that this neighborhood would have a shop making friezes for the many high-ceilinged apartments, he told Rejep to find a plasterer.

When Rejep had gone, Omar leaned against the wall, watching the nuns hover over the girl's body. The stone was warm against his back, having absorbed and saved up the faint winter sun all afternoon. He fell into a kind of trance. The garden was so tranquil, the light leaning in sideways and backlighting the leaves so that they seemed to glow from within. He was content, he realized, with a wife who put up with him and maybe even loved him, or at least had the compassion to let him believe so, and since last year the boy Avi, a street boy they had adopted and whom he loved as much as any of the sons he might have had but never could. Contentment was nerve-wracking, he decided. It made you always afraid of a fall from grace. What would it do to his famous willingness to take risks, to walk toward a blade or rifle barrel point-blank, as he had done many times as a soldier, intent upon breaking the enemy and uncaring whether he himself lived or died? Surprisingly, that kind of bloody-mindedness worked miracles. More than one enemy soldier had turned and run. He couldn't now remember which wars, but he thought of all of them with fondness and regret, not for his dead companions, some of whom he still mourned, but for the old Omar, who he feared was now truly dead.

He was startled by Sister Hildegard's voice close by his elbow. "You look tired, Chief Omar. Let's go sit on that bench." She was wiping her hands on a towel as she walked.

The girl was gone from the table.

"They're washing the body. Do you know who she is? She must have family."

"She might be a missing Armenian girl from Kurtulush called Sosi. That looked like it might be an engagement dress." And what does Sosi have to do with Kamil? he wondered, sliding his thumb over the domed surface of Kamil's watch in his pocket.

Sister Hildegard closed her eyes for a moment. "She was engaged? How terribly sad," she said. "The poor girl was strangled, but first she was raped and tortured. She also has what appear to be dog bites on her arms and legs." She glanced sideways at Omar to see how he was taking this narrative of harm.

"Go on," Omar said gruffly. "I've seen worse in the war." He took out his cigarette holder, hesitated, then offered the nun a cigarette. He thought she looked at it longingly, but she shook her head no. Omar returned the case to his pocket without taking one himself.

"Cuts, cigarette burns, bruises on her arms and chest," she continued. "Who would do something like that to a young girl?" After a few moments she added, "I too have seen war close up. Visiting such brutality on children is beyond evil."

Omar wanted to ask Sister Hildegard which war, but a certain delicacy held him back. He remembered hearing about an English-woman, Florence Nightingale, who had cared for wounded British soldiers thirty years earlier at the Selimiye barracks in Üsküdar across the Bosphorus. This nun didn't seem old enough to have worked with Nightingale. He had a sudden image of Sister Hildegard aiming a rifle that didn't seem at all incongruous. What did he know about women?

"We can still be shocked," Sister Hildegard went on. "That's the only good thing." She squinted at the apple tree, as if to find an answer there. "It means we're still human."

Omar nodded. Another saint, he thought, not unkindly. As for him, the horror of war had settled well into his bones. Having seen and withstood the worst gave him a kind of immunity, but he paid his tithe in bitterness. Everywhere around him he saw the potential for neighbor to brutalize neighbor, even after forty years of sharing tea and grazing sheep in the same pasture. No one was exempted, includ-ing himself. He knew what he was capable of. Except for the few saints like this nun that walked among them. If he allowed himself to be shocked by the girl's brutalization, Omar thought, he wouldn't be able to summon the rage he would need to find and castrate her murderer.

Just then Rejep returned with a man in a white-stained smock, followed by an apprentice struggling to carry a heavy bucket. Omar gave instructions, then watched while the plasterer carefully poured the pasty mix into the footprint.

"How long will it take?" Omar asked him.

"You can pull it out with these." The man pointed to two loops of string half buried in the plaster mass. "Best if it sets for a day." He thrust his beaked nose in the air. "Good thing it's not snowing."

"How about two hours?"

The plasterer shrugged. "Five, maybe. Not less." He nodded to the apprentice, who picked up the empty pail.

When they were gone, Omar put the stool back over the footprint and told Rejep to make sure no one disturbed it for five hours. Kamil wasn't the only one who could be clever, he thought with satisfaction, putting the question of humanity out of his mind.

51

AKUP BROUGHT A TRAY of food from the hospital kitchen, where Kamil had sent him to learn what he could from the staff about the events of the night before.

"The staff says that the orderly on duty last night disappeared before the murders were discovered," he told Kamil in a low voice. "Two of the policemen who were here this morning weren't from the local station. They arrived after the others, asked a lot of questions, and then left. One of the cooks has a brother who works at the Üsküdar station, so he knows everyone there. Also, there were reports of strangers asking for Huseyin Pasha at other infirmaries."

"Any idea who these people are?" Kamil could think of no conceivable reason someone would want to kill his brother-in-law. Perhaps the attack on Feride was in retaliation for Kamil's appealing directly to the sultan and upsetting Vahid's plans. But why the hunt for Huseyin?

"People are whispering about the secret police, but no one knows. A farmer has been spreading stories about a djinn in the vineyards. The townspeople are afraid to leave their homes."

While Yakup returned to eat with the staff in the kitchen, Kamil brought some of the dishes to Doctor Moreno and Vali. They both had regained consciousness, although the doctor was still very weak. Vali sat on a bench in his underwear, his head bandaged, a towel across his lap, sewing up a tear in his trousers. When Kamil entered, the driver jumped to his feet, clutching the towel, embarrassed.

Kamil addressed them formally, "I would like to thank both of you, and Boatman Nissim, may he be received into paradise, for protecting my sister and Elif Hanoum."

"I thank you, pasha, for honoring me." Vali bowed his head. "I did no more than my duty, and barely that."

Doctor Moreno tried to rise on his elbow, but winced in pain and let himself down again. "You needn't thank me at all, son. I was lying on the ground like a discarded broom."

"The doctor is right," Vali said. "It's Elif Hanoum who deserves our gratitude. I've never seen a woman wield a blade like that."

"What do you mean?"

"Allah knows, I thought it was all over. Nissim was dead, the doctor and I helpless on the ground. I was reciting the fatiha and preparing myself for the end when I saw Elif Hanoum walk over, calm as glass, and pick up a sword one of the attackers had dropped. She used it fast and with no hesitation. Those men weren't even able to raise their arms before she had already cut them off. She saved our lives."

"How is she?" Doctor Moreno asked.

Kamil was still digesting the image of Elif slicing off men's arms. "She's not well. Physically she seems fine, but her mind has turned in on itself. We're hoping it's only temporary."

Vali lowered his eyes. "I'm not surprised. I don't understand how a woman could do what she did, but even less how she could bear it."

"Women are hardier than men think," Doctor Moreno said, but he sounded unsure.

"Well, you might be right there, Doctor. My wife, Allah protect her, is as tough as month-old bread." Vali grinned.

Kamil called in an orderly to help the doctor eat, then stood in the waning light of the courtyard and thought about what to do. They'd have to stay the night. He hoped the patients would be well enough to move back to the city tomorrow. Omar hadn't arrived, so he had only Yakup and his boatman, Bedri, for security. That would have to be enough; he trusted no one else. He himself would stand guard over Elif and Feride.

52

THE NEW DAY DAWNED bright as a baby's eye, with a cloudless pale blue sky and the promise of warmth. A week had passed in which Vera alternated between a kind of blank-eyed existence helping Father Zadian's housekeeper, Marta, in the kitchen and a searing impatience to act. In frustration, Vera had stalked into the yard, taken an ax, and swung it over her head with all her might into the block. Her hands and shoulders still ached from the blow.

The following day, Marta asked Vera to accompany her on her weekly shopping rounds. Marta's figure was sturdy as an amphora, her graying hair braided and pinned in a circlet at the back of her head, but her red-cheeked face and eloquent brown eyes retained a youthful eagerness. Being Christian, she didn't veil her face. Marta hired a small boy who followed behind them with a big, cone-shaped basket on his back. In the mild air, the greengrocer had spread his wares on the sidewalk outside the door of his shop. He beamed with pleasure at Marta's approach.

"Just give me the best, Gosdan," Marta told him sternly. "We've been doing business for twenty years, and you always try to cheat me."

"Marta." Gosdan crossed his arms and puffed himself up in mock offense. "Never, never have I cheated you. I would rather cut off my right hand. Take these leeks." He held out one of the fat green stems. "Thick as a sausage and just as tasty."

Marta didn't take the proffered vegetable. "You've obviously never cooked anything"—she leaned in and peered at him—"and sometimes I wonder whether you even eat. You're getting as thin as that meager excuse for a leek you're trying to sell me."

Gosdan slapped his stomach with both hands. "Hard as a rock," he announced.

"Well, give me two okka of sweet apples," she relented. "Sweet, mind you."

"Like you." Gosdan selected the apples and put them in a bag made of folded newsprint. He filled another bag with Jerusalem artichokes. Into the boy's basket went three cabbages, a brilliant white cauliflower, and another two okka of onions. The greengrocer carefully placed the bags on top, then added a leek and an orange from the south.

"So you remember me and come back," he told Marta, who smiled and thanked him. "I'll add the rest to the parish bill. Come by again soon. You could fatten me up with one of your apple cakes," he suggested wistfully. He held the basket while the boy slipped his arms through the leather straps and balanced the load on his back.

Marta gave Gosdan a flirtatious smile, then lowered her eyes and stepped into the lane. Amused, Vera followed, trailed by the boy, plodding slowly under the weight of their purchases.

"Marta," Vera asked, "did you ever meet my husband, Gabriel?"

"No, but I've heard much about him."

Vera noted the caution in her voice and wondered what it was about Gabriel's mission that kept everyone silent. She stopped and swung around to face Marta. "No one will tell me anything," she burst out. "Why is that? He's my husband. Don't I have a right to know what he's doing?"

Marta wouldn't meet her eye but signaled to the boy to take a rest. He slid the basket from his shoulders and settled himself under a tree. Marta guided Vera into a wooded clearing beside the lane. "It's unseasonably warm today," she complained, wiping her face with her apron.

Vera turned her back. She didn't want to talk about the weather.

"Your husband and his friends have founded a socialist community in the Choruh Valley. It's called New Concord," Marta told her. "Didn't you know?"

Vera nodded. She had heard about the New Concord Project. Gabriel had collected money for it in Geneva and had encouraged people to emigrate there, but she had no idea that was the reason they had come to Istanbul.

Marta pulled Vera close. "Then you should know everything." She continued in a low voice, "The authorities captured a shipment of illegal guns and the Ottoman Imperial Bank was robbed. Someone blew it up. They think Gabriel was responsible."

Vera's shock was apparent on her face, and Marta tightened her grip on the girl's shoulder.

"There's more. Father Zadian says the palace sees these as signs of a revolt. The sultan might send troops to wipe out New Concord."

"That's terrible. Does Gabriel know this?"

"Probably not. Listen to me. Gabriel wasn't responsible for the explosion. Abel set it without his knowledge."

"What?" Vera took a step backward, tripping over a root and almost losing her balance. Sosi's brother, Abel, she had learned, had been Gabriel's driver before being murdered by Vahid's men.

Marta's voice was taut with urgency. "Some people think that if the sultan cracks down on Armenians, it will get Britain and Russia involved on our side. Your husband's commune is expendable. They're outsiders. Whatever happens, the socialists will be blamed for it."

"What people? What are you saying?" Vera shouted. "How could anyone want that?" A woman passed by in the lane, pulling a child by the hand. She peered at them curiously.

Marta looked after the woman with an anxious face. "I shouldn't have told you." She grasped Vera by the shoulders and shook her. "You mustn't tell anyone that I told you."

"Who is doing this? Who?"

Marta released Vera and walked away, shaking her head. The porter watched them from the lane.

Vera ran after her. "Is it Father Zadian?"

Marta made sure the boy was out of earshot. "People think we won't get an Armenian state without outside help," she answered in a low, hoarse voice. "But they're terrible, terrible fools."

"How far away is the Choruh Valley?"

"Several days by ship and then through the mountains. It's on the Russian border. You're not thinking of going there, are you?" Marta asked her in a concerned voice.

"Of course I am. Someone has to warn Gabriel."

Marta's face sagged. "Yes, you must go to your husband." There was resignation and a deep sadness in her voice. "Not knowing can destroy a person. I am married still, although I haven't seen my husband in fifteen years."

"But . . ." Vera stopped herself from saying that he must be dead.

"He might have been killed in the war, but he might also be in captivity. I dare not be fully alive until I know he is dead. Can you understand that?"

"You must love him very much."

Marta cocked her head and smiled quizzically. "That wasn't our way. I barely knew him until we were wed, and he left for the war ten days later."

"So, why?"

"Because loyalty is more important than love."

"Even if he's alive, your sacrifice is meaningless if he doesn't know about it."

"His relatives know. The Lord knows."

"But you're unhappy," Vera pointed out, wiping a tear from Marta's cheek. "What about Gosdan?" she asked. "He seems like a good man. After fifteen years, no one would blink an eye if you decided your husband wasn't coming back and wanted to marry again."

Marta blushed. "You don't know this community."

"There are worse things than some neighbors' unkind words," Vera told her. "Fifteen years is more than should be asked of anybody."

Marta looked up at the light filtering through the trees. Their dry leaves rattled in the breeze that had sprung up. "There's a lodos coming. I can feel it."

"What's a lodos?"

"When it gets suddenly hot like this in the winter, it means a wind will blow in from the southwest. It brings wind demons that dance on the water, kicking up their heels. They drill aches into people's heads and sit on their lungs. They can even make your eyes bleed. That's the lodos. We'd better get home. We still have to stop at the butcher."

By the time they got back to the road, the wind had picked up, a strange, airless breeze that felt suffocating. The boy was asleep under the tree, his legs sprawled in the wild sage.

AFTER THEY had walked along the lane for a while in silence, Marta said, "Your husband is a brave man. I don't know anything about socialism, but he's working for our people, and I respect him for that. Armenians have problems here, discrimination, unfair taxes. Sometimes the Muslims turn on us. We hear about it," she whispered. "Who can know why? Perhaps someone wanted his Armenian neighbor's land. It won't happen here. We get on well with our neighbors. But I sense a difference in the air, as if a lodos were coming. Sometimes your breath gets stuck in your throat." She looked around. The boy, with his heavy load, had fallen behind.

Just then a gust of wind sent the boy and his basket sprawling. Onions, apples, and cabbages rolled in every direction. The women ran over and helped him up. They gathered the produce and mounted the basket again gently on the boy's back. Vera hadn't realized how heavy it was until she held it while the boy inserted his arms into the shoulder straps. This too should end, she thought with a pang of pity for the skinny lad. They hurried, one on either side of him, back to the rectory.

53

"HAVE SOME MORE, my dear." Feride reached across the table and dabbed a spoonful of cream on Elif's plate. "Stop fussing over me as if I were an invalid."

Feride raised herself to her full, not very considerable height and feigned offense. "Well, you were an invalid." Elif had been in bed since their return from Üsküdar, sleeping or staring silently at the ceiling.

Elif tried to smile but winced instead, and Feride felt sorry for having brought it up. Elif had been away from her body, for lack of any other description, for two days, and then this morning, when Feride came down to breakfast, she had found Elif sitting at the table.

Feride sent a message to Kamil to tell him. The day before she and Kamil had attended Nissim's funeral at the Ahrida Synagogue. Surprised at the large crowd of mourners, they learned that Nissim had been a famous wrestler and respected for his wisdom. Feride sat with the women in the balcony and watched Nissim's wife shudder with grief. Her friends held her, while others cared for her children. Nissim's three girls sat frozen in place, unsure how to cry for something so big.

WHEN KAMIL arrived at Feride's, he found Elif in her suite, staring at a blank sheet of drawing paper. When she saw him, the pencil dropped from her hand. They moved together and stood entwined, Elif almost disappearing within Kamil's embrace.

"Stay with me," she said, and slipped her delicate fingers between the buttons of his jacket. She pulled at the woolen cloth, forcing Kamil to bend over, then pressed her lips against his.

Her abrupt embrace startled him. Kamil stepped back so he could look at her face. The strange light burning in her eyes made him uneasy. He caught hold of her hands, which had renewed their onslaught on the buttons of his jacket. "Elif," he said softly, "come and sit with me."

"No," she wailed, pulling her hands free. "No." She pounded his chest with her fists, her knees buckling.

Kamil caught her up in his arms and carried her to the bed in the adjoining room. She weighed little more than a child, sobbing in his arms. He threw back the covers, laid her gently down, and covered her. He sat holding her hand until she quieted, then walked to the door of her suite and flung it open. As he suspected, a group of servants had gathered there, alerted by Elif's cries. They stepped back, on their faces curiosity and disapproval mingled with shame at being caught eavesdropping. Kamil didn't care. "Where's Feride?" he demanded. "Fetch the doctor."

"VERA," MARTA CALLED as she came into the kitchen, where Vera was chopping cabbage.

"What is it?" Vera asked, suddenly anxious. Was there news about Gabriel or Sosi?

"Do you know someone named Apollo Grigorian? An Armenian Russian who claims to be from Geneva. He's been walking around the Armenian quarter, asking after Gabriel, so they sent him here to Father Zadian. He claims to know you. Can you vouch for him?"

"Apollo! He's my very good friend. He was supposed to join us for the trip to Istanbul, but he didn't show up at the train station, and we didn't know what happened to him. I'm so glad he's all right." Vera brushed past Marta, heading for the door, then stopped to take off her apron and smooth her dress and hair. "Where is he?" she asked, feeling suddenly shy. What would Apollo think of her, chopping cabbage while Gabriel was building his commune?

"He's in Father Zadian's study."

Vera hurried out, leaving Marta smiling after her.

AHID SAT IN HIS FATHER'S armchair and watched his mother's hands dance in her lap over the tatting for a tablecloth that he knew she would give to one of the neighbors. She would then begin a new one. His mother sat beneath a window, a square of sunlight illuminating her head and hands as if she were an idol from some unknown tribe. He tapped his finger on the armrest. Since Rhea's death and Yorg Pasha's disturbing revelations about his father, he had been unable to find peace in the usual ways, despite ever more frequent and painful attempts. He must do something to calm himself, he realized, before he made a fatal mistake. His middle finger drummed on the upholstery.

"Why are you fidgeting?" his mother asked suddenly, her hands paused in midair.

"I'm not fidgeting, Mama. I'm thinking."

"Well, think quietly." She returned to her tatting.

Vahid rose and went down the hall to his bedroom. After locking the door, he opened the wardrobe and pulled a large box from the top shelf. It was a presentation box of the kind that held expensive pieces of china. He sat down at a table and passed his hand across the

moth-eaten nap of blue velvet before opening the clasp. At the center
of the frayed satin lining was a depression where a serving dish had
once nestled. That dish, hand-painted with carnations picked out in
gold, rested on a shelf in a glassed-in cabinet in the sitting room. It
was his mother's prized possession, a wedding gift from her mother-
in-law, never used and dusted only by his mother's hand.

Within the depression lay three fist-sized switches of different-
colored hair, the curls neatly tied with a twist of ribbon. Beneath
them lay a sheet of parchment, torn in half. Vahid picked out the
pieces and laid them side by side on the desk. Together they formed a
charcoal sketch of a mother and her baby. In the image, the woman's
hair tumbled in black waves around a delicate face, with wide-set
eyes and a generous mouth that curled in the beginning of a smile.
Her expression was one of utter solicitude as she looked down at the
baby wrapped in a shawl in her arms.

Vahid adjusted the pieces so that the tear was less noticeable. The
edges were stained with finger marks. The night he had followed his
father to the bridge, Vahid had come home in tears and his mother
had insisted on knowing why. When he told her his father had called
him Iskender, she had marched into their bedroom and returned with
the sketch. She held it under her husband's nose and said in an angry
voice, "You think I don't know about this? This icon you pray to. She's
gone, dead." Her voice rose. "They're both dead, do you hear me?"

Vahid's father reached for the drawing. "You have no right . . ."

At this, Vahid's mother tore the sketch in half, threw it at her
husband, shouting, "We are what you have. We are all that you have,
or ever will have."

Enraged, Vahid's father grabbed her by the hair. He beat her with
his fists and, when she collapsed to the floor, kicked her savagely in
the ribs.

Vahid had watched in horrified fascination, every nerve alive with
feeling. He didn't try to help his mother, and for this he had felt enormous guilt. She had been bedridden for weeks and thereafter was
plagued with pains and illnesses that often made her take to her bed.
His father was absent from home after that, returning only to sleep

and sometimes not even then. It made little impact when one day he did not come home at all. They learned that he had been found dead, a drunk who in the early-morning hours had plummeted from the Galata Bridge into the oily water below. He had disappeared little by little over the years, and this was simply the final vanishing.

56

THE CANE SEAT IN Kamil's winter garden was low, and Yorg Pasha needed Simon's help to lower himself into it. Yakup brought in a tray of savories and a samovar of tea.

"This was the oasis of my youth," the pasha said, slightly out of breath and waving his hand at the leaves of the potted palm that arched above him. "In your mother's day, this was a terrace. We used to drink tea in these very chairs. But I like your glass house." He looked appreciatively at the ranks of colorful orchids on gravel-filled trays. "It looks like a kaleidoscope in here. A Swiss clockmaker sent me one of those last year. Have you seen them?"

Kamil, seated opposite him, said he hadn't. "What is it?"

Yorg Pasha explained. "Lovely, like watching women in colorful gowns dancing about a room." His voice betrayed his enthusiasm. Kamil knew the pasha loved calibrated mechanisms of every kind. "I'll show you the next time you come to Bebek." Yorg Pasha folded his hands in his capacious lap. "Now, my son, let's talk."

Kamil told him about his meeting with Vahid and what Omar's men had seen in the basement of Akrep. He handed him the torn paper with Russian writing. Yorg Pasha glanced at it, then handed it over his shoulder to Simon. The secretary took a magnifying glass from a small bag and began to examine it.

Kamil then told Yorg Pasha what he had learned from his meeting with Sultan Abdulhamid. "Through Vizier Köraslan, Vahid has convinced the sultan that the commune is a threat to the empire and that the Armenians are scheming with the Russians to take the Choruh Valley."

"It's plausible," Yorg Pasha commented.

"But not true in this case," Kamil asserted somewhat uncertainly.

"As far as we know."

"The sultan wants me to go find out the true nature of the settlement. If I fail, he'll wipe out the commune and, if Vahid has his way, the entire population of the valley."

At that, Yorg Pasha raised his eyebrows. "He's sending you, so that means he doesn't entirely trust Vahid."

"The vizier suggested it."

Yorg Pasha looked concerned. "It might be some kind of trap."

"I'll be all right. The sultan is sending troops along."

"When are you going?"

"He wants a report by the end of March."

"It'll be heavy going even then. Spring doesn't arrive in the Kachkar Mountains until at least May."

Kamil shrugged. The sultan's deadline was not negotiable.

"That fool Gabriel should be holed up in Trabzon by now," Yorg Pasha commented. "I hope he's not trying to get supplies through to his commune. I told him to wait, but he's a Russian. They're like large stones Allah has thrown down in the road. You can't go over them. All you can do is go around them."

Simon handed Yorg Pasha a glass of tea.

"Have you deciphered that scrap of paper yet?" the pasha asked him.

"It's part of a Russian travel document. There are letters, possibly of a name—*e, r, a*."

"Vera. What else could it be?"

Kamil thought about the room in which the paper had been found, the room with restraints and peepholes, but said only, "If it was Vera Arti who escaped, where would she go?"

"To other Armenians, no doubt. Simon, spread the word."

"I've taken the liberty of doing that, my pasha."

"Well, let's talk about your trip, Kamil. Who will take care of your orchids?"

Kamil assured him that his servants were well trained in the needs of his eccentric garden. "But to tell you the truth, I haven't fully decided if I will go." He told Yorg Pasha about Huseyin's disappearance and the attack on Feride. "I can't leave if she's in danger."

Yorg Pasha frowned. "That is very serious indeed. But you won't be going for another month yet. Surely your brother-in-law will turn up by then. The attack on Feride is another matter. I imagine we know who's behind that."

"I know you think it's Vahid." Kamil propped his head in his hands. "But what I don't understand is why."

57

VERA SLICED THE APPLES they had purchased at Gosdan's shop on a wooden board while Marta kneaded
dough. Her face was dusted with flour, and her powerful
hands plowed efficiently through the pale mass on the table. Apollo
sat on a chair near the stove, his prominent nose bent over a piece of
the apple cake that had just emerged from the oven. He was tall and
angular, with thick black hair and mustache, high cheekbones, and
a ready smile. His dark brown eyes glowed with pleasure.

"This tastes as good as my mother's cake," he told Marta, swallowing. "I give no higher praise than that."

"How is your mother?" Vera asked, basking in the familiar sound
of Apollo's resonant voice, as burnished and rich as caramel. She
wished for him to continue speaking, to extend the balm of his voice
over her forever. The afternoon light slanted into the room and lit
up ropes of crimson peppers, clusters of garlic heads, and bouquets
of herbs hung up to dry. Vera relished the rhythmic chopping and
the ever-growing pile of red-rimmed slices filling her bowl. She felt
content, she realized, though she found herself testing even pleasant
feelings as gingerly as if she were palpating a wound.

"She's not well, Vreni," he answered, using the diminutive of her name. Only Apollo and her own family had ever called her Vreni, Vera thought. Her knife slipped and the white flesh of the apple in her hand flushed red. Apollo rushed over. "Put your finger in your mouth," he told her. "Now give it to me." He pressed his finger on the cut, hard. "The pressure will stop the bleeding."

They stood facing each other, Vera's hand inside Apollo's. The hands of a philosopher, she thought, admiring his long, slender fingers. She had found Apollo less than an hour ago, and already he was comforting her.

"That's why I couldn't meet you on the boat as we had planned," he explained. "My mother had an attack of apoplexy. It happened while I was visiting her to say goodbye. She started shaking uncontrollably, and I could see something receding in her eyes. It seemed as though she didn't know me."

Apollo had dropped Vera's hand. She took his and pressed it. "That's awful. Has she recovered at all?"

"She's much better, a bit lame on one side, but she can care for herself again. Still, some part of her soul has left us. You can see it when you look into her eyes."

Marta clanged the oven door shut on the second apple cake, wiped her hands on her apron, and checked the samovar. "Let's sit," she suggested. "Father Zadian has gone to a meeting. He'll probably be away all afternoon."

When they each had a glass of tea in hand, Marta asked him, "What do you plan to do?"

"Father Zadian has invited me to stay at the rectory for now. Gabriel is at New Concord, so as soon as I can arrange transportation, I'll join him." Apollo looked curiously at Vera. "You decided to stay here?"

Vera's contentment evaporated. She nodded in assent, unable to say anything more.

Marta came to her rescue. "Vera was detained, so Gabriel went on without her."

"Detained?" Apollo looked to Vera for an explanation.

Vera flinched from his gaze. With Apollo she wanted to be the old Vera, before anything else had happened. The Vera with whom he discussed the debates of their Henchak comrades, the Vera who prepared picnics for her friends in the Bâtie Woods, the Vera who remembered how to laugh. When she looked up, it was to see Marta explaining something to Apollo in a low voice. The look on Apollo's face was enough to tell Vera that her old self was gone. Like Apollo's mother, some part of her soul was now missing.

58

Vahid strode into the Fatih police station, followed by three of his men, escorting a nun. They were not visibly armed, but their black uniforms caused a stir as the policemen whispered to one another, trying to guess which organization the visitors represented. Vahid wore a tightly tailored stambouline frock coat. With his high black boots and air of command, he needed no insignia.

Omar was sitting on his usual stool in a corner of the station. He recognized Sister Balbina from the Italian church, the one who had found Sosi's body. He watched as Vahid and his contingent moved toward the large oak desk that, although Omar never used it, boasted a plaque with his name. Someone brought a stool for the nun. Omar lit another cigarette and watched the group for a while. He wondered what Vahid wanted.

The policemen in the station, aware that their chief was not at his desk but observing his visitors at his leisure, couldn't resist an occasional snicker, and there rose a distinct murmur in the room. When Omar saw Vahid's face flare red, he got up and wandered over.

"What can I do for you?" he asked politely.

To his surprise, Vahid laughed out loud. "Public shaming, meant to break down your enemy. Not bad for a small-time policeman, but rather trivial and, dare I say so, childish."

"What do you want?" Omar asked, already sick of the man.

"The watch. Is this the man, Sister?"

Sister Balbina nodded. "Yes, I gave the watch to him."

"Let's have it," Vahid snapped at Omar.

"What watch?" Omar asked. He had sent a messenger to Kamil telling him about the watch, but hadn't had the opportunity to return it.

"The watch the dead girl had in her hand. The sister here said she gave it to you. And don't claim you never saw it. I've got ten nuns willing to testify. And you know nuns never lie."

His smile reminded Omar of a viper he had once seen in the desert that had swallowed a rat. Omar had killed it. "What's your interest in this case?" he asked Vahid. "Is it worth your while to be chasing around town after a watch?"

"What was the name on it?" Vahid asked the nun.

"Kamil. A gift from his mother. It was in French." She nodded officiously, her wimple moving up and down.

The station had fallen silent.

The reason for my interest is clear, Vahid's smug smile seemed to say. Omar wanted to punch his fist right through it. He realized that it was useless to deny that he had the watch. His word against ten nuns. If he were Christian, he would cross himself against the devil. If he didn't give them the watch, they would still implicate Kamil, and then he would be accused of destroying evidence—or of corruption and who knew what else. Omar didn't mind an accusation of corruption, especially if it was deserved, but he needed to be free to help Kamil. His eyes fell to Vahid's boots. They were the right size, new and of good quality, with a nick at the edge of the sole that matched the footprint in the churchyard.

He reached into his pocket, pulled out Kamil's pocket watch, and handed it to Sister Balbina. He wouldn't give Vahid the pleasure of taking it from his hand. "It means nothing," Omar told him, "unless we know how it got there." He gave Vahid a meaningful look. "And I know who put it there."

"You know nothing, and you can prove nothing." Vahid took the watch from the nun's hand and bounced it on his palm. "But this does."

THE MOMENT they were gone, Omar rode hard to Kamil's office. To his surprise, a line of gendarmes was guarding the front of the courthouse. They hadn't even waited to see whether he would give them the watch, Omar thought angrily. It was outrageous for someone of Kamil's stature to be arrested in public. Surely they wouldn't imprison him. Pashas don't appear in court and they don't go to jail. It would be as unthinkable as arresting the sultan.

Omar ran up the stairs into a scene of chaos. Kamil stood in the middle of a knot of people, looking calm but puzzled. The captain of gendarmes was explaining to Kamil in an apologetic voice that he had instructions to arrest him but that he hadn't been instructed as to the reason. A repeating rifle was slung across the captain's shoulder and a revolver stuck in the crimson sash around his waist. A scimitar hung from his sword belt. Kamil's assistant Abdullah was shouting at the captain to get out if he didn't have cause to arrest the pasha. The burly doorkeeper, Ibrahim, stood beside Kamil, scowling and ready for a fight.

When Kamil saw Omar, he raised his hands to calm the crowd and walked over to him. "Do you know anything about this?"

Omar leaned forward and whispered in his ear.

"I see," Kamil said, his expression unchanging. His eyes met Omar's. "Tell Yorg Pasha and Nizam Pasha. Do what you can. The only way to prove that I didn't kill the girl is to find out who did."

"We know who did it," Omar growled. "Leave it to me."

Kamil turned to the gendarme captain. "Let's go." He gave instructions to his astonished staff and then walked out of the office, surrounded by armed soldiers.

59

YORG PASHA AND FERIDE were in her sitting room, drinking coffee. The lamps were lit on this gloomy winter afternoon and the velvet drapes drawn to keep in the warmth. Flames from the fireplace threw twisting shadows on the walls.

"Think about my invitation to stay with us in Bebek. My family will be delighted to see you, and you'll be safe."

"Thank you, Yorg Pasha." Feride wondered how she could refuse without seeming rude. "I miss them, please tell them that. But I have to find Huseyin. Surely you understand." She remembered his great kindness and the attention he had lavished on her and Kamil when they were young, even though the pasha had four children of his own. But Yorg Pasha's wife was very pious and rarely went out, and Feride would feel obliged to keep her company.

"You can leave that to me, my dear," he insisted, putting down his cup with an age-spotted hand.

Yorg Pasha appeared much older than when she had last seen him. He reminded her of her father in the months before he died.

"But someone is trying to kill Huseyin." She blanched as she realized she had almost added, If he's not already dead.

"Kamil has told me this, Feride dear. And also about the attack on you. That's why I'd like you to come to Bebek."

"I can't. Please understand. There are"—she faltered—"reasons that I need to find him."

Feride could see the worry and consternation on Yorg Pasha's face. Finally he said, "Very well, but you won't object to my assistance, will you?"

"I'd be grateful for your advice, my pasha, and of course for your protection," Feride said, relieved.

"Would you permit?" Yorg Pasha took a fist-sized timepiece from the pocket of his robe and wound it with a key. "My secretary said he'd be here at four, and he's as punctual as any of my clocks."

Smiling in amusement at the old man's childlike delight, Feride drew her veil across her mouth in anticipation of a male stranger. The clock pealed a complicated pattern of silvery bells, and even before it ended, Simon stood in the room as if he had been there all along.

"Tell us," Yorg Pasha said, patting the timepiece and putting it back into his pocket. "You look fit to burst."

"We've found Huseyin Pasha," Simon told them.

Feride was on her feet. "He's alive?"

"He's in Üsküdar, just as you thought. When the people who took him from Eyüp realized he wasn't their relative, they took him to the home of a midwife who has been caring for him. He's awake, and we explained the situation to him. His lungs and throat are damaged and he's unable to speak, but I believe he understood."

Yorg Pasha turned to Feride. "You don't want Simon on your trail. Punctual, efficient, and as ruthless as a ferret." He looked pleased.

"When are you bringing him back?" she asked Simon.

"His condition seems stable, chère hanoum, and no one knows he's there. We didn't want to risk drawing any attention to him." He turned to Yorg Pasha. "What should we do now?"

"You will bring him home," Feride commanded, drawing surprised looks from both the pasha and his secretary.

"Of course we will, my dear," the pasha assured her. "But have you thought about his security once he's officially found?"

"I'm sure Kamil can arrange a guard," she said. "But why is someone trying to kill Huseyin? And who?"

"We believe it's a commander in the secret police. He's been asking after your husband."

She stared at them, not understanding." Surely it's not unusual for a member of the sultan's staff to ask after Huseyin. He works there."

"This is a very dangerous man, Feride," the pasha explained. "Your brother has been interfering with some of his plans and has darkened his name with Sultan Abdulhamid. It may be that the man is targeting your family out of revenge."

Feride stood in the middle of the room, her hands twisted in the cloth of her gown, thinking through her options. A servant entered and summoned Simon, who left the room for a few moments, then returned. Feride saw his shoulders had stiffened, and there was a fold between his eyebrows that she hadn't noticed before. He leaned over and spoke to Yorg Pasha in a low voice. The old man frowned.

"What is it?" Feride demanded.

"Kamil has been arrested."

"What?" Feride felt a sudden vertigo on realizing that Kamil too was under threat. She had always thought of him as the most solid part of the landscape of her life. If he was no longer there? The thought was insupportable. If she lost both Kamil and Huseyin, who would she be then?

Yorg Pasha signaled to the maids stationed by the door. They fluttered around Feride to steady her and helped her into a chair. One brought a cloth sprinkled with rose water and pressed it to Feride's forehead. Feride pushed it away and sat up. The maids retreated. "Why was he arrested?" she asked in a firm voice.

Yorg Pasha looked exhausted. "He's been accused of murdering an Armenian girl. Her body was found two days ago, and Kamil's watch was in her hand."

"That's preposterous."

"We know that, dear child. It was set up, probably by this same man. Do you see what I mean?" Yorg Pasha said earnestly. "This man is very dangerous. Let us handle it."

"What's this man's name?"

"Vahid."

She turned to Simon and asked, "Can you arrange to bring Huseyin here secretly?" She had a plan.

Feride saw Simon look at the pasha out of the corner of his eye, and the pasha give a barely perceptible nod. "Yes, chère hanoum," Simon answered.

"Then do it. I'll ask Doctor Moreno to be present to see to his wounds."

She walked over to Yorg Pasha and took his hand. Bending her head, she pressed the back of his hand to her cheek through the thin gauze of her veil. "Thank you, my pasha, for your offer of protection. I would welcome it." She stood before him, her back straight and her mind made up. "It would be better if the guards were invisible. That way no one will suspect Huseyin is back home. Perhaps they could paint the mansion. It needs quite a bit of work. The winter has been unkind."

Yorg Pasha laughed and asked Simon, "Can you tell we're related?"

60

"WHERE TO?" KAMIL ASKED the gendarme captain, a young man with professional bearing. Kamil had worked with him before on other cases, including the bank robbery, and he respected him as a good Ottoman officer—strong, educated, obedient, humane, and civilized. They were standing before a carriage surrounded by an escort of mounted gendarmes. A group of onlookers clustered at the top of the courthouse stairs. Kamil recognized his staff, one of the judges, and another magistrate. He saw the magistrate ask the judge something, then his surprised face. A crowd was gathering in the street, kept at a distance by the troops.

"Bekiraga Prison," the captain said, avoiding his eye.

"What?" Kamil was shocked. The prison was notorious for its squalid conditions and bad treatment of prisoners. He had assumed they were driving to the governor's office or to see the vizier or some other high official. "You're joking."

"I questioned it as well," the captain explained in a low voice. "The directive is from the palace, signed by Vizier Köraslan himself. There was nothing I could do."

This was the vizier's response to his humiliation, Kamil thought with rising anger. Only the vizier had the power to put a pasha in prison. But Bekiraga Prison? That was beyond the bounds.

"Thank you for inquiring, but there must be some mistake." He was grateful to the captain for taking the dangerous step of questioning his orders on Kamil's behalf. He turned to get into the carriage. "Take me to the palace and we'll straighten this out."

"Pasha," the captain said.

Alerted by a change in his tone, Kamil turned. "What is it?"

"I was commanded by the vizier himself to bring you to the prison and nowhere else." He hesitated. "Otherwise I am commanded to kill you."

Kamil felt for the young man. The very qualities Kamil admired in him had brought him to this point. "That would be assassination of a government official, are you aware of that?"

"Yes, pasha." The captain stepped back at attention. "Please, pasha, get into the carriage."

Kamil heard the note of pleading in the captain's voice. He didn't wish for the young man to have to make such a choice, so he put his foot back on the carriage step. "Very well," he said as he got in. "This will be cleared up soon." Kamil wished it were true. Justice, as he knew so well, had less to do with the evidence than with the people arrayed against you. In this case, Vahid and the vizier made a daunting combination. Who was on your side was just as important. He saw Omar on his horse, scowling, waiting to accompany the carriage. No doubt he had sent someone to inform Yorg Pasha and the minister of justice. His side was mobilizing, he thought with a rising sense of confidence as the carriage pulled away.

They clattered over the Galata Bridge, up Jalaloglu Street through Bab-i Ali, passing the two grand dowager mosques of Istanbul, Aya Sofya, formerly a Byzantine cathedral, and Sultan Ahmet with its six delicate minarets. The carriage crossed Beyazit Square and followed the high wall of the war ministry before pulling up outside a massive stone structure surrounded by a dry moat, inside which the tops of trees moved like restless brown water.

As soon as Kamil got out of the carriage, he was assaulted by the stench. Pulling his handkerchief from his pocket, he held it to his

nose. Stinking liquid flowed from a pipe protruding from the wall
into the moat. The pipe dripped, forming viscous pools in the lane.
Kamil had never before visited the prison to which defendants at his
court had so often been sentenced. The cesspool by the gate seemed
to act as its calling card and perhaps an intimation of worse to come.
Kamil put away his handkerchief and followed the captain through
the gate, stepping carefully around the sludge.

Although he thought himself modern and civilized, Kamil had
learned that he was capable of harboring a hatred and desire for
revenge so deep that it grew like a carbuncle into his very soul. Vahid
and his deadly schemes would not stand. And if he discovered that
the vizier too had acted callously, and not simply because he had been
misled by Vahid, he vowed to bring him down as well.

His thoughts thus occupied, Kamil followed the captain to the
warden's office, where the soldier handed over the arrest warrant to
a sour-looking man with yellowish skin and lank hair. He wore a gray
uniform and had wound a red-checked cloth around his fez. As the
man bent his head over the document, Kamil wondered if he could
read or whether he just was scanning it for the correct seal. The warden coughed, a wet cough that rattled in his chest, no doubt a result
of working in these surroundings day in and out, Kamil thought. The
man looked over the document for a long time, then glanced up at
the new prisoner. Kamil caught the glint of intelligence in his eyes,
or of wiliness.

Kamil could think of nothing to say. "I didn't do it" seemed a ridiculous claim, given the document in the warden's hand. He knew that
only proof of his innocence would get him out, or pull. It seemed that
it would always be so. When he was studying in England, he realized
it was the same there, that whom you knew was the deciding factor.
A young man at the university, the eldest son of a lord, had destroyed
the taproom of a pub on a drunken rampage with his friends. His
father paid the owner for the damage, but the rape of the pub owner's
daughter and her subsequent death were never investigated despite a
roomful of witnesses to both events.

Kamil had been at the pub the night she was killed, sharing
a pint with some fellow students. The young man came in with a

group of his friends, went straight to the girl, and pulled her from behind the counter. When her father tried to come to her aid, one of the men smashed a chair over his head. Customers fled for the door. The girl shouted that they were too late, she had told the police everything.

"Yes," the young toff had said, "that's what I heard." He grabbed her by the hair and punched her in the face and chest until she lay broken and bleeding on the floor. The men left, laughing and slapping each other on the back, as the anguished father bent over his daughter's body.

Kamil had tried to go to the girl's aid, but though he struggled, he made no headway against his fellow students, who overpowered him. "It's none of your business," they warned him. "We're not getting involved."

He had never spoken to any of them again. It was almost unbearable for him to think about this experience now, the deep sense of shame and dishonor he felt at having witnessed such a crime. In a roomful of people, no one had moved a finger to help her. They knew, he supposed, what he did not, that the outcome was preordained by the lord's power to manipulate all around him, including life and death. The others in the pub had accepted that they were nothing more than pieces on an aristocrat's chessboard.

Kamil had reported the incident to a bored policeman at the Cambridge station who clearly knew that the moment Kamil was out the door, the report would go into the trash. Kamil had to believe that the Ottoman system was more just than that, that the murder of an ordinary girl would not go unpunished because she was poor. Then, as now, he felt rage and a desire to seek vengeance against those he knew to be unjust. Yet here he stood in prison, wrongfully accused by a powerful man. He tried to believe that right would prevail, not because he too had powerful friends but because the system itself was just. He would be released because the evidence would show that he was not guilty. And when he was released, he would act. He was no longer a student in a foreign place, but a pasha and a magistrate, the sultan's special prosecutor. He would never again allow someone to hold him back.

The gendarme captain saluted, then turned. As he was leaving, he glanced worriedly over his shoulder at Kamil.

The warden coughed so hard it bent him double. He leaned out the door and spit a gob of greenish fluid on the ground, then wiped his mouth on his sleeve. "Welcome, pasha. Your staff will have to bring your food in from the outside, but otherwise you'll find your room as comfortable as the best hotel." His laugh was cut off by another fit of coughing. When he had regained his voice, he told Kamil, "Come with me. The warrant specified Number Eleven. You must have friends in high places." He laughed again, a nasty snicker that put Kamil on his guard.

Kamil followed him down a vaulted corridor smelling of damp, mold, and urine. They climbed a set of stairs. A sharp ammoniac reek and other foul odors Kamil couldn't identify became stronger until he almost gagged. He pulled out his handkerchief again, setting off another bout of laughing by the warden. The next corridor was low, so they had to stoop. The warden stopped before a thick wooden door set on iron hinges. He turned the key in the lock and pushed it open. A horrible stench wafted from the room.

"What is that?" Kamil asked, not moving. His head felt as though it were being torn to pieces.

"The cesspool is right outside this window," the warden explained, pointing to an opening high up on the wall. "Look," he said in a conciliatory voice, "your friends were playing a trick on you, that's clear. For a small commission, I can move you to a better cell." He winked at Kamil. "You'll find that anything's possible here for a man like you."

Kamil grabbed the warden by the collar. "How dare you address me in that manner. How dare you ask me for a bribe. I will not forget this, you filthy son of a bitch."

The warden must have seen something in Kamil's eyes that frightened him. He pulled himself from Kamil's grasp and scuttled down the corridor. "Here," he called over his shoulder. "I made a mistake. This is the one."

Kamil followed him, coughing into his handkerchief. The warden held open the door of another cell, and Kamil stepped over the threshold.

61

GABRIEL ARRIVED IN THE PORT of Trabzon and, as Simon had predicted, was unable to find porters who would take the supplies he wished to purchase into the mountains. What few roads there were, incredulous locals told him, were snowed in, and where he wanted to go there were no roads at all, only tracks. It cost him two precious gold liras to find a guide willing to take him and a hostler willing to sell him a horse and two mules. The guide was a bear of a man whose face was nearly hidden behind a bristling black beard, mustache, and thick eyebrows. His clothes were greasy and he stank. He grunted at Gabriel's instructions and took the coins, turning up a few hours later with the animals and supplies.

Gabriel decided to leave his trunk and extra supplies locked in a stone shed he purchased behind the guesthouse where he was lodging, and he paid the owner to keep an eye on it. The gold was hidden in the trunk beneath a false bottom. Despite Gabriel's fear that it would be discovered by some nosy townsman, he thought the gold safer there than strapped onto a mule with this disreputable guide and unknown dangers on the road. He would return for it as soon as he could.

They set off before dawn. Gabriel was excited about finally going to live at the commune, although he regretted that he didn't have more weapons and supplies to present to his comrades. In the spring, when the roads were open, he would purchase what they needed with the gold. By then Yorg Pasha would have found Vera and she would have arrived in Trabzon. They would pass through these mountains together.

The morning mist cleared, revealing layer upon layer of ascending ranges. The horses picked their way through the snow as the guide sounded the path before them with a six-foot wand to check for hidden fissures. They lost one of the mules when it stepped off the path and broke through a crust of ice hiding a deep streambed. At night, Gabriel and his guide put up in village houses that often consisted of only two rooms, one for the family and the other for their animals. Despite his being plagued by fleas, Gabriel's spirits remained high. Except for occasional instructions in a thick local dialect that Gabriel found hard to follow, the guide didn't speak to him at all. The journey from the coast took them fifteen days. Of the trip, Gabriel remembered the silence, broken only by the sound of distant avalanches and the glare of snow against a changing sky.

On his approach to the commune, Gabriel found a ghastly sight. The fields around the monastery were littered with dismembered corpses. When they arrived at the gate, the guide took the rest of his payment without dismounting, turned his horse, and disappeared back into the untracked expanse of the mountains. The gate was open. There was no sound, and Gabriel had the panicked thought that all his comrades were dead. He walked through the courtyard and pushed open the door to the building. It took a few moments for his eyes to adjust to the gloom. He was in a cavernous hall, a smoking fire at one end casting neither light nor heat. The windows were plugged with blocks of what appeared to be straw mixed with mud. Far above, he could make out a tiled roof. The commune's two dozen inhabitants, hollow-eyed and emaciated, sat or lay listlessly on straw pallets, barely taking note of Gabriel's arrival.

One man hurried toward him. Gabriel recognized Victor Byman, the medical student from New York. His distinctive head was round as a melon and seemed set directly onto his shoulders. When he got closer, Gabriel saw that his face was gray and sagged with exhaustion.

Victor broke into a grin when he recognized Gabriel. "The angel Gabriel come to save us," he quipped as the men embraced. When Gabriel stepped back, he saw tears in the man's eyes.

"What's happened?" Gabriel asked. "Why are there so many unburied bodies?"

Of fifty comrades who had made their way from far corners of the world to New Concord over the past eight months, Victor explained, only twenty-six had survived. "The ground was too frozen to dig, so we stacked the bodies outside the walls, first in a shed, then, when there were too many, buried under the snow. But the wolves dug down and dragged the bodies out and spread the remains across the fields, and we don't have the strength to stop them."

Victor led him to a stool by the fire and introduced the young Irishwoman sitting beside him as Alicia. Her face was mottled with freckles and her matted hair was the color of dry straw, but her blue eyes were clear as chips of ice. Alicia's hands were red and chapped, her dress tattered, but of good wool and embroidered at the sleeves. Gabriel wondered what had brought a girl of a good house all the way from Ireland to eastern Anatolia.

Victor brought them water and apologized that they couldn't offer more to a tired traveler. Gabriel told him about the supplies he had brought, although greatly reduced by the loss of one mule and its load.

Alicia got up hastily. "We thank you, sir," she told Gabriel, looking around the dark hall. "We are sorely in need. They've had little to eat these past days." She strode away, and Gabriel saw her speak to two men. They followed her into the courtyard, where his animals were tied up. After a few moments she returned.

Cradling his cup of water, Victor told Gabriel what had happened to the commune. The year had gone well enough. They put on a roof and harvested one crop; the hunting and fishing were good. New comrades arrived, bringing tools and supplies. Then their comrade Klaus Wedel died. Gabriel remembered him as a Swiss wool merchant, an avid skier who had come late to the movement.

"I thought it was pneumonia." Victor paused to take a sip of water. "That was in late autumn, when the ground was still soft enough to dig a grave."

The crackling of the fire was punctuated by coughs from the pallets. These makeshift nests of quilts, blankets, and straw were laid close together along an inner wall.

"My ma and pa and every blessed one of my siblings died of the pneumonia last winter." Alicia broke into the silence, her voice strangely dispassionate. "It took a mere two weeks to erase all their lifetimes."

"I'm sorry, Alicia." Victor leaned forward and pressed her hand with his own. "After Klaus, there were more," he went on. "We quarantined them, but this place is too small. It looked like pneumonia, but I'm not sure. Some had intestinal bleeding, so it could have been cholera, or even influenza. But it was faster than anything I've ever seen. You cough a bit, like something's stuck in your throat, you get a nosebleed, and next morning you're dead." Victor's hands, Gabriel noticed in the firelight, were clean and manicured, in contrast with his Shetland sweater and trousers, their colors camouflaged by dark stains. Gabriel wondered if the stains were blood.

Victor was examining his hands now, as if he were thinking the same thing. "There haven't been any cases in two weeks, so I hope it's over, but we need food. The weaker they are, the more susceptible they become. One more outbreak and we might as well give up."

"We have some ammunition left," Alicia said. "Ten cartridges."

"Alicia is the best marksman we have," Victor announced. "The source of all the game in our pot. Never wastes a bullet."

Gabriel saw his admiring look at Alicia, and her face lowered, a barely repressed smile on her lips. He thought of Vera. What would she think of him for abandoning her? He allowed himself to wonder for the first time whether she was still alive. He closed his eyes and willed the pain in his gut to subside.

"Something hurt?" Victor asked him with a concerned look.

"Life, comrade." Gabriel forced a smile.

THE NEXT morning, Gabriel and Alicia donned snowshoes that a Norwegian comrade, now buried beneath the snow, had brought with him.

"But you can't shoot." Victor pointed to Gabriel's bandaged right hand. "You'd be more helpful giving a morale talk to the comrades. Their heads are as starved as their bellies."

"Alicia can't go by herself," Gabriel insisted.

"I do all the time." Rifle slung across her shoulder, she was already swinging her feet, attached to the webbed snowshoes, across the field like a duck, heading for the forest.

"Alicia," Gabriel called out. "Stop. What if you're hurt? And how will you get the carcass back?"

"I'll go." Victor held out his hands for the snowshoes. "You're right, she might bag a deer instead of a hare."

Over several hours, Gabriel heard occasional shots ricochet through the mountains. He was stacking wood when he heard a shot that didn't sound like the others. It had a quicker report, like a snarl instead of the boom of the shotguns. He stared at the woods, then took up a rifle and stomped awkwardly though the knee-deep snow toward the line of pines, following the broad track of snowshoes.

He met Alicia and Victor stumbling through the woods.

"He's been shot," Alicia gasped.

As soon as they were back in the monastery, Victor shrugged off his coat and pulled back a blood-soaked sleeve. "Just grazed," he announced, his relief audible, but his face gray with pain.

Alicia cleaned the wound with an iodine solution.

"What happened?" Gabriel asked.

"I shot a deer," she said, her hands busy with bandages. "We were walking over to it when a man stepped from behind a tree with a pistol and shot Victor. He looked familiar. I think he works for one of the local landowners." She stroked Victor's forehead.

"Did he say anything?"

"I didn't understand him."

Victor sat up, wincing. "He said, 'Get out. You bring bad luck.'"

"In what language?" Gabriel asked.

"Armenian."

"I didn't know you spoke Armenian."

"My grandfather on my mother's side was Armenian. He moved to California, looking for paradise. He didn't find it and returned to New York, but I thought I should keep looking." He reached up with his good arm and pressed Alicia's hand against his lips.

"Wonderful," Gabriel declared. "Now the locals are after us too. Did you have any trouble with them before?" He wondered whether news of the bank robbery had reached this valley.

"A few months after we arrived," Alicia explained, "we were running short of money, so we stopped buying food from the Karakaya farmers. We had our gardens and a promising crop, and we hunted. The farmers left us alone. But recently we heard that the governor had paid a visit to the three biggest landowners, and after that it seemed like they turned on us. We had five goats, but one morning they were gone. When we hunted, sometimes there'd be the sound of a drum that would scare the game away. But nothing like this. They never shot at us before."

"Maybe we should think about leaving," Victor ventured. "There aren't all that many of us left."

"That would mean our comrades died for nothing," Gabriel answered crossly.

"The living are our responsibility too."

"Well, I'm staying," Gabriel insisted. There was nothing left for him in Europe, and he could never return to Russia or to Istanbul. There was only this valley. He saw Victor meet Alicia's eyes before he turned to stir life into the fire.

62

FATHER ZADIAN REMAINED CLOSETED with Apollo in the sitting room with the door shut for the entire morning on the day after he arrived. Vera had long since figured out that Father Zadian must have been the leader of Gabriel's cell. Gabriel had once complained to her that the men in his cell wouldn't take orders directly from him. Now she understood why. Father Zadian's rectory was visited, day and night, by all kinds of men, some who looked like wealthy merchants, some tradesmen, others dressed in rags. They spoke rapidly in Armenian, but sometimes in French. When their voices were raised, she could hear and sometimes understand.

There had been a fight over tactics, with some of the visitors objecting to provoking the government.

"Do you know how many lives will be lost if the sultan decides to strike back at our community?" Vera heard one man shout, but she didn't hear Father Zadian's response. It hadn't satisfied his visitor, who slammed the door on his way out.

Now Father Zadian was sequestered with Apollo and she could hear nothing, although she hovered by the door until Marta took her firmly by the shoulder and led her into the kitchen.

When Apollo emerged, he looked tired and unsettled. He went

outside without remembering to put on a coat and paced about the rectory garden. After a while, he came in and sat before the kitchen stove, shivering. Marta left, closing the door behind her, leaving him alone with Vera.

"How much do you know, Vreni?" Apollo asked her. He pulled a small leather pouch from his jacket, took a pinch of tobacco from it, and tamped it into his pipe.

She told him what Marta had said about Gabriel's bank robbery and the explosion.

"I don't think Gabriel knows that there might be an attack on the commune," Apollo said, "but he should be safe for the moment. Father Zadian heard that the vizier wanted to go ahead with an attack, but the sultan decided to wait. He's sending an envoy east to see for himself whether the commune is a threat."

"That's good news, isn't it?"

"Not if he decides it is one. Or if the vizier convinces the sultan to go ahead with the attack before the envoy returns."

"Why would he do that?"

"Another provocation like that bank explosion might make them think attacking the commune is necessary to protect the empire. We have to warn Gabriel, but it's not just about the commune anymore. Father Zadian thinks that if the sultan believes the Armenians are revolting, then the entire valley might be attacked. It wasn't what he had planned." Apollo gave a deep sigh. "I don't know, Vreni. People do the most awful things."

When Vera heard "we," her hopes soared. She was vaguely aware that the thought of seeing Gabriel gave her less pleasure than the prospect of traveling with Apollo. Gabriel might be furious if she followed him and became a liability again.

"We have to bring him the guns." Apollo opened the stove door and held a piece of kindling into the fire. It burst into flame, and he held it to his pipe bowl as he inhaled.

"Marta mentioned a shipment of guns, but it was confiscated." She breathed deeply of the fragrance of Apollo's pipe. It conjured memories of evenings in Apollo's apartment in Geneva with Gabriel and others in heated discussion that would go on deep into the night.

"For heaven's sake, didn't Gabriel tell you anything? That's why he was here—to get the guns and bring them to the commune."

"He didn't tell me what he was doing here." She bowed her head, feeling as though this statement had revealed her inadequacy, but also her resentment toward Gabriel.

Apollo stared at her. "That idiot," he said, shaking his head in disbelief. "That stupid, misguided idiot. How were you supposed to protect yourself if you didn't know against what? And now you're sitting here, doing what? Waiting for him?"

Vera crossed her arms. "No. I don't know." She felt put on the defensive. "Maybe I should just go back to Moscow."

Apollo reached out and took her hand. "What do you want, Vreni?"

No one had asked her that before. "I want to be part of something bigger than myself." She plucked at her skirt and said with a bitterness that surprised her, "Bigger than having a new wool dress." She examined Apollo's face to see whether he understood.

He looked at her solemnly and pulled on his pipe.

Encouraged, she continued. "I want to be part of some simple, worthy thing, like you and Gabriel. That's all I want." She faltered. "But I don't think I can do it. Everything I've touched has fallen apart." She started to cry. "I tried so hard, but I couldn't do it."

Apollo got up and embraced her. "Hush, Vreni. Sometimes bad things happen. We don't have control over everything. But if we give up, that means we've lost and they've won. I've never seen you as a delicate flower."

She laughed a little and wiped at her tears. "No," she agreed. "I'm not so delicate."

"Then let's plan our trip. You're coming along, aren't you?"

Vera nodded.

"Good. Now we have to figure out how to steal those weapons back. Someone called Yorg Pasha bribed the officials. The guns have been off-loaded and are in one of his warehouses. Ready for an adventure?"

63

THE CART ARRIVED, PILED HIGH with supplies for the renovation of Huseyin Pasha's mansion. The workmen hauled in ladders, several large crates of building materials, and containers of plaster and powders from which the paints would be mixed. One of these crates was carried directly into a windowless back room. It was furnished with a bed, comfortable chairs, a couch, and a large table. Still-life paintings adorned the walls. A pleasant fire crackled in the grate as the men gently deposited the box on the table.

They cut through the ropes and pulled off the perforated lid. Feride looked down into her husband's eyes, which winked at her before roaming the room. He was swathed in bandages, now none too clean. She reached down to clasp his hand, but realized that she had no idea where he had been burned. Instead she pressed her fingertip to her lips, then to his. She leaned over to say something, but the words stuck in her throat. Against her will, she visualized the man before her touching another woman. Unable to speak the terms of endearment that filled her mouth, she stepped away from the table and called, "Doctor?"

Doctor Moreno limped over using a cane, his leg not yet completely healed.

"He's here." Her voice was tipsy with joy. How odd, Feride noted, that her love for her husband could flow through a side channel but not fill its proper bed. Is this how marriages die? she wondered. Dams shunt the natural flow of feelings into ever-smaller conduits until one day the river dries up completely. She remembered how before his death her father had become more and more indifferent to his granddaughters, to all his loved ones, as if life already had evaporated, replaced by the opium that gave him the dream of being alive but excluded everyone else.

One of the workmen set Doctor Moreno's case on the table. Then he and the others, who, like all the supposed workmen, were Yorg Pasha's guards, set to work dismantling the box in which Huseyin rested. Only a handful of servants would share the knowledge that their master had returned and was recuperating in this out-of-the-way room. The rest had been told that Huseyin Pasha was still missing.

A steaming cauldron of water, bowls, and sponges were brought in. The workmen left, and Feride and Doctor Moreno began to peel off the bandages and clean Huseyin's wounds.

Feride sponged gently at her husband's ruined body, careful not to disturb the scabs. The touch of his skin and the compassion she felt at his helplessness summoned a sadness so desolate that she put the sponge down and went to straighten the coverlet on the bed.

Doctor Moreno watched her but said nothing.

After a while, Feride returned to her task. She was dabbing Huseyin's shoulder with a sponge and trying to avoid looking at his face when she noticed tears running down it. He was looking at her intently, the question clear in his eyes. Dropping the sponge, Feride ran from the room.

64

OMAR'S ADOPTED SON, AVI, followed him down the narrow streets, stepping carefully so as not to jostle the basket he carried on his back. Avi had insisted on carrying it, even though Omar and his wife, Mimoza, had been reluctant to burden the boy. They had given in when Avi knelt in front of the basket, slipped his arms backward through the straps, and swung it up onto his back like a seasoned professional. Omar and Mimoza had exchanged a glance. They had forgotten that before he joined their family the previous year, Avi had made a living on the street. He was a bit taller now and well fed, although still skinny. He carried the basket as if it were filled with air instead of tins of food, Mimoza's spinach börek, and two sealed clay jugs of water.

Omar stopped in front of Bekiraga Prison, careful not to step in the foul puddles on the pavement, lifted the iron knocker, and let it fall. A grill opened and a guard peered out. Omar identified himself and the gate swung open.

The warden came running down the path toward them, arms outstretched. "Omar, my dear friend."

"Abdulkadir, you pimp, you get younger every year. Tell me your secret."

The warden chuckled. "Come to my office."

When they reached the whitewashed one-room house set inside a miniature garden, Omar told Avi to set the basket down near the door. "This is Avi," he told the warden, "my son."

"Ah, ah," the warden cooed, "Allah be praised." He coughed violently and spit into the dusty geraniums at the side of the house.

Omar rummaged inside the basket and pulled out a clay container sealed with wax. "My wife made up an ointment for your cough. She knows about herbal remedies. Let me see, what were her instructions?" He passed a beefy hand over his mustache. "I don't remember."

"I remember," Avi said in a shy voice.

Omar and the warden grinned at each other, then at the boy. "Out with it then," Omar said, not disguising his pride.

"You rub it on your chest at night before you go to sleep and put a warm, wet towel on it. She also said to smear some below your nostrils."

Omar gave the clay pot to the warden, who peeled off the wax, sniffed it, and recoiled. "Allah protect us, if I smeared this on a prisoner, he'd confess immediately." They laughed.

"She also sent this." Omar gave him a paper-wrapped packet of fragrant börek, still warm from the oven.

"Bless her hands. You're the luckiest man in the world, brother. It's a wonder you're not fatter than you are."

Omar patted his not insubstantial paunch. "Shall we try them?"

The warden looked horrified. "You mean you want to eat some of my precious börek?" he cried out. "You'd tear the last scraps of food from the hands of a man dying of hunger?"

Avi looked confused and stepped behind the basket.

"I'll make you a deal," Omar said. They played this game every time he came. "If you let me see the prisoner, I'll let you have all the börek." He winked at Avi.

"You drive a hard bargain, but since you're an old friend, why not?" He called one of the guards over. "You'll see, I've moved him to one of our best cells, as you requested. That was a terrible trick to play on a man of such quality, ordering him to be put next to the cesspool. I didn't think that was right. I hope you give me credit me for that. If I had known he was a friend of yours, I would have put him in a different wing right off."

Omar said nothing. He was furious at the way Kamil had been treated. A small satchel of coins inside the packet of börek ensured that Kamil was comfortable. Omar knew that was the way the jail worked, but he found it hard to keep up the light banter when he wanted to stuff the avaricious warden's mouth with coins until he choked or released Kamil from this hellhole. He knew that Yorg Pasha was working assiduously behind the scenes to get Kamil out.

Omar followed the guard down the path, Avi trotting behind them with the basket.

"Come back afterward and we'll have tea," the warden called out.

Kamil's manservant, Yakup, had paid a large bribe to move him to a well-ventilated cell in a different wing and over the past two days had brought him supplies and meals, but without Omar's intervention with the warden, he wasn't sure what kind of treatment Kamil would receive in the prison. The warden might have been emboldened by the vizier's signature on the warrant to play cat to Kamil's mouse, despite Yakup's bribe, but Omar had a well-earned reputation for retribution if he was crossed. Omar was certain that the corrupt, luxury-loving warden would never wager his hide.

The guard turned the key and the door creaked open. Kamil looked up from the book he was reading by the faint light from a high window. The air was damp and smelled of mold, but the cell was in the part of the prison farthest from the cesspool. Kamil sat in a cushioned chair, a thick-piled carpet beneath his feet. A mangal brazier heated the cell but did nothing against the cold draft from the window, which had no glass. Kamil was wrapped in a fur cape, a rug draped across his lap, and wore his kalpak. Yakup had shaved him that morning, so the only difference in Kamil's appearance was the hard edge about his jaw and the black circles under his eyes.

"What news, Omar?" Kamil gestured to a pile of quilts stacked on the floor that he unrolled at night to use as a bed, the only other place to sit in the small room, no more than five paces across.

Avi set the basket down and squatted beside the door, shivering now that he was no longer exerting himself. Kamil took the soft rug from his lap and handed it to Omar, with a glance at Avi. Omar wrapped the boy in it. Then he took the containers out of the basket and stacked them on a low shelf next to some other covered pots. "I know you have food," Omar explained, "but the wife insisted." Placing his bulk between Kamil and the shelf, he lifted one of the lids of the containers Yakup had brought. Just as he feared, the food had been barely touched.

Omar sat down on the pile of quilts, sagging uncomfortably into the soft bundle. "I'd ask what you're reading, but it would be way above my head, so don't tell me."

Kamil's smile was forced. "Any news?"

"Your brother-in-law's back home. The house is full of Yorg Pasha's men, so I suppose it'll be fine." He looked unconvinced.

Kamil flung the book to the floor. "In Allah's name, what is this pestilence, and why has it infected my life, my work, and my family?"

"What can you do? You spit downward, it lands in your beard; you spit upward, it hits your mustache."

"That's very fatalistic of you, Omar," Kamil commented, unamused. "Surely you have a better idea."

Omar showed a sharklike expanse of tobacco-stained teeth. "I swear to you Vahid will regret he was ever born."

WHEN OMAR had gone, Kamil picked up his book, volume two of H. G. Reichenbach's *Xenia Orchidacea: Beiträge zur Kenntniss der Orchideen*. Kamil's German was rudimentary, but each orchid also was introduced by a description in Latin, the common language by which science ordered the chaotic munificence of life. The effort to understand the text made the time pass and gave Kamil the feeling that although his body was imprisoned, his mind was not. "*Sepala oblonga akuta*," he read, "*intus pallide orchracea, extus flavida maculis quibusdam . . .*" He shut the book and dropped it to the floor.

There was no point to trying to forget that he was in prison. For the worst crimes, someone of his status would be executed or exiled, but never locked up in a stinking hole like this. It had certainly opened Kamil's mind to what it meant when criminals were sentenced to prison. Perhaps the judge should allow them the choice of execution, he thought sardonically. The vizier was shaming him by punishing him with the lowest criminals. Kamil understood his motive, but he also sensed Vahid's hand behind this penance.

Kamil began to cough, a harsh, wet rasp that worried him. He had asked the warden to put glass in the window, but this request had been refused despite another large bribe. Yakup had fashioned a thick curtain that Kamil could draw at night, but the guard had torn it down and made off with it, claiming it was against regulations. More likely, he wanted to steal the woolen cloth. Bribes, Kamil had learned, did not automatically lead to services.

65

Two days after Apollo's arrival, twenty men gathered in the rectory after midnight. They conversed in hushed voices for several hours, then slipped out into the dark. Apollo tiptoed into Vera's room and sat beside her on the bed. He held her hand and leaned in. "I'm leaving, Vreni. Don't worry. I'll be back. Can you be ready to go in three days?"

Apollo's mellifluous voice seemed to her an oboe, his words a symphony. She hung suspended from the sounds until Apollo shook her shoulder.

"Wake up, Vreni, and listen to me. This is serious. In three days I'll come and get you. By then you'll need to have packed warm clothes for the east. Get some boots. Marta will help you." He leaned closer.

He smelled like cloves.

"Are you listening?"

Vera sat up, clutching the cover about her, and brushed her hair from her eyes. "Of course I am."

"Don't mention this to anyone else. Father Zadian doesn't approve of your coming along with us."

"I'll be ready." Impulsively, lured by the scent of cloves and the sound of oboes, Vera leaned forward and kissed Apollo on the mouth. He didn't pull back but let their faces linger so that first their lips, then their cheeks touched.

"Farewell, Vreni."

She couldn't fall asleep for a long while. When she did, she dreamed of the east. She was running through a barren landscape, falling to her knees, rising again, trying to outpace the creature chasing her. She could feel its foul breath on her heels, then the back of her legs. Her lungs were bursting. She tripped and fell headlong, her pursuer lunged, and then her breath was burned away as she was taken. She woke up screaming.

WHEN MARTA and Vera returned home from shopping two days later, they could see from the lane that something was wrong. The rectory gate hung askew and four unknown horses were tied to the fence. The streets were abnormally quiet. The boy they had hired to carry the basket of groceries bent over and dumped its contents on the ground and then ran away.

"They're looking for you," Marta whispered. "Hide in there." She pushed Vera into the neighbor's stable.

Shaken, Vera cowered among the bales of hay. Banging and loud voices came from next door. She heard Father Zadian say, "I will complain to the kadi about your desecration." Vera was so relieved that he was unharmed that she almost didn't hear the response.

"This isn't a church. You're not sacred, and neither is your house."

Vera shrank back against the wall of the stable and scrabbled frantically to pull a bale of hay over herself. She recognized Vahid's voice. Panicking, she slipped through the stable door and ran.

66

OMAR AND YAKUP STOOD BY while the guard unlocked Kamil's cell. It was early morning on the fourth day of his imprisonment. They found Kamil curled on a quilt, coughing. His face was sallow and unshaven.

"The warden wouldn't let me bring a doctor last night," Yakup said, his voice hushed with concern, "despite the bribe."

"The son of an ass doesn't want anyone to see how bad the conditions are in here." Omar turned to the guard. "Get the warden up here right now."

"I'll have to lock you in," the guard said officiously. "I can't just leave . . ."

Omar thrust his face into the guard's and bellowed, "Get that son of a whore Abdulkadir up here now or you'll lose your job." As the guard fell back, Omar smiled and added, "And if you don't hurry, you might lose your teeth as well." The guard paused a moment longer, hand on the baton hanging from his belt, but then retreated, cursing under his breath.

Yakup squatted beside Kamil. "Can you stand, pasha?"

Kamil struggled to sit upright, then began coughing again. Yakup helped Kamil to his feet. As they were going out the door, the warden appeared, followed by five guards, and blocked their way. The guard who had fetched the warden pointed at the cell door and said something, then stepped back when Omar filled the doorframe.

"What's going on?" the warden demanded.

"We're leaving," Omar said, unruffled. He pushed past the guards and cleared a way for Yakup and Kamil, who needed to lean on his servant as they descended the stairs.

"You can't just walk out," the warden shouted. "This is a prison!"

"Sounds like your cough is better, my friend. Don't forget who you have to thank for that. You might have shared some of that medicine with the pasha here."

"Allah damn you. Come back here."

They had reached the path to the main gate. While Yakup helped Kamil into the carriage, Omar turned to the warden. "We'll be back for the furniture. And I'll count every candlestick, you crooked son of a bitch." He thrust into the warden's hand a folded document that bore the large and impressive seal of the minister of justice, then pushed past him and went into his office. Omar grabbed the pot of ointment his wife had sent and brushed the food on the table onto the floor with his arm. He looked with interest at the warden's new wool curtains.

When Omar came out, the florid-faced warden confronted him, waving his fist. "How dare you. Never expect anything from me again."

Omar grabbed the warden's fist and stuck it into the clay pot, then smashed fist and pot against the side of the warden's head. The warden dropped to his knees, keening.

"You should be more careful," Omar admonished him, then went back inside and pulled down the curtains. Humming happily and trailing the material like a toga, he walked to Kamil's carriage.

LATER THAT evening at Kamil's, Omar told him about his attempt to use a plaster cast of a boot sole to prove that someone besides Kamil had put Sosi's body in the church garden.

"Very clever of you. Did it work?" Kamil sipped the warm chamomile and honey mixture Omar's wife had sent. He could taste other, more bitter undertones, but according to Omar, Mimoza refused to reveal her formula.

Omar looked sheepish. "Well, not exactly. The cast had dirt stuck in it, so it wasn't very clear. And I didn't have a chance to get an impression of Vahid's boot to compare."

"How did you talk them into releasing me then?"

"It seems you're a well-connected guy. How come I never knew that? Yorg Pasha and some other pashas, friends of your father's, it seems, ganged up on the minister of justice and forced him to sign your release."

Kamil couldn't imagine his superior, Nizam Pasha, being forced to do anything. He had a will strong enough to face down a division of Russian cavalry. The minister was of an age with his father, and Kamil wondered whether they had been friends. It seemed unlikely, given Nizam Pasha's dislike of Kamil, the source of which Kamil had never understood.

"It's not a full pardon, though," Omar explained, looking away. "Vizier Köraslan is insisting on a trial."

"That's absurd!" Kamil exclaimed, his hands grasping the arms of his chair. "I hope he doesn't expect me to stand in the dock in my own court. Donkeys will fly before I allow that."

"Think where we could go with rides like that, pasha," Omar said with half a smile.

Kamil frowned, thinking that among everything he had lost, the ability to laugh was not insignificant.

67

Terrified that Vahid and his men would discover her, Vera slipped into the alley behind the stable and made her way through the unfamiliar back lanes until she found Gosdan's shop. No one was there, but the door was open. She crept in and hid behind a stack of crates. Would they know to look for her here? After a few minutes, Gosdan returned, carrying a sack. He locked the door behind him and called out Vera's name.

When she emerged, he said in a troubled voice, "I went over to make sure Marta was all right. You can't go back. There's someone watching the rectory." He handed her the sack. "Marta thought you might come here. She asked me to give you this."

The sack was filled with neatly folded sweaters and other warm clothing. Gosdan went to the back of the shop and returned with a pair of thick-soled leather boots. Vera still wore the attractive but flimsy city shoes that the publisher's wife had given her.

"Thank you, both of you. Please tell Marta . . ." Her voice cracked.

He nodded distractedly and went over to the trays of vegetables arrayed against the wall and began to rearrange the leeks.

Vera didn't ask him where she should go. She felt ashamed at having caused trouble for so many people. She had always been lazy, she thought, launching herself into other people's lives as if they were a sea whose only purpose was to bear her up. She would spend the night in Gosdan's shop, if he allowed it, and tomorrow Apollo would fetch her and she would leave.

"Apollo!" she exclaimed. "He can't go near the rectory."

"He's been told. He'll come here." Gosdan pulled out a stool, then fetched a jug and two cups from a shelf. "Here, sit down." He poured something from the jug and handed her a cup. "Have some boza. It'll put flesh on your bones." Vera tried to sip the viscous liquid. Her hands were shaking.

He pulled up a stool facing her and, after a few moments in which he seemed to be trying to make up his mind about something, said in a gentle voice, "It's good that you're leaving, Vera. The darkness is drawing closer. The Agopian family has suffered a loss."

Vera stared at Gosdan. "Who?"

"Monsieur Agopian fell from a window. The neighbors across the street said it looked like he was struggling with someone before he fell, but the police claim no one was at home except the servants, and they saw nothing."

Vera moaned and covered her face with her hands. In her mind, she saw Monsieur Agopian wrestling with a man in a black uniform. He couldn't have told Vahid where she had gone. He didn't know.

Gosdan lowered his eyes. "And Sosi is dead."

Vera fell onto her knees. "I should have gone back for her," she wailed. "I shouldn't have left her alone." She curled into a ball of pain, the foul breath of the creature from the dream hot on her back.

68

THE SMALL STEAMBOAT DOCKED at the warehouse pier just after dusk, its outlines indistinct in the encroaching gloom, its deck in shadow. It appeared to be flying the Ottoman colors, although Vera hoped that, in this light, it would be hard for the men guarding Yorg Pasha's warehouse to make anything out for certain. Vera and fifteen comrades in makeshift Ottoman navy uniforms stood at attention on deck as a man in the uniform of a navy captain emerged and stepped from the ship onto the pier, followed by an armed lieutenant. The captain had a prominent nose, high cheekbones, and a trim mustache. As he approached the two guards, Vera saw them spread their legs and lift their rifles belligerently, and a chill went through her. They had researched what they could, but so much of their plan was based on chance, the quality of light and shadow, the inattentiveness of the guards.

Yorg Pasha, like the sultan, preferred Albanian guards because they were noted for their fearlessness and prowess with arms, but many had not learned the local language beyond what was required for their duties. Vera hoped they wouldn't notice Apollo's accented Turkish. Even if they did, Apollo had reassured her, Ottoman officers could hail from anywhere in the vast empire, so it wouldn't matter much.

"I have orders." Apollo's firm voice carried across the pier to the ship. She saw him whip out a case, extract a document, and hand it to the guard. The man took it but didn't look at it. Perhaps he couldn't read, Vera thought anxiously. Instead the guard barked out a name, and, after a few moments, a man emerged from a small house adjoining the storage area. The house was faced by neatly tended rosebushes, a contrast with the rumpled appearance of its inhabitant, an unshaven, jowly man in his fifties. He looked out at the ship, then shuffled over to the guards.

He said something to the captain as the guard handed him the document.

"This is urgent business," the captain responded tersely, his voice loud and officious.

The clerk took the document and twisted his head to read it in the half-light. Apollo and one of the men on board who was an engraver had labored hours over a forgery of Yorg Pasha's seal. The clerk squinted at the captain and waved the document. Vera couldn't hear what he was saying, but she feared their subterfuge had been discovered. She saw Apollo's lieutenant, a young Armenian named Yedo, adjust his rifle.

Apollo reached for the document. The clerk hesitated, then, to Vera's relief, gave it back to him and turned to instruct the guards. Apollo was already striding toward the warehouse doors. Vera saw the clerk shrug and pull his robe around him as if he were cold, then shuffle back to his house. As soon as the door shut behind him, a neat file of uniformed men emerged from the ship and marched in formation down the pier. Vera remained behind as lookout.

Before long, a line of men moved between the warehouse and the ship, where they wrestled the barrels onboard and stowed them. The Albanian guards stood idly by, smoking. It took less than an hour to load all fifty barrels.

By the time they were done and had cast off, it was fully dark. From the deck, Vera could see a light bloom in the clerk's window.

The tension was unbearable. She couldn't believe they had pulled it off and expected at any moment to see a pursuing warship in their wake.

"Hush," Apollo whispered to the excited group that clustered around him, all discipline forgotten. "Sound carries at this time of day." He grinned at Vera as he stripped off the captain's jacket that, at these close quarters, revealed its patchwork nature. The fifteen comrades embraced her and one another in barely restrained joy. One waved his fiddle in anticipation.

The engine huffed and the gears meshed as the steamboat headed up the Bosphorus toward the Black Sea and Trabzon. Strapped in its belly were a thousand rifles, pistols, and ammunition—the full shipment that had been confiscated by the police and then, to Apollo's great advantage, released by the authorities to be stored in Yorg Pasha's warehouse. This many rifles, he had told Vera, would ensure the survival of the commune. When they reached the open waters of the Black Sea, Vera allowed herself to breathe.

69

THE MINISTER OF JUSTICE, Nizam Pasha, received Kamil in his private suite at the ministry, which resembled a library. On every wall books and manuscripts climbed neatly to the ceiling. Kamil breathed in the familiar smell of leather and parchment that reminded him of his father, who also had surrounded himself with books. As a boy Kamil felt jealous of the books his father read and wished he would pay attention to him instead. But before long, Kamil had discovered an entirely new geography of feeling within those leather-bound volumes and found solace there. He felt little of that peace now, having been summoned by the minister of justice to discuss his upcoming trial for the murder of Sosi. He stood just inside the door, trying to marshal his thoughts.

The minister was dressed in an old-fashioned black wool robe and sat in an armchair beside a low table on which were piled papers and books, all of them clearly in use, the only sign of disorder in the office. He regarded Kamil steadily behind a curl of smoke from the chibouk pipe in his hand, his expression unreadable. Nizam Pasha gestured toward a chair facing him. "Sit, Kamil Pasha."

"Thank you, Minister." An invitation to sit in the presence of

Nizam Pasha was a good sign, Kamil decided, relaxing slightly and taking a seat. He kept his eyes respectfully lowered.

"So, how was Bekiraga Prison?"

"Not to be recommended, Your Excellency." A lingering cough still woke Kamil at night.

"You should know that there has been great outrage at your mistreatment. That includes myself. We cannot have men of our class subjected to such abuse. I can't imagine what possessed Vizier Köraslan to authorize it." He took a long pull at his pipe. "Yorg Pasha and some other powerful friends of your father, may he rest in peace, have opened a front to clear your name."

"I'm honored that they think me worthy of their attention," Kamil said, wondering who his defenders were and feeling an enormous sense of relief and gratitude.

"I'd like to know, between us, did you kill the girl, Sosi?"

"Of course not," Kamil's head jerked up in outrage. He saw a faint look of amusement pass over the minister's face.

"Then how did your watch get in the dead girl's hand?"

"I noticed my watch missing after I visited the Akrep commander, Vahid, the day before the girl was found dead."

The minister's pipe stopped halfway to his mouth. "How is Akrep relevant to this?"

Kamil wondered how much Nizam Pasha knew about what was going on in Akrep's basement behind the walls of Yildiz Palace. He thought about the room Rejep, the policeman, had described seeing, furnished with restraints, tools of torture, and a viewing gallery.

"I believe Vahid to be responsible for the murder."

"That's convenient. Did you give him your watch?"

"He collided with me at the door as I was leaving his office. He could have taken it from my pocket then."

"You're saying that the Akrep commander pickpocketed you?" The minister ventured a dry smile.

Kamil shrugged. "It's the only explanation."

"You understand that you're making a serious accusation. Do you have any evidence for it?"

Kamil took an envelope from his pocket and handed it to the minister. "This corner of a document was found in a room in the basement of Akrep headquarters," Kamil said. "We believe it's part of the passport of a Russian woman, Vera Arti, who we know was being held there."

Nizam Pasha approached the window and examined the torn piece of paper in the light. "How did you get this?"

"With the help of the police. We were looking for the woman." Kamil didn't explain who Vera Arti was or why they were searching for her. He saw that Nizam Pasha had noticed this omission.

"Did you find her?" Nizam Pasha asked, giving Kamil a long look.

"We believe she escaped before our arrival. However, the police examined the basement. One of the rooms appears to have been used for torture." Kamil described the viewing gallery. "That's where the police found this." He indicated the piece of paper in the minister's hand.

The minister said nothing, but Kamil saw his face tighten with anger and disgust. He held up the scrap of paper. "And what does this have to do with the girl, Sosi?"

Kamil had no answer. Yet he was certain that Sosi too had been held in Akrep's basement. He told Nizam Pasha about the cut wounds on the English nanny Bridget's arm made by a mysterious "policeman," whose description matched Vahid's exactly. "The cuts on the nanny's arm were similar to those found on the dead girl's body."

"You're usually more thorough than this, Magistrate. Your evidence is as insubstantial as moonbeams. None of it implicates Vahid directly or gets you off the hook."

Justice, Kamil realized with a sense of despair, depended not on big philosophical questions but on trivial details. He remembered Omar's failed attempt to preserve a footprint in the church garden. "That's all I have, Your Excellency," he answered, barely hiding his exasperation. "However, the evidence against me is just as slim. A watch, but no motive or evidence that I ever set eyes on the girl. So let there be a trial," he added defiantly.

The uneasy silence in the room stretched on. Kamil, seething, kept his eyes lowered. A servant brought a piece of live charcoal in a pair of tongs and placed it in the bowl of the minister's chibouk. After a few exploratory puffs, Nizam Pasha said, "If there is a trial, it won't be for a few months yet."

Kamil looked surprised.

"Sultan Abdulhamid is sending you on an assignment to the east. In addition to investigating this socialist settlement, he wants you to find out what happened to the weapons from the confiscated shipment."

Kamil was taken aback. "I thought the shipment was being kept under guard."

"The British wanted their ship back, so the weapons were moved to a warehouse, coincidentally owned by your friend Yorg Pasha, and then they disappeared."

At first, Kamil feared that Yorg Pasha had spirited them away himself, but as he heard the story of the men disguised as Ottoman soldiers who had brazenly stolen the guns, he chided himself for thinking badly of the man who was organizing his defense.

"I think it can be assumed," Nizam Pasha concluded, "that the guns are headed east toward this settlement that you and Yorg Pasha seem to believe is so innocuous. If they fall into the hands of the Armenians in that province, Allah only knows what will happen. Sultan Abdulhamid believes they would turn the guns against us and join the Russians." The minister laid down his pipe and walked over to one of the bookshelves. He drew his hand across the leather-bound spines, then turned back to Kamil. "Whatever the case, the wishes of our padishah, the Shadow of God on Earth, always take precedence. He is sending you east, and you can stand trial when you return. By that time, perhaps you'll have some evidence, instead of conjectures. And, let us hope, the missing guns and gold."

70

VERA STUMBLED ON DECK when Apollo told her they were approaching Trabzon. Her legs were weak from inactivity, but she felt elated. She had spent much of the four-day voyage in her cabin, out of the rain and wind, reading books in French, which Apollo had miraculously procured for her. He and the other men slept in hammocks in a common room. These comrades, Armenians from all walks of life in Istanbul, now crowded the deck. The ship had been "borrowed" by its captain and crew and would return to Istanbul immediately. That would leave only ten men and Vera. They would have to rely on local sympathizers to move the guns.

The men claimed to be socialists, but Vera by now understood that they did not understand socialism as she did, as a universal ideal of justice. This, she had come to realize, was an Armenian movement, and it was her Armenian heritage, not her ideas, that caused them to accept her. The men had obsessively planned the trek into the mountains, going over every possible scenario and danger. They had quarreled over each kurush of expenditure, since their means were limited by the money Father Zadian had collected.

"There's Trabzon," Yedo announced, pointing toward a cluster of red-roofed houses at the base of a steeply ascending forested slope patched with snow. Yedo, who had played the role of Apollo's lieutenant, was from Trabzon, and his face seemed chiseled in replica of some ancient Roman hero.

Vera gazed over the approaching rooftops at the ever-expanding cliffs and thought about Gabriel alone in this wilderness. She wondered how he was doing, a kindly concern, without the commotion she had expected in her heart now that she was so close. Apollo planned to send a messenger to tell Gabriel that they were coming. She felt a shiver of apprehension. How would Gabriel receive her?

A crowd of curious townspeople waited onshore, watching the small steamboat dock. Apollo had taken down the Ottoman navy flag, and their fake uniforms were hidden inside one of the barrels. Yedo peered into the distance, looking for his cousins, who had been sent a telegram asking them to meet the ship. It was a busy port, so before long the attraction of a new, unidentified ship wore off, and the crowd dispersed.

Vera watched from deck as Yedo approached a group of youths squatting against a warehouse wall. They jumped up and surrounded him, gesturing eagerly. As Yedo spoke, the men cast occasional sharp glances at the ship. Several of them left and returned with mule-drawn carts. Finally, the hold was opened and the barrels rolled down the gangplank and loaded onto the carts. "Cod," she read in English on the side of one barrel. The lids, she noticed, had been daubed with a crude symbol that might be a Henchak ax. That should be painted over, she thought, but probably no one here in the eastern mountains knew what it signified.

71

THE WEEKS BETWEEN KAMIL'S release from prison and his upcoming voyage to the east passed over him like the eye of a storm. It was early February, and the snow in Istanbul had begun to melt, coursing down the hillsides in brooks and waterfalls, overwhelming drains, and flooding low-lying basements. The crimson smears of geraniums in window pots burned through the morning mist.

Elif had set up her easel in Kamil's winter garden amid his orchids and was painting a fragrant, early-flowering *Pleione praecox*. The frilly pink-skirted flowers, she told Kamil, reminded her of ballet dancers. Since Huseyin's return, Elif came nearly every morning to Kamil's villa. Over breakfast, she shared news of Huseyin's improvement, then took out her box of watercolors as Kamil left for the courthouse in Beyoglu.

To his surprise, Kamil found that he didn't mind the loss of privacy in his winter garden, which he had thought of as his refuge. He had also overcome his anxiety that his orchids might be damaged. Elif always remembered to shut the door so that the temperature and humidity stayed constant. She drifted through his life light as a feather, and he found himself disappointed and out of sorts on the mornings when she did not appear.

He and Omar planned to embark on February 18, arriving in Trabzon just as the snow began to clear, but before the mountain roads were mired in mud caused by meltwater. Yakup was preparing their clothing and supplies, and Omar was seeing to the Ottoman navy steamer and the military guard the sultan had sent along with them. The police chief had insisted on accompanying them. He seemed convinced that Vahid's plotting extended to the east and that he might discover something there to undermine the Akrep commander. Kamil tried not to think about the murder trial he would face upon his return.

It was a Friday morning, a day of rest when the devout went to worship. Kamil stayed home to catch up on his work, read, and tend his orchids.

Elif lounged on the sofa in the sitting room, chatting idly about the week's events. She wore a cerise brocade vest over a white linen shirt and trousers. She had discarded her shoes at the door and, as usual, refused slippers, her toes burrowing into the thick pile of a tribal carpet. Kamil flung the French doors open to the garden, where as yet nothing grew, but the evergreen vines climbing the wall and the sparkling light of the strait beyond flooded the room with promise of spring. He came to sit beside her. Yakup had left a tray of coffee and savories on the table.

"Feride has changed," Elif was saying. "She even stood up to Huseyin's sisters the other day. When Feride told them that he was still missing, they descended on her like demons, demanding to know what was being done and blaming her for driving him away." Elif grimaced. "One of them told me, 'Your clothing is an abomination.'" Elif mimicked the woman's high-pitched voice.

They laughed, Elif's crystal voice joining Kamil's baritone. A breeze wafted in from the garden, carrying the scent of loam. A white kitten leaned against the door, too cautious to enter.

Elif took a deep breath and laid her head against Kamil's shoulder. "It's almost spring."

IT HAPPENED gradually late that morning, like a flower opening, not a momentous, drumroll moment but a gradual fruition of desires. They had run hand in hand up the stairs to his bedroom and behind the closed door had faced each other, grinning like embarrassed children. Kamil swept Elif into his arms and deposited her on the bed. He quickly stripped off his shirt and trousers, then sat beside her in his undershirt. She threw her arms around his neck and pulled him to her with surprising strength. He kissed her throat and cheeks and ran his tongue across the expanse of delicate skin where the top buttons of her shirt had come undone. He lapped at the hollow of her throat and traced her shoulders with his fingertips. She lay still as a doll as he unbuttoned the rest and peeled off her vest and then the shirt. She had bound her chest in a linen cloth and she sat up obediently while he unwound it. When at last her small, firm breasts filled his hands, he felt a beat take hold of his body, a metronome of blood that drove him forward. He pulled off her trousers and felt a jolt of tenderness at the sight of her slight body. It seemed to him as delicate as an ivory carving, fragile as the finest porcelain. He laid his hand on her belly and saw her flinch.

He noticed then that she lay on her back with her eyes closed, arms stiff by her side and legs pressed together. He sat back, allowing his hand to rest on her hip, and said, "You are magnificent, Elif." He traced her forehead with the tip of his finger, then leaned over and kissed it. "I love you."

She opened her eyes and tried to smile, but said nothing.

Kamil considered for a moment, then lay down beside her and drew the quilt over their naked bodies. In the darkness, Elif's resistance melted and their hands flew feverishly over each other's bodies. Kamil disappeared beneath the covers, kissing and licking until he found the soft fur of her sex. His tongue reached into the cleft and slowly her thighs parted and her breathing became ragged. Kamil repositioned himself and thrust into Elif, gently at first, then, submerged in the beat of his blood, hard against her raw cries that could have been pleasure or rage.

Kamil came, the stream of hot liquid cooling against his thighs. The quilt had fallen from the bed. He shifted his weight so he wouldn't crush Elif, and that was when he saw the pink scar like a sunburst on the inside of her upper thigh. His eyes met hers. She had noticed his surprise. To his relief, she gave him a shy smile. Encouraged, he kissed her cheek, then moved his head to kiss the inside of her thigh. There was a matching scar on the other thigh. He kissed them both.

"A firebrand," she said, her voice thick with emotion. "I wasn't cooperative."

An uncomfortable image came to Kamil's mind of another man doing to Elif what he had just done, torches pressed to her thighs to open them. Overcome with rage, he kept his face averted from Elif because he was uncertain what was displayed there.

Elif turned away from him. He noticed that her shoulders were shaking.

"Elif?" He touched her shoulder, but she didn't turn. "What's the matter?"

She didn't answer. Kamil didn't understand what he had done to distress her. Not knowing what else to do, he stretched out behind her and folded his body to hers, his arm around her shoulder. They lay like that until Kamil fell asleep.

Dust motes sparkled in the fractured sunlight streaming through the lattice that covered the lower half of his bedroom windows. In the days of Kamil's grandparents, the delicate wooden lattices had allowed the family's women to look out without being seen. Now they filtered the light for a row of potted orchids on a table.

Kamil lay on his back, arms behind his head and watched, mesmerized. It was as if he had fallen through the sky and these dancing points of light constituted an entirely different universe. Even his skin felt different, straining with sensation as if its surface were inadequate to hold it all in. He could feel the delicate puffs of Elif's breath against his side. Glancing down at the top of her head nestled beside him, he settled his arm in a slow embrace, trying not to wake her. Their act of love had not, after all, been what he had imagined. He had lain with women, a French actress, a concubine, but never before with a woman who he imagined might become his wife. He hadn't proposed marriage again, not since she had rejected the idea the previous year. She had said then that she wasn't ready. Now he could understand her reluctance and wondered what else she had endured. The barbarity of her scars had shocked him. He realized his imagination for evil was entirely insufficient.

He leaned over, cupping her head in his hand, and kissed her cheek. Still, the highly disturbing image of Elif killing those men in Üsküdar gave him pause. It didn't fit at all with his image of the vulnerable woman he desired more than anything to protect. There was much he didn't understand about Elif, who remained as opaque as obsidian, despite her reflected radiance. But it didn't matter. She was part of his life.

72

GABRIEL LAID THEIR GIFTS of three dressed fox pelts, a rifle, and a box of ammunition that he had brought from Trabzon on the carpet before the landowner's feet. Levon, the richest and most powerful man in the area, sat cross-legged on a fine Persian carpet draped over a raised platform in the center of the room. His deeply seamed face was framed by a russet beard. He stared down at Gabriel and Victor.

They were in the receiving room of the landowner's house, where men met to discuss the valley's affairs. A dozen men from the area, wrapped in furs and leaning on cushions, arrayed themselves beside and behind Levon. Other men sat on a divan against the wall. Their expressions were not welcoming.

"We're here to farm," Gabriel was saying. "You'll find us good neighbors if you'll give us a chance to prove it." He and Victor had come to ask for Levon's patronage, which would protect the commune from the other villagers in the valley.

The men began to argue. Gabriel had spoken in Armenian, but the dialect of the mountains was so thick he had trouble understanding the discussion. He thought he heard one man insist that since many of the newcomers were Armenians, the local community was required by the rules of hospitality to help them through the winter.

When an elder began to speak, the others fell silent. "It doesn't matter," he said in a quavering voice. "We are in a vise with the Russians to our left and the Ottoman army to our right. By spring we could all be dead, trampled in the mud between giants. No tree will bear fruit once its roots are cut. It would make better sense to welcome the strangers than to drive them out or let them starve. Why waste our bullets on each other?" There was a murmur of agreement.

Women in brightly colored flowing dresses and white kerchiefs carried in platters of rice and grilled lamb. The men sat cross-legged in a circle around the food. The landlord asked Gabriel to sit to his right. Victor was given a place alongside the older man, who introduced himself as Levon's father.

Pointing out a choice morsel of meat to Gabriel, Levon asked, "How many guns do you have?"

"Not enough," Gabriel answered bitterly. He thought angrily about the thousand rifles in the custody of the Istanbul authorities, thanks to the perfidy of one of his supposed allies. He chewed the meat, tasting nothing.

They rode back to the monastery through deep snow, trailed by two struggling donkeys laden with Levon's gifts—sacks of cracked wheat, dried chickpeas, apples, and an entire roasted lamb.

No NEW CASES of illness had appeared among the comrades of New Concord commune. That night their bellies were full of Levon's lamb and their spirits high. Someone had unearthed a fiddle and accompanied Alicia as she sang an Irish love song. She had an expressive voice that reminded Gabriel of his sister singing hymns beside him in church. After their parents died in a fire that destroyed their house, Gabriel had brought his thirteen-year-old sister to a hut in the forest that he had built as a secret refuge and furnished with scavenged objects. There he had tried to keep her from harm. It was the memory he most cherished. In the chill autumn nights they had huddled together. Every morning his sister had swept out the hut with a pine branch, sending out billows of fragrance. He had been a boy still, only fifteen, with a belief in miracles and magic circles that kept children safe. But then, while he was hauling barrels on the docks to earn a few kopeks, his sister had slipped into town to visit a friend. Some men had followed her back into the woods. Alicia's love song burnished Gabriel's memories so that, for a while, they outshone his shame at failing to protect first his sister and now his wife.

The comrades sat around the fire, huddled in their quilts and furs, eyes shining. There was the yeast of fellowship in the room tonight. If he could keep it alive, it would grow and nourish the commune. A young woman had baked a hazelnut cake with flour from the new supplies. She brought it out, a misshapen thing on a platter, but laced with honey and as sweet as the spirit in the room.

He allowed himself to think about Vera. She had longed to take part in his work, but he had kept her away—for her safety, he had told himself. He wondered at his motives now. Had he wanted to keep her innocent? Or had he simply not respected her because she came from a wealthy family?

As the fire died down and the hall was released to shadows, Gabriel saw Victor and Alicia disappear hand in hand into the darkness. A soft rustling like the brush of angels' wings rose in the room as its occupants settled into their straw nests. Gabriel continued to sit by the fire until late into the night, looking for Vera's eyes in the flames.

A loud pounding roused him, and he hastened out into a courtyard illuminated by starlight. Two comrades had also heard the noise and gathered by the gate. "Identify yourself," Gabriel called out.

"I come from Trabzon," the voice replied, "with a message from Apollo Grigorian."

73

FEBRUARY 18

"WISH US GOOD fortune, amja." Kamil kissed Yorg Pasha on both cheeks.

"Allah protect you, my son, and your companions."

Feride waited beside them, enveloped in a fashionable silk feradje cloak, a cloud of gauze covering her lower face. "I couldn't convince Elif to come. I'm sorry."

"No matter. Give her my love." Kamil kissed Feride's forehead. He was not as sanguine as his words. Elif had wanted to accompany him, but he had refused. He would be traveling through difficult territory with a group of soldiers and facing unknown dangers. "I need to go," she had said. That puzzling sentence had stayed with him. Did she feel such an intense need to be beside him? he wondered. Somehow he knew that wasn't what she had meant.

Behind them the steamer chuffed amid the voices of the crew and the snorts and whinnies of frightened horses being led belowdeck to be fastened by head-collars to the bulwarks. Kamil heard Omar's rumbling laugh. He had immediately made friends among the crew. Kamil suspected Omar was really coming along for the adventure and to protect him, as if the thirty Ottoman cavalry soldiers under Kamil's command were not enough. They had already boarded and were settled in their cramped quarters for the four-day voyage east along the shore of the Black Sea to Trabzon. Yakup was arranging Kamil's belongings in his private cabin. A cloudless sky promised fair weather. The blood-red Ottoman banner snapped in the breeze.

"May your way be open before you," Yorg Pasha murmured.

As Kamil turned and strode toward the ship, Feride spilled the traditional cup of water on the path behind the traveler. "As clear as water."

Later that night a weary Kamil unlatched the door to the commander's cabin that had been assigned him for the voyage. Omar had bedded down with the soldiers in the hold, and Yakup had been given a small cabin next to Kamil's. Kamil hung his lamp on a hook dangling from the ceiling and surveyed the room. The cabin was fairly large, decorated with gilded moldings, a Persian carpet on the floor. A broad ledge padded with quilts served as a bed. Yakup had put Kamil's things away in the cabinets built in beneath the bed and along one wall. There was a leather-covered table and four chairs. The iron cover to the porthole was screwed securely shut.

Suddenly a figure detached itself from the shadows. Kamil started and reached for his knife, then froze with shock. Elif stood before him, dressed in trousers and a man's jacket and greatcoat, holding a wide-brimmed hat in her hand.

He seized her and pulled her to one of the chairs.

"You're hurting me," she complained, rubbing her wrist.

"What the hell are you playing at?" Kamil struggled to keep himself under control. "This isn't a game. Why are you here?"

"Why not?" she responded coolly, looking directly at Kamil as if she were a man.

Her answer infuriated him. "I can give you a thousand reasons, but you know them all. We already discussed this." He paced up and down the cabin. "Allah protect us, what am I going to do now?" He stopped in front of her. "We will land at Shile and you will get off there and take a coach back to the city."

"No."

"I'm in command of this ship," he shouted. There was a knock at the door. Kamil stalked over and pulled it open.

Yakup stood in the doorway, a pistol in his hand, his eyes roaming past Kamil. When he saw Elif, his mouth slackened in surprise, but he said nothing. Eyes on Kamil's jacket, Yakup waited for instructions.

"Come in," Kamil said, his anger evident in his tone. "You know who this is." He indicated Elif. "She stowed aboard. I want her sent back to Istanbul."

"I'm not leaving," Elif repeated.

Yakup stood by the cabin door, looking uncomfortable.

Kamil nodded at him to go, then locked the cabin door and turned back to Elif. She sat with her chin out, one leg slung over the other like a man. Her small scarred hand on the table was held in a tight fist. She frowned at him and lowered her voice. "No one will know who I am. You can introduce me as your servant, Elias. Only Yakup will know."

"Omar is aboard too."

"So Yakup and Omar will know. The trip is four days. I'll stay in the cabin."

"And then? We're traveling into the mountains. Have you ever been in real mountains? Have you slept on the ground in the winter? You have no idea what's in store. You cannot come along."

"Why?" Elif rose and faced him, one hand on her hip, the other gesticulating. "Because I'm a woman? You think I have no balls? You think I can't put up with discomfort? You think I can't fire a gun or protect myself?" She reached under her greatcoat and pulled out a pistol, which she slammed onto the table. She added a small sword and a knife.

"Allah protect us," Kamil exclaimed, looking at Elif as if he had never seen her before.

Elif calmly pocketed the weapons and sat down again, crossing her legs. She took her hat from the table, dusted the brim, then returned it.

Kamil was alarmed at the change in the woman he saw before him. At the same time, he felt a stirring in his loins and realized to his consternation that he found this Elif just as attractive as the gentle woman he had sworn to protect. It made him angry.

They remained like this for a good minute, Kamil staring at Elif and Elif gazing nonchalantly into space.

"Fine. But you receive no special privileges. If you want to be a man, then be one." He turned on his heel and left, the iron cabin door clanging shut behind him.

FEBRUARY 24

SULTAN ABDULHAMID, dressed in a sable coat with broad lapels, waved at the crowd with both hands and then climbed into his carriage. With a deep bow an aide handed him his sword. Marshals, generals, officers, aides-de-camp, civilian officials, and foreigners, mounted and on foot, jostled and then settled into place at the side of the road.

Others lined up behind the carriage in the elaborate protocol that determined who had the honor of being a horse's length closer than the others to the Commander of the Faithful on his weekly ride to the mosque. Outside the gates, ordinary citizens of the empire gathered to witness their ruler and gape at the display of wealth and power that accompanied him, from the bejeweled and caparisoned horses to the brocade and gold-stitched robes of the courtiers. Vahid, whose duty it was to protect the sultan, rode just behind his carriage. His men were deployed in the crowd and at the mosque. Nothing could go wrong. Still, he was sweating profusely despite the cold.

When they reached the mosque, the sultan emerged from his carriage and began to climb the steps leading to the great gate. Vahid too dismounted and followed him as closely as decorum would allow. Suddenly a shot rang out. Vahid leaped and flung himself before the sultan, shielding him with his body. He looked anxiously for blood, but, as he expected, there was none. There was pandemonium as members of the court threw themselves down or began to run. Military officers formed a human shield around Vahid and their sultan. Soldiers in the sultan's entourage drew their weapons and plunged into the crowd, and hundreds more fanned out across Istanbul to hunt for the assailant and anyone who had assisted him.

LATER THAT afternoon, Vizier Köraslan bowed low before Sultan Abdulhamid and expressed his gratitude that Allah had spared the Great Lord's life. Dozens of officials arrayed by rank throughout the receiving hall in the sultan's private residence murmured their assent.

"He seems to have been a remarkably bad shot for an assassin, as they've found no bullet," the sultan noted, looking at his vizier with an unreadable expression. "I presume he's been arrested. Who is he?"

"An Armenian student at the imperial school. He confessed to belonging to the socialist Henchak organization. May I remind Your Highness that these are the same people our spies tell us are setting up a community in the Choruh Valley. We believe that this community is the kernel of an independent Armenian state and is being organized with the help of the Russians just across the border. If this movement isn't stopped, it will eat away the rest of our eastern provinces." Even as he recited these suppositions, Vizier Köraslan remembered Kamil's prediction that Vahid would stage an assassination attempt. He was certain the sultan remembered it as well. If the assassination wasn't real, the vizier wondered, how much of the rest of Akrep's information was reliable? He despised Vahid, but the man knew things that could destroy his family. Against his better judgment, he had allowed him command of Akrep. So far he appeared to have been successful, and now it seemed he had saved the sultan's life. Vizier Köraslan decided to rely on Vahid one more time.

"So the assassin wasn't working alone?"

"No, Your Highness. Akrep has launched an investigation into his network in the city. They will all be arrested. This organization will be eradicated."

"I'm unclear about what socialism has to do with this. It seems far-fetched to me that the Russians would support a socialist project when the socialists are trying to undermine the czar. Socialism is an international movement, not a Russian one. Or an Armenian one. I would like to speak with the prisoner myself."

The vizier faltered a moment before answering, "That won't be possible, Your Highness. He was killed trying to escape."

Sultan Abdulhamid was silent. His absolute stillness cast a pall over Vizier Köraslan.

Finally the sultan spoke. "Who arrested the prisoner and interrogated him?"

"Officers from Akrep, Your Highness."

"Vahid, you mean?"

"Yes, Your Majesty."

Sultan Abdulhamid's sharp black eyes rested thoughtfully on Vizier Köraslan, and he was silent for so long that sweat broke out on the vizier's forehead.

Finally the sultan spoke again. "You assure me that this is all true?"

The vizier's hesitation was not lost on the sultan. "Yes, Your Majesty."

"In that case, send the soldiers."

74

POLLO SHOUTED AT THE convoy to stop. The traces had snapped on one of the pack animals, and the saddlebags and supplies hung from its belly. The horse bucked and kicked at the weight dangling beneath it and then slipped on the icy trail, sliding down the ravine on its side, trailing the baggage. "Damn it," Apollo shouted, pointing at the lead mule that, spooked by the horse, had begun to balk. "Keep the other animals calm."

Vera worked her horse up to the mule. Holding the tether, she stroked the animal until it quieted.

Apollo dismounted so he could squeeze by the carts on the narrow road, in places no more than five paces wide. "Where did you learn to handle animals like that?" he asked Vera.

"My father has a dacha where he goes to hunt and to tame steppe horses. He used to take me along." As she spoke about her father, she missed him with a searing intensity. He wouldn't recognize her, she thought, in her broad wool shalvar trousers and fox fur cape and hat.

Behind them stretched a row of ten carts, each with five barrels strapped on and pulled by a team of mules or oxen. Before them, jagged cliffs rose to the summit, wreathed in clouds. On one side of the road gaped the deep ravine down which the horse had slid. Although the animal was lost from view, Vera could hear its screams.

Their group was made up of the ten men who had accompanied them from Istanbul on the ship and eight local men, Yedo's cousins, all from the same clan. So far they had made good, if slow, progress. Snow blocked some sections of the road, and the men were forced to dig their way through. The animals had strained upward to the Zargana Pass, but now the road had narrowed so much that the carts could pass only with great difficulty. Sheets of ice extended where meltwater had collected and frozen. The animals skidded and, together with their carts, threatened to follow the horse into the ravine.

Apollo told them to wait while he scouted ahead. Yedo handed him the long wand they used to probe beneath the snow for fissures. Vera insisted on accompanying Apollo. "My father always said there should be two people on an expedition. If something happens, one can go for help."

"Well, see you don't get into any trouble then, Vreni," Apollo answered, and kicked his horse's flanks.

They worked their horses through the pass, testing the ground before them, and finally emerged onto a bluff that overlooked a protected valley of meadows amid fields of snow. "The road looks open from here on," Vera noted. "But how do we get the carts this far?"

"There must be a way," Apollo insisted. "This is the main road through the mountains. People bring carts through here all the time."

"Not in winter. Remember, they told us in Trabzon that we were crazy to head out now. This is what they meant."

"Let's go back and look again. We can't stay up here at night. We'll freeze to death."

"Is there any salt among the supplies?"

"Three sacks. I know what you're thinking, but it isn't enough to clear the whole way."

"We don't need to clear the entire road, just tracks for the animals and the cart wheels."

Apollo thought about this for a moment, then yelled, "You get a

medal, Vreni!" and spurred his horse back through the pass. Vera
followed, smiling.

It was a long and grueling business, judiciously spooning the salt
into narrow channels, waiting for it to burn into the ice, then moving
the animals quickly before it froze up again. Two mules slid down
the ravine, together with the cart they had been pulling and five barrels containing a hundred rifles. The driver had jumped off but had
broken a leg, and his moans as the cart on which he lay jolted over
the rough tracks followed the party like an ill omen. It was almost
dark before they reached the other side of the pass. Vera could see
lines of smoke rising from houses in the valley below. Then it began
to rain, making the road even more treacherous.

They lost two more carts before they reached the village, although
they managed to retrieve the weapons. These lay bound together
under a tarpaulin, threatening to slide out of the vehicle at every
incline. It was a miserable parade of mismatched men, the Istanbulis
contemptuous of the locals and vice versa. The two groups had almost
come to blows several times, but Yedo had mediated between them.
The villagers greeted the local men warmly, and soon the warmth of
a fire, meat, hot bread, and wine eased the tensions.

EACH DAY that brought them closer to New Concord increased Vera's
excitement and apprehension. She began to avoid Apollo, disappearing for hours into a silent cocoon, collecting herself, trying to imagine
herself as Gabriel's wife. She would see her husband soon, she told
herself, relishing the word "husband," then immediately seizing up
with fear that Gabriel would no longer find her attractive or would be
angry at the trouble she had caused him. There were no visible scars
from what had been done to her at Akrep headquarters. Perhaps, she
thought, she shouldn't tell Gabriel. Then everything would be as before.
But she didn't believe that for a moment. By the time they came within
sight of the monastery, Vera felt confused and eager in equal measure.

Ten days after they had set out from Trabzon, they arrived at New
Concord. The heavy iron gate swung open, and Gabriel and several

others ran out to meet them. Apollo dismounted, and he and Gabriel embraced and pounded each other's backs. Vera remained on her horse, the collar of her fox fur cape and hat hiding much of her face. She could see Gabriel scanning the ragged group. Apollo's messenger would have told him that she was coming.

Gabriel walked over and peered up at her. "Vera?" He had grown a beard, brown with reddish patches at the cheeks.

She listened to her heart, which thundered beneath the cape. Was it passion or fear? Why couldn't she tell the difference? she wondered. "It's me, Gabriel," she answered, and slid from her horse into his embrace.

She heard Apollo shouting at the men to get the carts inside and unloaded. The sky was bruised violet. She could feel the darkness descending from the mountains like a cold breath on her neck. Gabriel took her arm and led her through the gate into the courtyard. They left the clanking of harnesses and rustle of tarpaulin being pulled from the carts and entered the main hall of New Concord commune. A fire burned in the grate, and a blond woman with freckles hurried over to greet her. She introduced herself as Alicia. When Vera turned back, Gabriel had gone without a word.

Alicia brought Vera a bowl of cabbage stew and sat beside her while she ate, telling her about the commune and occasionally laying her hand on Vera's arm. Vera wondered if the woman had sensed the pain that had shot through her when she saw that Gabriel had gone. Vera didn't like being the object of Alicia's pity but found the weight of the woman's hand comforting.

BY THE time Gabriel returned some hours later, Vera had recovered herself. Of course he had to help unload the carts and unharness the animals. Why had she thought he would immediately drop everything just to be with her? He always put duty first. She knew that about him, and she had married him. It was something she admired, she reminded herself. Her father, a general, also was often absent from home.

Gabriel came to sit beside her on the quilt Alicia had given her. He leaned back against the wall and closed his eyes for a moment. His beard gleamed in the firelight. Then he put his arm around her, the weight of it heavy on her shoulders.

"I'm so glad you're safe," he told her, his voice rough with emotion, his breath sour. She felt him looking at her and nodded without answering. She moved closer and began to shiver.

"I came back for you and you were gone," Gabriel said. "What happened?"

"They arrested me."

"The secret police?"

Vera nodded again.

"Where did they take you? Are you all right?"

Vera meant to say yes. "No." She forced the word out. "No, I'm not." She felt Gabriel tense, but he didn't ask. Instead he pulled her head onto his shoulder.

"I'm sorry, Vera. The police were after me. I had to leave Istanbul. But Yorg Pasha swore he would get you out, and he did. I wouldn't have gone if I hadn't thought he would do that."

"Who is Yorg Pasha?" Vera asked, lifting her head and meeting Gabriel's tired eyes.

Gabriel looked surprised. "How did you get out then?"

"I ran away."

Gabriel laughed, showing yellowed teeth. "Good for you. You didn't need me at all." Vera winced. He had aged since she last saw him, even though that was only two months ago. An eternity ago. She told him about the girl, Sosi, who had helped her escape and been killed.

"There were a lot of things I never expected I could bear." Her voice caught.

Gabriel glanced away, embarrassed. "Whatever happened doesn't matter to me. I'm glad you're safe." He held her close and pressed his cold lips against her cheek. "That's behind us now, my wife. You'll be happy at New Concord." He began to tell her his plans for the commune. His eyes shone, and Vera saw again the visionary with whom she had fallen in love. Perhaps it was possible, she thought, listening to the fervor in his voice.

75

T RABZON HARBOR WAS wreathed in early morning mist as the steamer approached, but Kamil could see a small crowd gathered on the pier. He heard the clash of drums and the nasal whine of a zurna. A band had been sent to welcome the distinguished representative of Sultan Abdulhamid.

The governor of Trabzon Province, together with all the notables of the town, the imam of the town mosque, and a long-bearded priest were gathered in the small plaza by the harbor. When Kamil stepped from the pier, they bowed deeply. The governor stepped forward and began to deliver a flowery speech of welcome. When he saw the soldiers and horses disembark under the standard of the sultan, his voice died away, but after a moment he picked up his speech where he had left it.

Kamil found this reaction remarkable, since it was usual for royal envoys to travel with a military guard. He noticed tension in people's faces and what he thought was fear.

The governor conducted Kamil to his house, which his family had vacated for the sultan's envoy from the capital. The staff was left in place, the governor explained, to see to the pasha's every need. He would personally supervise the billeting of the soldiers nearby.

Kamil thanked the man and directed Yakup to allocate rooms to Omar and Elif, whom, as she had suggested, Kamil introduced as his personal servant, Elias. Two days out of Istanbul, the steamer had encountered high winds and rocked back and forth like a baby in a swing. They had had to lay in at the Black Sea port of Zonguldak to avoid the worst of it, delaying them by two days. Elif had suffered a great deal from seasickness and, her face green, curled up under the quilts in Kamil's cabin through the entire voyage. Kamil and Yakup had taken turns tending to her. Kamil's anger had abated somewhat.

Omar knocked perfunctorily on the sitting room door and barged in, holding a piece of yellow paper. Kamil turned from the window, where he had been considering the height of the cliffs ringing the town.

"A telegram." He handed it to Kamil.

Kamil read it, his expression darkening. "It's from Yorg Pasha. There's been an attempt on the sultan's life by Henchak Armenians. The sultan was spared and is in good health, praise be to Allah."

"You think your friend Vahid set that up?"

"Of course. It was just the push the sultan needed to send his army east." Kamil waved the telegram. "It says here that a punitive expedition is being sent. Not just to the commune but to the region."

"Just coincidentally while the sultan's envoy, Kamil Pasha, is here," Omar said venomously. "Vahid's after you too."

"He's after much bigger prey. Vahid thinks he can get the sultan in his pocket by warning him that he's in danger, that the empire's in danger, and then miraculously saving them."

"He already plays Vizier Köraslan like a puppet." Omar danced his fingers around. "I wonder what he has on the old fellow." He told Kamil about the kidnapping and murder last year of a young man, a friend of the vizier's son. "There was never any evidence that he was kidnapped, but there are plenty of rumors that Köraslan's son killed him."

Kamil frowned. "I can't believe Vizier Köraslan would go along with a cover-up."

"Not even if the alternative was arresting his only son and losing his family's reputation?"

Kamil held up the telegram. "We have to warn the commune. Those people must leave immediately."

"Fine, we tell the socialists to pick up their tails and wag them out of here. But what about the local people?"

"I'll inform the governor, but I can't imagine the army would attack peaceful towns like Trabzon or Ispir." Kamil took out his map. He estimated that the town of Ispir was about seven days' travel, not far from the site of the commune but separated by mountainous terrain. "All right," he announced, putting the telegram aside. "We'll stop here for a day, then push on to Ispir."

Omar picked up the telegram and read it again. "Did you see the date?" he asked, his voice tense. He held it out to Kamil. "This arrived a week ago. If the sultan sent troops, they could be here by now."

Kamil looked at the date, then called out, "Yakup." When his servant appeared at the door, Kamil told him in an urgent voice, "We move out tomorrow at first light. Get everything ready. We'll need animals and supplies." He began to fold the map. "Omar, go tell the soldiers. We'll need a local guide."

"Damn. I could have used some decent food," Omar announced, patting his belly.

"You, the tough old soldier!" Kamil teased him. "I thought you could live on boiled boot leather. You've become too fond of your wife's cooking."

Omar didn't respond and stalked out, leaving Kamil wondering whether the police chief had taken offense.

LATER, OVER a meal of stewed lamb, Omar said between bites, "That explains all the goodwill and offers of free merchandise in the shops. The whole town has known about the contents of the telegram for a week. They're expecting the worst. They probably think we're the punitive expedition. People are practically throwing their valuables at me as I walk down the street."

Kamil was appalled. "I hope you didn't accept any of it."

"Of course not," Omar announced in an aggrieved voice, turning away. "What do you think I am?"

"If we convince Gabriel and his associates to leave, that should solve the problem. They're the ones Vahid has accused of starting a rebellion. It's absurd. They're socialists. Why would the Russians help the very people threatening the czar's government?"

"That's why Vahid is calling them Armenian rebels and not mentioning the socialist part to the sultan. Our padishah isn't dumb."

"That puts the rest of the Armenian population here in danger too."

"Didn't you say the sultan was sending Kurdish irregulars?" Elif's voice startled the men. They hadn't heard her enter the room. She sat down and picked up a spoon. "You can't put a boiled sweet in a child's mouth and then hope to take it out again. The only thing that will stop men like that is a direct order from Istanbul, and even then . . ." She let the sentence dangle. "Some men just can't let go."

Kamil and Omar stared at her.

76

ALMOST ALL THE COMMUNE gathered by the fire to listen to Apollo's lecture. Tonight he was discussing the philosophy of fate versus free will. Vera sat outside the circle, wrapped in her quilt, watching Apollo's profile and eloquent hands as he held his audience spellbound, as much with his charisma and melodious voice as by what he had to tell them. The lectures had begun informally. Whenever Apollo explained something, a group had gathered around him. Two weeks later, they had become regular events. Only Gabriel was absent, haunting the storerooms, chopping wood, like a spooked horse, too restless to think about anything other than survival. They had not made love since Vera's arrival. He came to her every night after she had fallen asleep, curved himself around her, and held her close. When she woke, he was already gone, but she felt the trace of warmth where he had pressed against her. They had had almost no time to talk, beyond exchanging the most necessary information. She had begun to want him again. Her blood coursed more freely as his warmth and his presence, faint though it was, became familiar.

There was a commotion at the door. The landlord, Levon, strode into the hall, followed by five tall, broad-backed men dressed in furs, their heads wrapped in red cloths.

Gabriel hurried over to welcome them. Vera watched from the shadows.

"This is my son, Taniel," Levon announced, indicating the young man beside him. Father and son resembled each other, both sporting enormous mustaches, Levon's yellow with age and nicotine, his son's brown and luxuriant. Neither smiled, their hard eyes roaming the room. Vera could see that they weren't impressed by what they saw.

Gabriel seated them near the fire on the best quilts. The commune had neither carpets nor proper cushions. Victor and Apollo joined them, and the men talked for a while in Armenian. To Vera, the visitors' tone seemed peremptory.

A platter of rice and grilled game was placed before the men on a low tray, but they didn't eat. This, Vera knew, was a bad sign.

Instead Levon said, "We have news from Trabzon. There was an attempt on Sultan Abdulhamid's life by Henchak Armenians. The sultan is going to attack us in revenge." He fixed Gabriel with an accusing stare. "Why are we being punished for something that happened on the other side of the empire?" Levon pushed the tray aside and stood. The platter of food clattered to the floor. His voice rose accusingly. "We know who these Henchaks are." He looked around the hall, where members of the commune were rising to their feet in alarm. "They're right here, playing innocent farmers. Do you think we're stupid shepherds, that we don't know what's going on in the world?"

He marched over to a barrel top that was being used as a tray and held it up. "This is Henchak," he said, pointing to the figure of an ax daubed in red on the wood. "You are Henchaks." He dropped the tray and regarded the stunned faces in the room. "You are all fools. You are dead fools."

"Please calm down," Gabriel said. "I don't know what you're talking about. I told you we are socialists. Some of us are Armenians, that's true, but not Henchaks. Look at us." He swept his hand about the hall. "We're from everywhere."

Taniel approached Gabriel, his hand on his knife. "You're lying."

Apollo conferred with Gabriel in rapid Russian.

"Why are you speaking Russian?" Taniel demanded.

Vera heard the click of rifles being cocked. Levon's men had taken up positions at the back of the room.

"Let's just leave them to be killed, Father," Taniel remarked over his shoulder. "Why bother with them?"

"Because your grandfather says we should bother," Levon snapped. "And because we need fighters."

"I don't know what you're talking about," Gabriel insisted, hands outstretched. Vera could feel his despair leaking into the room and willed him to be strong, instead of reasoning with these men as if they were in someone's living room in Geneva. "We have nothing to do with an assassination attempt. You must believe me."

Levon shrugged. "Whether you do or not, the end is the same. How many guns do you have?"

"Why?"

Levon spoke very slowly, emphasizing each word. "Because any hour now a contingent of Ottoman soldiers is going to ride into this valley and slaughter every one of you, and probably us. That's what sending Kurdish troops has always meant."

Vera felt the hairs on her arms rise. She had no way of knowing it was Vahid, but she could feel him approaching the valley.

"Tell him," Apollo commanded Gabriel in Russian.

"Nine hundred rifles and pistols."

Levon stared at him. "Were you planning an invasion?"

"To protect ourselves," Gabriel responded gruffly.

"Why didn't you tell us this before? You said you had only a few guns."

Gabriel indicated Apollo. "My friend brought them over the mountains two weeks ago."

Levon regarded Gabriel steadily. "I have no choice but to trust you, even though it sounds like lies. You'll see that once this storm is upon us, we will require one another. There's no other way. Ten years ago, war came to our villages. We recognize its face, and I feel its breath on my forehead again. Nine hundred guns are better than a hundred but are no guarantee of anything. There will be death." He glanced around the room at the thin men and women in their shabby clothes huddled in nests of straw and quilts. "Fools," he muttered. "A paradise of fools."

He motioned to his men to leave and told Gabriel, "We'll be back at dawn tomorrow. Have all the guns ready to load. And remember, when we use them, we protect you too. Guns piled in a storeroom protect no one." He turned again at the door and added, "It would be much better for us all if you left. Look at you. What are you doing here anyway?"

After Levon and his entourage had gone, the hall was still. Fear had choked off everyone's breath. That night, Vera was awake when Gabriel came and lay down behind her. She turned and placed her lips against his, and Gabriel crushed her in his arms.

THE REFUGEES began coming before dawn. Vera heard a pounding on the main gate. She and Gabriel woke the others and ran out into the courtyard. A dozen women and children crowded into the yard, some screaming and pulling their hair, others weeping. One woman held together the tatters of her dress with one hand and gripped the arm of her daughter with the other. The little girl clung to her mother's bare leg, which Vera saw was smeared with blood and coated in mud. The women had used head scarves to bind their wounds, the bright tatted edges strangely festive against limbs streaked with dirt and blood.

"They're from a village just up the valley," Victor exclaimed, holding up a lamp. "I recognize the headman's wife. They once asked me to come and look at a child who fell in the river." He approached an old woman supported by a teenage girl at each elbow.

"Siranoush Ana," Victor said. "What has happened?"

One of the girls at her side fixed Victor with a glare and spit at him. "This is your doing. You brought the evil eye to this valley. You brought the djinn, and now we'll all be dead."

"What nonsense are you spouting, girl?" Siranoush Ana panted, laboring to catch her breath. "They were Kurds." She sat down in the dirt suddenly as if her legs had given way. Her daughters squatted beside her. "I'll get you some water, Mama," one said, and gave Vera a pleading look.

Vera called over two women from the commune and asked them to pass out water. She brought Siranoush Ana a cup, then listened with growing horror while one of the daughters told them what had happened. Gabriel, Apollo, and the others stood nearby, their eyes straying to the barred gate.

"They broke our neighbor's door down," the girl said, her voice shaking. "Baba took his gun and went outside. We locked the door, but they broke it and dragged us out. They ripped off Mama's bracelets." She looked toward her mother, who sat on the ground, hands clamped together in her lap, staring straight ahead. "They did other things." The girl started to shake. Vera brought a blanket and draped it over her shoulders.

Vera found it hard to look at anyone. It was as if her own experience in the basement of Akrep had been exposed on her face for anyone to see. She kept her eyes on the tatted flowers edging the girl's head scarf.

"Baba must be hiding. If I'd had a gun," the girl wailed, "I could have fought them." Vera put her arm around the girl. We're all hiding, she thought miserably.

She saw the headman's wife grab Gabriel's leg as he passed and, without looking up, say in a matter-of-fact voice, "Our men are dead. They bludgeoned them in the square. I saw the dead. I know their names. You can rely on me as a witness."

The old woman's words made a powerful impression on Vera. She was so tired of feeling afraid. Drying her eyes, she rose to see what she could do for the other women.

AT DAYBREAK, a guard on the battlement reported the approach of Levon and his men. The gate was opened, and Levon and Taniel charged in on horseback, followed by a line of creaking carts pulled by horses. Levon jumped from his horse and strode toward Gabriel. "Well?" he said impatiently. "Where are they?"

"The women?"

"What women? Don't waste my time. I'm here for the guns."

"Something has happened," Gabriel told him. "Come with me." He led Levon, trailed by his son, into the hall where Victor, Alicia, and others were tending to the frightened women and children. When Levon saw Siranoush Ana, he let out a shout of dismay and fell to his knees beside her. "Why are you here? What has happened?"

"They're all dead," Siranoush Ana said quietly.

Levon grabbed the arm of one of her daughters. "Tell me."

When she finished her account, Levon bowed his head. "May God have mercy on us."

Taniel stood behind him. "Baba?" Vera could see he was fighting back tears.

"We'll take care of this," Levon promised the women in a voice raw with feeling. He went back into the courtyard and confronted Gabriel. "You see now what I meant. These Kurds aren't soldiers, they're bandits. They're like locusts destroying an entire village and then moving on to the next place." He squinted at the mountains. "If this is the first village they attacked, they must have come from the south. That means they'll come here next. We still have time to arm the rest of the valley."

Gabriel led him to a storeroom and pointed to the barrels. "Leave us a hundred and fifty and take the rest. There's also ammunition."

Vera had followed and now whispered something in Gabriel's ear. "Are you sure?" he asked her.

Vera could hear the reluctance in his voice and couldn't help wondering whether he was worried about her safety or annoyed at her interference. Her chin and the tip of her nose were scraped raw from his beard. "Please," she insisted, "it's important."

"My wife wants to come with you when you distribute the weapons to the villages," he told Levon. "She wants to teach the women how to use a firearm."

"That's ridiculous," Taniel snapped, stepping forward. "We can't have a woman riding with us. It'll slow us down. We don't have time."

Levon, however, appeared to think it over. "Did Siranoush Ana suggest this?" he asked Vera.

"Her daughter."

He nodded. "They're wise, those women. Very well. We leave as soon as these guns are loaded. It'll take several days to reach all the villages. Pray God we have time."

77

AMIL AND HIS SMALL army left Trabzon before dawn on the following day. A bearded, taciturn man in a fur coat named Sakat Ali had been recommended by the governor and hired as a guide to lead them through the mountains to Gabriel's commune at Karakaya. He rode a short-legged gray horse that appeared, like its owner, to be all scrawny muscle. The thirty Ottoman soldiers wore kalpak caps and cinched coats, crossed with ammunition belts and bristling with weapons beneath their wool cloaks. They looked young and eager. Kamil thought that many of them were probably on their first field assignment outside the capital. He felt oddly cheerful, leading brave men on a challenging mission. He wished it were summer, so he could witness the famous orchids of Choruh Valley.

Yakup remained behind in Trabzon, which had a telegraph, to await any further messages. Elif rode at the rear with Omar, in charge of the supplies. The streets of Trabzon were deserted as they passed through. The road wound back and forth along the cliff face, becoming steeper and narrower so that the horses had to go single file. They would be easy targets for an ambush, Kamil worried, and hoped the road would improve. Instead it burrowed ever deeper into the mountains until it was no more than a slim pass between staggering cliffs. A distant boom announced an avalanche. The governor had warned him about the Zargana Pass, and they were prepared to dig their way through snow blocking the road. To their surprise, they found the road open. Someone had come through recently. The ground had been churned up as if by the wheels of many heavy wagons.

"Well," Omar commented cheerfully, "I'm always happy when someone else does my work for me. Probably delivering barrels of wine. The customers couldn't wait until the road opened." He laughed. "Not too different from Istanbul."

Kamil pointed out a smashed carriage and broken barrels deep inside a ravine. Next to it was the dark mass of a dead horse. Sakat Ali too halted and peered down at the wreck.

"Wine barrels. Just as I predicted," Omar said smugly.

Kamil didn't see the body of a driver. "It must have slipped off the road. What are those sticks lying next to the barrels. Can you see?"

"No." Omar squinted. "It's too far down. Probably wheel spokes."

As they descended into the valley, they saw further evidence of a troubled journey, a dead mule and another smashed barrel. This time the barrel was closer, and Omar and Kamil clambered down to investigate. To their surprise, the inside of the barrel was empty and dry. "It says 'cod' in English," Kamil noted. "Who would import fish into this area?"

"Foreign fish? That makes no sense. People just open their mouths around here and fish jump in." Omar sniffed at the wood. "There were never fish in this."

Kamil held up part of the smashed lid and showed it to Omar. It was marked with the sign of an ax.

"Allah protect us. The missing guns."

"What would a small group of socialists want with a thousand guns?"

As they emerged from the gully, they saw Sakat Ali staring down at the wreck.

TOWARD NIGHTFALL, the road opened out into a valley, and they were able to proceed more easily. The air was milder here and in places where rock faces reflected the sun even felt warm. Small stone houses perched precariously on the hillsides amid barren orchards. They made camp in a sheltered area beside a meadow, and Kamil sent Sakat Ali and Omar to contact the residents.

After some time they returned. "No one's home," Omar reported to Kamil, a worried look on his face.

"What do you mean? There's smoke coming out of that chimney." Kamil pointed to a house in a high meadow.

"No one answers the door. Unless you want me to break it down?"

"Of course not." Kamil sat on a folding stool and tapped his riding crop against his boot.

Omar squatted beside him. "Do you think a pack of armed socialists passing through here just ahead of us could have had something to do with the locals' lack of hospitality?"

"Maybe. Or maybe they heard the news that Sultan Abdulhamid is sending troops. Everyone in Trabzon seems to know."

Omar hunched further into his ancient wool greatcoat. "Maybe they're already here."

An orderly had set up Kamil's tent and built a fire on the ground before it. A light drizzle chilled him, and he moved closer to the fire. He glanced at Elif, who had joined them, to see if she was fatigued by the ride or cold, and was relieved to see that she seemed fine and in oddly good spirits.

Kamil scanned the darkening hillside. No light showed on the green verges. He imagined the villagers lying in the dark, waiting for the army camped on their plain to ride on. He was angry at their stubbornness, but then wondered what he would do if he thought his family were in danger. Would he lie low, or would he join other men organizing a resistance? He imagined that these villagers were doing both.

The irregular Kurdish regiments the sultan had threatened to send to the region were tribal militias given the distinction of official rank by the state in order to keep them from rebelling against it. But they were paid little and lived off plunder. Would the Kurds break down the doors to this peaceful village? And why would the sultan countenance that? Was it possible that the padishah didn't know what was being done in his name? Kamil found that hard to believe. An image of Huseyin, pointing a wineglass and calling him naïve, came into his head. "One knife has to be sharp," he remembered his brother-in-law saying.

The soldiers rolled themselves up in their greatcoats near the fire. Wrapped in a blanket inside his tent, Kamil fell into an uneasy sleep, tormented by dreams in which someone cut Elif's throat, then Feride's, as they slept, and he tried to cry out to warn them but could make no sound.

They remounted before dawn, and it was with great foreboding that Kamil led his troop through the valley and back up into the mountains. Every village appeared deserted when they arrived. The weather was freezing at this altitude, so they slept in stables with the bawling, neglected livestock. They drew water from the village wells and slaughtered some of the animals to supplement their dwindling supplies, boiling the meat on abandoned hearths. Kamil left coins on the doorsteps of families whose animals they had taken, imagining the press of bodies on the other side of the door, hearts pounding in fear.

They traveled in the shadows of snowcapped peaks through a landscape of lakes and waterfalls, and crossed rivers seething with snow-fed rapids, the roar of which could be heard at a great distance. The forest was thick, with endless shades of green. The regular boom of avalanches kept them alert. Often they saw evidence of the group traveling before them, whether roads churned up by their wheels and hooves or splintered wagons and dead animals by the side of the road. They never saw any of the guns they knew the carts were carrying.

After ten days, hollow-eyed from fatigue, they neared Ispir, the closest town to Karakaya, where the commune was located. The continual change in temperature had made some of the men ill.

While the weather in low-lying areas had been wet and misty, high in the mountains they were buffeted by icy winds and struggled through snow that at times reached up to their horses' withers. The approach to Ispir was a steep switchback up a cliff face overlooking the Choruh River.

When they reached the plateau, the men and animals were spent. Elif, insulated in a fur coat and hat, had kept up without complaint. Kamil admired her calm endurance. He was looking forward to a warm room and a bath, and was about to send his orderly to see if the town had a hamam he could reserve for his men when he hesitated. What should he do about Elif? She was as tired as the rest, and he was sure she would like to bathe. They had not had a moment alone since they left Istanbul. On the ship Elif had suffered from seasickness, and during their one night in Trabzon they had spent the hours readying for their journey the following morning. Kamil had almost come to believe his intimacy with this severe-looking woman dressed in men's clothing had been a dream.

The mayor of Ispir and the town dignitaries had hurriedly collected in the central square to welcome Kamil. They looked less dismayed than the Trabzon dignitaries at the sight of thirty soldiers under the sultan's standard, he noted, perhaps because now his men looked so tired as to appear harmless. Whatever the case, Kamil was grateful when the mayor placed at his disposal a house that had a private hamam. He set up Omar and Elif in their own rooms, then had the servants throw wood into the stove that heated the baths. In the garden at the back of the house, Elif pointed out tracks of small animals etched in the snow. The sky was a brilliant blue, so hard it seemed it might crack.

After they had bathed, they shared a pot of soup made of dried yoghurt and mint and a dish of boiled cracked wheat with lamb. The blessed ordinariness of everything soothed Kamil's jangled nerves so that he could almost believe that they were out of danger. He could almost believe in Gabriel Arti's golden dream of paradise. When Omar retired, Kamil took a jar of wine and two cups into Elif's room.

78

ANIEL IGNORED VERA for the entire afternoon it took to ride to the northern end of the valley, leading a string of mules laden with rifles, pistols, and ammunition. Taniel's father, Levon, had taken half the guns to the south. He had ordered a reluctant Taniel to take Vera along and allow her to teach the village women how to use a firearm, but he hadn't ordered Taniel to talk to her. This hadn't bothered Vera or stopped her from talking, whether he answered or not. Astride her horse in woolen trousers, Marta's hand-knit sweater, and boots, wrapped in a fur coat and hat, a rifle and a bag of ammunition across her saddle, she felt almost lighthearted, absolutely certain that this was where she ought to be.

In the first village they came to, the bearded headman categorically refused to allow Vera to teach the village women to use guns.

"Just leave the guns here and we'll take care of it," he told Taniel, eyeing the boxes and bulging sacks strapped to the donkeys.

But to Vera's surprise, Taniel stood his ground. "My father, Levon, requires this of you," he said firmly.

"Our men will never agree to it," the headman insisted, glancing at the line of men squatting at a respectful distance. "It's out of my hands."

"Not if your wife is the first to volunteer," Vera told him, ignoring Taniel's irritated frown.

The clearing was so still that she could hear the wind soughing in the pine branches above her. Without another word, the headman walked away. Taniel threw her a disgusted look and went back to the mules. "We're leaving," he told his men. Seeing their incredulous faces, he snapped, "My father's wishes are law to me. It's not required that I agree."

Ashamed of having interfered and, in her ignorance of local culture, wrecked this village's chance to arm itself, Vera mounted and turned her horse back toward the forest. Thankful to Taniel for keeping his word, she vowed she would say nothing more.

The headman came rushing across the clearing, yelling for them to stop. A heavyset woman in tow was so thoroughly wrapped in a woolen shawl that Vera could barely see her eyes. The headman thrust the woman toward Vera and hurried over to Taniel.

Vera dismounted. "I want to teach you to use a gun to protect yourself," she told her. "Will you bring the other women?"

The woman didn't respond. In frustration, Vera wanted to pull the shawl away from her face but instead told her, "My name is Vera. Do you know Siranoush Ana?"

The woman nodded and let her shawl fall open, revealing a face leached of beauty by age and hardship but strong and resolute. Her eyes met Vera's.

"Does Siranoush Ana desire that we do this?"

When Vera nodded yes, the woman told her to wait. Before long, she returned with twenty other women, some as young as fifteen.

While the men were unloading, Vera took the women into a meadow and showed them how to clean, load, and reload a rifle and a pistol. The women were shy and hesitant at first, but Vera found them to be physically strong, hardened from carrying water and baskets of firewood on their backs up and down the steep hills. The recoil of a rifle hardly budged them, and once they decided to learn, they put their backs into it. Some of them turned out to be very good shots.

Taniel and his men slept in the headman's guest room and stable, and his wife took Vera into the women's quarters that night. They fed her and gave her the warmest quilt, but despite sharing a room with a dozen women and children, Vera felt lonely. She was dressed in dun-colored man's trousers, while these women wore brightly patterned gowns, torn and stained, but attractive nonetheless. One woman reached out and squeezed Vera's breast, making her hot with embarrassment. "Just like us," the woman called out approvingly.

The following day, Vera, Taniel, and his men moved on to another village. The mountains flung great columns of water from their flanks and breathed the valley full of mist. As they rode along the trail, Vera caught glimpses of flowers—magenta pinks, deep purple grape hyacinths, primulas, and others she couldn't name. Her mood lifted at the prospect of spring and her own feeling of accomplishment. At each village, they repeated their transaction—the women learned to shoot, and the villagers received rifles and ammunition. A messenger had come from Levon telling them that the Kurds hadn't attacked again, although their scouts had been seen near the monastery. They began to think that perhaps the danger was over. A week passed quickly. Taniel remained taciturn, but Vera began to think that he and his men respected her. He assigned one of his men to escort Vera back to New Concord. Before she was out of earshot, she thought she heard Taniel say, "Go with God."

79

KAMIL WAS RELIEVED when he came within sight of the ancient monastery where the New Concord commune had settled. Meltwater streamed from the cliffs and had turned the road into a quagmire through which Kamil and his men rode with difficulty, their horses slipping and stumbling into holes hidden beneath the mud. The monastery was a large structure, half in ruins, but protected by an intact stone wall with a heavy iron gate. As they approached, Kamil could see that the building had a new tiled roof. He dismounted before the gate just as it opened and a ragged group of men and women emerged, pointing rifles.

Behind him, he could hear his own men drawing arms.

"I'm looking for Gabriel Arti," Kamil announced.

A bearded man in a mud-napped fur coat stepped forward, unarmed. "I'm Gabriel Arti." He had lanky hair the color of sand and a beard. His right hand was bandaged, and Kamil thought he looked unwell. His face was white and slick with sweat. A young foreign woman, dressed in a hand-knit sweater and a man's shalvar, held on to his elbow as if helping him to stand.

"Kamil Pasha. Allow us to enter."

"Well, if you're knocking at the door and introducing yourself, I suppose you're not here to kill us," Gabriel responded, his sarcastic tone giving way to a deep, rattling cough. Looking confused and frightened, the commune members slowly lowered their guns.

"If you're referring to the troops sent by Sultan Abdulhamid, I've heard that report too, but I know nothing more about it. We're here because the sultan wishes to know what your community means to accomplish." As he said it, Kamil realized how ludicrous that sounded. The sultan is sending someone to understand you and someone to kill you. The prospect of having to explain made him feel exhausted. He hoped these misguided people would just agree to leave the country. He wished to be back in Istanbul.

Two men stepped forward, one disheveled with a round head and wearing a stained jacket, the other tall and distinguished, looking a bit like a mad scholar. Kamil caught himself, aware that his mind had been drifting. The immediate danger may have passed, but he was responsible for what followed.

"This is my wife, Vera," Gabriel was saying, "our surgeon, Victor Byman, Apollo Grigorian, our other comrades." He pointed to each in turn, finally sweeping his arm at the thirty or so people behind him. Then he seemed to tire and let Vera lead him back inside.

"Come in," she called out to Kamil in English, which seemed to be the language of the commune. He took a long look at Vera Arti, the woman he had sought in Istanbul and a torn corner of whose passport now rested on Nizam Pasha's desk. She had amber eyes in a childlike face, and her hair fell in a shower of auburn curls around her shoulders. He imagined her in the room in Akrep's basement and shuddered. He marveled at this young woman's courage and fortitude in escaping such a place. She might be a witness to the fate of the Armenian girl, Sosi, but that conversation would have to wait.

As he led his men into the courtyard, he noticed that the monastery walls had been patched with clay and bricks, and some of the windows plugged with bales of straw. The yard was neatly swept, and there was a well and a big stack of firewood. The inside of the monastery, though, was in a shocking state. It had almost no furnishings, no cushions or carpets, just straw pallets scattered around the room, as if a flock of storks had nested there. A group of women and children sat clustered in a far corner of the hall. A fire roared in the hearth, lending the hall some warmth. Yorg Pasha was right—the commune was in no shape to start a revolution.

Apollo led him to a stool by the fire. "The soldiers can bed down in the storage rooms off the main hall," he offered, but admitted that they didn't have enough to feed them.

Overhearing him, Omar picked up his weapon and left with several soldiers.

Gabriel sat near the fire, wrapped in his fur, coughing. His teeth chattered.

"What's wrong with him?" Kamil asked Victor, the surgeon, who had joined them.

"I think it's pneumonia. A week ago, some refugees from a village came to us." He indicated the group of women sitting together. "One of their children was ill and died. Gabriel held him and must have become infected."

"Refugees from what?"

Victor told him what had happened. "We thought your men were the soldiers that had attacked the village."

Kamil was appalled. "I had no idea the soldiers would attack women and children." Of course you did, Kamil scolded himself. You're not naïve. Huseyin, his colleagues, and presumably the sultan himself believed that what they called punitive expeditions acted as a deterrent to rebellion. Actually meeting the victims was a different matter.

"The women say they were Kurds. We thought they'd come here next, but it's been a week now and we haven't heard of any further attacks, although people have seen strangers in the area watching the roads. It's almost as if they're waiting for something."

A couple of hours later, Omar and the soldiers returned, each with a dressed deer slung over his shoulder. The women made stew in cauldrons over fires in the yard. A young woman with yellow hair oversaw the serving of the food and, after the meal, sang ballads that entranced the soldiers and all the others in the great hall, their faces shining in the firelight. Some of the village women began to cry. Kamil watched Gabriel, who lay with his head in Vera's lap, eyes closed, his breathing labored. This was the famous terrorist and bank robber, he thought with sardonic bemusement. Captured at last.

His eyes sought out Elif across the room. She seemed spellbound by the music. A smile played around her lips. If this was happiness, it was all the more precious for being fractured and fleeting.

Kamil could see flashes of the dream community that had entranced Yorg Pasha. Apollo had explained their plan to him, the need for more land, animals, and equipment so that the commune could become self-sustaining, the need for guns to defend themselves against a Russian attack. Gabriel admitted that when their weapons were confiscated, they needed to quickly acquire the money to replace them. But the explosion and the deaths at the bank had been the work of traitors, he insisted, nothing to do with the commune. Apollo had been the most eloquent defender of their vision. They wished only to prove, he said, that it was possible to create a society in which all members were equal.

It was a worthy experiment, Kamil thought, but carried out by unscrupulous means. He spoke to them about leaving. Gabriel seemed unwilling to consider it, but Kamil had the sense that the others knew the commune had no future now. It was urgent that the commune disband immediately. If he drew the stinger, perhaps the sultan's venom would dissipate. Tomorrow he would make arrangements to escort the commune members back to Trabzon, where ships would take them out of Ottoman territory. The village women could accompany them, if they wished, to the safety of Trabzon.

80

FERIDE HANDED HUSEYIN the day's newspaper. He had moved to a sitting position as the scabs that covered his body had begun to give way to scars. His face was marred on one side by a plane of puckered skin that extended from ear to nose. His eyebrows had not grown back. Feride thought he looked like a newborn and her heart ached for him. They spoke little, except what was necessary.

His lungs had healed enough that he could whisper, "Thank you."

Feride nodded in acknowledgment and leaned over to kiss his good cheek, then turned away before he could say more.

It was an open secret now among the household staff that Huseyin Pasha was back and recuperating from a horrible accident, so they had moved him into a room with a view of the garden. The repairs on the house were finished, and the guards, now dressed in Huseyin's livery, stood at attention beside windows and doors.

Doctor Moreno came once a week to look in on Huseyin. Afterward he sat with Feride in deep discussion over an accounts book. Feride's attention was absorbed by a new project she had conceived together with Doctor Moreno and Amadio Levy. She would provide the money to set up a foundation for the Eyüp hospital, including a children's wing. Feride's donation would seed the project and attract other donors.

Bored, Huseyin had begun to wander about the house, leaning on a cane and frightening the servants who hadn't yet seen his ruined face. Two guards always accompanied him on his rambles, increasing his irritation.

"I'm not an infant," he croaked to Doctor Moreno on his next visit. The doctor reminded him of the attempt on his life and Feride's. Huseyin quieted and nodded assent. Feride saw him look around for her, but she was standing near the door, where he couldn't see her. Because of the scar tissue, he could no longer flex his neck.

She felt a deep pity for her husband. She wanted more than anything to soothe the pain from his face, from his soul. She would even be willing to take some of the pain onto herself to spare him the fear she could see in his eyes when he tried to speak and could only whisper. But she found herself shackled by resentment and anger, for which she berated herself endlessly. In penance, she brought him tea, adjusted his cushions, and chatted idly about the daily adventures of their daughters, who, after their initial shock at seeing him disfigured, had immediately forgotten and treated him as they always had, a benign presence to be propitiated and taken advantage of.

81

The following day, Feride sent a message to the vintner, asking him to come by that afternoon at a time when
Huseyin usually napped. While she waited for the vint-
ner's arrival in Huseyin's receiving room, she ran her fingers curiously
along the spines of books on the shelves and peered into the morocco
leather folders of documents that covered his desk and the two side
tables. She understood nothing about her husband, she realized, not
what he did nor where his appetites lay, besides good wine and the
occasional jest with his family. Was that her fault?

A servant announced the vintner's arrival. Dressed in black, the
man was short and plump, much like a barrel of his own wines, with
red-rimmed eyes that looked as though he had been weeping. His
short-cropped hair was blond mixed with white and circled his head
like a halo. He stopped awkwardly just inside the door and looked
down at his stockinged feet, clearly confused at being received not
by the pasha but by his wife.

"My husband is traveling," Feride explained. A thin silk veil swept
across the bottom of her face but did little to hide the grim set of her
mouth. "I'd like to ask you about something."

The vintner looked surprised. "Madame, I sent this month's supply of our best wines. If there was something wrong with it, I humbly beg your forgiveness. I will immediately replace it."

"That's not it." Feride faltered. "The quality is fine." She didn't know how to proceed. It wouldn't do to ask the man outright if her husband was having an affair. "I have heard of Rhea," she said non-committally, allowing the statement to refer to a woman or a type of grape.

"Vah," the vintner exclaimed, falling to his knees. "You are so kind to remember my daughter." He buried his face in his hands. "It's been a terrible shock to our family. Our beautiful daughter." He looked up at Feride, his anguished face streaming with tears. "So beautiful. A kind and dutiful girl. She was going to be married."

"Married?"

"Huseyin Pasha arranged it. He has known her since she was a child when he used to visit the vineyards. He always had a space for her in his heart." He stood and wiped his face with the back of his hand. "You are both very kind," he mumbled.

Feride was stunned. It was worse than she had feared. Huseyin had planned to take a second wife. He must have been meeting Rhea the night he disappeared. They would have been in the restaurant together. Had she died in the fire? Seeing the grieving father, Feride didn't feel triumphant. She grieved with him for everything she had lost, her husband, her marriage. This would be true whether Huseyin was alive or dead.

"I should tell the pasha myself about the tragedy that has befallen us," the vintner said softly, "When will he return?"

"Not for some time. I'll let him know. What is it you wish me to tell him?"

"That if Rhea were alive, she would thank him a thousand times for his kindness and efforts on her behalf. That I and my family are eternally in your debt."

"What efforts?"

The vintner's eyes appraised the servants arrayed around the room. "May I approach, chere hanoum?"

Feride wondered if he thought she would be shamed by speaking of this second marriage. She signaled her maids to withdraw to a distance, leaving them both alone at one end of the room.

The vintner knelt before her, his eyes on the carpet. "Our daughter was engaged to a friend's son, a clever lad who would have taken over our business. More important, my daughter wanted him as her husband. But marriage was impossible as long as Rhea received unwanted attentions from a powerful man who also wished to marry her. I wouldn't have allowed it. He appears cruel, and I feared he would use her badly. He had begun to demand her presence in compromising circumstances, and I was afraid for her, so I approached Huseyin Pasha for advice. I didn't know where else to turn. Huseyin Pasha kindly offered to intercede so that our daughter could get married."

At this, Feride's breath caught, and she felt the heat rise to her face. She had been such a fool, she thought, with no concern for anything but her own pride.

"I'm sorry," she said. It came out in a hoarse whisper.

"She was to have met the pasha at my cousin's taverna that night to plan what to do. It was where she died, along with my cousin and his wife." He was unable to go on. His mouth hung slightly open and his eyes stared blindly at the wall behind Feride as if at a great distance he could see his daughter there. His eyes widened. "Is the pasha also . . .? I thought he had been delayed."

"He was badly injured but is recovering."

"Praise be to God, who rewards the just and leads the innocent to paradise."

Feride rose and softly uttered words of condolence. "May you be well. Our family is united with yours in sorrow. I'll let the pasha know of your visit."

82

THE NIGHT KAMIL ARRIVED, another group of women and children poured in through the monastery gate. These had come farther than the first group, through the forest, without coats and shoes. They were cut and bruised, freezing and in shock. Their men had been killed or escaped into the hills.

Everyone in the commune was mobilized to cook and pass out water, to tend to the wounded and comfort those who could be comforted. Some of the children sat listlessly, thumbs in their mouths or twisting their hair, while others swarmed together and squealed and bickered, as if nothing out of the ordinary had happened.

The refugees came all through the following morning. By noon there were at least a hundred people taking shelter at New Concord commune. The stench of excrement, mixed with blood and fear, spread a pall over the grounds.

Kamil climbed halfway up the stairs that led to the top of the wall that circled the property. He looked over the crowded yard, worried about what to do with all these people. The new refugees were a complication in his effort to disband the commune. They couldn't just abandon them, and he doubted they'd be able to make it through the mountains to Trabzon on foot.

Omar climbed up beside him and said, "From the women's description, I'd say the attackers are Kurdish irregulars.

"What we expected."

"They'll come here next. It's almost as if they were waiting for you. The refugees are their calling card."

"We have to protect these people."

Omar nodded and climbed back down. Kamil saw him speaking to Apollo, who then called for attention. In a voice that carried across the yard, Apollo made a statement in Armenian, which Kamil didn't understand. Omar told the villagers in Turkish that they should organize the cooking, cleaning, and managing the outhouses. Seated on an overturned trough, Siranoush Ana rapped her cane against the wall and, when she had everyone's attention, began to issue assignments. The women looked relieved to have something to do, to have been called out of themselves and the unbearable memories of their own arrival a week earlier. Yedo and his cousins began to dig latrines.

Meanwhile able-bodied members of the commune took rifles from the storage room and placed stockpiles of ammunition at strategic points. The monastery had been built for defense. One of its two towers remained, along with a sturdy crenellated wall that ringed the property.

Kamil called his thirty soldiers to order. "You are Ottoman soldiers," he reminded them. "You are representatives of the most civilized empire in the world, serving a sultan who cares for every peasant in his land as much as for every pasha. It is your duty to obey the orders given by your superiors, but it is also your duty to fight for civilization. The refugees that have arrived appear to have been driven here by the sultan's irregular troops. These troops were given orders to keep the peace, and some have exceeded those orders by terrorizing the population. But I don't want to hide from you that these troops were sent by our great padishah, just as you were. I see our mission as protecting the people in this compound. If these troops attack us, then our missions will conflict, and you must decide for yourself whether you are willing to remain here under my command. If we end up fighting them, that might be considered treason. As your commanding officer, I assure you that you are free to leave my command, and I will note it down as a transfer, not a desertion. You are free to go." Kamil pointed to the gate. Not a man moved. The soldiers remained at attention. "Have you understood me?" Kamil asked. "If we fight, we may be fighting the sultan's army."

"Yes, pasha," they responded briskly in unison. "As you will it."

Kamil allowed himself a smile at the loyalty of the men who had accompanied him through such hardships already. For many this would be their first battle. He prayed it wouldn't be their last. He hoped it wouldn't come to fighting. If he could speak with the other troop's commander, he was sure they could escape bloodshed. Perhaps the excesses were the work of rogue soldiers, not the central command.

Still, it was prudent to be prepared for the worst. He stationed some men along the protected walkway at the top of the wall and others by the gate. Since the ground-floor windows had been bricked up and others blocked with insulation, once the door was locked, those inside the monastery building would be relatively safe.

The afternoon passed as slowly as if it were mired in clay. More refugees arrived, including a dozen or so local men, out of ammunition or having lost their weapons. Kamil issued each man a firearm, grimly aware that the guns were from the stolen shipment, and posted him at a station. The refugees all told more or less the same story. A group of armed Kurdish tribesmen had swooped in unannounced, rounded up whatever men and boys over the age of ten they could find, and shot or felled them with an ax to the back of the head. They had broken down the doors to the homes and taken gold and other valuables and carried off some of the young women, then left. Some reported meeting a man in a black uniform who had asked them in broken Armenian whether any strangers had traveled by in recent weeks.

❧

KAMIL HEARD the thunder of hooves before he saw anything on the road. From the sound, he estimated at least a hundred men. As they came closer, Kamil saw that they filled the valley. He scanned the battlements to make sure his soldiers were in position. He had set men to guard the doors and windows of the monastery and some of the older boys to fetch ammunition.

"Two hundred, at least," Omar commented. He checked over his weapons, a rifle with extra bandoliers across his chest, a pistol and an ax tucked into his sash, and a large curved knife in a scabbard at his side. He grinned. "Well, I'm ready." The police chief's face was charged with anticipation.

Kamil too had a rifle in his hand, extra ammunition slung across his chest, and a pistol in its holster at his side. He bent over and checked that the knife in his boot slipped out easily. But he still hoped that the troop commander would approach the monastery first to parley or to allow them to surrender. All Kamil needed was one chance to identify himself as a representative of the sultan. Surely then they wouldn't attack. He had set the sultan's standard, a pole topped with the regimental insignia, high on the wall where the approaching troops could see it.

Apollo and Vera, both armed, climbed up beside Kamil and looked out over the battlements. He heard their sharp intake of breath. Elif emerged from the monastery, and Kamil noticed with a stab of apprehension that instead of a gun, she carried several knives, one tucked into her cummerbund, another in a scabbard at her side. When she turned to speak to someone, he saw the large curved knife in a scabbard on her back, where she could reach over her shoulder to draw it. Kamil's heart beat rapidly for a few moments, and then he calmed himself and focused his mind. He accepted a cup of water from Vera and, after drinking, let a few drops spill to the earth to inaugurate this final journey. "May our path be open," he whispered to whatever gods inhabited this wild place.

Just then he noticed a blur of motion at the gate. Sakat Ali was unlocking it and pushing it open. A moment later Elif descended upon him. Sakat Ali doubled over, clutching his right arm, and Elif and several soldiers pushed the gate shut again and locked it.

83

"WHAT?" HUSEYIN CROAKED. "Why haven't you told me this before?" He stood up, steadying himself on the arm of the chair. It was the time of day that he usually took a restorative sleep, and he felt tired. He wondered where Feride had gone. He hadn't seen her since she had brought him his tea that morning. Something was bothering her. Since his return, she had refused to look him in the face. He caught sight of himself in a gold-framed mirror on the wall and saw the pink scar that stretched across his cheek from his ear to the side of his nose. Did Feride find him ugly now? Too ugly to love? He felt suddenly incapable of standing and sat heavily on a chair.

Yorg Pasha was dismayed to see that he had overtaxed and upset Huseyin. Doctor Moreno had told them that although Huseyin was able to move about with a cane, his lungs were still not healed, and it wouldn't take much for the toxins in his lungs to infect other tissues. Huseyin was not to leave the house, Doctor Moreno had impressed upon his family, and he was not to be distressed.

"Kamil still has two weeks to report back before Sultan Abdulhamid sends troops to the valley," Yorg Pasha lied. He didn't tell

Huseyin about the reports Simon had been receiving that the entire region was preparing for an attack, or that after the recent attempt on his life the sultan had decided not to wait for Kamil's report. The troops were on their way to the east. Yorg Pasha had sent Kamil a telegram in Trabzon warning him of the impending attack, but Kamil had inexplicably continued on to New Concord. He hoped Huseyin would know a way to help but hadn't wanted to upset him by telling him the full extent of the danger Kamil was in.

"Get my coat," Huseyin told a servant, "and get the carriage ready. I'm going to my office." He rose from the chair and leaned on his cane.

"Really, Huseyin. There's no need." Yorg Pasha reached out a hand to stop him.

"You don't understand. I'm the sultan's minister for the east."

He looked at Huseyin in surprise. "That doesn't matter. You need to stay home and rest. Write a letter and I'll take it to the palace."

"Bah," Huseyin growled, and hobbled from the room.

Yorg Pasha hurried after him. Wrapped in furs, they stepped out onto the drive, where Vali waited with the carriage. It had rained overnight and the air was chilly. Huseyin stopped for a moment and swayed, then took a breath, which Yorg Pasha could see was painful for him. Vali helped the two men, one after the other, into the carriage, which he had padded with felt against drafts.

"Is this really necessary?" Huseyin rasped, indicating the ten Albanian mounted guards following the carriage. "I'm not afraid of Vahid."

"You should be," Yorg Pasha told him.

84

"THE ATTACK IS ALREADY under way?" Huseyin wheezed. "Why didn't you keep me up-to-date?"

His secretary stood before Huseyin's mahogany desk, head bowed and hands clasped before him. "We couldn't discover where you were, Your Excellency."

"All right. But now I'm here, so I expect to be kept fully informed."

"Naturally, Your Excellency."

"Arrange for us to see Sultan Abdulhamid." He included Yorg Pasha with a wave of his hand.

"When?"

"Now." Huseyin tried to shout and instead began to cough. He cringed until the pain subsided.

Yorg Pasha sat silently in an armchair at the side of the room while Huseyin was briefed by his staff. Gilded high-backed chairs with gold brocade cushions rested near several tables and crowded desks, presumably for Huseyin's secretaries. It was a well-appointed office, occupied by a man who kept on top of things. It was not what Yorg Pasha had expected of Huseyin, whom he had always considered a sharp-tongued bon vivant. He had heard good reports of him from the palace from time to time, but had never given much thought to Huseyin as a minister. It had always seemed so unlikely from the boy and then the man he thought he had known. He was pleased to have been proved wrong. He needed his competence now.

When the secretary had gone, Yorg Pasha said, "Allah protect him. Kamil is in the middle of it."

"The rumors of massacres. Do you think they're true?"

Yorg Pasha didn't respond. They both knew what the Kurdish irregulars were capable of.

SULTAN ABDULHAMID was holding court in the Great Mabeyn. He was seated on a throne between gilded pillars at one end of the high-ceilinged hall. Stained glass windows with flower-shaped panes threw bouquets of light against the walls. An enormous silk carpet covered the entire floor. A crowd of officials and petitioners waited at the far end of the hall, precisely positioned by protocol according to rank. The sultan's first secretary led Yorg Pasha and Huseyin Pasha slowly to the front of the hall, two scribes hovering at their elbows.

When the sultan saw them approach, he motioned to his vizier and stood. Those waiting fell to their knees and pressed their foreheads to the carpet. Huseyin remained standing, leaning forward as far as his scars would allow. Yorg Pasha simply bowed his head respectfully before the young man standing before the throne, whom he had known since he was a boy. If he knelt, Yorg Pasha thought, even two able scribes wouldn't be able to get him to his feet again.

Accompanied by a phalanx of officials, Sultan Abdulhamid proceeded into a side room. It was equally opulent but had the advantage of privacy, if one overlooked two dozen officials and the servants whose duty it was to serve him. Vizier Köraslan waited nearby.

Sultan Abdulhamid sat in a simple high-backed chair, one Yorg Pasha knew the sultan had made himself. He had shown it to the pasha with pride on a previous visit.

"Welcome, Yorg Pasha," the sultan said. "Please be comfortable. We are old friends." He indicated two armchairs.

"Thank you for your kindness, Glorious Majesty." With the assistance of the scribe, he settled himself gratefully into the chair. Huseyin sat down beside him. Yorg Pasha could hear his raspy breathing and began to worry that this outing would rekindle his illness. The poor child Feride might well lose her brother. He didn't want her to be a widow as well.

"Huseyin Pasha, you have been missed," the sultan said. "I've heard you've been ill. I hope your health has improved." The sultan showed no reaction to Huseyin's scarred face.

"I'm honored to have had some small space in your thoughts, Your Highness."

A servant handed each man a tiny porcelain cup set in a gold slip encrusted with diamonds. As they sipped their coffee, they made obligatory small talk. Finally, when the cups were taken away, there was a brief silence as the sultan waited for them to state the reason for their visit.

"Huseyin Pasha's illness makes it painful for him to speak," Yorg Pasha began. "With your permission, I would like to present his request for him. It is also my request."

The sultan nodded assent.

"We understand that Your Highness has ordered an attack on the Choruh Valley." The sultan didn't respond, so Yorg Pasha continued. "Your Highness also sent a special investigator to the valley, Kamil Pasha. He's there now. He was under the impression that no attack would take place until the end of March. We are concerned about his safety."

The sultan turned to Huseyin. "I don't need to justify my decisions to you, but I understand your concern about your brother-in-law. It was unavoidable, and I extend my sincerest wishes for his continued good health. What is your request?" he asked Yorg Pasha.

"We respectfully petition Your Highness to call off the attack until Kamil Pasha returns with his report."

"You told me you had warned Kamil Pasha about the early decision," the sultan said to Vizier Köraslan.

The vizier narrowed his eyes. "I sent a message, Your Highness. Perhaps it never reached him."

Yorg Pasha knew he was lying. Simon's sources would have remarked on such a telegram.

The sultan looked at his vizier's face a moment longer than necessary. Had Sultan Abdulhamid understood that his vizier was playing a double game? Yorg Pasha wondered. To know about this distrust between the sultan and his vizier was an advantage that he might be able to use.

The sultan turned back to his guests. "You are aware that members of this Armenian Henchak group tried to kill me? Is this not the same group that set up an infidel settlement in the valley?"

"We don't believe they're revolutionaries, Your Highness. They're a naïve group of socialists trying to set up a utopian community."

The sultan interrupted him. "Even if this group had nothing to do with the attempt on my life—of which you have yet to convince me—what is to stop them from trying to annex the valley to their cause? Artvin was Ottoman territory until ten years ago, when we were forced to cede it to the Russians after my predecessor's disastrous war. I will not let the Russians take one more blade of grass or a single stone. And I certainly won't let the Armenians get it in their heads that they can form their own state there." His voice rose by a notch. "It is Ottoman land, and it will remain that way. Tell me, if these so-called socialists wanted a utopia, why did they go all the way out there to the mountains on the Russian border to start their settlement? Why not set up near Smyrna or Bursa? The weather is much more suitable."

"I understand that the Choruh Valley has certain advantages. It's fertile and relatively unsettled, unlike the areas you mention. The settlers hoped to be welcomed there, as it is heavily Armenian and some of the settlers are of Armenian heritage. But they're first and foremost internationalists, not nationalists. This socialism is a crackpot idea of youth, Your Highness. A candle burns only as long as its fuel, and their only sustenance is ideas. How long can that last?"

Yorg Pasha wondered suddenly if they all were dead—Kamil, Gabriel, Vera, who Simon had learned had made her way to the commune, and the headstrong Elif, who had left Feride a note saying she was stowing aboard Kamil's ship—and whether he was to blame for encouraging them. Would it have been better to crush their dream in the palm of his hand, as he had had the power to do since Gabriel's ship of armaments had first docked in Istanbul?

Huseyin opened his mouth to speak but managed only a painful cough.

The sultan looked at him with concern and held a handkerchief up to his mouth. "Are you well, Huseyin Pasha? Nothing contagious, I hope."

"The pasha was injured in a fire," Yorg Pasha explained. "His lungs."

"I understand. May you be well." The sultan nodded politely at Huseyin.

Huseyin tried again. "There have been reports of massacres in the east."

There was a moment's tense pause while Huseyin put down his cane and pulled a newspaper from his jacket. He held it out to the sultan.

Vizier Köraslan took it from Huseyin and presented it to Sultan Abdulhamid. "What is this?" the sultan asked without looking at it.

"*The Times* of London," Huseyin said. "The headline is OTTOMANS SLAUGHTER ARMENIANS IN EAST.

The sultan lifted the paper and looked at the front page. They watched his face move from curiosity to rage as he read. Finally the sultan laid the newspaper in his lap and turned to his vizier. "You knew about this." His voice was low and deadly as a blade.

Vizier Köraslan blanched. "These are lies, Your Highness, fabricated by foreigners. I didn't want to distress you needlessly."

Yorg Pasha knew that the sultan was extremely sensitive to any foreign criticism.

"Who fed them these lies?" The sultan's voice rose. "How can they know about this so soon?"

"The Armenians in Istanbul are well connected abroad," the vizier said in a tone full of innuendo, seizing the opportunity to deflect blame. "All it takes is one telegram and a photographer, and the Europeans are on our backs."

"This attack on Christians, whether true or not, will give the

British and Russians the opening they're waiting for. They'll send troops into the heart of the empire on the pretext of protecting the minorities," Huseyin told the sultan. "There's still time to stop this before it spirals out of control." Huseyin's voice was so weakened from exertion that the sultan had to lean forward to hear him.

"Where was your advice earlier, Huseyin Pasha?" Sultan Abdul-hamid replied scornfully, although there was a tinge of compassion in his voice for his unfortunate adviser. "It's too late now. The cow is out of the shed."

"We can still save the shed, Your Highness," Yorg Pasha broke in, bringing a humorless smile to the sultan's lips.

Sultan Abdulhamid rose from his seat and went over to the window, where he stared out at the bright day, the newspaper dangling from his hand behind his back. No one in the room moved or spoke.

When Sultan Abdulhamid turned around, his face was in shadow. "Call it off," he told his vizier. He threw the newspaper at him. It fluttered to the floor between them, and Vizier Köraslan crouched to retrieve it.

FERIDE RECEIVED the news that Huseyin had gone to the palace with trepidation about his health but also relief. It signaled the return of his self-confidence and an end to her pity. She could think about what she meant to do next in this marriage. She went to her dressing room and found the ruby and silver hairpin Huseyin had given her. She put on the red velvet gown she knew Huseyin liked, then had her maid arrange her hair and draped a light silk veil across it, held coquettishly in place by the ruby pin. She called for a glass of wine, then took a book Doctor Moreno had given her about hospital administration to her private chamber to wait for Huseyin's return.

85

THIRTY PROFESSIONAL SOLDIERS, thirty-seven comrades, and fifteen local men manned the battlements against a seemingly endless mass of mounted tribesmen forming and re-forming outside the walls. Kamil examined them through his field glasses. The Kurds rode tough, spindly-legged horses that seemed too small to carry the weight of the men astride them but were agile and fiery. Above the men's long mustaches, they wore turbans of tasseled cloth and fur hats. Bandoliers of ammunition crossed their chests, and their sashes bristled with daggers.

Suddenly the Kurds drew up and shouted among themselves, pointing at the regimental standard of Kamil's imperial troops atop the wall. Then they wheeled about and galloped some distance away to a clearing by the forest. Kamil adjusted his field glasses. The horses clustered around two mounted men arguing. One of them, a Kurd, gesticulated angrily. The other was hidden by the mass of riders. After a few minutes, to Kamil's bafflement, the Kurds turned and resumed their attack. Kamil kept his field glasses trained on the place where he had seen the argument occur, but by the time his line of vision cleared, the second man was no longer there. Before he could scour the countryside more closely, a bullet smacked into the stone beside him and he ducked for cover. They were under attack.

Kamil ordered the men and women on the monastery wall to fire only when the enemy was so close they could see their mustaches and not simply to spray the ground with bullets. Kamil sensed that the troops were playing with them. They would storm in like a wave on the shore, fire at the battlements, then retreat. He could hear them laughing and joking among themselves in their own language. Kamil could see the effect of their own efforts as a man here and there fell from his horse, but it was as ineffectual as shooting at a swarm of gnats.

A bullet grazed Apollo's shoulder, but he insisted on remaining at his post. Victor had set up a medical station in a corner of the court-yard near the well, but at the moment he too was on the walkway that circled the top of the wall, crouched behind a piece of masonry with his rifle pointed at the men circling on their horses just out of range.

Kamil pointed. "They're lighting torches."

"The walls are stone and the roof is tile, so we should be all right," Apollo told him, "although some of the windows are sealed with clay and straw."

Kamil shouted to the men to aim at anyone carrying a torch before the rider came into throwing range. The torches that made it over the wall were immediately doused with water.

Victor ran back and forth, his left arm, which had been wounded while hunting, held stiffly by his side, sweat streaming from his face, as one after another of the defenders fell. Apollo was hit again in the shoulder. After the wound was bound up, he returned to his post, his face crumpling with pain at each retort of his rifle.

Vera went to check on Gabriel. He was barely conscious. She took the cloth from the woman caring for him and wiped the sweat from his forehead. She trickled water between his cracked lips. "Gabriel," she whispered, "I'm here, but I have work to do." She kissed his mouth. "Don't worry. I'll be back." With tears in her eyes, she lowered his head back onto the quilt and took up her gun.

"I taught some of the women to use these," she complained to Siranoush Ana, thinking about all the idle weapons in the storage room, "but Apollo says they're not needed." Several hundred women and children were crowded into the central hall. "Maybe he's right. There are so many children."

"Why should we wait?" The old woman stamped her foot. "We have eyes and we have hands. What do breasts have to do with it? Others can watch the children." She summoned her daughters.

They assembled about forty able-bodied women. Vera demonstrated the basics of using a rifle and pistol, then grouped the inexperienced women around those she had trained in the villages. Men passing through the hall stopped in startled contemplation of a troop of armed women, but no one spoke against it.

Siranoush Ana held out her hand for a rifle. "My eyes are as sharp as a hawk's."

KAMIL TRIED to stay near Elif during the battle but lost sight of her in the pandemonium. The tribesmen had set up a ladder against the outer wall. One of the comrades was killed as he pushed it away, but it was immediately set back in place. A face with a large mustache under a red-checked turban appeared over the wall. That's when Kamil saw Elif again, as she swung her curved sword and neatly severed the Kurd's head.

Stunned, Kamil stared at her. She saw him and flushed, then ran at him with her sword. He steeled himself, then felt a movement behind him and swung around just as Elif's sword sliced into the arm of a man attacking him. Elif's eyes met Kamil's, and he shuddered at what he thought he had seen there. Bloodlust? Yet was hers any different from the faces of the men around him? He watched Omar gleefully kill one man after another, as if he were on holiday.

Other invaders were dashing down the stairs from the battlements now, their dun-colored cloaks billowing about them, rifles and daggers in hand. Their faces too had a look of satisfaction. Kamil wondered how they had scaled the wall, but the monastery was so old that they might well have clambered up some of the rubble surrounding it. He looked for someone who was commanding the invaders but saw only a maelstrom of jagged motion, glinting steel, and the startling crimson of fresh blood. Despite the frenetic activity, the air seemed caught up in silence, the shouts and screams of anguish background notes to a timeless hush.

Kamil took aim at a man running along the top of the wall toward Omar, an ax in his left hand, a knife in his right. His shot missed, but it alerted Omar, who spun around and ducked the ax. Grabbing his rifle by the barrel, he swung it at the man's head. In a corner of the courtyard, Victor was kneeling over a wounded man, bandaging his arm, while Alicia held a cup to the man's mouth. A Kurd appeared behind Victor, knife in hand. Kamil raised his rifle, aimed, and shot him. Victor jumped up and grabbed his rifle, placing himself in the path of three other men approaching, their eyes on Alicia.

To Kamil's surprise, just then the monastery door opened and a troop of armed women emerged, grim-faced, others hesitant. A few glanced back, panicked, at the sound of the key locking them out to protect those still inside. Then they opened fire on the Kurds. Those who were too close or too inexperienced used the rifles as clubs. They were cut down by the amused tribesmen, but not before inflicting damage of their own. The stairs and courtyard were slippery with blood and blocked by bodies of men and women, some still alive but too weak to move out of the way.

The diminutive Siranoush Ana and her daughter leaned their rifles against a piece of masonry, firing their weapons over and over, as the younger daughter reloaded for them. When the eldest daugher was cut down, the old woman turned her gun on the attacker. He took hold of the barrel to wrench the gun out of her hands, but found her hold firmer than he expected. In that instant, she pulled the trigger and his blood spattered over her. Her other daughter ripped the scarf from her head and laid it over her fallen sister's face, then wiped her mother's gun clean and reloaded it.

Omar was rolling some of the enemy's bodies over the side of the wall to clear a space for fighting. Kamil saw him jerk back and fall. He raced up the stairs. An axe protruded from Omar's upper thigh.

The police chief grinned at him and joked, "Those dogs can't aim."

Kamil used his knife to cut Omar's trousers away, then tore a long piece of linen from his own shirt, which he tightened around the top of Omar's leg.

"Ready?" he asked.

"What are you waiting for?"

When Kamil pulled the ax out of Omar's leg, the wound started to bleed heavily. Omar tried to get up, but his face turned white and he passed out, crashing to the ground. Kamil shouted down into the courtyard but couldn't get Victor's attention.

He pushed his shoulder under Omar's chest and grabbed his leg. The police chief was short but stout. Kamil staggered to his feet, with Omar balanced precariously over his shoulder. He made his way down the stairs, trying not to slip on the blood, some of which flowed from Omar's leg.

AMID THE desperate hand-to-hand fighting in the courtyard, Vera moved among the women, helping them load their weapons, comforting the wounded, and trying to pull them to the side so they weren't trampled. Guns had given way to knives and bludgeons. One woman ran at a tribesman with a stick from the latrine. She managed to shove it into his eye before he shot her down. Vera stopped to help a girl of no more than thirteen in a torn shalvar, whose face was swollen from bruises. Her gun had jammed, and she was pulling blindly at the trigger. Vera took it from her hands and laid it aside. She recognized the rage and pleading in the girl's eyes and handed over her own gun, showing her how to make sure it didn't jam again.

Vera turned to see Apollo and Kamil open the gate leading into the courtyard. She ran over, shouting a warning, wondering whether they had gone mad. Why were they letting the enemy in?

As Levon and his son, Taniel, galloped through the gate at the head of a small army of villagers, Vera bent over, dizzy with relief. The riders who were wounded clutched at their mounts so they wouldn't fall. Those who were able jumped from their horses into the fight, wielding axes and swords, unable to use their firearms at such close range. Before long, the remaining Kurdish tribesmen fled through the gate. When the firing stopped, Vera dared to hope they had driven off the Kurds.

Levon's men searched among those lying on the ground for members of their families. Levon embraced his wife and daughter, and Taniel reverently kissed his mother's hand. The gate closed onto cries and imprecations to God from the lips of men who had found their loved ones.

As soon as the monastery door was unlocked, Vera ran inside to see Gabriel. His eyelids fluttered. She leaned over and pressed her lips to his. His breath smelled of hyacinths. "Gabriel," she whispered. His lips moved, and she pressed her ear to his mouth. "I love you." Had she heard him say that? Or had it been her voice? His breath rattled. She could no longer see his chest move. "No. Don't go." She wrapped her arms around him and, pressing her face to his, rocked back and forth.

After a while, she realized that Apollo was kneeling beside her. He pushed her away gently and checked the pulse at Gabriel's neck. He laid his hand over the dead man's eyes and murmured a prayer. Vera had no prayer in her heart, just a scream that she could not release.

86

KAMIL TRIED TO ORGANIZE a united defense in case the tribesmen returned, but to his frustration the villagers answered only to Levon. Kamil wasn't surprised they were suspicious of him. After all, he was an envoy from the same sultan who had sent the Kurdish troops.

The women and the wounded were inside the monastery, while the men had organized a watch and were taking turns sleeping. Of Kamil's thirty men, sixteen were dead, three others severely wounded. Victor had sutured Omar's wound and told him to remain still so it wouldn't reopen, but the police chief fashioned a cane from a branch and used it to climb the stairs to the top of the wall. Levon's men spread out across the battlements. Kamil had been impressed by their ferocity during battle.

Kamil invited Levon to sit with him by a small fire in the courtyard and, to gain the man's trust, tried to explain why he was there, that he had been sent to discover whether the commune was the center of an armed rebellion or an experiment in communal living.

"Does it matter?" Levon responded, breaking a stick of firewood in his hands and feeding it bit by bit to the flames. "White dogs, black dogs, they're all the same. These people"—he spit out the word—"have brought disaster to our valley. If you represent the sultan as you claim, why don't you stop these bastards?" His voice was hostile.

"They ignored the regimental standard. Did you expect me to walk out there with a letter of invitation?"

"Talk to their commander."

"It was impossible to tell who was in command. Have you learned anything about their leader?" Kamil asked.

"He's a coward, stays at the back. But he wears a uniform."

"Describe it." Kamil was prepared for the answer.

"Black greatcoat, black uniform, imperial army issue. A kalpak with some kind of gold insignia on the front." Levon's eyes fastened onto Kamil's. "Maybe we should just kill him and blame it on you. Or kill you and blame it on him. Black dog, white dog." He chuckled, then got up and went back to his men.

THAT NIGHT the Kurds returned. One of the first casualties was Taniel, shot in the head as he looked out from behind the wall to take aim. Levon rushed over. He carried his son's body down the stairs and laid it on the ground beside the fountain. Kamil watched, sick with pity, as Levon scooped up a handful of water and let it flow across the young man's shattered forehead, unrolled his turban, and draped it across his son's face. He then returned to his post.

Kamil aimed his field glasses out into the night but saw only the occasional flash of a face as a torch was lit. As the night wore on, the Kurds shot many defenders on the wall but, hampered by darkness, proved unable to reenter the monastery. Omar had propped himself in a corner, his weight on his good leg, and shot one tribesman after another. Noting Omar's skill, Levon sent a young farmer over with a second rifle that he reloaded while Omar fired.

By the time this battle was over and the Kurds retreated in the early hours of the morning, Kamil had lost three more soldiers. Levon's daughter also lay dead. Stroking her hair, Vera told Kamil that she had been among the best shots. Their mother threw herself wailing across the bodies of her children, but Levon seemed preternaturally calm, speaking to his men and seeing to those who were wounded. Yet he shouted at Victor to hurry up—the first time Kamil had seen Levon lose control.

Kamil took the loss of his soldiers hard, but found an odd comfort in Omar's steady stream of curses as they prepared the bodies of the fresh-faced young men for burial at the back of the courtyard. Kamil added their identity documents to the twelve that were already neatly folded in a leather envelope he kept in an inside pocket of his coat against his heart.

The hall echoed with the sound of weeping. He looked for Elif and found her asleep in a dark corner of the monastery. The desire to lie down beside her was overpowering. Instead he let his hand rest on her shoulder. It came away sticky with blood. He lit a flare and in its light examined her. Although covered in blood, he saw no obvious wounds, and she seemed not to be in distress. He extinguished the light and kissed her cheek. "Sleep," he whispered. "I'll come back later." It had been enough just to see her. He saddled his horse and, opening the gate, slipped out.

The path was slick with mud, but the stars bright enough that he could follow the churned tracks left by the attackers' horses. He heard hoofbeats behind him and pulled up, gun drawn, until Omar's familiar bulk materialized beside him.

"Running away, Magistrate?" Omar asked.

"Levon saw a man in uniform giving orders. I'm going to find him."

"And do what. Make him apologize? It's too late."

"I have my own plans."

"I'm coming with you." As Omar spurred his horse forward, his face turned white and he almost slipped from the saddle.

"Go back, Omar," Kamil pleaded. "You can't ride with that leg. You'll just be in my way."

Omar sat hunched over, panting with pain. "You'll get in trouble."

"I'm only going to observe. I want to know what this commander plans to do next."

"We gave those bastards a good beating today," Omar commented.

"Yes, we did. Now go back." Kamil waited for Omar to turn his horse before riding into the darkness.

87

*V*ERA WAS HOLDING UP a small flare to guide Alicia as she examined the wound on Apollo's shoulder that had reopened. Omar had returned and sat beside them, tense and silent, his eyes on the gate. No one had lit torches, unsure of what attention the flames might attract. The courtyard was illuminated only by a brilliant cover of stars that flowed like an icy river across the sky.

"Look how bright the stars are," Vera said in order to distract Apollo from his pain and herself from the memory of Gabriel's death that accompanied her everywhere.

Apollo leaned his head back and gazed upward. "That's Hartacol, the Straw Thief's Way," he told her. "According to the legend, the god Vahagn stole some straw from the Assyrian king Barsham and brought it to Armenia to protect the people from a cold winter, just like this one. When he fled across the heavens, he spilled some of the straw along the way."

"So Vahagn stole the straw but managed to drop most of it along the way? What a useless deity!" Vera exclaimed, her voice bitter. She extinguished the flare now that Alicia had finished bandaging Apollo's shoulder, and they all sat back to gaze at the stars.

"In another legend," Apollo continued, "the straw was dropped by Saint Venus after she was stolen from Saint Peter. And an even earlier legend says that the stars are corn ears dropped by Isis in her flight from Typhon. It's an ancient name. The Arabs call it Darb al-Tabanin, the Path of the Chopped Straw Carriers, or Tarik al-Tibn, the Straw Road. The Persians call it Rah Kakeshan. And even in China, it's called the Yellow Road, from the color of the dropped straw."

"We call it the Milky Way, as if a cow had knocked over a pail," Alicia said. "To me, though, it looks like a field of diamonds. I don't think I've ever seen this many stars at once."

"All those clumsy gods and heroes, where are they now?" Vera complained.

"When we need their help," Apollo added softly, scraping up a handful of straw from the ground and scattering it in the air.

"Do you know all those languages, Apollo?" Alicia asked admiringly, getting up to help Victor tend to the other wounded.

"I'm a philosopher, my dear. We collect the cream clotted at the rim of every civilization. We don't need to see it milked and churned."

88

KAMIL FOLLOWED THE TRAIL of the Kurdish tribesmen to the nearby village of Karakaya, the scene of one of the massacres. He tied up his horse and walked through the forest to the edge of the village, his boots of special soft leather making no sound. He heard their voices and saw a fire in the village square. He edged his way through the forest until he had a better view. The men had opened a barrel of wine and were feasting on the carcass of an animal, part of which still hung in tatters from a spit over the fire. From the size of the pile of bones and trash, Kamil guessed they had camped in this village for days. Why hadn't they attacked the monastery sooner?

He waited for a while, changing position every so often to get a better view, and was about to give up and return to the monastery when he was rooted to the spot by a woman's high-pitched wail. It ended abruptly. The men around the fire laughed uneasily. The sound had come from one of the houses—the headman's house, to judge by its size. The door opened onto the square where the men were sitting. Kamil ran silently to the back of the house and crept up to a window. He lifted a corner of the hide that covered the opening and peered inside.

The room was brightly lit by a lamp. A naked girl of around fifteen was splayed out on the floor, her arms and the inside of her thighs sheathed in blood. A thatch of hair had fallen over her face. A man in a black uniform knelt hunched over her, knife in hand. Kamil couldn't see his face, but he knew. Vahid raised a fistful of the girl's hair and cut it off. She moaned and turned her head.

Vahid wrapped the hair in a piece of cloth and slipped it into his jacket pocket. Then he turned his attention back to the girl, as if wondering what to do next.

Kamil thought furiously. How could he save the girl with an army of Kurds at the doorstep? He drew his pistol and hoisted himself through the window. He landed on his feet, gun aimed at Vahid. The Akrep commander was still on his knees. His gun was pointed at the girl's temple.

"You are so predictable, Kamil Pasha." Vahid smiled. "Look." Vahid ran his free hand over the girl's breasts and then, to Kamil's outrage, plunged it between her legs. She bucked but seemed unable to move. Kamil wondered if she was drugged. As long as Vahid had his revolver pointed at the girl's head, he could do nothing.

"Would you like a turn?" Vahid grinned at him. "No?" He moved the gun from the girl's head but kept it trained on her body. "That's too bad." Vahid shoved the mouth of the revolver between the girl's legs. "Because no one will know whether you did or not."

Vahid twisted and aimed his revolver at Kamil just as Kamil fired.

Expecting the Kurds to rush through the door, Kamil leaped out the window and ran into the forest, keeping to the tufts of grass that he knew wouldn't take the impression of his boots. But he didn't go far. The pistol still smoked in his hand. He planned to return for the girl. And if the tribesmen were going to take retribution on the surrounding countryside for his rash act, he had to know and do what he could to stop them, or at least to warn people. Much to his surprise, the Kurds hadn't charged into the house after the shot had been fired. When Kamil looked back from the forest, they were still sitting around the fire. They thought Vahid had shot the girl, Kamil realized.

He wedged himself into a cleft of rock, close enough to see the men with his field glasses. One stood and shouted something at the others. An argument ensued, with some of the men gesticulating toward the mountains. Finally one of them knocked on the door of the headman's house. Hearing no response, he went in, then hurried back out and strode angrily to the edge of the square, staring out at the forest. The others crowded in and emerged, shaking their heads in disgust. Within minutes they had saddled up, strapped their wounded to their mounts and set off at a rapid pace along the lane in a direction that led away from the monastery. Still, Kamil couldn't be sure they wouldn't return once it was daylight. Perhaps they were simply going to a less blood-soaked village to spend the night.

89

THE DAY DAWNED without another attack, and the survivors peered carefully over the monastery battlements. A light mist blanketed the trampled field outside the gate, and they heard birdcalls and the sound of water running. Levon took Siranoush Ana aside and told her, "Ana, I bear dreadful news. When we passed through your village yesterday, we found your husband in the square with nine others. They'd been dead at least a week. We buried them."

"May you be able to bear it, Levon," she responded. "And what of your father?"

Levon grimaced and shook his head.

"I'm sorry about all your losses. Your son and daughter were enormously courageous. Each had the heart of a lion, like their father." They stood in taut silence for a moment. "I know you were a great friend of my husband," Siranoush Ana continued, her voice a calm murmur. "Before I left our village last week, I went to the square so that someone would bear witness to our men's deaths. I closed all of their eyes onto this world, so henceforth they will see only paradise." She laid her hand on Levon's arm. "You will see your children again in paradise."

When no further attack had occurred by late afternoon and the day had become unseasonably hot, the survivors decided to bury their dead and set some men to digging in the meadow behind the monastery. A quarrel broke out about whether to bury the enemy dead as well, but it was decided to move those that had died inside the monastery walls out to the side of the road, where the Kurds could retrieve them. A search was made for the guide, Sakat Ali, but neither he nor his body could be found.

Victor had barely slept since the attacks began. Inside the monastery hall, he loped stiffly from one wounded person to another, treating them with whatever was at hand. He had long since run out of supplies, so Alicia had set several women to work boiling strips of cloth and collecting lengths of twine, needles, and thread. Alicia helped him clean the wounds and, with the help of Omar and one of the soldiers, held the patients down while Victor sewed them up and, in two cases, amputated. There was no anesthetic and no alcohol. Victor cauterized the wounds with the flat of a sword that had been heated in the fireplace.

KAMIL HAD returned to the monastery shortly after dawn, a different man from the one who had ridden out hours earlier. Propped in the saddle before him, wrapped in a blanket, was the unconscious girl. Now I really am a murderer, he thought, feeling neither regret nor shame. Omar and Levon hurried to meet him, but he would tell them nothing except that he hoped the Kurds wouldn't return. What Kamil had seen in that room was etched into his eyes, and he refused to make it any more real by telling someone else about it—not even Elif.

He searched inside the monastery and scoured the courtyard for Elif, but no one had seen her. Numb with anxiety, he slammed through the gate and walked to the back of the monastery, where the meadow was cut by a raging stream fed by waterfalls hurtling from the cliffside. The sun was hot on his back and the meadow steamed. Whenever he stepped into the shade of a tree or boulder, the chill of winter returned.

He found Elif lying on her back beside the stream. Her eyes were open, and for a heart-stopping moment he thought she was dead. But she smiled up at him, and he found that he hungered for her as badly as he had ever wanted anything. Her face and hands and clothes were entirely covered in blood, as if she had bathed in it. The bare branches of a willow tree formed a yellow cage around them, letting in the sun. Kamil knelt beside her and, sliding his hand behind her head, leaned over and kissed her. He tasted iron, and his lips clung to hers through the stickiness of someone else's blood.

"Come on," he said, indicating the stream that sparkled yellow and green in the sun.

She grinned, her teeth white in her red face. "Are you mad? We'll freeze our hides off."

"I could use a new hide," Kamil answered, stripping off his clothes. He unbuttoned her shirt and slipped it over her head, then removed her trousers and her undergarments, remarkably white despite the mud and carnage. Hand in hand, they walked into the stream. It was fed by rapids upstream and swollen with snowmelt, deep enough for them to walk in up to the waist. The water buffeted them and pulled them off balance. Holding hands to steady themselves, they squatted and dipped their heads under the rushing torrent. Despite the sun on their backs, the water was freezing cold, so they didn't remain long.

By the time they got back to the willow, Elif was shaking. Kamil rubbed her body with his wool undershirt until her skin glowed. Then they pulled on their clothes, still dirty and stiff with blood. Their eyes met for the first time since Kamil had found her under the willow. He felt as though he were looking into a deep, clear pool. He had no more understanding of what kind of woman Elif was, but he felt somehow that they understood each other. He was no longer sure he understood what kind of man he was.

When they returned to the monastery, they found Levon raging over the bodies of his children. It was as if now that the danger was over, all of the powerful man's reserve had broken like a dam under a flood. Kamil wished he could tell Levon that his children had been avenged, but he knew that was a meaningless statement. The dead are not less dead when they are multiplied.

Levon saw Kamil. "Welcome, oh representative of the sultan. Take a look at what you have brought us." He threw out his hand to indicate the sea of wounded men and women lying on the flagstones of the hall.

Kamil walked toward Levon. "To all of you," he said loudly, "may you be well. I'm sorry about the loss of your families. I came here to investigate this community. Clearly I wasn't here to kill anyone. Or did you not notice that I was inside the walls, not out there with the Kurds?"

Levon aimed his rifle at Kamil. "One more dead body won't be noticed," he snarled.

The room froze. Kamil heard the click of a cane and looked down to see Siranoush Ana standing between him and the barrel of Levon's gun.

"We've all lost more than we can bear, Levon," she said in an even voice.

Levon slowly lowered his gun and nodded. "We want these people out of our valley." He flung his hand at the hall. "Right now," he bellowed.

"These are mostly your people," Kamil pointed out.

"I mean the socialists, the Henchaks, whatever they are," Levon answered wearily. "No, pasha, you're right. We all have to leave. The villages have been destroyed, all the food looted, and those devils might return at any time. There's nothing to go back to. And it is true that without this community's guns, we wouldn't have survived at all." He nodded to Apollo and Vera. "Thank you," he told them in Armenian. He hobbled from the room, shoulders bowed. Siranoush Ana watched him go, and Kamil saw tears in her eyes.

THEY SPENT a last night in the monastery. Kamil grabbed a quilt and stretched out on the floor. He was too exhausted to look for where Elif had bedded down. The sleep of the dead, he thought just before he fell into a profound slumber.

Sakat Ali crept through the monastery hall in the early hours.

The fire had died out. No one was on duty this night after the battle to feed the flames, as on other nights. The hall was pitch black and cold. The guide knelt beside Kamil and looked down at his dreaming face. The man was smiling in his sleep, Sakat Ali realized. Akrep was going to pay him handsomely for killing the pasha, but he would enjoy it too. No man should be happy amid the misery of his fellows. It showed that the pasha had no honor and deserved to die.

With his good arm, Sakat Ali drew a knife from his sash. "You thought you won, didn't you?" he whispered. He had followed Kamil out of the monastery and almost been discovered when that fool Omar arrived. But Sakat Ali was clever and remained undiscovered, even after the pasha had shot the Akrep commander without provocation.

Killing Kamil now would be nothing more than executing a treasonous murderer. That is, if Vahid had died.

90

THEY FINISHED BURYING their dead, including Yedo and five of his cousins. The body of Sakat Ali had been found that morning in the stable, his throat apparently cut by his own knife, still clutched in his hand.

Omar told Kamil that he had heard Sakat Ali approach him in the night. "I took him outside for a little talk before he said good night. As we suspected, he was an Akrep agent. He followed you to Karakaya and saw you shoot Vahid." Omar looked at Kamil appreciatively. "At first he thought Vahid was dead, but regrettably he wasn't. Looks like you blew off part of his right hand, though. Our spy fixed his boss up and hired someone to take him to Trabzon, then came back here to kill you. And that was his last assignment."

"Thank you." Kamil found the words inadequate for the immensity of saving his life.

"Vahid might die on the way, but I don't see it. The devil has a thousand lives."

A priest from among the refugees said a prayer for the dead. Vera placed a bouquet of meadow hyacinths on Gabriel's grave, one of a long row marked only with piles of stones. Then they focused on organizing the living.

Kamil set out at the head of the column of close to two hundred frightened and desperate men, women, and children who had no homes to return to. They passed the Kurdish corpses by the side of the road. Mothers hid their children's faces in their skirts.

Rapids from the early-spring melt had made the river unnavigable and cut off the road to Rize on the coast, closer to them than Trabzon. Levon and his men rode ahead of the train of refugees, checking the road and forest for ambushes and foraging for food and supplies to feed the mass of fleeing people who had once been their neighbors. Omar and the remaining soldiers brought up the rear, making sure no one was left behind. In this manner, they plodded through the mountains. Kamil sent one of his men ahead to alert the governor of Trabzon that they would need food and shelter when they arrived. He wondered whether Vahid had arrived alive or whether they would pass his carcass on the road.

The road followed the river until the flat land gave out and they were forced to climb the hills along narrow paths, passing through ravaged villages blazing with rare yellow rhododendrons. Their numbers swelled as they moved through the valley and survivors from isolated communities joined the refugees. Most of them either had relatives in Trabzon or wished to escape the province on one of the ships in the harbor.

The journey to Trabzon was long and miserable. Although the end of March, it was still winter in the mountains. Winds ripped through the gorges, and clouds settled so low that they drenched the skin. Days were warm as long as the sun shone, but then they were plagued by swarms of biting insects. At night the temperature plummeted, and people built small fires or dug themselves into the forest loam for warmth. Children whimpered in fear as wolves howled and jackals yipped on the hillsides. Levon's men occasionally brought sacks of clothing and boots that they distributed. Kamil assumed they had gathered them from abandoned villages along the way. There was no sign of the Kurds. Were they not willing to fight without Vahid?

When the refugees reached the town of Ispir, the mayor put them up in homes and stables, and the town's women baked bread almost continually. The mayor insisted on billeting Kamil with his own family.

Some of the refugees who had relatives in Ispir decided to stay, but after a few days it became clear that the town couldn't sustain its generosity toward the rest. The townspeople were running short of food, and tempers flared. Kamil ordered those who wished to go on to Trabzon to resume their march through the mountains.

Levon's men hunted wild boar, goat, and deer, which they roasted and then distributed among the refugees, along with bread and leather sacks of salted olives, cheese, dried fruit, and whatever they could forage. Fish were plentiful in the river and easy to catch in nets. Still, it wasn't enough for the enormous number of refugees as others joined the column. Fights broke out.

Elif, Alicia, Vera, and others rode back and forth along the long line, handing out food and looking for stragglers, people who were too weak to go on. When the terrain allowed, they used carts to transport the old and ill, but some of the passes through the mountains were too narrow or too steep and treacherous, and they had to be carried on donkeys or on people's backs. At times they waded through mud up to their knees. The rocky terrain destroyed the horses' shoes, and some of the animals fell lame and had to be left behind. Omar had insisted on walking with his stick, in order to free up transport for others. But after two weeks on the road he fell ever more behind.

"You're too proud to be seen on a donkey?" Kamil taunted him.

"I'm too proud to throw an old woman off a donkey so I can get on," Omar retorted, sitting on a rock by the side of the road. His face was red and sweating, and the bandage around his leg was crusted with blood. "Just leave me here."

"You'd rather die here?"

"Why not? It's as good a place as any." He looked around. "The sweet smell of pine, the sun on my face." He grinned, but Kamil saw the effort behind it.

"It's not very heroic after all you've been through to die at the side of the road like a hare that's been hit by a cart."

Omar frowned and focused on a woman sitting in a patch of vivid blue hyacinths breast-feeding her infant. She had deep circles under her eyes and the blank look of exhaustion. "My definition of heroism has undergone some revision."

"As you like, you stubborn, selfish old mule, but think about your wife and Avi. Don't you have some responsibility to them? You're just too lazy to live." Kamil stalked off.

THERE WAS plenty of water. It fell in sheets from the side of the mountain, surged in the rivers, and trickled in streams amid the stones. But the mass of people made sanitation a problem, and some became ill with diarrhea. When Victor fell ill, Alicia tied him to his horse so he wouldn't fall off and stayed by his side. Omar rode on a donkey, up front where Kamil could keep an eye on him. When he became delirious, he too had to be tied to his mount. Too ornery to die, Kamil hoped, casting anxious glances at his friend's slumped form.

It took them almost a month to get to Trabzon. The road behind them was studded with fresh graves, particularly toward the end of their journey. One of them was Victor's. Another belonged to Siranoush Ana. Her daughter had carried her mother's body on her back for five days before they convinced her to allow Siranoush Ana to be buried. At each burial, one of the surviving priests said prayers and they erected a wooden cross, hastily carved with the deceased's name. At Siranoush Ana's burial, the grim-faced Levon had cried like a baby.

The following afternoon, they passed through a meadow where hundreds of tiny yellow blooms had forced their way through the sheet of snow. Kamil rode off alone and dismounted on the pretext of examining the flowers—marsh marigolds, tiny goblets of sunlight. He picked one of the flowers and wrapped it in his handkerchief, then placed it inside his coat alongside the dead soldiers' documents. He walked far enough away that no one could see his shoulders heave or hear his sobs.

WHEN THE minarets and church towers of Trabzon were in sight, a roar went up among the refugees and people began to push forward. Levon rode up next to Kamil and, pressing his fist against his heart in a gesture of friendship, met Kamil's eyes. Kamil nodded his head in acknowledgment. Levon spurred his horse around and, together with his men, melted into the forest. Kamil wondered whether they would go back to their land or stay in the forest as outlaws. They had a thousand guns after all. He wished them well.

At the edge of the city, Kamil was met by the governor, this time not with a band but with a contingent of gendarmes. The governor looked stunned to see the train of refugees.

Kamil dismounted and went to speak with him. It didn't escape his notice that it took the governor a good few moments before he bowed and uttered words of respectful welcome. Kamil realized that the governor hadn't recognized him at first. No wonder. He was filthy, his clothing in tatters, and he now had a full beard.

"Thank you for meeting us," Kamil responded. "These people need food, lodging, medical care. I presume you had word of our arrival. I sent a messenger some weeks ago. What have you been able to prepare?"

"The city elders have refused permission for them to enter, my pasha. They'll have to go back."

Kamil stared at the governor in disbelief. He flung his hand at the crowd behind him. "Take a look, sir," he said, trying to keep his anger in check. "They are in no condition to go anywhere, and there is nowhere for them to go back to. They will remain here."

At a signal from the governor, the gendarmes spread out and blocked the road. "I'm sorry, Kamil Pasha, but we've heard that they carry disease. We can't risk letting them into the town."

That, at least, was a legitimate concern, Kamil thought, his anger abating somewhat.

"I understand," he said. "If they are not to go into town, perhaps a camp can be set up for them outside, where they can receive medical care."

"We hadn't expected such numbers. How many are there?"

"I don't know. Two hundred? Three hundred? Quite a few died along the way."

"We don't have enough to feed them," the governor stuttered, "or the resources to build that many houses. And we have only one doctor."

"Surely as governor you can meet the expenses. This is a human disaster for which you are responsible."

The governor shook his head and looked embarrassed. "These people are rebels. The government won't allow me to pay a kurush to help them."

Kamil flung his riding crop down in rage and strode up and down the row of gendarmes while the governor waited, his face twitching with anxiety. He could send a telegram to Istanbul, Kamil considered, but to whom? And what would that accomplish if the administration believed these people were rebels? He could pledge his own considerable wealth, but he worried that it would take too long to arrange. Still, he decided to try. He'd send a telegram to Yorg Pasha.

A crowd of residents began to gather behind the troops and on the hillsides. Surely they would help these people, Kamil thought. He saw several prosperous-looking men advance on the governor. They appeared to be arguing.

Kamil heard Vera say his name. Her face was gaunt, her eyes caked with pus from an infection, and her lips were chapped raw. She had trouble articulating her words. "I might have a solution," she said. "Come with me."

Kamil told the governor that he had business in town and asked him, for humanity's sake, to distribute bread, clothing, and blankets to the refugees.

The governor nodded. "The residents are eager to help." Shoulders sagging with relief, he went to consult with the local men with whom he had just been arguing.

VERA LED Kamil to a guesthouse near the port. "Gabriel told me he stayed here when he first arrived in Trabzon. Because the roads were still bad, he left his trunk behind. He gave me this key," she said, pulling it from her pocket, "and told me that if anything happened to him to get the trunk. It was almost as if he knew he wouldn't survive." She regarded the house and then led him around the back and through a gate. "That must be it." She pointed at a windowless stone shed. The key fit in the lock.

They squeezed inside. Kamil lit a lamp he found by the door, revealing a jumble of boxes and barrels and, behind them, a chest as high as Kamil's waist.

"Gabriel said the gold from the bank would be in the chest." Vera ran her hands across the dusty lid, her voice thick with feeling. "He didn't have a chance to tell me what he wanted me to do with it. I know he'd approve of using it to help these people." She looked at Kamil, concerned. "You're not going to return it to the bank, are you?"

Kamil had no answer. Vera didn't have a key to the chest, so he forced the lock. They drew open the heavy lid. The chest was crammed with furs and other household goods. Puzzled, they pulled everything out and examined it, piece by piece. When the chest was empty, Kamil climbed inside it with the lamp to examine the bottom. With the tip of his knife, he scored the leather lining and pulled it up, revealing a recessed latch. He manipulated it until a soft click revealed the outline of a panel, which he pushed aside. An extensive false bottom opened to view. Kamil reached in and extracted a necklace set with large emeralds, which he gave to Vera, then pulled out a handful of gold liras.

Vera stared at the jewelry draped over her hand. "God save us," she exclaimed.

Kamil took in the sea of gold lapping at his feet. "It seems he has."

KAMIL DIDN'T tell the governor where the gold and jewels came from. It was about half of what had been taken from the bank, and he wondered where the other half was. With some shame, but seeing no other solution, he let the town think it was his personal fortune. He implied that it had been left with Yakup, who had stayed behind in Trabzon. He had removed the emeralds from the necklace so they couldn't be identified. Neither the governor nor the residents seemed to think it unusual for a pasha to travel with so much wealth. Perhaps they were simply too relieved at having the problem solved to inquire too closely.

He sent Yorg Pasha a telegram to tell him he was safe and a longer letter to him and one to Feride with a ship leaving that morning for Istanbul. There was no sign of Vahid in Trabzon, although a local doctor said he had treated a man who had lost part of his hand. The sultan's Kurdish irregulars had vanished.

OVER THE next few weeks, Kamil worked together with the governor and town leaders to erect shelters and purchase food and other supplies that had to be brought in by ship. A cold fog still enveloped the town in the mornings, but later the sun burned it off, revealing fields of forget-me-nots and wild tulips amid brilliant green meadows. Birdsong mingled with the sounds of sawing and hammering. The women refugees, now mostly widows, sat outside the doors of their communal shacks in flecks of sunlight, staring into space. Only the children, resilient as spring flowers, ran exuberantly underfoot.

Some of the money from Gabriel's chest was used to hire ships to take people to Istanbul or other Black Sea ports where they had relatives who might take them in. Some families had decided to return to their villages under Levon's protection. A photographer disembarked from one of the ships and, carting his box and tripod through the town, took pictures of the remaining refugees.

Kamil began to think of leaving. He trusted the governor and the sizable Armenian community in Trabzon to continue the relief effort as long as the money held out, as it would for some time yet. Kamil reminded himself that he faced a murder charge. The thought was so ludicrous that he laughed out loud.

$\mathcal{V}$ERA CRADLED the Henchak pin in her hand. She had found it wrapped in a piece of flannel in Gabriel's chest, along with her passport, and, pressed between two pieces of cardboard, a dried daisy she had given him before their marriage as a memento of a lovely day they had spent picnicking in the Alps. He had brought this simple, fragile flower all the way from Geneva to Istanbul and from there to Trabzon. She had been married only a single night, and all the rest had been misunderstanding and needless pain. Why had she immediately assumed that her husband would abandon her?

He was like the Straw Thief, she thought, a hero who loved her and his people and took great risks to help them. He had embarked on a long road across the globe and had produced something new and wonderful for them but had made mistakes along the way. One by one, his successes had slipped through his fingers, numbed by this savage winter. She pressed the flannel parcel to her chest and gave way to her grief, whether for herself or for Gabriel, she didn't know.

"COME WITH US, Vera." Alicia pleaded, her eyes dull with the pain of losing Victor. Her freckles looked almost black in her pale face, and her hair blazed in the sunshine. She and Apollo and some other comrades were boarding a ship to Batumi the following morning, then traveling overland to Tiflis.

"This is just a harbinger of things to come," Apollo told Vera. "They'll go after the Armenians whenever the wind blows the wrong way. The villagers don't have any coordinated defense, just bands of young men with outdated rifles. They would barely have been armed if Gabriel hadn't brought in weapons."

Vera didn't point out that it was Apollo who had brought the weapons to the east.

"We have to organize." Apollo took her hand. "Come and help us do that, Vreni. It'll be in Gabriel's name. He would have wanted us to do this."

Vera thought about the women and children huddled in hastily assembled wooden shelters at the edge of town, coughing in the smoke from their braziers. Would forming an armed revolutionary group help them? Or could justice be had without violence? Gabriel had always wanted peace, yet his actions had led to the deaths of so many people.

"I need to think on it," she told Apollo, her hand lingering in his. "Kamil Pasha has asked me to return to Istanbul to testify in a court case. I should do that first. Send me a message when you're settled and tell me where you are."

Kamil Pasha had told Vera about Sosi's murder and the attempt to blame it on him. She had failed Sosi once, and she promised herself that she wouldn't fail the courageous girl again. The idea of bringing Vahid to justice for what he had done to them was immensely satisfying.

Apollo drew Vera to him and kissed her on the lips. "Promise me you'll come, Vreni."

Vera nodded, mute with joy, now and forever adulterated with regret.

92

THE FOLLOWING MORNING, Kamil stood on the pier and watched a group of refugees and the surviving members of Gabriel's commune board their ship. Omar had learned that they planned to organize an armed resistance against the Ottomans, coordinating and arming all the small village-based groups like Levon's. As an Ottoman official, Kamil knew he had a duty to stop them. As a representative of justice, he had no idea what the right thing to do was.

He was spending the empire's wealth—the proceeds of a robbery that he had been charged with solving—on saving these Armenian refugees, who in the future might well turn on the empire. He had helped them while they used illegally obtained weapons to defend themselves against the sultan's irregular troops. Worse yet, he had subverted his soldiers to fire on their own. The sultan could exile him or even have him shot for any of these offenses. Yet he felt he had done the right thing. Did moral decisions have to be worked out along the way, or could one rely on a set of moral principles that applied under every circumstance? He found himself thinking that what was right today might not be right tomorrow depending on the circumstances. He wondered uneasily where such a relativist attitude might lead him.

Kamil raised his hand in farewell, then turned and walked away through the morning mist. "A magistrate without principles," he muttered to himself, shaking his head. "What's left?" he asked, louder. His voice echoed between the houses in the early-morning stillness.

ELIF HAD returned and was waiting for him in the dining room, where Yakup had laid out breakfast. The sight of her slight form and keen eyes was as heartbreakingly lovely as the flower-strewn meadow outside his window.

Elif stirred her tea. Kamil sat down and for a moment was captivated by the delicate clink of her spoon against the glass. "So fragile," he said, half to himself.

"What is?" she asked, handing him the glass of hot tea.

The best-brewed tea is the color of rabbit's blood in the glass, Kamil remembered his mother saying. Not knowing what to answer, he drew Elif close, then closed his eyes and sipped the scalding liquid.

VERA SAW Chief Omar on the docks that morning, supervising the loading. Now clean-shaven except for his extravagant mustache, he leaned on his staff and bellowed orders. The local doctor had cleaned his wound and rebandaged it. It seemed to be healing, but the police chief had been warned to watch for infection. Vera was amazed that after all their travails, the eight remaining soldiers from the pasha's force of thirty were still willing to march in formation as if they made up a company. In two hours they all would embark on new lives, but, she was sure, not lives any of them would have recognized two months earlier.

93

SULTAN ABDULHAMID RECEIVED Kamil in his private quarters. Kamil could hardly believe three months had passed. Everything looked the same: the furnishings of the receiving hall, the sultan's formal gold-braided suit, the tip of his sword embedded in the pile of the carpet. Enormous gilt-edged mirrors at the sides of the room reflected each other, as if opening a tunnel into the void. Dozens of officials and servants stood in formation along the walls, with Vizier Köraslan by the sultan's shoulder. Only this time the French doors to the garden stood open, admitting a soft breeze. Birds rioted in the hydrangeas.

Kamil bowed before the sultan, then stepped back, keeping his eyes lowered.

The vizier walked over and closed the French doors. Kamil's ears rang in the sudden silence.

"I'm glad to see you returned safely, Kamil Pasha." Kamil thought he heard a trace of genuine concern in the sultan's voice. "If you would be so kind, sit and tell me your account of events in the east." The sultan indicated a brocaded chair.

As Kamil sat down, he felt the full weight of the exhaustion that had dogged him since his return. He straightened and took a breath. "From my inquiries, I estimate three to four hundred dead, most killed by the Kurdish irregulars, but many refugees died on the road of hunger, cold, and disease." He couldn't think what else there was to say.

The sultan waited for Kamil to continue. When he remained silent, Sultan Abdulhamid asked, "And what of the revolt? That was your purpose, was it not, to investigate the revolt?"

Kamil looked up into the black eyes of the sultan. He could read nothing in them, neither concern nor interest. "There was no revolt, Your Highness."

"We have reports that there were hundreds of weapons in the villages as well as in the monastery where your supposed socialists set up their commune. I suppose those weapons all grew in the meadows like spring flowers."

"The guns were taken from the arms shipment the police intercepted in Istanbul in January."

"I thought the police had confiscated those," the sultan exclaimed, turning to Vizier Köraslan for explanation.

"The cargo was moved to Yorg Pasha's warehouse," the vizier admitted. "The British company wanted its ship back, and we thought that was the best place to store the guns. As far as I know, they're still there."

"You didn't know they had been stolen?"

The vizier flushed.

"What of your Akrep sources?" the sultan asked impatiently. "Surely they knew. This was under their jurisdiction."

Vahid had let the vizier down, Kamil thought with satisfaction. The Akrep commander had been away in the east. Did Vizier Köraslan know that?

"Perhaps Yorg Pasha didn't report them stolen. I'll find out, Your Highness."

"Do." Sultan Abdulhamid turned back to Kamil. "Hundreds of weapons in the hands of Armenians in the east, right on the border with Russia, and yet you claim there was no revolt."

"The weapons were distributed only after word spread of an impending attack on the villages."

"How do you know that?" the vizier snapped.

"The news of the attack was in a telegram waiting for me in Trabzon. I have it here." He handed the vizier the telegram. "By the time I arrived, the entire region had learned of its contents."

"The villagers, led by these Armenian socialists, attacked our troops." The vizier's face was flushed with outrage.

How do you explain a massacre, Kamil wondered, except in parables? "Your ten-year-old son is feeding the cow," he began, "and a soldier kills him with an ax to the back of his head. You go to protest, and you too are brought down. All the men of the village and older boys are herded together in the square and killed. Not shot, but axed, to save ammunition. Then the soldiers break down the doors shielding the women and girls. Their fate is worse."

"What in Allah's name are you talking about?" Vizier Köraslan shouted. "How dare you profane the padishah's presence with such nightmarish lies?"

"If you could get hold of a gun, what would you do?" Kamil continued calmly.

"That is not the behavior of an Ottoman soldier," Sultan Abdulhamid said, his voice tight. "Are you insulting our army?"

"No, Your Glorious Majesty. The Ottoman army is a professional force. The soldiers you sent with me were obedient, dutiful, and fought bravely."

"Who were they fighting?" Vizier Köraslan asked triumphantly, so that Kamil knew Vahid was back in Istanbul and had told him.

Kamil lowered his eyes and answered in a soft voice, "The wolves of the steppes devour the lambs and blame the shepherd." He felt very weary and incapable of explaining.

"Stop talking in riddles," the vizier snapped. "You suborned the sultan's household troops to fight against the empire."

Kamil raised his eyes and looked Vizier Köraslan full in the face. He saw fear behind his arrogance. "The Akrep commander led the offensive against the population, so you can place blame either way."

Kamil saw the sultan glance sharply at Vizier Köraslan, and the vizier grow thoughtful. Vahid was rapidly becoming a liability, Kamil reflected with a trace of smugness.

"Kamil Pasha"—the sultan leaned forward, and Kamil heard a thin vein of compassion in his voice—"I understand you have been through a difficult time. I have also heard that you used a great part of your own fortune to save the lives of the refugees that descended upon Trabzon. Let us leave aside the question of who shot at whom and deal with the matter immediately at hand. I commend you for your humanity and your generosity. You are a true Ottoman.

"Once the engagement was over, the women and children deserved bread and a roof over their heads. If you hadn't stepped in, the loss of life would have been tremendous. The empire has already come under attack by foreign journalists for supposedly attacking defenseless villagers. Whether or not they were defenseless is a question it seems we must disagree on. But if many more had died on the outskirts of Trabzon, the consequences for the empire would undoubtedly have been severe. Britain or Russia might have felt called upon to intervene. As it is, the newspapers took note of your admirable efforts and the world has already forgotten the Choruh Valley. You are quite an international hero, you know."

Kamil looked confused. He had disembarked only a few hours earlier and had come straight to the palace. He saw the sultan motion to the vizier, and after a few moments, the man returned with a stack of foreign newspapers.

Although the vizier's every outward motion was unfailingly polite, as he bent to hand Kamil the papers he caught his eye, and Kamil felt a wave of hatred and fear communicated in that look. Kamil wondered what could make a formidable man like the vizier so afraid. He recalled the rumors that the vizier's son had murdered his friend. If Vahid had engineered a cover-up, he would be in a position to threaten the vizier's family and reputation, and that was a threat that could bring low the most powerful man.

Kamil flipped through the stack of newspapers in his lap. The front page of the *The Times* of London showed a grainy photo of makeshift

shelters in Trabzon. The headline announced: PASHA PAYS FOR ARME-
NIAN RELIEF. The *New York Tribune* read: OTTOMAN LORD RESCUES
ARMENIANS. A rather inaccurate drawing of him with an oversized
nose and bristling mustache showed him protectively holding his fez,
in which a miniature huddle of threadbare women and children were
sheltering. There was more of the same, in every language.

Kamil was stunned. "This is wrong."

The sultan smiled at him. "Enjoy your fame, Kamil Pasha. To
thank you for your service to the empire, I am bestowing on you
the High Order of Honor and a yali mansion in Sariyer. May you be
happy there."

Vizier Köraslan held out a velvet-covered box, its lid open. Sultan
Abdulhamid asked Kamil to approach. The sultan stood, took the
High Order of Honor from its case, and lifted the sash over Kamil's
bowed head. It was an eight-pointed gold star with a central medallion
bearing the seal of Sultan Abdulhamid II. It was surrounded by four
green enamel banners on which Kamil read the words "patriotism,
energy, bravery, fidelity."

"I congratulate you and thank you for your service to the
empire."

"Thank you, Your Majesty," Kamil stuttered, overwhelmed and
greatly disturbed. He bowed his head.

The sultan sat back down. "Oh, and did you discover the missing
gold from the bank?"

"No, Your Highness. I've failed in that. The perpetrator is dead,
so we may never know what happened to it." Kamil noted dispassionately that he felt only a slight twinge of guilt at lying to the sultan.
What else could he have said? The truth, that he had spent half of
that stolen gold saving the lives of hundreds of people, presented
a moral conundrum that he felt unable to solve. He had chosen
life over honesty, one kind of justice over another, but he knew not
everyone would agree that he had chosen well. He was certain that
the vizier wouldn't agree, but he wondered what the sultan would
think.

"I see." The sultan tapped his fingers on the chair arm and regarded

Kamil thoughtfully but said nothing more. He lifted his index finger, and the vizier stepped forward to signal an end to the audience.

As Kamil backed out of the room, his mind was on something Vera had told him. "Karl Marx," she had said, "believes that money is like a living being that divides and multiplies, so that those who have it gain ever more, while sucking the life from those who have none and never will." At the time he had thought it an exaggeration.

94

"AYALI! HOW WONDERFUL." Feride clapped her hands at the thought of her brother living in a seaside mansion. Sariyer was north of Bebek, where Yorg Pasha lived, and accessible only by boat, but she knew the wives of several pashas who summered in the area. The mansion Sultan Abdulhamid had given to Kamil had belonged to the late Sultan Abdulaziz's daughter. When she married and moved to her husband's mansion, the house on the waterfront had reverted back to the palace. "I've seen it," Feride told Kamil. "It's lovely, a huge place. Much too big for you," she concluded with a smile.

Feride was already making plans to visit. Her daughters would love to be closer to the water. Their mansion in Nishantashou had a big garden, but nothing was better than being able to step directly from your terrace into a caïque on a moonlit night and picnic on the water. It would do Huseyin good too to get away from this house that had been his prison for so many months. After his visit to the palace, he had developed a painful cough and for a time had become so incapacitated that she had worried he might die. Now he was on the mend, although still weak. There had been no opportunity for the reconciliation she had planned with her husband, but the tension between them had disappeared, replaced by an awkward caution.

"You'd better put your name on the door, Kamil," Huseyin joked. "Your sister is already arranging the furniture."

She leaned over and kissed her husband's brow, leaving her lips in place for a moment to feel the warmth of his skin against hers. He smiled in return and squeezed her arm, but she saw the hesitancy in his eyes. There was a smear of puckered pink flesh across his cheek. He still walked with a cane, and his body was seamed with scars. He had insisted on sleeping in a separate bedroom. He hadn't understood her tears and protests over his doing so, she thought. Had she become his nurse and nothing more? Did he no longer wish her to see his body? Perhaps she should have acquiesced quietly, but she was determined to win her husband back.

She stood by her husband's chair and wondered when, if ever, he would draw her onto his lap again.

95

THE MINISTER OF JUSTICE, Nizam Pasha, fitted the torn scrap of paper against a page in Vera Arti's passport. It was written in Cyrillic, with stamps and signatures, and at the bottom a translation in French. They were in his private chambers, sitting in armchairs before the minister's desk.

Kamil handed the minister another document. "This is Vera Arti's deposition, her account of being forcibly abducted by Vahid and kept in Akrep's basement, along with the murdered woman, Sosi. The passport fragment we found confirms she was there," Kamil continued. "And it gives credence to her claim that she saw Sosi also being held there and that the girl probably died there."

"There's no proof of where and by whom Sosi was killed," Nizam Pasha corrected Kamil, "but this evidence is very indicative."

"The girl feared for her life. Vera reported seeing wounds on Sosi's hands of the kind documented by the autopsy, the same kind of wounds that I saw had been inflicted on Bridget, the British governess. They clearly were made by Vahid," Kamil insisted. "These are the actions of a man with no respect for human life."

"You think it was Vahid. But there's no proof that he killed Sosi or anyone else. It could have been one of his men."

It took all of Kamil's willpower not to rise from his chair and smash something. It was as if all the violence of the past months had crept into him and now threatened to uncoil. But respect and protocol required him to remain seated in the presence of the minister and to hide his uneasiness. He needed Nizam Pasha's help to hold Vahid to account for his cruelty. If not Vahid, then who was responsible for all the deaths in the Choruh Valley? He felt a deep personal grudge as well. Kamil hadn't forgotten his four nights in Bekiraga Prison or Sakat Ali's attempt on his life. If Omar hadn't been awake to stop the Akrep agent, Kamil would be dead.

"This should be enough to exonerate you." Nizam Pasha waved the documents in the air. "The Order of Honor alone will make this charge go away. The sultan isn't in the habit of rewarding his subjects with the empire's highest honor one day and throwing them in jail the next. You should take care, though. Vizier Köraslan has taken a special interest in you, first jailing you in that outrageous manner and then pushing for a trial. Aside from the fact that it's an affront to our class, I don't approve of officials from the palace messing about in the business of the courts. The vizier should stick to matters of state." He pointed his pipestem at Kamil. "You've made a powerful enemy there, Kamil, but you seem to have a talent for that."

"What about Vahid?" Kamil asked, trying to mask the desperation in his voice. "I want him punished."

"There's no evidence to link him to any of the crimes. I'll bring Madame Arti's testimony to the attention of the vizier, but my guess is that he'll succeed in explaining it away. After all, she's a foreigner of the worst kind, a Russian."

"Vahid and the vizier are covering for each other."

"Of course. That's life, Magistrate."

Kamil felt a helpless rage twist inside him. This, he noted almost dispassionately, was how men are pushed beyond their natural boundaries to take violent measures. This is how a man feels when he kills the man who has dishonored him. He must find a way to hold Vahid accountable for what he had done.

"That solves the robbery as well, doesn't it?"

"Yes, the bank robber, Gabriel Arti, was killed in the fighting.

The guns from the confiscated shipment probably will never be retrieved."

"And the stolen gold and jewels?"

"They disappeared in all the madness."

The minister shook his head. "It's a big loss. Eighty thousand British pounds. Perhaps Arti sent it abroad. I suppose we'll never know. Allah be praised that the bank was insured. The managers didn't even lose their posts. In fact, Mr. Swyndon has been promoted."

Kamil couldn't mention that he had found only half that amount in Trabzon. He had no idea what had happened to the rest of the money. In the larger measure of things, it didn't seem to matter anymore. He had come face-to-face with an evil greater than lying, stealing, betrayal, or even, he thought wonderingly, murder. Three months ago, he would have argued on principle that one life was worth the same as many. Every unnecessary death, every killing was equally reprehensible. But that was before New Concord, before so many innocents had been trodden underfoot. Hundreds of people killed, and for what? As fodder for men's ambitions. Whether that man was Vahid or Gabriel was immaterial. Or Kamil himself. Now he was being honored for all of it, he thought with despair—for his treason, theft, deception, subverting the army, and killing the sultan's men, and for the loss of hundreds of lives that he had set out with hubris and naïveté to save, but had failed to do so. He had compromised everything he believed in and failed. An image flashed through his mind of Siranoush Ana's daughter carrying her mother's body on her back through the mountains, loyal beyond reason.

Kamil left the ministry of justice and turned down a narrow lane. He had no idea where it might lead, but he felt as though he couldn't breathe. He walked faster until he finally broke into a desperate run, fleeing blindly through the winding lanes.

Omar found him hours later, sitting on the rocks beneath the spire of the Ahirkapi lighthouse. It was dark, and the Sea of Marmara spread out before Kamil like a black bowl. Every six seconds, a light slashed the darkness as a screen pulled by a weight rounded the crystal that cradled and refracted the lighthouse's kerosene heart.

96

"CAN'T YOU KEEP YOUR PERVERSIONS at home?" Vizier Köraslan slammed his fist into the veneered tabletop, leaving a hairline crack. "Did you think no one would find out about your games in the basement?" He strode to the door, opened it, and slammed it shut again. Then he circled Vahid, who was standing in the middle of the carpet, eyes down, hands clasped before him. A thick bandage covered his right hand.

"I know everything. There is nothing I don't know." He grabbed Vahid's arm and pushed back his sleeve, revealing a tortured field of old scars and new cuts.

Shocked, Vahid hurriedly pulled his sleeve back down. How could the vizier have known about his cutting? No one had ever found out, not since as a ten-year-old boy he had discovered the peace such regularly administered measures of pain could bring him. Deeply ashamed, he kept his eyes on the carpet. His wound beat in his hand like an anvil, but it was useless pain, runaway pain that did nothing to calm him.

Vizier Köraslan sat down in a satin-upholstered armchair and looked him over slowly. "They have proof that this girl was murdered in your headquarters. What do you plan to do about it?"

Vahid grasped on to this appeal to his competence. "One of my men has been charged with the girl's murder."

"You realize that everyone will know it was you who killed her."

Vahid looked up. "Do you know that, Your Excellency?"

Taken aback, the vizier said, "Well, not directly, but from the evidence, it can be assumed."

"You don't know it," Vahid told him, "and neither does anyone else. They can think whatever they like, but they don't know."

"It will damage you politically, nonetheless. Who would follow someone who makes an innocent man take the punishment for his own crimes"—Vizier Köraslan held up his hands—"whether he actually committed them or not?"

Vahid took a step closer to the vizier. "And what of your son, Your Excellency?"

The vizier's face flushed red. He rose to his feet. "You backstreet scum, you son of a whore. You dare threaten me?"

Iskender is the whore's son, Vahid wanted to cry out. I am the good son. He stood unmoving, glaring at the vizier.

Perhaps having noticed something unpleasant in Vahid's eyes, the vizier stopped shouting and was regarding the Akrep commander with disgust. "I should never have gone along with your stupid scheme. You told me the troops would wipe out a small group of socialists that no one cared about. Instead they ran loose and massacred entire villages that had nothing to do with the Henchak revolt you sold me. Now I know why you disappeared. You went to lead them yourself, and undoubtedly to engage in more of your unpleasant digressions." Vizier Köraslan's mouth screwed up in distaste. "The Franks are looking for any excuse to invade. By allowing such madness, you gave them the pretext to come in and help the embattled Armenians. If Kamil Pasha hadn't stepped in to save the refugees and if I hadn't sent reporters and photographers east to make sure the world knew about it, it could have been a disaster. I was a fool to trust you."

"You've never trusted me, Your Excellency," Vahid pointed out reasonably. "We had an arrangement that until now has suited us both."

"You said you'd increase my influence with the sultan, and instead now he suspects me. You were going to sideline Kamil Pasha, and now he's a hero. Why? Because you enjoy giving pain and you don't know when enough is enough."

Vahid smelled the old man's must emanating from the vizier's mouth. It reeked of death. He, on the other hand, was young, vital, untouchable. When Vizier Köraslan was deposed, he, Vahid, would be promoted to be the head of the Teshkilati Mahsusa. He would build a secret service for the sultan that would deprive all his enemies of air. He would be the guardian of the empire. Not the sultan, not this vizier, not his father's favored son.

"You go too far," the vizier said, visibly unsettled by the smile on Vahid's face and no doubt remembering that Vahid held evidence linking his son to murder. "You are mad."

"No, Your Excellency. I am not."

Vizier Köraslan stared at him a moment and seemed to come to a decision. "Get out," he said.

Surprised, Vahid hesitated, then turned and left the room.

AFTER VAHID had gone, the vizier called in his secretary and asked him to summon Nizam Pasha and Kamil Pasha. "Tell them to bring the file on the Armenian girl's case."

The two men were surprised to be summoned. Vizier Köraslan listened to the pasha's evidence that placed Sosi in Akrep's basement. He further surprised them, saying, "I have absolutely no doubt that Vahid committed this murder and probably others. He is an unscrupulous character who has been clever enough to pin the blame for his misdeeds on others. Why, he's even tried to blackmail me with trumped-up evidence against my son. We cannot have a scoundrel of this magnitude commanding a force like Akrep. That institution will be shut down and replaced by a more efficient secret service, and I want Vahid arrested and charged with murder and treason."

"Treason, Your Excellency?" Nizam Pasha inquired.

"Kamil Pasha, did you not witness Vahid leading a group of bandits in the massacre of innocent civilians in the east and attacking your imperial troops that were protecting the population?" Without waiting for Kamil, who seemed at a loss for words, the vizier answered his own question. "That, gentlemen, is treason."

97

*V*AHID TENDERLY STRAIGHTENED the tine of Rhea's hairpin, then put it in his pocket. It took only a short time to
walk from Akrep headquarters across the grounds of Yildiz
Palace to Huseyin Pasha's office in the Great Mabeyn.

The secretary announced him and then asked him to wait until
Huseyin Pasha had finished his meeting. Vashid paced impatiently.
After half an hour, several well-dressed men emerged, followed by
their secretaries and a scribe. Finally Vahid was shown into an office
more luxurious than his own. He strode in, his eyes seeking the man
he had sworn to kill, the one who had stolen Rhea from him and
caused her death.

The sight of Huseyin's scarred face brought back memories of
Rhea's charred body on the sidewalk. He started when he saw Kamil
standing by the open French doors. Vahid smelled the cloying scent
of lilacs enter with the breeze. An invisible bee buzzed insistently as
the two men glared at each other.

"Selam aleykum, Vahid." The note of satisfaction in Kamil's voice
caused Vahid more concern than the hostility. His wound began to
throb.

"Aleykum selam," he answered cautiously. He hadn't expected to ask about Rhea in front of Kamil and wondered if he should return another time.

"If you have something to say," Huseyin snapped, "let's hear it, or don't waste my time."

Kamil shut the door and came to stand beside his brother-in-law.

"These have been trying times." Vahid began in a neutral tone, wishing Kamil would leave.

"The times have certainly been treacherous for Armenians," Kamil agreed in a hard tone, "and for socialists. In fact, for a lot of ordinary, innocent people. Their graves line the road from the Choruh Valley to Trabzon. But you know that, don't you? You put them there."

Kamil's tone was sarcastic, but Vahid was satisfied to hear the anguish beneath the magistrate's words. Undermining Kamil emotionally and morally was almost better than killing him outright. The cruelest death was the slow rot of self-doubt.

"I'm amazed to hear you criticize His Highness's decision to send troops to put down an armed rebellion," Vahid responded, "but what else can one expect from a traitor?"

Kamil stepped toward him, but Huseyin pulled him back. "There's no point," he told Kamil.

A man who can be baited, Vahid thought, smiling inwardly. Passion made men weak.

"Do you deny that you ordered Ottoman soldiers to fire on the sultan's troops?" Vahid asked. "And this charade about using your own fortune to help the refugees," he scoffed. "No funds have been withdrawn from your bank. Nothing was sold to account for the sudden, mysterious appearance of forty thousand British pounds in gold and several large emeralds in your hands in Trabzon. Did you steal them? Perhaps from the Ottoman Imperial Bank?"

"You are a mass murderer," Kamil responded in a cold voice. "Worse than that, you are a man who kills for a calculated reason, as if he were slaughtering pullets to sell at market. Did you get what you wanted? Were the deaths sufficient to get you promoted?"

"I don't answer to you," Vahid said offhandedly, and turned to Huseyin. "I want to know something."

"What?"

Vahid wondered if the men were armed. He presumed Kamil was. He reached into his pocket and saw Kamil's hand slip inside his jacket. Vahid slowly withdrew Rhea's hairpin. The magistrate's hand emerged empty.

Vahid placed the pin on a small table by Huseyin, then watched jealously as he picked it up. The sight of the precious artifact in Rhea's lover's hand was unbearable. He felt a desperate need to pierce his own skin until all the poison had run out.

"My wife's hairpin!" Huseyin exclaimed. "Where did you get this?"

No wonder Rhea wouldn't marry him, Vahid thought. She had already married this bastard. "Rhea was your wife?"

"Of course not," Huseyin exclaimed. "Rhea was a young girl I was trying to help." He dropped the pin on the table. "You harassed the poor girl. If it weren't for you, she'd still be alive."

"That's a lie," Vahid snarled. "She died because of you. You brought her to that taverna."

"How dare you insinuate anything. Rhea was like my daughter."

Vahid snatched up the pin and held it in Huseyin's face. "Is this what a father gives his daughter?"

"Her fiancé asked me to buy something special for her. What business is it of yours?"

"What fiancé?"

"I ask you again, what business is it of yours? You did your best to destroy her life. I won't let you destroy her reputation after her death." Huseyin hobbled to the door and held it open. "You've caused enough tragedy for us all. Leave now."

Overcome by confusion and an inchoate rage, Vahid slammed the door shut behind him.

Turning to Kamil, Huseyin explained, "Rhea's father asked me to get rid of Vahid's unwanted attentions. They were making it difficult for the girl to get married. Vahid threatened her father."

"He misunderstood your relationship, but that explains why he was trying to kill you and why his men attacked Feride." Kamil frowned and pressed his fist against his mouth. The thought of Vahid harming Feride made him want to finish the job he had left undone. He would have gone after him if he hadn't already laid a satisfyingly malicious snare for the Akrep commander.

"What a viper," Huseyin exclaimed. "We have to do something about him. Imagine the damage he could do if he were promoted to head up the new secret service?"

"It's been taken care of," Kamil answered, his jaw tight. He had come to Huseyin directly from Vizier Köraslan's office, but Vahid had arrived before he could tell Huseyin about the meeting. Better even than shooting off Vahid's other hand was the thought of the man shivering in the special cell Omar had reserved for him at Bekiraga Prison, where Vahid would wait, perhaps for a long time, for his trial.

98

*V*AHID WALKED THROUGH the gardens of Yildiz Palace, unseeing, trying to understand what Huseyin Pasha had meant by "Rhea's fiancé." How could she have become engaged without his knowledge, and to whom? Turning down the drive leading to Akrep headquarters, he quickly halted. Dozens of gendarmes surrounded the building. Vahid ducked behind a shrub. Through the window he was outraged to see men moving about his office. He was certain they were there to arrest him. But on what charge? They had no evidence that he killed Sosi or anyone else. He would brazen it out, he decided, and almost moved from his hiding place. But what if the vizier had concocted evidence against him? He clutched his bandaged hand. Kamil Pasha had seen him with the girl in Karakaya. That must be it.

Seized by an unreasoning terror, no longer able to see where the threads connected, Vahid stumbled through the wooded palace grounds. If news of his arrest hadn't reached the guards at the back gate, he might still escape. He had never told anyone where he lived, so he calculated that he had time before anyone noticed he was not at the palace and managed to track him down in the backstreet warren of Fatih.

Less than an hour later, Vahid sat at the table in his room at home and, fumbling slightly with his left hand, opened the velvet-covered box. He could hear his mother snoring down the hall. He lifted out the swatches of hair and the torn drawing of his father's Greek mistress and his half brother, Iskender. Beneath it, in the folds of satin lining, his fingers found a pin with a narrow piece of satin attached. He pulled it out, licked his thumb, and rubbed at where it had begun to rust, although that just made it flake more. It was his award for graduating first in his high school class. He remembered that his father had received the news silently, nodding once, and gone back to reading his paper.

Later his father had gone to the coffeehouse, returning home long after he and his mother were in bed. Vahid, though, had been awake and saw his father pull the award from his shirt pocket and place it on the table. Vahid had felt a piercing joy at knowing that his father had shown the pin to the men at the coffeehouse.

"Baba," Vahid whispered, gently replacing the award in the box. He added Rhea's hairpin and the other objects and closed the lid. Then he went into the kitchen and shoved the box into the stove, waiting until the flames had bitten securely and were devouring it. He went back to his room, pulled a suitcase from the top of the wardrobe, and hastily packed.

99

The six oarsmen pulled in unison, sending the caïque skimming over the water north to Sariyer. Kamil and Huseyin sat in the bow deep in conversation, while Elif and Feride and her daughters nestled on a platform of carpets and cushions in the stern under a velvet awning that kept out the wind. Another boat followed with their luggage, but Elif had insisted on keeping her painting materials with her. Her boxes, canvases, and the easel filled most of the space. The two women sat close together, Elif's head resting on Feride's shoulder. Her eyes were closed and she seemed to be asleep. Alev and Yasemin trailed ribbons in the water.

Feride's eyes focused on Huseyin with a greed and desire that shocked her. She had always prided herself on keeping an even keel, while others rocked the boat around her. Now that she felt herself coming frighteningly alive, Huseyin seemed to recede from her in equal measure. At the summerhouse, she was determined, they would find each other again.

When the yali came into view, she roused Elif. They excitedly commented on its attributes, pointing out to each other the peaked gables, the balconies traced in lacelike fretwork, the tower, and the terrace right on the water.

"I wonder what plants are in the garden. It will be wonderful to draw them, like the gardens in France." Elif's eyes were crystal-clear ponds.

"Kamil will be able to tell us, no doubt," Feride responded, feeling suddenly chilled and wrapping her cloak more tightly around her shoulders. The women, with the twins, planned to spend the spring and summer at the yali, Kamil visiting on weekends.

They disembarked, Kamil helping Huseyin climb from the boat. Yakup, his mother, Karanfil, and some other servants from both households had come ahead. The servants helped the women and children ashore and carried their belongings to the house.

Doctor Moreno was to come up the following week with the paperwork for the foundation Feride was setting up to support the Eyüp Mosque hospital and fund a new children's wing. Kamil was bringing an Austrian nun, Sister Hildegard, who had some ideas for establishing a children's hospital in Galata.

To Feride's surprise, Huseyin had been interested in her new project and pledged a considerable amount to supplement her own portion. She had seen the pleasure in his eyes when she told him what she planned to do. There had also been pride. Then he had kissed her cheek and gone to his own bedroom that night, as on all the other nights since his return.

Their entry into the new summerhouse was festive and full of laughter. Elif, Feride, and the girls dashed into rooms and leaned from windows, giddy with delight. The men watched them, bemused, but Feride could tell that they too were bewitched by the light reflected from the strait through the tall windows and the charm of the place.

She saw Kamil join Elif on the balcony overlooking the garden and put his hand on the small of her back. Elif stepped closer until her body touched his, yet she remained distinct, straight-backed. Feride wondered what the relationship was between Kamil and Elif. She knew that they had been intimate with each another before they left for the east. The thought pleased her but also made her uneasy. Kamil had never been interested in marriage. Would he marry Elif now? And she was no longer sure whether Elif, so unpredictable and sometimes so frighteningly violent, would be the ideal partner for her brother. Elif was saying something to Kamil and pointing. Feride wondered what had happened between them in the east. It was as if their connection had snapped apart and been replaced by a different kind of understanding. They were always together, yet she sensed that their pleasure in each other was restrained by wariness.

Feride turned and caught Huseyin looking at her, and before he could look away, she winked at him inexpertly and stretched out her arms.

100

ARTA AND GOSDAN'S wedding was held at Father Zadian's church late that spring. Vera ground out the cigarette beneath her shoe and entered the cool dimness of the church. All of Kurtulush seemed to be there. Gosdan stood beaming by the altar. Roses spilled from every vase, scenting the air.

Marta wore a white lace gown with a long veil that covered her face and billowed behind her. Vera thought she saw Marta nod in her direction as she passed. The bride held a bouquet of white roses, and when Gosdan lifted the veil, Vera saw a young, vibrant woman whom she barely recognized as the rectory housekeeper. They placed crowns on each other's heads and drank wine from the same goblet.

Father Zadian blessed them, "Christ protect them under the shadow of thy holy and honorable cross in peace." Guests tossed rose petals over the new couple as they swept from the church down the street toward the taverna where they were to have their wedding meal.

As Vera stepped out of the church into the light, she felt faint. Gabriel's dying face interposed with that of Victor. She thought of

Siranoush Ana's corpse clinging to her daughter's back. Vera's heart began to race, trying to outrun all the horror it had witnessed.

She sat down on the steps of the church and began to cry. She was crying for them all, for herself, for the rage that now resided within her. When Vera looked up, she saw Marta hastening toward her, the veil billowing in the breeze so that she seemed a marvelous, iridescent creature.

This is what I will cling to, Vera promised herself, when I'm in Tiflis with Apollo.

101

KAMIL WATCHED ELIF put down a dish of food for the kittens that stalked about the gardens of the yali. Knots of them lay in every sunny spot, their fur a tapestry of shade and light. Elif had put on some weight, and Kamil appreciated her shape as she bent over. He went to her, laid his hand around her waist, and pulled her to him. She unbent slowly in his arms. There was always the initial resistance, then he felt her relax. We've learned the way there, Kamil thought, his chest tight with compassion. If only we didn't have to walk the same stretch every time. Time, he scolded himself. She needs time.

Arms around each other, they wandered through the garden to the door that led into Kamil's part of the house. He felt Elif tense, then soften as they crossed the threshold. When they entered his bedroom, they drifted apart. He locked the door and drew the curtains. By the time he turned around, she had slipped off her pants and tunic and was already under the duvet in Kamil's bed. He wanted to see her body, but she had never again allowed it after the first time. He slid beneath the covers, reaching for her pliant warmth, then dived into the darkness that held her secrets.

When he woke, Elif was still in his arms, breathing evenly. In the shadowy room, he could see that her eyes were open. "Elif," he whispered against her head, his heart beating hard with trepidation at what he was about to do.

"Yes?"

"Have you reconsidered about marriage?" Kamil was furious with himself at this awkward start. "I mean, would you consider marrying me?"

When Elif didn't answer, Kamil began to despair. She had refused him the previous year. What made him think that just because she had given her body, she would now be willing to tie herself to him? He drew away. His hands were slick with sweat.

Elif turned so that their faces were almost touching. He couldn't see her expression. "Will you take me as I am? Half a woman?" Her voice was gravelly with emotion.

"What do you mean?" Kamil exclaimed. "You're not half of anything. In fact, you're more of everything than most women are." He wasn't sure what that meant exactly, but he believed it, and it seemed to satisfy Elif.

"Then we should try it."

Kamil was grateful for the dark that hid his tears of relief. They remained silent for a long time, entwined like the kittens. The enormity of what he had just done expanded in the room about him. Soon he would have to tell Feride. Arrangements would have to be made. Elif would need her own studio, apart from his precious winter garden. The sitting room by the garden had good light and could be adapted. He should tell Yakup to hire workmen. He lay on his back, eyes wide open, increasingly anxious, assailed by the consequences of his proposal.

102

THE FOLLOWING DAY, Yorg Pasha arrived at the yali in a gaily decorated caïque rowed by eight men. They showed the pasha around the house and garden, and then, over a festive luncheon on the shaded terrace, Kamil took Elif's hand and announced their engagement, aware that the words were irrevocable and glad of it.

The twins squealed with delight and then ran into the garden. As he listened to the assembled group—Feride and Huseyin, Yorg Pasha, Sister Hildegard, and Doctor Moreno—cheer and call out congratulations, Kamil felt relieved. He no longer had to worry about whether it was the right decision or not. He had found over these past few months that the calculus that decided whether or not decisions were right was unreliable and predicted nothing. What was precious and right was life and the joy one was able to give to others as well as partake in oneself. He leaned over and kissed Elif on the cheek. Just then Alev and Yasemin returned with fistfuls of flower petals that they strewed over the couple. Kamil laughed and hugged the girls. Then he walked to where Feride was sitting and, leaning over, cupped her head in his hand and kissed her forehead, letting his thumb linger like a benediction.

He saw Huseyin's smile, the happiness and pride in his eyes when he looked at Feride, and he was glad that his sister and brother-in-law had reconciled and recovered whatever had been lost between them after the accident. Feride was radiant. She had spent the afternoon closeted with Doctor Moreno, Sister Hildegard, the family accountant, and an architect, drawing up plans for the renovation of the Eyüp Mosque hospital and discussing the seed money needed to draw donations to build a children's hospital in Galata on the site of Sister Hildegard's infirmary. The property for the hospital, Sister Hildegard explained over lunch, had been donated by the Austrian Embassy. Feride planned to ask the wealthy women in her circle for donations to construct the building. Once the hospital was built, the embassy would maintain it.

Elif spoke little, but Kamil could tell that it soothed her to sit at the center of her new and unexpected family.

After luncheon was finished, Yorg Pasha motioned Kamil over to a carpet spread under a blooming Stewartia tree. Kamil helped Yorg Pasha sit and arranged the cushions behind him. Yakup handed them tiny china cups of coffee, then withdrew.

Yorg Pasha took a sip. "We haven't found him," he announced. "His mother has been no help."

Kamil wished he had stopped Vahid in Huseyin's office. What had tipped him off? Kamil had gone through the conversation in his mind a hundred times but could find nothing. "You said Vahid's mother is blind. Who's looking after her?"

"He paid the daughter of a neighbor to look in on her. Their agreement was that if his mother became unwell, the girl would move in and take care of her. He gave her some money and promised her a lot more."

"And you'll be watching when it's delivered."

"The house is under surveillance. When the payment comes, they'll trace it, hopefully back to Vahid."

"Do you think he left the country?"

Yorg Pasha thought for a moment. "This is his habitat. I doubt he'd stray far from it."

"So Akrep is going after its own chief?"

"The sultan has disbanded Akrep, although he still has his own secret police. He's moving ahead with an even bigger secret organization, the Teshkilati Mahsusa."

"An intelligence service," Kamil observed. "I understand they plan to send spies abroad." He set down his cup and stretched his legs out. "If it's run well, it might benefit us. We need better information about what the British and the Russians are planning."

"And the French, Germans, Armenians, and Greeks. Just spit in Istanbul and you hit a foreign spy. We need our own sources." Yorg Pasha focused on Kamil's face. "Your father would be proud of you."

"What do you mean?" A breeze ghosted through the branches of the Stewartia tree, dislodging a torrent of white petals.

"The hero of Trabzon, celebrated in European capitals. Wouldn't that be the perfect front for an intelligence chief? Sultan Abdulhamid has mentioned your name in connection with the position."

Kamil was taken aback. "I've heard nothing about that. I'm not sure I'm interested." His eyes strayed to the terrace, where Elif sat beside Feride, stroking a white cat in her lap.

"You may not have a choice."

Kamil closed his eyes and let his head fall back against the trunk of the tree, his lips pressed tightly together. Petals drifted down and cooled his cheeks like the false promise of paradise.